livelifeaberdeenshire.org.uk/libraries

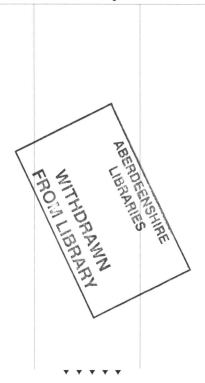

♥ ♥ ♥ ♥ ♥

Acknowledgements

Procrastination was my enemy when it came to writing this book. When I eventually stopped talking about it and started writing that's all I wanted to do. Thank you to my family who indulged me- you have my full attention back now.

Thank you to my wonderful husband Mark for all his hard work getting this 611-page document ready to be published- I don't know what you did but you are amazing, especially after a hard day at proper work and even sometimes sacrificing your evening run.

Thank you to Elliott and Evie for inspiring me each day and giving me enough material to write the next two books- should I ever get time to write those.

Thank you so much to the wonderful ladies who read my humble first pages and chapters, especially Joanne, Yvonne and Laura. It was nerve-wracking asking you to read what was essentially the contents of my head. Thank you for giving me your time, encouragement and feedback it meant a great deal.

Thank you to Sian from Ion Creative for taking my hopeless silhouette and turning it into a wonderful front cover that I just love. Thank you for getting back to me when you were on maternity leave too!

Thank you also to Jon for answering technical questions and always having an answer that worked when nobody else was around.

Finally thank you to all the even more amazing ladies who so far have bought and read my book and continue to give me encouragement and positive feedback! That you should spend your hard earned cash on something that I have written is flattering to say the least and I hope that it was money well spent. I have appreciated every share and like, every positive word. Thank you so much.

I wrote this book with the intention of simply making people laugh. I had a story in my head and I thought that it might be quite a hoot- a piece of escapism to lighten the mood as life can be awfully serious these days. Thank you for buying it- I hope you enjoy it! If it makes you chuckle, then I will be thrilled!

Here's to the memory of wearing trousers on a skirt day.

Prologue

"So, who have you brought with you *this* time?" The grey haired man chuckled hoarsely giving away his 40-a-day habit. "I think you bring a different man to every family occasion!"

Sophie inwardly groaned at her drunken uncle's topic of conversation.

He's off his face, she thought.

She looked apologetically at the man standing next to her who smiled back, amused by her eccentric family. Before she had a chance to answer another voice piped up.

"Mummy's had *lots* of boyfriends!" a small boy said.

"I have not!" She protested feeling her cheeks starting to flush under the sudden spotlight of attention. Looking to the man next to her she adamantly repeated, "I've not, he's making it up..."

"Yes, but who was that man you brought to London that time?" The uncle who had clearly taken advantage of the free bar was not in the mood to let the subject pass. He pointed at her accusingly, "I saw you in London, didn't I, that time... well, not just *me* it was the whole *family*..." he slurred, "for someone's birthday... or was it a christening... or, well, whatever it was... when *was* that? I'm sure you had a different gentleman with you that time," he looked closely at her partner, "or was that *you*?"

Sophie couldn't believe it. She wanted to clamp a hand over her ancient relative's mouth as he started to recount the time, many years ago, that he met her in London with the rest of her family, and her ex.

"Who was that Sophie?" the man next to her asked with a twinkle in his eye, "It wasn't me," he added, addressing her uncle.

"I have no idea," she said slightly crossly, wanting to bring the conversation to a close, "That was *years* ago anyway…"

"And then there was that *other* time?" The uncle raised his glass towards Sophie and peered at her over his half-moon glasses, "I have another memory of you with *someone else!*"

"Photos!" A faint voice in the distance was heard, interrupting the interrogation, much to Sophie's relief.

"Ollie, are you staying here or coming with mummy?" she said briskly, addressing the small boy who stood in their group looking in awe at the elderly uncle, hanging on his every word.

"Staying," he stated firmly not averting his gaze, hoping to be entertained further.

"Right. Let's go for the photos then, they're in the gardens I think," She turned and smiled at her partner indicating that they were leaving the company of her son and uncle. He held his arm up for her to take and they made their way outside. Holding the door for her the man led her through and over to a quiet area of the lawn where the wedding party were milling around sipping champagne and waiting for the group photographs. Sophie tried to put her weight on her toes so that her heels didn't sink down into the soft grass.

"Oh I'm sorry, they were talking about *years* ago and I really *haven't* had a lot of boyfriends..! Oh..!" Her partner had suddenly gone very quiet and had a look of disapproval on his face. She had a horrible feeling that he was getting entirely the wrong impression about her.

A smile then started to play on his mouth.

"Its fine," he said gently kissing her forehead, "I'm just not really a fan of these things, I've always avoided family gatherings..." He gazed at her fondly. "You look so beautiful, I just want to take you to our room and make love to you."

Sophie beamed lovingly at him, sighing deeply. This was like a proper happy ending. She sipped a flute of orange juice having discreetly abandoned her champagne at a nearby table after feeling the first mouthful going straight to her head. The moment was disturbed by a lady wearing a bright blue floppy hat who tapped her on the shoulder.

"Why are you drinking that filth? Have some *champagne!*" she hissed. "You might as well, it's *free!*"

"Mother!"

Sophie looked at her partner trying to convey her utter dismay at her mother's brashness. He took over the conversation.

"We have our marathon next weekend- it's Sophie's first so we're looking after ourselves. She's been training really hard," he looked proudly at Sophie who smiled back adoringly.

"Sophie's sister did the *London* marathon a few years ago," her mother said.

"Did she?" the man asked. "We didn't want to do that one because it's too busy. We're doing one way up north, away from all the crowds," he smiled back at Sophie. Her mother carried on.

"We watched her all the way round; we were jumping on and off the tubes! And I saw this funny thing, a lady there, a runner, with a note pinned to her top. Do you know what it said? It said, looking for love. *Looking for love!* Advertised like that on her top! With her *phone number!*" Sophie's mother looked incredulous, "A bit desperate wasn't it?"

Sophie rolled her eyes up to the sky. "I don't think so mother. I think that sounds like a very *sensible* thing to do. She was obviously just doing something that she loved- running- and was single and so thought she might meet a like-minded person along the way. Better just to get on with your life and do the things that you always do and *want* to do rather than waste time on date after date after date after *useless* date…" she stopped talking, aware that she was becoming rather animated, "I would imagine."

"Someone sounds like they know what they're talking about," the man joked.

"Well, we did wonder if Sophie was *ever* going to find a man," her mother stated, "she had enough chances! Tell me what you think of the book, by the way," she said addressing Sophie's partner, flirtatiously Sophie thought, "I've always enjoyed those ones."

Sophie waited for her mother to be out of earshot.

"What book has she lent you?" she asked sounding horrified, "Have you any idea the sort of books my mother likes? Don't read it! Oh look!" she pointed over to the bride and groom who had just come into view having their photo taken under a trellis of red roses, making their way back to the gathered guests. Sophie smiled wistfully.

"I *love* weddings," she sighed.

Chapter One

Sophie drifted out of sleep as the daylight shone through the edge of the blackout blind, drawn down over her bedroom window.

I wish I'd measured that properly before I put it up, a random thought registering in her sleepy head.

With a contented Saturday morning feeling she pushed her feet as far down to the bottom of the bed as she could and reached her hands up to the headboard, stretching out her whole body.

I love Saturday's, she thought, no alarms, no rushing around, no stress, no dull work, no school runs, no nothing if I like. Love Saturdays…

She pulled the duvet up around her shoulders and snuggled back into her cosy bed. Her eye's felt heavy again and she slipped back into a deep sleep. Colin Firth was there in her dreams and he loved her completely- what an amazing feeling to be in love and to be loved, especially by Colin Firth. He looked at her tenderly, his gorgeous smile playing on his lips. Was he going to kiss her? She longed to be kissed. Were they getting married, she wasn't sure...

"Is it school today?"

A voice in her head, in her morning muddled dream. In sleep her body felt heavy and exhausted. It needed at least a day to catch up on some rest. Colin pulled her towards him.

"Is it school today?"

She was in a semi-conscious sleep but aware enough to drink in the total relaxation of a weekend lie-in. Colin moved his face towards hers.

"Mummy is it school today?"

The voice she heard suddenly urgent and piercing through the morning peace. Sophie woke up with a jolt and sat bolt upright in bed, a movement that was only possible by the sudden realisation that it may in fact not be the weekend after all. Her son lay next to her in the space his Daddy had vacated three years previously and looked at her with wide awake eyes. He copied her movements and sat up too and changed his expression to the same one of panic and confusion that was now registering on her sleepy pillow marked face. The massive feeling of disappointment that she was *not* about to kiss Colin Firth was fleeting as reality kicked in.

"School!" she exclaimed, "I don't know! Is it? I can't think. What did we do yesterday?" Her head was heavy with sleep and completely blank of all thought. For a few seconds if you had asked her to tell you her name she would have struggled.

"I think it is school today…" her son thoughtfully stated, "because Mrs Newman said yesterday that we need to dress up today."

"Oh fffffflip. Shhhhhhhhhhugar puffs."

"I *love* sugar puffs!" the little boy's eyes opened wide and sparkled at the thought of something different for breakfast rather than his usual organic porridge.

"What? No sorry darling, we don't have any sugar puffs they are very bad for your teeth."

"Mrs Newman says that it's OK to have a little bit of what we fancy if we clean our teeth afterwards. We talked about sugar in healthy schools' week."

"Mrs Newman is quite right but we don't have any sugar puffs," Sophie replied through gritted teeth, Mrs Newman had become a righteous influence in their household since the boy had started school. "Oh b…other. What can we remember about yesterday?"

Both looked thoughtful for a moment.

"Kerry let me stay up late," the boy offered.

"Thursday! It was Thursday! My gym night! So that means today is Friday. Oh fffffflip."

The little boy sitting in bed giggled at her use of funny words.

"Sugar flip and bother," he copied

Sophie jumped out of bed and cast a cross glance at her son, "Don't copy mummy please Oliver. Mummy shouldn't say those words," she made a mental note to try harder not to do so in future. "It's 8 o'clock. Darling we've slept in!"

A whirlwind of activity began. She picked up the clothes she had cast off on the floor the night before in her state of exhaustion, too tired to lift the washing basket lid next to her bed. She ran into the bathroom and turned on the cold water tap, peering into the mirror above the wash hand basin; her puffy tired red eyes peered back.

"This has got to change," she thought.

Her son appeared in the bathroom doorway wearing a pumpkin dressing up costume with a big smile on his face, his little eyes sparkling bright.

How can children go from sleep to wide awake in such an easy one step she thought? There was no trace now of sleep on his perfect angelic face. The pumpkin costume suddenly made an impression on her muddled mind.

"Why are you wearing your pumpkin costume darling? Come on mister I've just said that we've slept in so we really don't have time for... Hang on a minute- did you say something about dressing up?"

There was silence. The boy's little face was still but his eyes moved from side to side and up and down like there were little men in his head controlling them as he thought.

"Ollie!" Her voice came out harsher than she meant. She hated herself for being impatient with her precious son. She cupped his chin in her hand and gently planted a kiss on his nose. "Sorry darling but it's now 5 past 8 and we need to leave for school in half an hour. Did you recently mention dressing up?"

As she spoke she ran into her bedroom and found her phone on the floor next to her bed where she must have dropped it after she switched her alarm off and went back to sleep. Jules would know. Jules always knew what was happening at school. Jules only worked two days a week and had time to read newsletters. She also had time to volunteer at the school, make cakes for the monthly Cake Sale, be on the P.T.A. and do face painting at the summer fair. She started texting as she returned to her pumpkin of a son in the hall and asked him calmly, "Have you remembered yet darling?"

The eyes were still shifting around. Moments later they stopped and looked up to the left for what felt like an eternity and then it seemed his thought process was complete. He looked at her seriously.

"We have to take in one pound and Mr Smith will give all our pounds to poor people."

"Who's Mr Smith and why do you have to bring in a pound?"

"Mr Smith is the Head Teacher mummy and we need to pay a pound for not wearing our uniform."

Sophie held her head in her hands and squeezed her eyes shut, hoping to bring some clarity to her thoughts.

"Mrs Newman said that we have to dress up today for World Book Day…." he stopped and considered this for a moment, "… we have to come to school dressed as our favourite book character…"

"Oh for the love of God."

Her phone pinged twice to tell her that Jules had text back. The information was the same. Today was World Book

Day and the children should go to school dressed up as their favourite book character, with a pound for a non-uniform day and the book to justify the costume.

Sophie started her soap box rant.

"Why do they spring these things on us? Don't I have enough to think about without having to now come up with a dress-up-able book character in half an hour? I am a full time working single mother. Well part time but it feels like full time! *Why* do I have to be involved like this?"

Another text came through suggesting that if she had time they had a Harry Potter costume in Tesco last week.

"Great. If I'd have known yesterday then you could have been Harry Potter…"

"I don't like Harry Potter mummy."

"Well that's good then because you're not going to *be* Harry Potter! Why can't they give me notice of these things?"

Sophie turned into the bathroom and started to busy herself getting ready. She directed her son to go back to his room, take off the pumpkin outfit and put on some underwear while she thought.

"Charlie Bucket!" she called out a few seconds later feeling pleased that her first suggestion was a good one and from a book that they had just read.

Silence.

"Nah," was heard from the bedroom.

"But darling Mummy doesn't have long now to make you a costume and Charlie Bucket would be easy as you can just go in old clothes *and* we have the book!" she said this patiently staying true to her belief that children must be involved in the decision making process.

"Nah…"

"Oh I know, George from 'George's Marvellous Medicine'! You could take my mixing pot and wooden spoon!" Thank goodness for their Roald Dahl box set, she thought.

"Nah I don't really like Roald Dahl."

"What about Harry from 'Harry and the Bucketful of Dinosaurs'?"

"Nah, that's for babies."

Sophie sighed.

"OK mister can we stop saying 'Nah' please? What about Mr Bump! I can quickly paint you blue with our face paints and wrap you up in bandages! We have that book!" Sophie began to feel frustrated with the negotiation process. She frantically sent a text to all her friends to triple check that the children did need to dress up and one to her mum to see if she had any better ideas. Within minutes everyone text back, 'yes' and 'Harry Potter'. She felt her frustration bubbling up again.

"If Mrs Newman had told me about this when I picked you up yesterday then we wouldn't be in such a rush now! All it needed was a note up on the classroom door! I have never heard about this before! How can I make you a dressing up costume in such a short time? I could have done a lovely one last night!" her exasperated voice came out of the bathroom as she flapped around trying to think of a character that didn't require too much preparation.

I wonder if it would be terrible to call the school and say the boy is poorly, take a sickie and go to the zoo instead, she thought.

"Mrs Newman said that it was in Parent Mail so Mummy's should know about it."

"Mrs bloody Newman…" Sophie muttered under her breath as she pulled her dark brown hair into a pony tail. Everything she said made her feel like a bad mother. She went into her room and switched on her lap top which was on her bedside table. Life at home seemed to revolve around bed.

"Parent Mail…" she thought. It didn't ring any bells.

As she waited for her computer to fire up Sophie began to think of reasons to give to her work for needing the day off; there was a sick bug going around the school and she had been up all night with Ollie perhaps. She sighed. That was a non-starter. She already spent her time making up for the fact that she had a child- a day off would only confirm to her strict boss that they had been wrong to employ someone on a part-time basis when everyone else worked full-time.

Resigned to the fact that she was going to have to go into work she opened her Inbox and scanned her eyes down the many emails finally resting on an unopened communication from the school. It was dated two weeks previously and stated that today was indeed World Book Day and the children did, in fact, have to dress up as a book character and bring a pound in for non-uniform day.

She stood with a puzzled look on her face, not remembering receiving the message and not remembering ever giving the school her email address. Parent Mail was new to her. Good idea though.

The boy appeared at the doorway dressed up as Buzz Lightyear, one of his few actual dressing-up costumes. Sophie sighed again. If only it was that easy.

"Today is apparently *book* day, darling and Toy Story is a *film* as is Wall-E and Transformers for which you also have an outfit."

The boy trotted back off to his room. Sophie heard clatters and bumps then rustling and he appeared again with a big smile on his face holding open his Disney annual. Open at the page with a story about Buzz Lightyear. Sophie gasped and clapped her hands with glee. She picked up her son and gave him a tight cuddle and squashed a huge kiss onto his cheek.

"You are *such* a clever boy!" she exclaimed," We have a dressed up boy and a book! I would call that a success. Well *done!*" she sighed happily.

"Can I have a treat then?" the boy tried his luck.

"Well, you can stay up a little bit late tonight and say 'Hello' to Mummy's friends when they come round? That's a special treat. You always want to say 'Hello' to the girls on Friday," The look on her son's face told Sophie that this was not the sort of treat he was hoping for. "Well, maybe we can get you a magazine on our way home too because I am *so* happy with you."

The boy considered this.

"Some sweets too?" he replied.

"Maybe."

"A toy?"

"Don't push it. Let's be happy with a magazine and see what happens."

Oliver admitted defeat.

"What would *you* dress up as if *you* had to dress up for work?" he asked with a thoughtful look on his face.

Sophie pulled her own thoughtful face giving his question serious consideration.

"I think I would dress up as Cinderella and then we might meet our handsome prince," she said and smiled at her son, ruffling his hair playfully. "Although I think that I already have a little handsome prince."

Twenty minutes later they arrived at school and Sophie cast her glance around the playground. Pirates, cowboys, fairies, angels, devils, a pumpkin even but not many costumes that she could recognise from a work of literature- apart from several Harry Potters in their Tesco outfits and one 'Where's Wally'. The Deputy Head stood at the gate welcoming the children dressed up as Minnie Mouse and Oliver was the only one that Sophie could see clutching a book. Feeling rather smug and intellectual she gave her son a big squeeze of a cuddle and kiss and sent him off to join his line waiting to go into class. As she waited by the gate she could see in the distance his little friends greeting him excitedly pointing at his costume and the boy holding up his book showing them the page that Buzz was on. Sophie quietly congratulated herself for the achievement. I can do it all, she thought happily, I am pretty damn close to being Wonder Woman.

Sophie hugged her cardigan around her body to keep out the early morning chill and watched her son as he lined up with the rest of the Reception class. She always had to wait until they had all marched into school, the little boy needing to turn round one last time before entering the building to wave to his doting mum. Some mornings they went in first and Sophie was on time for work. Other mornings they went in last after Years 1, 2, 3, 4, 5 and 6. She would very slowly edge her way towards the gate, remaining in sight of the boy's line so that she could give him one last wave before hurtling towards her car- past other Mum's who ambled along chatting with each other- and racing over to the other side of town where she worked. By this time the spaces within two streets of the city centre school where she was employed were taken and so she had to park a good ten minutes away and run as fast as she could in her suit and heels up a steep hill, arriving at work quite a bit dishevelled and perspiring slightly. This morning the boy's class went in unusually efficiently giving her a spare moment to pass home on her way into work, the early morning confusion making her forget her work bag. As she opened her front door she saw that the postie had been already and picked up the letters that lay on the Welcome mat.

"Junk, junk, junk…" She flicked through the bundle of leaflets to check there wasn't anything important and found a small envelope beautifully inscribed with her name and address but bursting open with its contents. She opened it as she walked through the house to dispose of the bundle of leaflets that she still held and realised what it was.

Standing in the kitchen she felt a pang of sadness for her own situation. She held a white card on which there were two thistles tied together with a little black watch tartan ribbon. The calligraphy writing told her the occasion. Her elder sister's wedding.

"The perfect sister with the perfect life to become the perfect wife," Sophie muttered.

She chided herself for being so mean. "I didn't mean that…" she said out loud, her years of attending Sunday school making her think that someone might just be listening.

She read through the invitation. She had forgotten that it was on its way. Her mother had told her on the phone last week but the information had got lost somewhere in between running out of food, trying to find a reliable washing machine man, realising the car needed an M.O.T. and having to find a last minute babysitter so she could go back into work. A Friday in May 2012. Just over a year away. That sort of long term planning was entirely alien to Sophie now. Once upon a time she had planned her life out, perfectly she thought, but that had all gone wrong so now she planned from day to day. She read the details of the invite dutifully; she was to be the only bridesmaid. She continued to read the invitation.

'Plus one', it read.

"Are they trying to tell me something?" Sophie sighed. She stood the invitation up on the mantel piece. I have been single for about three years, she thought, maybe it *is* time I found my plus one. I don't have *time* to find a plus one.

The cuckoo clock hanging above the fireplace signalled nine o'clock. Sophie snapped out of her daydreams and shook her head. Work! Never mind trying to find a plus one, she thought. Getting a day off work will be more difficult. I already have a little plus one anyway.

***

Sophie arrived at work with the usual flustered clattering entrance that the office staff had become accustomed and not quite meeting the expectation that she should arrive at least fifteen minutes before her start time of nine thirty. They heard the door bang and then her footsteps through the main hall of the exclusive private school before she made her entry into the office.

"For someone so small you sound like a heard of flipping elephants…" one of her colleagues commented.

"Morning!" she said with false cheer in her voice looking around at the stony faces blankly gazing at her. "Another fun-filled day at the…" she noticed the school principal sitting at the far end of the communal desks, "…The Elm Tree Preparatory School and Nursery- good morning Mrs Wright," she muttered and busied herself finding the signing-in book under the vast bundles of branded paperwork.

She signed in and hurtled back out into the hall and up the four flights of winding stairs that took her to the top of the school and her office, situated in the loft area of the Victorian structure. She stopped at the top of the stairs to take a breath and straighten her hair before casually opening the fire door and heading towards the room beyond a second door where her four colleagues sat, trying to imply an air of organised efficiency. Usually she paused at the second door having learnt to listen to make sure the principal wasn't there, lest she should become involved in one of her day long monologues about education, but today she breezed straight in. She ignored the cursory glances at the clock and the tutting from her line-manager Enid and her despised colleague Laura, the office grass who sat in the corner of the room observing; waiting for someone to slip up.

So I'm only ten minutes early and not fifteen, she thought, what a *big deal*.

The two other ladies who worked in the office, Pam and Ruth, looked at Sophie and smiled. They were sympathetic to her, having both worked at the school for longer than she had and at one time both being the object of Enid's bullying.

"Good morning!" Sophie said again determined to remain the happy individual that she generally was and not be dragged down by the oppressive atmosphere in the school. "Enid, can I talk to you for a minute later please about holidays?"

Enid, the training manager, peered over her computer at Sophie.

"Have you started work? I was under the impression that you started at nine thirty. I'm rather busy at this moment."

"Oh um no…" Sophie's voice trailed off and the office fell silent.

"Are you aware of our new holiday policy?" Enid shuffled her papers, obviously deciding that she wasn't so busy after all, "It was reviewed and updated at the beginning of this month so I'm assuming that you are."

Sophie nodded her head to indicate her awareness of said policy although she had no knowledge of it at all.

"Well as you will know there is a holiday form that you must obtain from the office before requesting your holiday from me so I would advise that you complete that first before we waste our valuable time in discussing the matter," a superior smile flickered over Enid's face and she switched her attention back to her computer screen to indicate that the discussion was over. Ruth, sitting at the desk next to Enid, glanced at Sophie and smiled to say she had been there, she had also tried to get time off.

"Right yes I did know about that form but I've not managed to get one yet so I'll do that and…" her voice trailed off, it wasn't important enough to finish the sentence. Getting a day off was maybe more complicated than she had initially thought…

Enid nodded and looked smugly at the computer screen. She had the power to make everyone in the office turn into mumbling imbeciles.

What a bitch, Sophie thought and scowled at her like a child.

She went through to the tiny kitchen area and hung up her coat and put her lunch in the even tinier fridge. As she came in last every morning there was never enough room left and so her lunch was usually of minute proportions. She felt organised that she had actually managed to make a sandwich last night and not just brought items meant for Ollie's packed lunches as she normally did.

She took a glass back into the office and sat down at her desk in the corner, opposite Enid. She reached into her bag and put her phone on 'Silent' mode but rested it on top of her wallet so that she could see it flash if she got any texts, mobiles being forbidden in school. She then got the first of many Diet Cola's out, opened it and poured it into the glass, ducking behind her computer to swig the last drops out of the can- drinking out of bottles and cans was also not allowed. She needed some caffeine to prevent her from nodding off at her computer.

"You're having your first cola early!" Pam observed, "Think I'll have my ten o'clock crisps early too!"

"Sorry Pam, I've disturbed your crisp equilibrium! It's Friday, I'm feeling a bit crazy and I've had a bit of a morning so far," Sophie joked. "I'll give it up next week as I'll be going on a detox. I need to find a partner to take with me to my sister's wedding. My family clearly won't accept that I'm alright as I am."

"You look lovely," Pam replied, "Any man would be lucky to have you!"

"I'm not sure I have time in my life for a man anyway," Sophie said ignoring the compliment, "and my life does tick along just fine without one."

"I thought you were holding out for your one true love, an old romantic!"

"Can we have less of the old please? No, true love only happens in films."

"OK ladies this is all very nice, team building and all that I'm sure, but we do have a lot of work to do so maybe we could cut the chit chat now!" Enid looked up at the clock above her desk which now said half past nine. "Sophie we have a conference next month and I have left you out the paperwork that needs to be photocopied. All staff will attend and so we will require one hundred conference packs. Mrs Wright would like the red Elm Tree folders to be used and each one will need one name label, one pencil, three sheets of Elm Tree headed paper, the power point paperwork and one each of the worksheets that I've left on the table next to the photocopier next door. Also I need you to make one hundred copies of the school conference evaluation form on which Laura is still working and individually fold each one. The conference is on mental health issues."

"That's a cheery topic to get everyone in on a Saturday for," Sophie mused.

"The main thrust of the topic will be how to maintain a healthy work life balance to *avoid* mental health issues…" Enid added.

What a joke, Sophie thought, getting the staff back in at the weekend when most of them have done a fifty-hour week already, not including the extra three hours training on a Wednesday night, to listen to a man drone on about their work life balance!

"We're thinking also that staff should wear name badges so make two sets of name labels," Enid continued.

"Can't they just wear their name badges that they usually have to wear to work?" Sophie boldly asked.

Enid looked up from her computer screen and fixed her stony stare on Sophie.

"Most of the girls will be crawling in after a heavy night on the tiles so I don't think we can trust them to remember to bring in their name badges as well as themselves. They're already being asked to wear their uniforms and so name badges might just tip some of the more nervous ones over the edge. If we have name badges here, then we will be sure that they all have one."

"We all know the staff anyway…" Sophie again volunteered.

"Sorry?" Enid looked at her harshly with raised eyebrows and pursed lips. "Are you *questioning* my decisions?"

Sophie shook her head vigorously. "I didn't know we had a conference next month. I'm not sure I can find anyone to look after Ollie…"

"*All* staff will attend," Enid said firmly, "let me know what your time-scale is on that as we have staff First Aid training coming up in the next few weeks and Laura needs her resuscitation dolls ordered, the new qualification launch is coming up soon- you need to do presentation packs for that- and then we're being inspected at the end of the month and so you need to do our standardisation meeting minutes…"

"We've not had any standardisation meetings?" Sophie asked.

"You will be *required* to do the minutes. You have a lot of work to get on with. The study needs to be set up for visitors arriving at ten and it's now nearly twenty to. Oh and we need to catch up with some of our own teaching staff and make appointments as some are not achieving and some of them quite frankly are a waste of space."

Sophie sat with a blank look on her face, her head buzzing with all the information that had just been thrown at her.

"Shall I do that first then?"

"What's that?" Enid raised her eyebrows again.

"Set up the study?"

"Well, what do *you* think?" Enid asked the question back.

Sophie thought and took a very deep breath, "I'll set up the study."

Enid smiled at her, an emotionless smile, and turned her attention back to her computer screen.

* * *

Later on in the day, just before she was due to leave, Sophie obtained the holiday request form and quickly filled it in.

"Enid," she asked hesitantly, "I've completed the form, the holiday form. Do you want me to leave it on your desk?"

Enid got up briskly and smoothed down her navy suit.

"No let's do it now. My office is free so we might as well use this opportunity. I want to talk to you anyway about your commitment to the school."

"Uh ok," Sophie replied sure she was about to get another telling off. She cast another glance towards Ruth and rolled her eyes towards the ceiling. Sophie hated her chats with

Enid in her private office. She was sure that Enid could kill her with her bare hands.

Sophie reluctantly followed Enid with a sinking heart.

"Holidays holidays…" Enid murmured as she flicked through some paperwork on the desk. "Ah here we go, 'Staff Request for Holiday According to the Request for Leave Policy Discussion Form…' So! I believe that you have completed a holiday request form?"

"Yup."

"And from whom did you obtain this form from?"

Sophie was used to the Spanish inquisition.

"I asked in the office and Tim gave me the form," she instantly cursed herself for mentioning names. Names were never mentioned as the policies changed so regularly that staff had trouble keeping up with their roles and responsibilities. Generally, if you took the initiative to do anything it would be the wrong thing to do.

"Tim?" Enid clicked her tongue. "Does Tim have the authority to issue holiday request forms now? Interesting…"

"Well I don't know but I just asked for a form and he gave me a form as they were in the drawer next to him…"

Enid scribbled notes on her form in her spidery handwriting. 'Tim- forms???' it read. Clearly this was outside his normal duties. Sophie made a mental note to apologise to him on her way out for any bollockings he may receive in the next few hours.

"I can see," Enid held up the holiday form by its corner with her thumb and forefinger,"...that you have filled in the details...." She scribbled on her meeting record as she spoke, "... and that you have requested.... One day off in May 2012.... That day being next year and in approximately fourteen months' time, I will find out the exact time between now and then."

Sophie rolled her eyes and sighed unable to hide her frustration. Why did everything have to be made so difficult?

"I need to leave in a minute Enid to get Ollie from school..."

"There is one section of the form that I need you to complete before I can consider your application and submit it to your employer," she said turning over the form and ignoring Sophie completely, "it details the implications of your absence and if I could just get you to complete that now..." Enid passed Sophie the form.

"Oh I thought that bit was for you to fill in."

"Well I wouldn't be asking *you* to fill it in if it was. The implications of your absence are for *you* to identify."

"The 'implications of my absence'? What- how you're going to manage without me?" Sophie asked slightly incredulously as although vastly experienced and qualified she had basically been working her way through piles of photocopying for the last six months, not even allowed to answer the telephone for reasons unknown to her.

Before this job she had worked in Adult Education at a college in town, finally using her brain as her mother had said. She had been forced to find a much better paid job having the mortgage to pay by herself and Oliver to support. The pay was good but the workload was something else and she found herself working all hours of the day to keep up, often staying up well into the night marking or getting up at the crack of dawn to finish off things from the day before. She had seen this job advertised in the local paper. It had been a small and brief advert merely saying that the school required a qualified individual educated to degree level to work as part of the team delivering in-house training in the school. She applied for the job but then found out that the hours were unmanageable for her, her college work being fairly flexible. They were looking for someone to work from eight until six daily and then a Wednesday night as well as some Saturday's and she just couldn't imagine how she would manage those hours with Oliver, although the pay was much more than she was getting at the college. Sophie was offered the job but she turned it down saying that she was very sorry but the hours were more than she could do with a young son. She thought nothing more about it and then a couple of weeks later she received an email from the principal saying that after careful consideration she would like to offer Sophie a part-time job and what hours would suit Sophie the best. She couldn't believe it and emailed back asking if half nine until half two every day would be possible. Those hours were offered to her shortly after for a very good wage and Sophie accepted the job and was excited that she was going to work at such an exclusive school. There were rumours around town about the way that members of staff were treated but she didn't pay much heed to them. She was still expected to come back in on a Wednesday night but she couldn't have everything she decided and the rest of the job seemed just perfect. The uniform list arrived in the post and she thought she would look smart and sophisticated in her dark suit. She was brought down to earth with a bump on her first day when Ollie told her she looked boring and Enid cut her off as she started to explain about her previous job and was told that nobody cared what she had done before, she was in the real world now. It turned out that to deliver the qualifications that they wanted to the school needed a degree educated person and Sophie was just that. She soon decided that the wage was only just enough to put up with the bullying and harassment.

Sophie looked at the form in her hand and repeated the question.

"Implications of my absence…"

"Well yes," Enid said, "when any member of staff takes annual leave then we have to consider the implications of their absence before granting the time off. If any implications are not stated and are raised at a later date, then your leave may be cancelled and so it is better to be upfront with it now. Of course, if there are no implications of your absence then your employer might wonder why she is employing you at all…"

Oh great, Sophie thought to herself, so now I need to justify my continuing employment! One pesky day off and now I'm pleading to keep my job, typical of this place. She started writing.

"I'll leave you to it. Just pop the completed form on my desk. I'm out for the rest of the day now so I'll see you tomorrow."

"Bye then," Sophie forced a smile and held it until Enid had left the room. She visibly relaxed and slumped back in her chair.

"Implications of my absence..." Sophie wondered out loud. "... the photocopying will have to be done by someone else... my workload will be shared between the remaining four members of staff... I don't have a workload, not an important one anyway," she picked up her pen to start to write. "I will inform my colleagues of any duties that I may need to fulfil during my time off... hmm like washing up the coffee cups! I know, I will discuss my absence with my line manager and agree any handovers that need to be made. I will have a follow up meeting when I return to identify and important areas that I need to reflect on when returning to work. There. That's Enid implicated!" Sophie smiled and folded up her request form and put it in an envelope. She sometimes thought that she wouldn't care if her employer did decide that she was surplus to requirements but then remembered the money and reluctantly decided she'd rather she didn't.

She popped her head around the office door and said a quick 'Goodbye' to her colleagues who were glumly sitting at their desks- she always felt a little bit guilty that she was allowed to leave the miserable place a whole three hours before anyone else.

"Have a nice weekend! Remember drinks at mine later if anyone fancies it!" Sophie chimed, suddenly happy and excited that it was the weekend. She had never had a job before where she had felt *so* good leaving on a Friday afternoon. She knew that only Ruth would come but she always offered anyway.

She hurtled back down the stairs taking two at a time, in the same rush now to get to the school to collect Oliver but now with a skip in her step. At this time every afternoon she congratulated herself for making it through another working day. On so many occasions during the last six months she had just wanted to get up and leave, always shocked by the rudeness of many of her superiors in the school, but she needed to work. The one thing that always persuaded her to stay in the job was that it had been the only one she could find where she could work school hours and the fact that she could earn enough money *and* be around for her son was invaluable to her right now.

Ollie's school finished at quarter past three which gave her a little more time than the morning. She had a chance to catch up with her friends as they waited outside the classroom. She saw the notice on the classroom door stating that it was World Book Day and that the children should dress up.

"I will never again forget the date of World Book Day," she said out loud to nobody in particular. "Has that been up all week or have they just put it up today to make me feel stupid?"

She saw her friends Tina and Jules walking towards where she stood.

"My turn to forget!" she called to them cheerfully, "What amazing costumes did you make for today then? Tell me, make me feel rubbish."

The two ladies came through the gate and joined her outside the class.

"Lydia was Cinderella!" Tina smiled. "It's easier for the girls. We've all got princess dresses so take your pick! Beauty and the Beast, Cinderella, Sleeping Beauty- I could go on."

Sophie turned to Jules who had boys. "Harry Potter?"

"I'm afraid so- both of mine were Harry Potter! Cost me a fortune! What time do you want us round tonight? I could really do with getting out. Steve is being a right pain just now. We were meant to be going out together tomorrow afternoon but now he's going to watch the football with his friend leaving muggins here to look after the boys. Don't get me wrong, I'm not complaining but sometimes I just wished he would spend some time with us."

"Well they are his boys too," Sophie said. She felt sorry for her friend whose husband never seemed to be around. She'd rather be single than have that. "Tell him that you want to spend the day with him- although, I'm not sure why you would want to spend time with such a selfish pig."

"Sophie!" Tina was shocked by her friend's frankness, "that's Jules's husband you're talking about!"

"It's alright, she's quite right you know," Jules said.

The school bell rang signalling the end of the day.

"Sorry but you know I'm anti-men right now."

"You've been anti-men for the past three years," Tina scolded her friend. "I think it's time that you got back out there- not all men are *that* bad!" The ladies giggled.

"Have you seen your vanishing ex lately?" Jules asked.

Sophie scowled. "I wish people would stop asking me about him!"

"Sorry," Jules said genuinely apologetic and squeezed Sophie's arm gently.

The teacher opened the door and Sophie craned her neck to see if she could see her little boy lined up ready to come out for the weekend.

"I've been invited to the wedding of the century actually," Sophie told her friends, "I need to bring a Plus One apparently so I might need to be a bit more pro man if I'm to find one! You can give me your worldly advice later. I need to rush off with Ollie and get him some clothes in town on our way home before you lot get round. Say around half seven which will give me a chance to get him into bed and sort myself out? I'll text Lou, she must be running late. See you later!" She smiled as the children started to tumble out of the class all running excitedly to their grown-ups. Sophie crouched down to give her boy a big cuddle as he ran into her arms.

"Was that a good day?" Sophie asked, beaming at the boy who was still dressed up as Buzz but now without his helmet.

"Are we going to buy a magazine?" he immediately asked.

"Yes we are, plus some clothes but that won't take long," she lied. "Did you have a nice day?"

"You *always* say that we're getting one thing and then you get more!" the boy complained. "You said that we were just getting a magazine! You *always* say 'Just one more shop just one more shop.'"

"No I don't darling and I don't remember saying that. I said that we *would* get a magazine but I didn't say that we *wouldn't* be getting anything else! How was school?"

Oliver looked glum. "I don't *want* to go shopping now."

Sophie sighed.

"Why do I always collect Mr Grumpy when I dropped off Mr Happy? I don't want to talk to Mr Grumpy now that it's the weekend so make him go away please!" I bet Mrs Newman doesn't need to put up with all this grumbling she thought ruefully.

"Shopping is *boring!*" the boy continued to protest.

"OK but we *will* need to get you some clothes on Sunday otherwise you won't have anything to wear! Let's go past the newsagent shop on the way home and get your magazine. Then Mummy can have a nice bath before her friends come round. Is that a good idea?"

The boy nodded happily, pleased that the shopping trip had been delayed by at least a couple of days. Sophie was pleased that he was pleased.

***

Later that evening Sophie enjoyed a brief moment of contemplation in the bath before her girlfriend's came round for their Friday night drinks. She closed her eyes and allowed her body to sink down into the bubbles of the slightly too hot water, the whole bathroom filled with steam and condensation. She had taken Oliver to the shop and bought him his promised magazine. He had asked for a toy as well and Sophie had told him that she didn't have enough money for a magazine *and* toy. The innocent-looking boy had told her that when they got home he would give her all his money in his money box so that she *did* have enough money and she had felt so guilty that in the end she bought him both. He probably had that planned all along, she thought cheerfully, clever little thing.

She lay in the water with her head half submerged and closed her eyes, her thoughts drifting to weddings. In her mind she pictured herself walking down the aisle behind her sister and meeting the gaze of some handsome stranger in the congregation. She of course was immaculately made-up and had curls in her hair, tumbling around her pretty face and down her back. Or maybe he could be the best man who would look over his shoulder and catch her eye making her smile as she walked towards him. He would say something witty as they signed the register looking at her with his twinkling eyes and she imagined blushing slightly and laughing with him. As best man he would ask her for the first dance and then they would dance all night. Other men would watch from the sides of the room and think how stunning this mysterious bridesmaid was but none would get a chance to catch her attention as she only had eyes for the handsome best friend of the groom. As the night drew to an end he would tell her how beautiful she was and that he had had the best night with her. He would meet Oliver and ruffle his hair and make a coin appear from behind his ear then look back at Sophie and smile making her feel weak at the knees. Maybe as they said their goodbyes at the end of the evening he would steal a kiss and make her heart skip a beat and give her the most glorious feeling of butterflies in her tummy.

Sophie snapped herself out of her daydream and sat up in the bath. Silly stupid daydream, she scolded herself. Thoughts like that hurt too much when you remembered they weren't true. Her heart had had enough heartache for one lifetime.

Her mobile rang on the floor next to the bath bringing her back to reality. She reached for a towel and dried her hands and the bubbles from her ear before answering. She registered with slight dismay that it was her mother.

"Oh good timing," she thought, aware that her friends would be round soon, "Hi Mum!" She answered the phone in a brighter tone than she felt, "I can't talk for long! I'm in the bath and the girls are coming round soon."

"I'm fine darling thank you for asking although my knee has been rather sore after my fall. I'm only calling because I've not heard from you today and my handsome young man."

Sophie instantly felt guilty for being too busy to talk.

"Sorry Mum I meant to call. I'm just always so busy. You got my text this morning about Oliver having to dress up. I'll get him to call you in the morning. You really should go to the doctor if you're knee is still sore by Monday."

"Yes well I might do that darling. There's a rather dishy young doctor who's started at the practice apparently, according to Mrs Donaldson and she said that he had a terribly gentle touch."

"Mum!" Sophie cut her Mum off short. "You should be going to the doctor because your knee is sore *not* because there's a hot new doctor! Oh my goodness if he *knew* why he was getting so many repeat visits from the same older ladies. What about Dad?"

"I'm sure your Dad wouldn't mind darling, he's a very liberal man. Anyway did you get it?"

"Get what?"

"*Darling!* The *invitation* of course! Did it come?" her mother spoke as if this was the most exciting event of her life so far. "*Gorgeous* isn't it?"

"Oh *that*. Yes, it came this morning. I didn't get much of a chance to look at it though, to be honest, as I was late for work as usual. I'll look at it later. I'm sure it's lovely."

"Lovely? It's *beautiful.* Your sister has exquisite taste. I know where she gets that from."

Sophie could hear that her mother was smiling with pride. She often felt like second best daughter.

"It was alright. I wouldn't have chosen it myself but it does the job."

"Well it isn't *your* wedding darling, is it?" Sophie's Mother replied. "Maybe if you prettied yourself up a bit and found a man then you would get to send out invites too!"

"I already did that mother, didn't I, but the man did a runner so I'm not really in a rush to do it again," Sophie's voice was flat and emotionless.

"Oh darling, don't sound so down in the mouth! This is your sister's special day so please don't ruin it by being selfish and moody."

"I'm not planning on ruining anyone's day!" Sophie said hotly, "it just reminded me of the wedding that *I* was supposed to have. It's fine."

"And how is Ben?" her mother asked. Sophie flatly ignored the question and there was silence on the phone. "Well," her mother continued eventually, 'it might give you a kick up the backside to find yourself someone to bring to the wedding. We're hoping that you will. Dad and I do worry about you being all on your own."

"I'm not on my own Mum. I have Oliver and I was planning to take *him*."

"Oh I know *that* darling. He's going to be a page boy anyway so of course he's coming. I mean that we're hoping that you'll have a *partner* by that time. A good looking woman like you should have someone by her side and, you know, look after her in lots of different ways. It doesn't need to be a man darling. Mrs Jones has moved in with her lesbian lover after being married for forty years to Mr Jones and having three children. She's very happy now and I think she's being satisfied in a way that she never has before."

"*Mum!*" Sophie snapped at her mother. "Mum I really don't need to know about that. Poor Mr Jones."

"Well I'm sure it's his fault for not keeping her happy in the bedroom department."

"*Mum!*"

"We just worry for you darling. Your dad and I would hope that you are being satisfied in that way too."

"Mother you have not had a conversation about this with Dad. I am about to terminate this phone call."

"Oh OK. No I've not spoken to Dad. While he was at choir practice last night though I borrowed his computer and had a look at this amazing website where you can buy all sorts of things to, you know, satisfy yourself..."

"*Mother!* That's it. I've got to go the girls are coming round. Oliver will call tomorrow. Bye!"

Sophie hung up and shuddered. I hope Dad doesn't check his browsing history, she thought.

She lifted her slightly pink soapy body out of the bath and stepped onto the fluffy white bath mat on the grey slate floor of her bathroom. Wrapping herself up in a matching white towel she padded through to her bedroom leaving wet footprints on the carpet as she went.

Weeks were so busy that by Friday Sophie was usually exhausted, unless she had managed a rare early night in the week. The thought of her bed right now was more appealing that sitting up until all hours watching her friends drink wine. They didn't mind though the odd occasion when she would actually doze off on the sofa, at least her house was a man-free haven. Life usually got in the way of them meeting up every week but it was always noticed if a while went past without a girl's night.

Jules would often let off steam about her absent husband as the rest of them wondered if he was having an affair- Sophie couldn't imagine anyone else wanting him though. Tina's husband worked away and she often compared herself to Sophie as a single mum. A couple of years before he had had an affair and Tina always joked that she should have one too- just to make them all square. Sophie couldn't imagine trusting someone again who had cheated. Lou had a happy relationship. She was married and had two children and a lovely house. Her husband Simon was the one that the Mum's fancied at school with his boyish good looks and expensive casual clothes. He was a freelance graphic designer and would often work from home on the days that Lou worked and be there on sports days and for school fairs and nativity plays. Sophie often thought how lucky her friend was to have such a devoted husband. Ruth had recently started to come along too and back up Sophie's unbelievable stories of rudeness and threats of violence at work. It had become a personal challenge to see how long each could stay at the place. Ruth's boys were older allowing her to work full time at the school. She jokingly resented Sophie being allowed to leave at two thirty when she had to stay until five. With Sophie sticking to soft drinks the remaining ladies managed to put away an impressive amount of wine and she enjoyed sending round the Saturday morning text detailing the number of empty bottles in the recycling.

She pulled on a simple grey dress and some tights and pulled her damp hair up into a bun. Nobody would care what she looked like. She put on some lip balm and went through to check up on Oliver who was quietly playing with his cars, winding down himself after his busy week at school. Sophie sat down next to him and chose a car to drive around the car mat, making 'broom' noises as she went.

They played in companionable silence for a while before the doorbell rang, interrupting the moment of peace.

"That will be the girls darling," Sophie said, "Mummy is going to let them in. You can come and say 'Hello' and then I'll read you a quick story. Maybe Jules will read you a story too like last time!"

"Everyone can read me a story!" the boy stated with glee.

"Well, maybe not everyone. Let's see," she placed a kiss on the top of his head, breathing in the smell of his hair that she loved, and went downstairs to open the door to her friends.

Her phone beeped as she welcomed in Jules, Tina and Lou who had all walked round together. She sniffed the air comically as they trooped in past her arms full of wine and crisps.

"Have you lot been on the booze already?" she asked incredulously, "it's only half seven and you smell like you've been on it since lunchtime."

"Cheeky!" Lou laughed. "We may have had a little aperitif as we were waiting for Steve to get home but nothing compared to what we're about to have! I'm pissed off with Simon because he's working again tomorrow morning which should be our family time, Tina has the hot's for her plumber and Jules is being abandoned by her husband again this weekend. What's Ruth up to- I love your stories from work."

"That's Ruth who's just text me now," Sophie replied looking at her phone, "she's running late. I think she got locked in the office by Enid at home time. OK ladies. Who wants a drink?"

"Me! I do!" the ladies replied and followed Sophie through her lounge and into the kitchen. Jules paused at the mantelpiece.

"Is this it- the wedding of the century?" she asked, picking the invite up and holding it up for all to see. "What a pretty card!"

"It's alright," Sophie said flatly.

Jules looked at her indulgently. "It's *lovely*. It's so unique. You'll have a great time too. I *love* weddings!"

"I hate them," Sophie responded, taking a bottle of wine out of the fridge and holding it out for Tina to inspect, "I absolutely hate them. Maybe if my own hadn't been so rudely cancelled then I would feel differently. I normally manage to duck out of going to them but I have to go to this one. I have no idea who I'm going to take with me though. I guess I've got a year to think about it."

"I'm sure you'll find someone by then. If not, I'll come with you! It's in Scotland- I've never been to Scotland before. I've *always* wanted to," Jules put the invite down and joined the rest in the kitchen.

"Well you can be my plus one then Jules. Glad that's sorted. Mother will be pleased I'm sure that I've turned to lesbianism."

"Will she *really?*" Jules asked.

"Not really. She's just rather desperate for me to find a life partner! I don't know though she's going through a bit of a funny time right now," Sophie shuddered at the thought of her earlier conversation. "As long as I'm there with someone I don't think she cares."

"Oh I'm sure she does. She'll want you to find someone nice to look after you and Ollie."

"I'm not sure that I need someone to look after us!" Sophie said defensively. "I'm doing fine by myself. Listening to you lot sometimes I think I'm lucky being single..." she paused then added thoughtfully, "I suppose it *might* be nice to have someone to cuddle up with at night after a busy day or just to help me find things in B&Q..."

"B&Q... and they say romance is dead!" Jules interjected.

"Anyway," Sophie continued smiling, "second time around and my standard are *very* high. I can't imagine ever meeting anyone who would live up to them!"

"You will," Tina said, passing out the glasses of wine that she poured while listening to Sophie talk. "What's your sister's fiancée like then? Where did they meet?"

"Oh they seem perfectly matched," Sophie replied, getting herself a bottle of alcohol free lager out of the fridge. "They met speed dating but by some fluke they seem to be just right for each other. I wouldn't have ever thought that you could meet your life partner *speed dating* but..."

"Well there you go- there are *so many* ways to meet a partner these days," Tina said, "you could try one? There are lonely hearts columns in the papers and dating sites online or radio stations run ads or there's speed dating or blind dates or social networking or you could take up a new hobby or have a holiday romance…"

"*That's* not going to happen anytime soon," Sophie interrupted, shaking her head and thinking about her earlier attempts to get time off from work.

"Or you could have an office romance…"

Sophie continued to shake her head.

"Or there's supermarket dating..?"

"*Supermarket dating*," Sophie asked incredulously. "*Supermarket dating?* What's *that?*"

"I've seen them do it up the road," Jules replied. "Anyone can go shopping on the night but all the single people have to wear a little rosette- blue if you're a man and pink if you're a woman…"

"Do I *really* need a *rosette* to identify me as a woman?" Sophie asked incredulously.

"No but you *do* need one to identify yourself as a *single* woman," Jules replied shortly. "Anyway, you just do your shopping on that night and if there's a nice man wearing a blue rosette…"

"Just in case I can't tell he's a man..." Sophie interrupted.

"If there's a nice *single* man," Jules continued, "then there's no embarrassment in going up and saying 'Hi'!"

"I'm not so sure about that…" Sophie looked sceptical.

"The contents of a man's shopping basket could tell you a *lot* about him! If he's got cat food that would be quite sweet or if he's got oysters and wine even better..."

"Or condoms!" Lou added.

"Corn flakes would say 'dependable'; Honey Nut Loops might say 'exciting...'"

"Really- *exciting*?" Lou interrupted again. "Or child like?"

"Or a variety pack would tell you to steer well clear," Jules finished, ignoring Lou's suggestions. "I guess then you just start chatting to them, a little bit of flirting at the fresh fish counter... I think they do food and wine tasting too so you can stop and have a chat."

"Just remember on that night not to need to buy anything embarrassing like loo rolls or tampons!" Lou laughed.

"It just sounds so *difficult* now. Why don't I just put a big sign on my head that says 'I need to find someone by May 2012'? I've been single for *three years.* I wouldn't know where to start these days. The first time I didn't try, it all just *happened.*"

"How can you have been single for *three years* Sophie?" Lou asked. "Have you had your head in a box all that time?"

Sophie shrugged. "I don't know. I just have. It's no big deal, not to me anyway. I've just been getting on with bringing up Ollie and sorting out my career."

"You've only been single for three years because you don't actually go out!" Jules replied. "You could get back into practice. When you go out and start looking I'm sure you'll find loads of nice guys. You just need to look in the right places."

"Actually you can meet *more* people by staying in!" Tina offered.

"I *do* go out but usually just running or to the gym. I'd rather do that though anyway than have to sit in a restaurant somewhere with a random man, I'd go mad if I didn't get out for a run. It's my 'me' time. I have Ollie to consider too now- I can't just go out with any old bloke."

"Well it wouldn't be *any old bloke* anyway would it? You're not just going to *bump into* Mr Right. You can *plan* to meet him though," Tina said her eyes twinkling with mischief. "There are *loads* of different web sites where you can meet *all kinds* of men- or women!"

"A man would be fine," Sophie frowned at her friend.

"There are web sites to meet older men, younger men, intellectual men, rich men, men with children, men *without* children, good looking men, vegetarian men, men in *uniform,* men in *specific* uniforms…" Tina took a gulp of wine and looked like she might continue.

"You're very knowledgeable on this subject!" Lou observed. "Is there something you'd like to tell us?"

"Oh a girl can look can't she?" Tina said defensively. "I'm not ever going to try and meet someone! My husband actually touched another woman- I'm just looking at pictures."

"It's quite shallow to look for a guy *just* because he wears a certain kind of uniform… isn't it?" Sophie asked. Tina looked at her incredulously.

"*No!*" she said as if it were the most obvious place to start. "Most people have a Top Five uniform list… don't they?" she said, looking around at the others. "You *do*! Don't try and pretend you don't!"

"Who's number one then?" Sophie asked. "Firemen..?"

"*Obviously..*!" Tina replied.

"I disagree!" Lou chipped in. "What about a pilot."

Tina considered this. "You have a point there… I'm sticking with firemen though- they save people's lives," she pretended to swoon.

"I might have to say the army," Joules joined in. "Definitely the army. Although, what about the police?"

"Good call!" Tina said. "It is difficult to put them into Top Five order isn't it..?"

"Let's go and sit down anyway, my feet are killing me," Jules interrupted. "Hello little man how are you?" she smiled at Ollie who had silently appeared in the kitchen, "did you have a nice time today dressing up?"

"Yes thank you," the little boy replied, "but I wanted to be Harry Potter and Mummy wouldn't let me."

The group looked at Sophie for her response.

"Now that's not true is it darling? For a start there was no way you were going to be Harry Potter anyway as we left it so late but you told me that you *didn't like* him!" Sophie was used to her son's tall tales. "Anyway, I better put you to bed properly. All of Mummy's friends have been naughty and had too much wine so I will read you a story tonight. I can read your new magazine. Say goodnight to everyone."

"Goodnight," the boy dutifully said and Sophie picked him up and took him to his room while the girls made themselves comfortable in her lounge. Jules pulled a couple of stools out from under her table to put their nibbles on and Sophie heard the chink of glasses as they said 'cheers'. She smiled and shook her head like their indulgent mother.

She placed the boy in his bed and tucked the sheets around him and his favourite teddy bear, Mr Ted.

"Is there space for me too?" she asked, raising her eyebrows. Ollie moved Mr Ted to the other side of him making a small space for Sophie to squeeze in.

"Right I'm going to read one story from your magazine and then I'm going downstairs to talk to my friends. You need to think of what you want to do tomorrow as well darling. It's you and me this weekend. Aunty Jo is coming to see us next weekend and tell us *all* about what we need to do for her wedding so that will be nice but this weekend it's just us." She loved the weekends when they had no plans. She lay down next to her son and flicked through his magazine to find a suitably short story. Twenty minutes later she was woken up by the sound of her friend's laughter from downstairs.

"Damn it!" she thought. Ollie snored gently beside her.

After their hectic morning and her week at work she could have easily slept there all night, cuddling her son's little warm body. It was with a great effort that she managed to get out of his bed and take herself back downstairs to her cold living room. The laminate floor and open plan lay out looked modern but was not cosy at all. Conversation, laughter and wine were in full flow. Sophie squeezed in next to Jules on her little two-seater sofa and blinked her tired eyes.

Lou was holding the Sunday newspaper that Sophie always got but never read. She folded back the paper and flattened it down on her lap.

"OK let's see who we've got here then," she studied the print for a moment. "Here we go, here's one. 'David, solvent male, fifty-two…'"

"What are you *reading*?" Sophie asked in a horrified tone.

"Just the lonely hearts adverts. You've inspired us to have a little look. Anyway where was I? David, solvent male, fifty-two…"

"What- does that mean he's pissed all the time?" Jules interjected and laughter ensued.

"I believe it means he has shed loads of cash. Anyway there's more. 'Looking for fit female, looks unimportant, will try anything'. I bet you will you dirty dog!" Lou snorted with laughter and took a gulp of her wine. "Let's try another one. OK this might be better. 'Milo, forty-eight...'"

"The Tweenies' are getting on a bit!" Jules interrupted.

"Milo, forty-eight, no major issues! Yeah is that apart from your name?"

Laughter rang out through the room once more. Lou held out her empty glass.

"Any more wine going?" she asked trying to locate the opened wine bottle. Jules poured the last into her own glass and disappeared off to the kitchen to open their second. Sophie clutched her alcohol-free lager, hiding the label with her hand.

"Hmm Kyle, good name, enjoys the simple things in life and looking for the right lady to share them with."

"*Bo-ring*!" Tina sang out. "*Everyone* says that." She took another large swig of her wine aware that she was showing too much knowledge on the subject for a married mother of two.

"How about this," Lou continued. "Loving, caring, loyal, romantic, trusting, protecting..."

"How many adjectives can one man be?" Jules interrupted.

"*As I was saying..!*" Lou continued, "… all I want is to be loved and to love and share my heart and soul with my wife to be," she comically stuck her fingers in her mouth. "No thank you Malcolm- too wet."

"He sounds lovely," Sophie mused.

"Sixty." Lou added.

"*Sixty?* Go a bit younger!" Sophie giggled, "At least about my age? I don't really see myself with someone that old- go, like, thirty years younger."

"Oh *here* we go this is more like it," Lou sorted out the paper on her lap and started to read. "'Gorgeous twenty-six-year-old…'" she began.

"If he's so gorgeous what's he doing in the lonely hearts?" Jules interjected as she came back into the room holding a fresh bottle of Rose.

"Well Sophie's going to be in them and *she's* totally gorgeous!"

"No I'm not!" Sophie protested. "I can't think of anything worse than putting an ad in a newspaper. I'd rather just meet someone, if I'm going to! I can't imagine dating again. Anyway, nobody's going to describe themselves truthfully in these things are they? They're all making themselves sound more amazing than they are."

"Really..? What, even Milo?" Lou raised her eye brows quizzically.

"They could be *anybody* though and I can't decide if I'm going to like someone on two lines of text- especially when there's no accompanying picture!"

"Ah if it's pictures you want then you need to be online!" Lou triumphantly stated, "Some of these sound OK though. You don't need to date *all* of them! Listen," she focussed her attention back on the paper, "'Michael, thirty-four, seeks genuine lady to enjoy nights out and maybe more. GSOH.' *He* sounds OK!"

"That says nothing at all!" Sophie exclaimed. "How can you say he sounds OK from *that*?"

"Well then *you* could put an ad in then you can say exactly what *you're* looking for. What's your type?"

"I'm not sure if I have a type," Sophie replied thoughtfully. "I'd know it when I see it."

"Of course you've got a type! *Everyone's* got a type!" Lou looked round the room. "Tina's type is a muscle bound labourer- not too clever but nice to look at, Jules's type is someone who is physically present, my type is George Clooney although I'm happy to put up with Simon for now…"

"I've never thought about it. *Honestly!* I just met Ben and we got along and that was it- I didn't think about if he was my type or not."

Lou rolled her eyes. "Sophie we are going to have our work cut out with you! Let's come at it from a different angle then. We need some kind of preferences for an advert. What do you like?"

"Oh I'm not putting an advert in the paper! I'm sure the only people who'll reply will be complete Psycho's," Sophie protested.

"Psycho's who can't use the internet," Tina added.

"You don't need to put an advert in the paper then. Let's just make one up. Come on, just for a laugh," Lou said.

"I'm glad that my situation is causing you so much hilarity!" Sophie said getting slightly tired of the subject.

"Oh go on humour me just this once," Lou pleaded. "Come on, what do you like?"

"Reading?"

"Oh come *on* Sophie what do you want him to do- take you to the library? Sex it up a bit."

"Well I *like* reading," Sophie complained. "At least we'd have something in common. I like *running.*"

"Yes that's good then they'd know how fit you are."

"Actually, I have a friend who is single," Jules suddenly joined in the conversation after studying the wine label for some time, "he's so sweet but was messed around pretty badly by his ex."

"Join the club," Sophie said.

"Well exactly. He's really funny, has me in stitches all the time. Look him up online. Why don't you see if he wants to go out for a drink?"

"I can't just randomly ask someone out for a drink," Sophie said, "He doesn't know me."

"Well I'll see him tomorrow when he picks Steve up for the football. I could just mention something, you know, using my subtlety."

Sophie looked dubious.

"Well you know I could just mention you? Or we could all go out for a drink? I'll sort it out," she smiled. "How lovely would that be for two of my best friends to get *married*?"

Sophie laughed at her friend's optimism and went into the kitchen to get some more food. They'll need it to soak up all that wine, she thought. She poured some crisps out into various bowls and took some dips out of the fridge. She went back into the lounge carrying the whole lot, bowls of crisps in both hands and the dips balanced on her wrists. The doorbell rang as she held out her hands for someone to help her put the food down.

"Oh that'll be Ruth! I'd given up on her coming now, it's quite late."

Sophie went to the front door and opened it with a smile. Her friend from work was there.

"That woman is *unbelievable*!" Ruth said without saying hello. She kissed Sophie on both cheeks as she spoke. "She *knows* that I work until five and gave me a *massive pile* of photocopying to do at ten to! I was there until just gone six!"

"Oh that's *my* job!" Sophie joked.

"On a *Friday..!* I mean, what's going to happen to it anyway over the weekend?"

"You should just say that you only work until five and do the rest the next day," Tina suggested, "she sounds like she needs to chill out a bit."

"You don't question Enid. She does need to chill out a *lot!*" Sophie told her friends. "I think we need to find *her* a man and not me and then maybe she wouldn't be so mean to everyone! She's in that office every day at about six and doesn't leave until late. She's probably in this weekend too... Anyway, Ruth, what would you like to drink?"

Ruth joined Sophie drinking soft drinks and the two chatted while the other's continued thinking of ways to find Sophie her plus one. Sophie left them to it deciding that they didn't need her input.

"What's your email Sophie?" Lou asked, "I just want to email you a link to something."

"What do you want to send me?" Sophie asked.

"Oh just a link to, um, a new gym I saw has opened in town."

Sophie recited her email address, thinking it was slightly odd that Lou couldn't just tell her, but then was distracted by Ruth telling her that Enid once actually locked her in the cupboard that she forgot to ask any more about it.

It was late by the time she got to bed. She checked on Oliver before she went into her own room, leaving the door slightly ajar so that he could creep in with her in the night- a habit that she knew that he would have to get out of but at the moment was happy for him to take up the empty space. She flopped into bed just before two in the morning, hugging her arms round her pillow and finally being allowed to close her heavy eyes having made it to the end of another frantic week.

Chapter Two

It was half past six when Sophie woke up the following morning, her body clock always doing at the weekend what her alarm clock should do in the week. She groaned when she saw how early it was. She rearranged her pillows and snuggled back down, cuddling her son who slept soundly next to her and closed her eyes, hoping to drop back off to sleep herself as she had done successfully the previous day. Her mind was awake now though and thought's flickered through it about weddings and dating and work and the washing machine.

Damn, the washing machine, she thought. I meant to call someone about that yesterday, as if I have the time for the washing machine to break down.

Trying not to now look at the overflowing washing basket she carefully sat up and twisted her legs around, putting her feet into her slippers at the side of the bed, mindful not to wake up the quietly snoring boy next to her. Quietly opening the door, she crept out of the room and down to the kitchen to make a pot of coffee. She ignored the glasses in the sink and empty bottles that sat on the kitchen side left from the previous night when she had been too exhausted to tidy up. The ladies had offered to help but they had opened a new bottle of wine at half past twelve and by the time they eventually left, just before two, Sophie was ready to crash in her bed. She loved having time to catch up with the girls properly, it kept her sane, but *sometimes* she did wish they would leave a *little* bit earlier.

I'm so unsociable really, she said to herself with a smile, though I'd better *get* more sociable if I'm to find a man. Humming a tune, she decided to have a continental breakfast as a treat as it was the weekend, or as continental as she could manage. She stood up on her tip toes, trying to reach inside the highest cupboard to find a new packet of ground coffee and then jumped up on the kitchen side to retrieve a cafetiere that was tucked away on top, an engagement present that was rarely used. She felt guilty now that people had bought presents for her engagement when the marriage didn't take place- even though it wasn't her fault. There were random things around the kitchen to remind her of her cancelled wedding- a tray, a cheese board, some key hooks, a mortar and pestle, some pasta jars and a cafetiere. All items that were fairly useful but nothing she would want to spend money on replacing and so she kept the sad mementos.

Sophie paused for a few seconds, remembering the excitement that she had felt about being the bride to be. She had been such a book worm as a child and adored her books of fairy tales and stories of princesses, daydreaming about one day meeting her very own handsome prince. Her favourite story was Cinderella and she would urge her parents to read it night after night. As she got older she was allowed to stay up reading for a while and she would lie and gaze at the pictures of Cinderella in her beautiful ball gown and dream of one day being a princess like her.

The handsome prince had come along in the shape of Ben Sharpe, an accountant who she met at a friend's party a couple of years after she graduated. The inconvenience of real life had forced her to get a job and she had taken a summer job as a nanny abroad, much to her parent's distress after paying her through university and hoping for her to follow her sister in building up a successful career, and when the family returned to their home in the south of England she had gone too and the job carried on. Sophie and Ben had got on instantly, they went out together, drank together and made each other laugh and soon became inseparable. Thinking back, it had all happened so easily. It didn't take long for Sophie to move in with Ben and she spent the next ten years wondering if he would ever propose. She had asked him one year and he had laughed and said it was too soon and she laughed too saying it was only a joke anyway. *One day,* he had said. She longed for that *one day.* Then *one day* she had a tooth abscess and the dentist didn't tell her the antibiotics might affect the pill that she was on and she became pregnant.

Sophie was overjoyed at being pregnant, it wasn't an issue for her that it was completely unplanned or that they had never spoken about children because she knew that she was with the man that she wanted to spend the rest of her life with. She bought all the pregnancy magazines, started taking folic acid, told *everyone* when she was due, started buying tiny socks and cut out anything that was bad for baby. It was during the first weekend of being pregnant that she suddenly realised that all she and Ben did together was go out to pubs and drink. There was a big rugby match on and he wanted to go to their regular pub and watch it with their friends but Sophie wanted to go to a baby shop and look at tiny clothes. Suddenly they had nothing in common anymore despite the fact that she was carrying the child they had made together. As she stood on the kitchen side, pondering on what had been she wondered if she had become so wrapped up in being pregnant that she hadn't noticed the signs that she and Ben had just grown apart. He had, however, asked her to marry him soon after she had found out that they were to be parents and when Oliver was born Sophie got to work on getting back into shape and helping her mother arrange the wedding that she had always dreamed of, set for Oliver's second birthday. It was such a wonderfully busy time with her new son and gym visits and the wedding preparations she hadn't noticed that anything was amiss. But three months before the marriage was to take place the groom went AWOL, leaving a letter saying how sorry he was but he wasn't ready for all this. Still not ready, after all this time Sophie had thought. Ten years and you're not ready. She wished he had said earlier, years earlier so that she hadn't fallen in love with him so much or wanted so much to have his children or wasted so much of her time. She was devastated but with a baby boy to look after Sophie shed little tears and got on with it resolving to never let anyone hurt her or waste her time like that again. She numbly got on with the life that she now had. The wedding plans were cancelled. Cake shops and flower arrangers and musicians and drivers and seamstresses and hoteliers and ministers of the cloth were all discreetly called to say that their services would no longer be required and the many guests who had been invited were informed that the wedding was off. Sophie sighed at the memories.

Six months later Ben had reappeared with longer hair and stubble, wearing wooden beads around his neck and wrists with a new tattoo bearing the name of his son and a bunch of flowers for the bride he dumped saying he was *so sorry* and he wanted to be a part of Oliver's life.

Sophie remembered it vividly. It was a Saturday morning and she and Ollie had slept in, as they had a tendency to do. She'd just got out of the shower and was walking around the house with her towel wrapped around her head and her very old white dressing gown when the doorbell rang. She contemplated leaving it and pretending that they weren't in, not feeling that sociable and fully expecting it to be either an energy salesman or someone from the local church but then she remembered that she was expecting a parcel and rushed downstairs to open the door. Ben was standing there, his handsome features having been improved by a tan and looking more youthful with a head of floppy hair compared to his usual short, back and sides. Sophie had been dumbfounded at first, not knowing what to think or say and not quite believing that it was actually him standing before her. It had been such a long time since she'd seen him and for a moment nothing had seemed real. She stared at him, still speechless, before he had broken the silence and said, 'Hi' and smiled, the smile that had melted her heart all those years ago. She couldn't remember her reply exactly but it included lots of single words and unfinished sentences; 'What…?', "Why…?", "Where are you…?", "What did you…?", "Ollie…"

She had dumbly taken the flowers and listened to the words that were coming out of his mouth; he was sorry, he didn't mean to hurt her, how was Ollie, could he see him, he'd missed him so much, they'd been together so long, he didn't know what he wanted anymore, he'd met somebody else.

Those last words had struck her like a kick in the stomach. She still felt that feeling when she thought back. He'd met someone else, he said, Sarah. They'd been together for so long, he said, and things had gone a bit stale. Sarah had made him laugh and remember who he really was and was just so much *fun*.

"I was fun," Sophie had said, "I made you laugh…" She looked at Ben pleadingly and then all the words that had been building up in her head over the past three months had come tumbling out. "You told me that I was the only one who really knew you. I wanted to grow *old* with you. That's why we were together for so long. That's why I wanted to marry you and have your child. I wanted to be with you for *decades* more. I wanted to be with you *forever!*" As she spoke her voice rose and her body began to shake. She felt the tears stinging her eyes and her heart was banging inside her chest. "How could you *leave* us? How could you *leave me?* How could you? *How could you?*"

Ben had seemed shocked by Sophie's reaction, like he was expecting a big hug and to be welcomed back in for a cup of tea and a chat. He said that it was obviously a bad time and was Sophie having a bad day and did they laze around in bed every morning until eleven o'clock at which point she muttered that she really had other things to do and started to push the door shut before Ben put his hand up to stop it.

"Listen Soph. I've come back to see Ollie. I'm sorry about everything but I don't know what else to say. That's it. He's my son and I want to see him."

Now, Sophie had thought. You want to see him now. You left with no warning and didn't contact him for six months but you want to see him now.

And that was the worst part of it all, she thought, that he had come back. She wished that he had never come back. If he had left and they had never heard from him again then she could have grieved then moved on with her life. She could imagine then meeting someone else and being happy again. Instead he was still there, living two streets away so that he could be close to his boy. He called her randomly to ask how Oliver was and popped by sometimes on his way home from work. Some evening's he would text to say how much he missed his boy and could he come round to read a story to him. When he arrived he'd kiss her on both cheeks because Sophie was far too polite to say 'No, bugger off', and ask how she was and comment on how she was looking and how she'd done her hair. He asked about her family and how her job was going and seemed to want to be involved in everything again, except from being with her. And then, like a final lasting dig at her, everyone started to ask after him. When she spoke to her parents they asked, 'How's Ben? Are you seeing much of him these days?' as if nothing had happened. Her sister asked, 'How's Ben?' Her friends asked, 'How's Ben?' The people who had been there for her and helped her through those months were now asking how the man who smashed her heart to pieces was. Oliver was supposed to be seeing him in a couple of weekend's time but Sophie didn't tell him until it happened as these visits often got cancelled or moved depending on what Ben and Sarah had planned. Texts often arrived ten minutes before he was due to pick him up saying that something's come up and could he get him in the morning. Sophie felt bitter that her life now revolved around Ben and his new girlfriend's.

Stupid bloody man, Sophie had thought. You decide one day that you were going to abandon us for someone else, leaving me to support and raise our son and then you waltz back into our lives and tip it all upside down again, just as everything had settled down, demanding to see Ollie now you've had a think about it. This isn't how I had wanted to raise my child, passing him back and forth between parents, having to be apart from him every other weekend. This is not how I wanted my life to turn out.

Sophie suddenly realised that her body was shaking with anger and she felt like she was about to cry. She was gripping the handle of the cafetiere so tightly that it was starting to hurt her hand. She put it down and took a deep breath, letting the tension that she felt leave her body. I've wasted enough time and tears already on that man, she thought, I have more important things to worry about now like breakfast and the washing machine. She shook her head and dismissed all thoughts from her head. Back to today. She lowered herself carefully down from the side and filled the kettle to boil and took a croissant out of the freezer to toast, switching the grill on.

I could put a quick face mask on now, she thought, seeing as mother thinks I should be prettying myself up.

With a sudden feeling of optimism Sophie went upstairs to the bathroom to find the pot of face mask that she knew she had but hadn't used for months. She listened at her bedroom door and heard the soft sound of Oliver's breathing, at least one of them making the most of the weekend lie in. She carried on past to the bathroom and rummaged around in various drawers of a white wicker unit until she found a white tub of expensive face treatment- a present from her sister the Christmas just gone and from a company that Sophie would never be able to afford to buy from.

What a treat, she thought. I really should spend more time looking after myself.

Taking off the lid she smelt the cream and wrinkled her nose at the slightly odd aroma.

It must be good if it smells so bad, she thought and started to smooth the white cream over her face starting around her mouth and jawline. She pulled funny faces at herself in the mirror as she rubbed the face mask under her nose. The silky texture of the cream felt luxurious. As she studied the blurb the scent became more noticeable, probably because it's right under my nose she thought.

A shrill piercing sound suddenly shattered the still morning peace.

What the… Sophie thought and instantly remembered her continental breakfast was still on the go downstairs.

"Mummy!" her son's frightened shriek came from the bedroom and the door opened. *"Mummy where are you?"*

"I'm here darling! I'm here in the bathroom," the little boy scampered into the bathroom still clutching his teddy bear as the alarm continued to scream out. He stopped and stared and started to laugh despite the smoke detector's cries.

"Mummy you're like Father Christmas!" he exclaimed with glee, "Are you dressing up like Father Christmas?"

"No," Sophie said ruefully, "No I'm not I was just trying to make myself look pretty."

"*That* doesn't look pretty Mummy," the boy responded, "that looks silly!" and he looked pleased with himself at his own little joke.

Sophie hurried past him and ran downstairs, Father Christmas beard on, to put an end to the racket and possible fire in the kitchen. She pulled out the grill pan to reveal a black and smoking croissant, switched off the grill and opened the back door which led onto their garden. She put the croissant in the sink to join the empty wine glasses to add to her, 'Things to Do Later' list and ran back into the lounge looking around quickly to see what she could fan the smoke away from the detector with. The first paper item that she saw was the wedding invitation that had caused so much discussion the previous night and she grabbed it and sped to the smoke detector at the bottom of the stairs. Jumping up and down she frantically waved the card back and forth below the little white box on the ceiling and seconds later the noise abated and the house fell silent once more.

And that, she thought with resignation, was my relaxing continental breakfast.

"Do you know how you could be really helpful?" she said to her son who had followed her down the stairs to witness the whole proceedings.

"How?" he said without much enthusiasm in his voice.

"You could make your own breakfast?"

"I don't know how to make my breakfast," he replied.

"Yes you do. You get a bowl and put some porridge in it and some milk then eat it with a spoon," Sophie said, annunciating each word clearly.

"I don't know where the porridge is," the boy was suddenly being less that helpful.

"Yes you do because you were being helpful yesterday and got it out for me. It's in the cupboard next to the fridge isn't it?"

"What if it's a new packet and I can't open it?"

"I know it's *not* a new packet but if it was you could try and then if you couldn't open it you could ask for help," Sophie was determined not to let this one pass.

The boy stood thoughtfully.

"What if I spill the milk?"

"You won't spill the milk if you're being careful!" Sophie explained patiently, "Listen. You get a bowl out of the bottom cupboard- the one you use every day. You get your spoon out of the drawer- the blue one with a little train on the end. You go into the cupboard next to the fridge and take two spoonful's of porridge out of the packet which I happen to know is open because it is on my shopping list for today and so it must nearly be finished," she held her hand up to stop his protests at the word 'shopping'," You then *carefully* take the milk out of the fridge and pour a *little* bit on top of the porridge which you have put into your bowl. You then *carefully* take your bowl of porridge and spoon into the dining room and *carefully* sit up at the table where we eat our food every day and *eat* your breakfast. If you were being *super* helpful you would then take your bowl back into the kitchen, pushing your chair under the table and wash up your bowl and make sure the porridge and milk was away."

There was a long silence while the boy digested all this information.

"I'm not hungry."

"Right, go upstairs please. I'll make your breakfast."

The boy smiled at another victory and trotted off happily. Sophie shook her head, sighed and looked around at everything in the kitchen, wondering where to start. She scowled as she remembered the half applied face mask and went upstairs to take it off. At least my chin will be radiant today, she thought.

She returned to the bedroom a little while later, after tidying the kitchen and disposing of her chargrilled breakfast, with a tray containing the boy's porridge, a carton of his juice from the lunch box supply and a cup of instant coffee. Oliver was sitting on the bed watching a DVD that seemed to have been on repeat for at least two weeks.

"Don't you want to watch something else today darling?" Sophie asked, "I think you've watched the Lion King about twenty times!"

"Only twelve times Mummy," he responded without taking his gaze away from the screen, "I like the Daddy lion."

Sophie sighed. Every so often he would come out with a little comment as if to remind her that she might be OK but that he'd quite like a daddy around. She placed her modest breakfast tray on the bedside table and got back into bed, leaning over to give her son a hug and kiss. She then reached for her laptop which was on the floor next to her side of the bed and switched it on making a mental list of all the things she had to check. She searched 'Washing Machine repairs' in her locality and numerous links came up. Unsure of which one to choose she scrolled up and down the screen reading each advert in turn. One caught her eye as the person was close by and she scribbled down his number on a piece of scrap paper that she kept in the drawer next to her bed. She noticed that the advert said, 'Single Mother's Welcome' and was puzzled momentarily but decided that he must do some kind of discount and thought nothing more about it. Checking her social networking sites she saw instantly that she had a friend request from a Paul Dudley.

"Wow that was easy," she thought, assuming he must be Jules's friend. She studied his picture. "I've never even met him and he wants to be my friend. What the hell," she thought and, in a moment of sheer abandon, accepted his request. Sophie was the sort of person who had thirty-eight friends and knew each one. "Nothing to lose I guess. Let's see if he's my type."

She immediately had a look through his photos. She could hear herself saying the night before something about looks not being important, it being the person that counts. She had decided that her type was someone with a sense of humour. Looking through his pictures now she turned into someone who could be called superficial. She studied the few pictures that he had on his page, squinting at them and trying to imagine him in person. None of the pictures were that close up though and she sat on the bed feeling slightly perplexed as she now wanted to study this random man in fine detail. She thought for a moment then remembered about a magnifying glass that Oliver had been given last Christmas by her Dad and which was normally used for inspecting poor spiders and other small beasts who unsuspectingly wandered into the young boy's path. That should do the trick. She nimbly jumped out of bed and went through to Oliver's room and rummaged around in a box of miscellaneous junk. With every room clear out Sophie suggested that most of this stuff could be thrown away but the boy always insisted that he needed it all- charity shop toys, tiny plastic trinkets from Christmas crackers, items from party bags, various bits from broken Transformers and other random items. She found the magnifying glass in the box.

"Bingo!" she thought and took it back through to where tiny Paul was pictured on her laptop.

"Not *bad..,* " she thought, peering through the glass and trying desperately to like the pictures, "He must be nice if he's Jules's friend anyway."

She carried on studying his photos for a few minutes longer, trying to imagine this man in her life. She couldn't tell exactly but he looked alright. He *looked* like he might be good with children- she got that impression from a photo of him on a bouncy castle and Jules had said that he was great with her boy's. There were a few photos of him with groups of men, mostly with a beer in hand, some with Jules's husband Steve. He looked fairly harmless and normal and the more she looked the more she liked him. Her imagination started to work overtime as she thought about dates with him, maybe to the cinema or out for a meal, or the three of them- Sophie, Ollie and Paul- being invited to Jules's for a bar-b-q or a trip to the beach.

She checked her emails and saw that she had a new message from the Times Dating online.

"What the…" Sophie thought as she opened the mail and started reading its contents. "Oh my goodness. Oh my flipping goodness what have they *done?* I'm definitely going to have to ration their wine intake next time."

She read the email which was from Michael, who Sophie could only imagine was the guy who had advertised himself in the lonely hearts that had caused so much laughter the night before. She instantly picked up her mobile and sent a text to her three friends asking them which one had done this dastardly deed. I don't expect I'll get a reply for a few hours though, she thought, thinking about the empty bottles of wine she's just put outside in the recycling bin. She re-read the message and was horrified that he mentioned that she was nice. If they have sent him a photo of me I'll *kill* them, she thought. He also seemed to be thinking that they were meeting up soon.

"Hi Sophie," the message read. "Good to hear from you, thanks for getting in touch. I thought I'd give this a try- didn't ever think someone as nice as you would get back to me! I'll tell you a little bit about me before we meet up if you like although obviously I'd love to meet such an attractive woman. I'm a freelance journalist, I write stuff for outdoorsy magazines. I'm into anything that's extreme. I've just come back from mountain biking over the Himalayas and in a few months I'll be diving and biking again this time in Vietnam. I did my first bungee jump earlier on this year- awesome. Life is pretty good- just obviously looking for a similar-minded individual to share the ride with. Would love to hear from you again- stay in touch. M. xx"

Sophie sat and thought for a second, never before had her own life seemed so boring. As she sat next to her five-year-old with the strains of 'Circle of Life' coming out of the telly she struggled to know how to reply to that email, if she was going to reply at all, though now that she'd been introduced into Michael's life she probably should respond. Would I even want to go diving in Vietnam though, she thought? Paul seemed like the safer option. She decided just to reply anyway and see what happened, beginning to warm to this contact with the outside world that she had been starved of for three years. I'll see what he looks like and go from there she decided and sent him a brief reply saying she was rushing out for the day but that she'd be back in later and how it would be nice to see who she was chatting to. She pressed send before she had a chance to change her mind, scrunching up her eyes and grimacing to the point that Oliver's attention was diverted away from his DVD.

"Mummy shall I call 999? Is this an emergency?" His little voice sounded like he was man enough to cope with anything. She relaxed her facial muscles and took a deep breath.

"No it's fine darling. Well done for asking if it was an emergency. What would you do if Mummy didn't reply?"

"Dial 999 and tell them that Mummy's not moving."

"Well *done* darling. Mummy's fine I was just sending a scary email."

The boy's face lit up at the word 'scary'.

"Ooh *scary*? Was it an *alien* or a *monster*?" He asked with anticipation. "Was it a *dinosaur*?"

"No darling I was just sending an email to a normal person."

The boy turned his attention back to the telly deciding that there was nothing more in the conversation that was of interest to him. Sophie turned her attention back to her emails and saw, amongst the junk there was one from her sister titled 'Next Weekend' and continued reading. She sent a brief reply that she would call her later and shut down her lap top.

"OK Mister I'm going to get ready and phone someone to come and fix the washing machine. Then we can go out to the park and if you're extra good you can have a turn on the little train *and* some ice cream. Sound good?"

The boy nodded his head frantically, smiling broadly.

***

She wasn't that sure what time it was OK to call workmen on a Saturday or if they would come out anyway. She was sure that if they did come out it would cost her a small fortune whatever time it was.

Mike arrived at the door at about half past nine. He told Sophie that he didn't usually work on Saturday but that he could pop round as he lived so close and at least tell her if the washing machine could be fixed. A rounder man Sophie had never seen. His head merged into his neck which merged into his body with his arms resting on the sides. She would have described him as a Weeble which she remembered from her childhood- even his face was similar with his pin-hole eyes and cheeky grin. He held a tool box in one hand and extended his other to Sophie who looked doubtfully at his grubby fingers but decided it would be too rude not to shake them. She ushered him in and through to the kitchen to inspect the patient, cringing as he walked over her immaculate floor with his shoes still on.

Mike placed his tool box on the floor which caused the layer of dust that covered it to sprinkle down to join his grubby footsteps. Sophie instantly felt annoyed that she hadn't asked him to take his shoes off, long gone are the days that I spend my time tidying up after messy men, she thought.

"So, this is it…" he said importantly.

"Yeah..!" Sophie replied. "This is it!" She looked at him expectantly.

He opened the washing machine door and held it by either side with his stubby fingers and looked into the barrel. He gave the thing a shake, spun the barrel round and had a look in the drawer. He stood up to his full height of five foot two and clicked his tongue before crouching right down to pull out a section of the machine that Sophie didn't know existed, peered into the dark space that it filled and then placed his hands on his legs and, with some difficulty, pushed himself back up to standing. He stroked his chin with his fingers and looked thoughtful for a while. Sophie stood silently, trusting this funny little man to solve the problem on the basis that he had an advert that said that he could. He shut the door and put a wash cycle on and they both stood and watched while the barrel filled up with water. Then the noise of whooshing and gurgling stopped and they listened to the silence. I could have told you it would do that, Sophie said to herself, it's broken, that's why I called. Finally he spoke.

"It's hard," he said seriously 'when you're by yourself and things start going wrong."

Sophie stared at him, not really sure if he meant that it's a pest when something breaks down or something entirely deeper. She immediately decided to assume the former as the latter seemed too problematic.

"Yes it's a nightmare when the washing machine breaks down especially!" she said lightly, almost hysterically she thought later. "I'm *so* busy I really don't have time for things like this so I'm hoping it's not a serious problem! I could do without having to fork out for a new one right now!"

She suddenly stopped herself jabbering and wondered how he knew that she was by herself. Maybe he meant that she was just by herself in the house at that moment but it didn't *sound* like that.

"I can get a beautiful woman like yourself a new one at cost price if it would make it easier for you."

Sophie immediately felt her defences going up. How *dare* he be so smarmy when all I want is for him to fix the bloody washing machine, she thought? Make it *easier*. What a creep.

"It would be easier if you could just fix the one I've got, thanks all the same. Can you fix it?"

"Well," he sounded like there was a reason why he couldn't, 'the problem with machines these days is that you can't really fix them. They're so technical that really only the manufacturers can do that but even *they'd* probably just send you out a new one. Once something goes wrong then that's it really, they don't last like they used to. In that respect they're quite like relationships."

The man obviously had things that he wanted to talk about but Sophie didn't comment, not wanting to engage in any more conversation now than was absolute necessary. She felt a sudden urgency to get this man out of her house. She didn't even question his advert which said that he could repair washing machines, 'Any make, and model'. She wished she'd called the other one she had considered which simply said, 'Washing Machine Repairs', how stupid to call one that said 'Single Mother's Welcome'! Maybe she'd pass his details onto Tina, she thought.

"I could take you out to dinner though to make up for it?" Mike added.

"I'm really quite busy," Sophie replied, not sure how else exactly to reply to the sudden dinner invitation, "If it can't be fixed then it can't be fixed never mind! Not to worry, um, my friend's moving house and did say that I could have her old one if I needed to so I'll do that," she lied.

"Do you need any help plumbing it in?" Mike asked hopefully.

"Oh no that's fine I can do that! Well, at least, my *boyfriend* can do it, later, when he gets back from, um, the football! In fact, we might just go and get a new one, later, when the football's finished..." she started to back out of the kitchen towards the front door in order to eject this man from her house.

"Sophie," Mike looked at her seriously with what Sophie later described to Jules as being 'lust in his eyes', 'here's my number," he held out one of his business cards and she felt obliged to take it. 'If you need any help with *anything* then give me a call. Even if it's just to talk- I'm a good listener."

OK, Sophie thought, this is weird now. She continued to make her way to the door, thanking Mike for making the trip out and how sorry she was that he couldn't fix the problem but that she had plenty of other options so she'd probably be fine. Oliver appeared at the top of the stairs as Mike was on his way out. Mike saw him and smiled and asked him if he was going to watch the football with his Daddy.

"My Daddy isn't seeing me this weekend," he replied, "He only sees me when he's not busy."

Quite a few seconds passed while the group digested this information.

"Well, that's his loss," Mike eventually said. He extended his hand to Sophie, "Remember, if there's *anything* I can do."

He took himself and his redundant tool box out and Sophie shut the door firmly behind him and breathed a huge sigh of relief. She stood with her back against the door and suddenly laughed. She ran upstairs two at a time and gave her son a tight cuddle.

"I have all the time in the world for you Oliver Bridges," she said, "You are the *most important person* in my life. Who wants an ice cream?"

Sophie loved these days. No definite plans, just a whole day ahead with her son. She smiled to herself as they left the house, not even ten o'clock and I've been practically propositioned by three men already. Although, she thought, I'm sure Mother has her hopes pinned on someone a little richer than a washing machine repair man. Sophie's tummy fluttered with excitement, something that it hadn't done for a very long time.

The country park was busy on the bright springtime morning it being one of the few green spaces in the built up area where Sophie lived, very different to the Scottish countryside where she grew up. Sophie spent the morning following Ollie around, wherever he wanted to play; on the swings, running around on the open field, down on the small pebbly beach and for a ride on the little steam train. By lunchtime they were both ready for a rest and Sophie spread out the picnic rug on the grass. She sat down and handed Ollie his lunchbox casting her eyes around the park. These were the times when she felt most sad- when she had time to stop and think and watch couples with children, enjoying their time together. On these occasions she felt like the odd one out, the only single mother in a world of happy families and as she sat observing she saw many a blissful scene.

She watched as a man threw a football back and forth to who Sophie assumed was his son and a woman clapped and cheered when the small boy eventually caught it, the two adults exchanging proud smiles. Another couple walked in front of them into Sophie's view, the man pushing a buggy and a woman holding onto his arm and looking up to him lovingly. Further away in the distance there was a large group having a picnic, four couples that Sophie could see and their children- one of the men handing round some food and gestured to his other half to sit down, maybe saying today was her day off and that he had everything covered. Another taking a blue balloon from a boy and swapping it for a chocolate ice cream, licking the drips from around the edge before handing it over causing the boy to protest. Sophie sat dreamily watching the snippets of family life through the hazy sunshine and suddenly felt the tears threatening, the sense of aloneness engulfing her thoughts.

That's all I want, she thought, to be a happy family doing happy family things.

Her gaze travelled further off into the distance and she saw a group of runners gradually getting closer to where she sat. She wondered if she should join them one day and take Joules up on one of her ideas about how to meet a man. She spent so many hours running alone; maybe running with others would be good for her once in a while. She cast her gaze over all the members to see if there were any men that looked nice then rolled her eyes at herself and shook her head; most of them were women anyway she observed. A man was leading the group; about as old as Sophie was she thought, maybe younger who kept turning round encouraging them all, occasionally running back to those further behind to keep them all going. They all looked like they were having fun anyway, she decided, even if I didn't meet anyone to go out with.

Her mobile rang disturbing her daydreams.

"Hi..!" she said answering the call from her sister, "How are you?"

"Good thanks. More to the point though- how are you? Mum said that you were a bit low and your email sounded a bit like you were."

"Did it? It wasn't meant to! I'm fine thanks- really good actually. I'm at the park with Oliver right now, we're just having lunch. I can't believe Mum said that to you! I had to cut her off the other night because the girls were coming round so maybe she thought I was a bit off with her but really, she was telling me about one of her lesbian friends and making references to sex toys so I really had to go."

"Yes I had a conversation like that with her too- I think Dad's working quite a lot."

"Yes clearly. Anyway, how's it going?"

"Well, where shall I start? I've got *loads* of wedding magazines for us to look through next weekend. The first thing we need to do is decide what colour your dress is going to be because then I can go ahead and order flowers and I can maybe have the table decorations matching too and the ribbons around the chair covers and, well everything really depends on your dress. I'm bringing down a CD for you to listen to as well to help me choose some of the music. I've got some pictures of cars and cakes and, well, there's *so much* to think about! I might get a wedding planner actually- I'm so busy with work that I think it would be easier if I decide what I want and then just get someone else to sort it all out. Next weekend we can start to look at dresses and make up though, just to get the ball rolling."

"What, already? It's still over a year away!" Sophie thought, after her own experience that the plans were all rather premature.

"Well, if we can at least get a *colour.* I need some make up anyway and that big department store near you has the *best* counters so we might as well go there too- they have a wedding shoe department too don't they? In fact, we might be able to get everything from there. What colour do you think, for your dress?"

"Um," Sophie thought, "Any colour really. Not reddish though as I don't think it suits me *at all,* or orange or pink. Maybe dark green or dark blue…"

"Oh," her sister sounded disappointed, "They sound a bit dull! I thought maybe deep pink- I've already seen a dress actually that we can have a look for next weekend."

I love it when people ask for your opinion but have no intention of listening to it, Sophie thought.

"Sounds good," she said, "I'm sure that it will be *lovely,* even if I do look very pink. Why don't you email me a link to the dress that you like so that I can mentally prepare myself? Let me know when you're boarding so that we know if you're on time or not. See you next weekend!"

***

Later that evening when Oliver was settled in bed Sophie got herself ready too, also for bed, and went downstairs to the kitchen to make some hot chocolate. If I'm to go on dates with men, she thought, does that mean I'll have to stay up past 8 o'clock? She imagined herself sitting in a restaurant with some faceless man yawning uncontrollably and restlessly shifting around in her chair trying to stay awake while trying to take a subtle peek at her watch under the table. At that moment, standing in the kitchen in her pyjama's and slipper socks, stirring her hot chocolate she couldn't think of anything worse.

She took her drink upstairs and got into bed despite the early hour and switched on her computer again deciding to see if Michael had sent her an indication of what he looked like yet. I'm not going to encourage him until I know that, she thought. She went straight to her emails and saw that she had three unread messages. The first one was from her sister and had an attachment which she supposed would be of a dress so she left that, not feeling in the mood. The next one was from Michael and she felt a buzz of excitement in her stomach. She opened the message and clicked on the attachment, suddenly not interested at all in what he had to say, just what he looked like. Her tummy was positively fizzing. The guy had sounded fairly cosmopolitan and very active. She imagined he must have some money to be able to travel so often to such far flung places. She waited impatiently as the attachment opened, her laptop being annoyingly slow, the little circle on the screen going round and round and round and round…

Eventually the photo opened and Sophie slammed her laptop shut in fright.

"Ugh!" she exclaimed, "Ugh… what was that?" she shuddered, "That wasn't *him* was it?" The image she had been building up in her head all afternoon was wildly off the mark.

Gingerly she opened her lap top back up and peered under the lid at the photo that she had anticipated all day. She gasped and drew away again, unable to look at it for any amount of time.

"Oh this is silly," she thought and lifted the lid completely. She turned her head away from the screen and slowly moved her eyes back to look at the photo then breathed in sharply. The photo was black and white. It showed a skinhead, his face covered in piercings; his nose was pierced, his eye brows were pierced, his cheek seemed to be and he had a row of piercings across the top of his lip, where a moustache would be. I wonder what *other* places he has pierced, she thought, out of those we cannot see.

"Ouch" she said and made a face of disapproval, "I hope Ollie never decides to do that."

To add to this art work he had a web tattoo covering his smooth shiny head and he glared out of the screen at her the way she imagined a convict would. Sounded nice, looks scary, she thought, and not how I would have imagined your typical Times reader to look like. She felt slightly disappointed but also a little relieved- he had sounded fairly exhausting and she would have had to go to great lengths to make her own life sound as exciting as his. He could at least have smiled though, she thought a little crossly, instead of glaring like he has some kind of vendetta.

She returned to her inbox and considered her reply, the thought of just leaving it and not getting back in touch didn't cross her mind. She wrote back that she had just taken on a new contract at work, whatever that means she thought, and because of this she couldn't see any time in the near future when she would be able to meet up and so she was sorry that she was not going to keep in touch. She felt bad for letting someone down like that and text Lou to tell her, in order to try and make herself feel better about it, a problem shared. Lou soon replied saying that Sophie shouldn't worry about it because he probably wasn't. A bit harsh, Sophie thought but deleted his email and the ones that she had sent him which left no trace of Michael at all apart from the impression his image had left on her mind.

Opening the last email, she saw that she had a message from Paul on her social network site. She followed the link and read the inoffensive message. It said that he was sorry for taking a while to get in touch but that he'd been working all day- he didn't work every weekend- and had only just got in. I wonder what he does, Sophie thought. He said that he wasn't working in a couple of weekends and that did she feel like meeting up for a drink as he couldn't bear to communicate by email.

"Well there, a very normal sensible person", Sophie said out loud, "I couldn't agree more".

She started to compose a message back to him agreeing that emails were rubbish and how you couldn't possibly get to know someone like that. She asked where he lived so that they could decide where they were going to meet up, hoping that that wasn't too forward or make him think that she was going to come round and pester him. At the end she added that it would be lovely to meet him. She pressed send and smiled. Much better, she thought.

***

Monday mornings came round too quickly. The 'Monday approaching' feeling of dread generally started on Sunday evening about seven when she put Oliver to bed. It was in sharp contrast to the feeling of complete joy and elation that she felt on leaving the office on a Friday afternoon when she ran skipping out of the main doors and down the street humming 'The Sun Has Got His Hat On'. Everyone hates Monday's, the girls had said during one of their drinks nights. You don't know what Monday's *are* until you've worked at the Elm Tree, Sophie and Ruth had insisted.

On Monday's the training team did their own 'development work' and so instead of being out and about with the teaching staff doing their job of training they sat in their little office at the top of the school and, well, Sophie wasn't sure what everyone else was doing but generally she spent her day getting away with doing as little as possible. That part was fine and it had become a challenge between her and Ruth to see who could do the least amount of work without being noticed. The problem was that as they all sat at their computers Sophie had to spend her five-hour day sitting opposite Enid, her every movement being scrutinized, her every word being questioned. She still spent most of the time looking on the internet for other jobs but the atmosphere was suffocating.

This Monday started particularly badly. Sophie sensed that something was wrong as soon as she entered the office-there were always undertones of hostility but today it was particularly noticeable. As she signed in the staff in the office downstairs gawped at her in silence with dumb looks of total shock on their faces.

"I didn't think I looked *that* bad!" she joked as she sped through and up the stairs, used to everyone behaving slightly strangely.

She took the stairs two at a time and stopped at the top to smooth down her hair. Looking down she felt pleased with herself for actually ironing her black trousers for once, managing to finally get them washed by giving the temperamental washing machine a sharp kick meaning that she could put off the expense of forking out for a new one right now or having to make further contact with Mike. Breezing through the fire door she stuck her tongue out and fingers up in the direction of the office and then had to stop for a moment to giggle for being so childish. Wish I could do that to her face, she thought and entered the training office.

"Morning!" she said as cheerily as she could manage and made her way to her desk, not registering the silence that had met her entrance. She squeezed past Pam who smiled at her wanly, dumped her bags down on the floor and sat down, leaning forward to switch her computer on. It was as she did this that she looked up and suddenly realised that Enid was staring at her, her already popping eyes looking like they would actually leave her head this time. Sophie glanced around the office and was surprised to see that everyone was looking at her with similar expressions, even Ruth looked surprised.

"What?" she asked. "Do I have something on my face?" she looked to Ruth to answer the question and started to wipe around her mouth with her fingers. Ruth shook her head with what now looked more like respect for her mixed in with a little amusement.

"What?"

Laura pursed her lips and smiled an emotionless smile.

"Did nobody tell you?" she asked with what looked quite like smugness.

"Tell me what?" Sophie was losing patience, "What have I done wrong *this* time?"

Ruth and Pam suddenly became engrossed in whatever work they were doing and there started a great deal of paper shuffling and tapping at keyboards from their desks. Laura continued to look at Sophie across the room with the contented look of someone who liked it when someone else got a good kicking. Enid stood up and buttoned her jacket.

Sophie immediately noticed that she was wearing a skirt. Everyone usually wore trousers. She was about to joke about how smart she looked when she noticed that Pam next to her was also wearing one and even Laura. She looked at Ruth with pleading eyes as if to say, what have I done now, what have I forgotten?

"Skirt day?" Enid asked, raising her eyebrows at Sophie as if she were meant to know what she was talking about. Sophie looked back blankly. Enid sighed.

"As you will be *aware,* as you have worked here for some time, we have a policy which states how we are to behave and *what we are to wear* when we have a visitor in school. As you know, we have a visitor in school today…"

"Do we?" Sophie asked.

"You were told on Friday that we were expecting a visitor, in fact she will be arriving any time now and so we are all wearing *skirts*. If I could just remind you of the actual wording of the Visitor policy..." Enid produced a paper copy of said policy as if she expected that she was going to need it, "which states, 'When the school plays host to a visitor it is the policy for all staff to be dressed as the policy states. Men shall wear…' well we don't need to know about *them!* 'Ladies shall wear their normal uniform of a white shirt, black or navy suit jacket and matching *skirt*. In the winter months- from the beginning of the autumn term to the Easter weekend *black* tights shall be worn, in the summer months- Easter weekend to the beginning of the autumn term- American tan tights shall be worn. Hair shall be tied back unless cut above the shoulder in which case a black or navy hairband should be worn to keep it off the face. Nails should be short and may be painted with clear nail varnish. Make up shall be subtle. Black or navy shoes should have a heel of one inch or less, any higher being a contravention of the policy and a danger to the wearer and others- see also Health and Safety policy..."

Sophie awkwardly shifted her feet under her desk aware that her heels were above the regulation minimum.

"Anyway, that is by the by. It clearly states that a skirt should be worn. It would appear that you have decided that the visitor policy does not apply to *you* as you seem to be wearing trousers..." Enid stated and fixed her withering stare on Sophie.

Sophie's mind raced, she couldn't remember ever being told of such a policy and she certainly wasn't told that they were having a visitor today. Why couldn't they have just said to me on Friday, we'll have a visitor on Monday so wear a skirt, she thought? Why does everything have to be made into such a *drama?* Why do we need to wear a skirt anyway just because there's a visitor? Who are they expecting anyway, she thought, the bloody *Queen?* She felt her tension levels suddenly rocket.

"Oh," was all she could manage in response.

"Oh indeed!" Enid almost sounded triumphant. She looked at Sophie as if to say, so what are you going to do about it then?

"I'll have to phone downstairs if we need anything, "Enid continued, making reference to one of Sophie's main tasks-

fetching things when they ran out. "It's just not going to be *appropriate* to have someone, you, in here wearing trousers! If the visitor makes their way upstairs you will have to go into the cupboard and shut the door."

***

Half way through the morning after being confined to her desk lest she embarrass the school by wearing trousers, Sophie made a hasty excuse and followed Ruth into the photocopying cupboard. Enid had nearly burst a blood vessel when Sophie had suggested she pop down to the office to collect some printer paper when they ran out, despite the fact that Enid needed to print out some work herself. Wearing trousers on a skirt day was clearly a big deal.

"I'm having a break," Ruth whispered.

"OK!" Sophie whispered back. "I'll have one with you. I was going to talk to you anyway. I can't go to the conference next month!"

"What? Do you have a death wish?" Ruth giggled. "Actually, I was trying to think of excuses myself- I just can't be *bothered.*"

The two women stood in the store room giggling like teenagers. Their hushed cupboard chats had become a regular feature of their day, it being impossible to talk about anything of importance in the office itself. Not long after Sophie had started she had found a Dictaphone which seemed to have been taping their conversations and she found a file on the computer where these were saved. Any discussions about work or general grumbling about Enid were now mostly done in hushed tones in the cupboard.

Sophie noisily opened the filing cabinet.

"I think I'll just say I'm sick," she whispered. "They can't really say anything about that at the weekend. Original, I think you'll agree."

"Oh I was going to be sick!" Ruth complained in hushed tones. "I suppose I could be sick too- there could be some bug going round the office? Either that or one of my distant relatives might have to, you know, sadly pass away."

The two ladies started to giggle again.

"I can't believe we're standing here whispering about what excuses we're going to use to get out of coming into work at the weekend! I'm thirty-six years old!" Sophie whispered. "If this place was normal you'd just say, sorry I can't come in! The conference will be a load of rubbish anyway! They're always total crap and everyone's always so pissed off to be in on a Saturday that they just can't wait to go home!"

When Sophie had to go back into work at the weekend it heightened her feelings of hatred for the place especially as she never got paid or got any time off to make up for it.

Sophie held her finger to her lips as she listened, thinking that she heard somebody coming. Mark from the office came through the fire door backwards holding three boxes of printer paper and looking a little flushed.

"Here you go ladies, to feed your photocopying addiction that you clearly have- you're *always* in here!" He put down the boxes and threw an empty sandwich wrapper into the bin. "I was send out to buy it and managed to grab a sandwich on the way back..." Mark smirked, "I know it's not allowed..."

"Do we know what the policy is for stopping for a sandwich?" Sophie asked. Ruth's body started to shake with uncontrollable giggles which she tried to contain.

"Ah yes, that will be the Lunch Policy," Mark said. He put on a high and very well spoken voice. "The health and well-being of our staff is of upmost importance and as part of this it is recognised that staff nutrition is to be considered. It is the policy of the school to allow all staff to be placed on a hospital drip when they become dangerously malnourished."

Sophie and Ruth struggled to stifle their laughter. Mark played up to his audience.

"Lunch will of course be available to the children but it is considered a waste of time for adults who have already reached their maximum growth and so all staff will be required to work through any time referred to as 'Lunch time' as stopping for food will require their attention to be diverted from the important job of education."

"… and photocopying…" Sophie added.

"I'm impressed that you're still alive actually…" Mark said. "… coming into work wearing those trousers! You owe me one- I've been fetching and carrying all over the place this morning because you're not allowed to be seen."

"Who's the visitor anyway?" Sophie asked. "Nobody's told me yet!"

"Just some woman trying to sell us an e-portfolio system. She's running quite a bit late actually so I expect she'll get turned away anyway."

"So I'm meant to be wearing a skirt and American Tan tights for a *sales person?*" Sophie asked. "If she ever makes it she'll wonder what all the fuss is about."

"Actually I'd better get back- I'm supposed to be waiting at the front door to greet her," Mark said.

He gave the two ladies a wave and returned downstairs leaving Sophie and Ruth alone again.

"Have you met Jules's friend yet?" Ruth asked.

"Not yet but I think we might be going out or a date next weekend! I'm now his friend on my social network site and I've had a look through his photos- he doesn't look too bad at all. I'm not sure what he does for a living actually." She shrugged her shoulders. "Well, I've got nothing to lose have I and he might just be Mr Right. What's the worst that could happen? Have you heard anything about my day off yet? Nobody's said anything to me."

"No nothing. You won't hear anything though. Just assume that it's fine. Laura had a week booked off before you started here and only found out on the Friday that it was

OK for her to have the next week off. I won't tell you the bit about her being called up on the Monday morning and told that she had to come in after all. She had to cancel her holiday!"

Sophie's face displayed disbelief.

"What? This place is crazy- you can't cancel people's holidays the week before, can you?" She momentarily looked worried then shook her head. "All I'm asking for is a day off anyway and it's over a year away so I'm sure *that* will be OK…"

The two ladies jumped as they heard the office door opening and Enid walked into the store. "Got your paper alright?" she asked. Sophie nodded and started to open the photocopier drawers and load them all up. Ruth picked up a random folder from one of the shelved and went back to her desk. Enid looked satisfied that everyone was still working.

***

Later on at school Sophie had words to say to her friends about Michael.

"I can't *believe* that you did that to me!" she said to them with mock crossness in her voice. "I switched on my computer on Saturday morning and there was a message from a certain Michael saying how much he'd like to meet me!"

The girls looked at one another in amusement.

"It was a perfect example of why I would *never* use the lonely hearts columns to try and find a man. His email sounded perfectly fine and normal- apart from the bungee jumping and diving in Vietnam, granted- but his photo was something else. He looked like a convict glaring out of the screen at me! He was actually frowning and looked quite scary, it just instantly put me off because I'd already built up a mental picture of a ruggedly handsome and fit adventurer and then I see his photo and he looked like a druggie. You should have rigorously vetted him before you let him loose with my contact details. Lonely hearts are a no go."

"It *was* only one guy," Lou sensitively suggested, "and there are hundreds out there."

Sophie was shaking her head vigorously. "No- absolutely definitely not. It's put me right off."

"Oh well back to the drawing board. Did Paul get in touch?" Jules asked.

"Yes, on Saturday morning as well. Really I'm going to have to watch your wine consumption next time. I got a message from him and *then* I was invited to dinner by a washing machine man! I tell you, it's suddenly all go in my love life."

"Ooh what's he like?" Tina asked her eyes wide with anticipation.

"Oh he was... just not my type. I'll pass you his number if you like?" she smiled at her friend.

"Oh no better not," Tina sighed. "Was he a dish though?"

Sophie thought back to the little round man and put her finger up to her lips looking thoughtful. "He's not such a dish, more of a bowl," she smiled, "Anyway ladies I'm really sorry but you might have to find another venue for your drinking because there is the distinct possibility that I might have a hot date!"

"It's started already," Lou said jokingly. "A little bit of interest from the opposite sex and she's dumping her real friends."

"Don't be silly!" Sophie protested, "To be fair, you lot have set me up and so it's your own fault that your drinks night has been hijacked! It's easier to go on dates when I don't have Ollie and I know he's definitely going to see Ben next Friday night and so if Paul asks me out I'm going to suggest then. My sister's coming about tea time *this* Friday and so it's just going to be quite hectic."

"That's OK I'm sure we'll forgive you but only as long as we get *all* the gossip!"

"I will definitely keep you informed! Just don't pass on my details to anyone else!"

***

Once home she signed into her email account and saw with a flutter of excitement that Paul had replied already to her message. As with his previous communications the message was brief, to the point and- most pleasing to Sophie- polite. He asked her that if she wasn't too busy this weekend could he give her a call- Sunday evening perhaps- and then maybe they could go out the following weekend. He was free on Friday night and wondered if she might like to go out then. The email finished with him saying, 'but we can chat about that if you're free.'

Well what a nice man, Sophie thought, thank you Jules, my friend. Maybe this was going to be easy after all. This man sounded very lovely, his photos didn't look too bad and now she was going to have a chat with him on the phone- next thing was to meet him, get along and hey presto- one boyfriend aka a plus one. Her tummy fizzed as she looked forward to meeting this random person and emailed him back. She told him that Sunday would be perfect to chat and the following Friday would be good to go out. She hit send and felt a buzz of excitement.

Chapter Three

Oliver's Aunty Jo arrived on Friday evening in a taxi from the airport with a holdall full of wedding magazines. She had been in the house for barely five minutes before she was showing Sophie pages she had folded over during the journey. There were pictures of dresses and flowers and hair styles and rings and shoes and cars- Sophie looked and nodded and showed interest although her heart ached at the memories that it conjured up.

Her sister went into the kitchen to make herself a cup of herbal tea and Sophie sat and casually flicked through the magazines. With all the talk now about weddings she had noticed that the painful feelings that she had felt back when she had read Ben's letter were beginning to resurface after three years of her successfully bottling them. Everything for her own wedding had been decided and now looking through the magazines she remembered each detail of what she was to have for her special day- the white roses and greenery, the classic cars, the traditional setting, the invitations that she was going to make herself with the calligraphy pen and silver ink that she still had in a drawer in the kitchen and the ivory dress, cut to show off her slender and petite frame. She let the magazine drop into her lap as she closed her eyes and remembered the day that she tried it on, still being able to see her reflection in the mirror as she gasped in wonder and spun herself around watching the skirt swish around at her feet as her mother clasped her hands together and told her how perfectly beautiful she looked and that Ben was a lucky man.

"I've arranged for you to have a make-over tomorrow as well!" her sister called through from the kitchen. Sophie shook her head to dispense with the daydream.

"A make- over?" she replied reluctantly. "Why? What's wrong with the way I do my make-up already?"

"You hardly wear make-up!" her sister teased her as she came back into the room. She flicked through the magazine that she was holding and eventually found the picture that she wanted to show.

"I thought you'd suit *that* kind of make-up!" she said and held up a page that showed a bridesmaid with heavy dark eyes and red lips. Sophie screwed her nose up.

"It doesn't look very me!" she protested, "Isn't it a bit much for a wedding? I thought something subtler would be nice."

"It's just exactly how I had imagined that you'd look!" her sister told her, "The lips would look amazing with the dress that I saw and the eyes would look really dramatic in the photos and it would just suit the colour of your hair," she looked at Sophie's reluctant face.

"Oh go on Sophie it'll be fun!"

"Oh OK fine, it's *your* wedding."

"Well you could at least sound a little bit enthusiastic," her sister had sulked. "I think you'll look great."

"I am enthusiastic," Sophie had lied, feeling guilty that she was putting a damper on her sister's plans. "I really can't wait."

***

The next morning Sophie, her sister and Ollie arrived in the department store where Sophie was to have her make-over done. It was a busy Saturday in town, more so than usual as it was pouring with rain outside. Sophie kept a tight grip of Oliver's hand, worried that he'd get lost amongst the crowds of shoppers. Taking him shopping in town was the last thing she would normally choose to do with him on a Saturday and she wasn't sure how long it would take for him to get horribly grumpy and bored.

"Let's try and do this as quickly as possible," she said to her sister. "Shopping with your children for make-up at the weekend has got to be in the top five lists of 'Things to avoid for a stress free life'."

As they approached the counter where Jo had booked the make-over the sales assistant turned to them and smiled.

"How she can smile with all that make-up plastered to her face?" Sophie whispered to her sister. The girl looked like she had applied every conceivable product. "I don't want to look like *that!*"

"You're not going to look like *that!*" her sister hissed back beginning to lose patience with Sophie's reluctance. She ignored her and smiled at the assistant as they reached the counter. She explained that they had booked a make-over and were looking for products to use on her wedding day.

As she told her what products she used already Sophie cast her eyes around the array of pallets, pots and tubes of every conceivable colour. She saw a rainbow of powders and creams and glosses and glitters most of which she didn't know how or where to apply. She picked up one of the tester brushes and dusted a little eye shadow on the back of her hand and admired the sparkle it had as she moved it around in the light. She took the lids off pots of eye creams and night creams and day creams and felt their silky smooth texture with her finger and noticed the tub of face mask that her sister had bought for her. She picked it up to see if there was a price on the bottom.

"No price," she thought. "Wow it must be *really* expensive!"

As she was exploring around the beauty counter she became aware of the two pairs of eyes that were following her every movement belonging to her sister and the shopping assistant. She looked up to meet their gazes. It's OK, she thought, I'm not shoplifting!

"Is this the one?" the shop assistant asked Sophie's sister, pointing at Sophie with a perfectly manicured nail.

"Yes Sophie's the bridesmaid and she's the one having the make-over today."

"Yes," the girl replied as if to say, I can see this is the one who needs a make-over. She turned her attention to Sophie. "So what would you say is your main concern at the moment- so that I can decide what products to use?" she picked up two different pots of creams, "Is it first signs of ageing and dehydration or fine lines and wrinkles?" she asked, holding the latter closer to Sophie as if to make her choose that one. "As we get older our skin loses *elasticity.*"

Sophie looked as though she'd never given it much thought, which she hadn't. She objected to the word 'Old'.

"Hmm I think maybe just dehydration?" she said hopefully. "I'm still in my thirty's." The girl raised an eye brow as if to say, dehydration, in your dreams. Sophie looked helplessly at her sister.

"I don't have wrinkles yet!" she protested. "I don't think…"

"Our cream for fine lines and wrinkles does also deal with dehydration so that would maybe be a good choice."

Sophie felt annoyed that, just to rub it in, she was getting advice about this from someone who looked young enough to be her daughter.

"I usually use that brand over there," Sophie said pointing across the walkway to another counter that sold much cheaper products in much bigger pots. "To be honest I'm not sure I could afford to get this stuff all the time."

The sales girl pounced on an opportunity to grab a new customer.

"You only need to use a *tiny* amount of our products so they really should last for a long time! I think you'd notice a *big* improvement too, although," she added, suddenly aware that she might have offended her new customer, "you really do have *very* good skin. How do you *usually* do your make-up?" This was an easy question for Sophie to answer.

"Oh I don't usually have time for make up! I have a five-year-old boy," Sophie gestured towards Oliver whose eyes were transfixed on a huge aquarium full of tropical fish that was providing a perfect distraction for him at that moment. It won't last long, Sophie thought. "I also work somewhere that you're not really meant to wear make-up so in the week I guess I don't really wear it. At the weekend I probably just really use lip gloss…"

The girl behind the counter looked at Sophie with a mixture of pity and complete incomprehension as if not wearing make-up and having children was an alien concept. She turned her attention towards Sophie's sister who seemed to be more on her wavelength.

"What is your colour scheme going to be for the wedding? Have you chosen bridesmaid dresses or flowers yet?"

Sophie drifted off.

She looked around at the other shoppers, wistfully watching the couples who walked through, some hand in hand or with their arms round each other or with the man holding all the shopping bags while the woman looked at make-up. She wished that she had that again, someone to love her and hold her hand, although she wouldn't want to go shopping. She'd rather be outside somewhere away from all the crowds- her, Ollie and whoever. She imagined them being somewhere like the country park, in her imagination it was autumn and they were kicking bundles of leaves, picking some up and throwing them in the air and laughing and being in love…

"*Sophie!*" her sister's voice harshly interrupted her thoughts. She looked at her dumbly.

"What?"

"We're ready! Come over here and sit down. We've decided what colours would suit you."

Her sister twisted a tall black chair around so that Sophie could clamber up onto it.

"What? Am I sitting in the middle of the shop to have this done? I thought I'd be in a little room somewhere!"

The counter assistant looked towards Sophie's sister helplessly hoping that she would sort out this unwilling model.

"Oh come *on* Sophie! Really, Mum was right! She said that you were being miserable about the wedding on the phone. You're being so *unhelpful.* I came all the way down to see you and you're just being so un*enthusiastic*! You weren't bothered about the magazines and you don't care about your dress and now we're here and you have a face like *thunder*! Please, I know this must be difficult for you but it's my *special day.* It won't be fun at all if I think you hate it."

Sophie instantly felt guilty and selfish though she hadn't realised that she was being quite so bad. The shop assistant looked on with a look of shocked interest taking over from the one of boredom that he had previously had. Oliver turned his attention away from the fish for a second to ask why Aunty Jo was cross. Sophie suddenly felt like it was all too much for her now and burst into tears.

"Oh I'm sorry Jo I had no idea I was being like that. Really I had no idea," she managed to say through her sniffles, "It's just, with all the talk of weddings, it's made me remember the one that I was supposed to have and I guess the feelings have been difficult to deal with. I'll forget about it, it's fine. I'm sorry of course I'm bothered about your wedding." She was suddenly aware of a small group of people who had paused their own shopping to witness this live show of family drama and emotion.

"Oh I'm sorry too!" her sister responded, "I had no idea that you still felt like that! But really, it was *three years* ago Sophie! Ben's moved on, you should too. Stop wasting your time feeling sad and get back out there and meet someone else, someone who's worthy of you not some idiot who could walk away from the two people who loved him most." She stopped talking and also realised that they had an audience. "Her fiancée cancelled their wedding," she told them, feeling that they needed to have the full details, "leaving my sister here to bring up their baby son alone."

The gathered crowd murmured sympathetically, some shaking their heads.

Oh great, Sophie thought. She felt her skin redden at the embarrassment of it all. She jumped up on the seat and asked if someone could recommend a foundation with good coverage.

The sister's had left the department store with bags full of make-up and free samples, Sophie's lack of knowledge about what type of skin she had or what suited her finally tipping the young sales assistant over the edge, causing her to give them every possible sample she had in the hope that one day Sophie would come back and know exactly what she wanted. She had made two purchases- a pink lip gloss and some eye cream as she felt obliged after the girl had spent so long explaining each different type to her- and had also received a free gift of a small make-up bag containing yet more samples. The make-over had improved the way her skin looked, she agreed with the sales assistant, and the dark circles that were usually present under her eyes had disappeared under concealer. Her deep brown eyes were accentuated and she had loved her black eye lashes, comically fluttering them at Ollie who had told her she looked pretty. She had rubbed the red lipstick off as soon as she was out of the shop and replaced it with her new subtler pink lip gloss but she was surprised that on the whole she had been pleased with the results.

"I need to practice that now," she had said to her sister, "so that I can recreate it on your wedding day."

They had gone into the dress shop where Jo had seen the bridesmaid dress that she liked and luckily they had one more in Sophie's size. She had been doubtful about the deep pink colour but when on the dress was stunning and Sophie admired her reflection in the changing room mirror. The gorgeous silk dress reached the floor and clung flatteringly onto her figure with an asymmetric shoulder and sash that tumbled down the back. She called her sister and Ollie into the changing room and they both looked pleasantly stunned at her beauty.

"Wow you look like a *real* princess!" Ollie had stated.

"Oh that's beautiful," Jo had added. "It's just perfect on you. Please say that you like it Sophie, you look absolutely stunning."

Sophie didn't think she had ever looked so elegant.

"I love it, actually!" she smiled, "It's really lovely and I think it suits me," she twisted around to look at the back in the mirror. "I'll be very happy to wear this dress."

Her sister started to think out loud about getting some shoes dyed to match the colour of the material and Sophie suddenly felt inspired to be a bit more pro-active in finding her Plus One.

***

Sophie and Ollie had taken Jo to the airport on Sunday evening. Sophie promised to start looking for shoes and think about what Ollie was going to wear, her sister suggesting full Scottish dress but Sophie worried that he would find it uncomfortable, especially the itchy socks, to the point that the whole day would be ruined by his complaining.

"Believe me- you didn't witness the nativity play when he had to wear leggings. Never have I seen a person fidget and grumble so much. We might have to compromise and get him some tartan trousers."

On returning to the house Ollie's bedtime routine had been put into practice promptly allowing Sophie the rest of the evening to experiment with the various creams, serums and glosses that she had been given, dabbing and smoothing them onto her face feeling how silky soft they made her skin. She inspected the literature that they had come with; there was face cream and eye cream and neck cream and bust cream and hand cream and body cream and serum to go *under* the cream and serum to go *over* the cream and day cream and night cream... Sophie wondered what order they should go on.

The problem with this *upping* of my skincare, she concluded inspecting her new more-youthful face in the mirror, is that it will be very difficult to go back.

She had arranged to talk to Paul at half past eight. At twenty past she randomly powdered her nose, brushed her hair and applied some lip balm. How silly, she thought, when he can't even see me! At half past eight she checked her reflection again and applied a little lip gloss and checked that her phone was on. She repeated this process for the next ten minutes and at about twenty to nine she got a text message asking if it was still OK for him to call. Waiting for a few moments to reply, so as not to appear too keen she said yes she was free whenever he was. The phone rung soon after and she instantly felt awkward about answering to someone she had never even met before.

"Hi!" she said aloud before she answered then altering her tone slightly, "Hi!"

She shook her head and smiled at herself, took a deep breath and answered.

From his initial 'Hi' Paul had put her at ease and she found it easy to talk to him. In the end they had chatted for nearly an hour. Both had given each other brief outlines of their life histories and just generally chatted, Sophie omitting most of the details after meeting Ben but explaining that she had a son. Paul said that he had known that already from Jules and Sophie smiled at the thought of her excited friend giving Paul all the gossip. She had told him a few stories from work and he said he'd never heard of anywhere that sounded so ridiculous. He told her how he knew Jules and Steve; they met at a football match, and talked about her boys as if he were their adopted uncle. She felt happy talking to this easy-going sounding man and agreed to meet him on the following Friday.

"Where do you want to meet?" he'd asked, "I can pick you up if you like? I've got a *really cool* new car and could take you for a spin!"

Sophie wasn't sure about the dating etiquette and didn't know if it was alright for someone who was essentially a stranger to pick her up from home- at the same time this was Jules's friend and she didn't want to offend him. He must be OK if Jules put him in touch, she thought. Paul must have sensed her hesitation though as he suggested that instead they meet at a pub that was quite local to her- I go there with Jules and Steve sometimes, he had told her. This gained him even more brownie points with Sophie and she put down the phone at the end of their conversation feeling more than a little excited about her forthcoming date.

She had one last look through her goodies before going to bed and went to sleep with a white face, thickly smothered in eye cream and night cream, beginning a week of pampering in preparation for her date.

***

In an attempt to cheer Monday morning up and in her new optimistic state she applied some of her new bright pink lip gloss and some mascara. She was pleased at the difference even such a small amount of make-up made to her pretty features. The Elm Tree School was so strict about appearance that she had given up trying to look nice for work. Her beauty regime consisted of face wash and lip balm and her hair usually got tied back, occasionally it was allowed to stay down with an Alice band keeping it out of her eyes but those days were rarer and rarer with each week that passed.

"You look different," Oliver had stated before school. Sophie was flattered that he noticed.

"Is that good different or bad different?" she had asked.

"Good different," he said.

"Thank you darling," Praise indeed, Sophie had thought and ruffled the boy's hair playfully.

For once they had arrived for school in good time and Sophie managed to have a chat with her friends before her race into town. The three ladies commented on how nice she looked today and Sophie had lied and said that it was due to some proper sleep.

"I've got a date this Friday! It's my first date in *three years!*" she announced to the group almost triumphantly, "I must be mad. So this week I shall be trying to get some sleep and making myself look nice," she added.

"Ooh!" Jules squealed. "Is it Paul? *How* exciting! Oh Sophie I hope that you love him! He's so sweet and funny- I must tell Steve!"

"I wouldn't tell too many people about it!" Sophie warned her friend. "Not until I know how it's gone anyway; it might be a disaster you know! We might have absolutely nothing to say to each other."

"Oh I doubt that," Jules said cheerfully. "Paul's a r*eally* interesting guy, I'm sure you'll have loads in common…" she paused, thinking of an interest that they might share. "I'm sure there'll be something anyway." She said, unable to think of anything in particular at short notice.

Sophie glanced at her watch.

"What's up with the teachers today?" she asked nobody in particular. "They're running quite late! Bloody hell, I'm not going to make it in to work for quarter past at this rate!"

"I thought you started work at half nine?" Jules asked.

"Yes but the *expectation* is that we get there fifteen minutes early. I'm not going to make it! Where are the teachers?"

"Maybe they had a heavy weekend?" Tina suggested.

"I don't care about their weekends!" Sophie wailed. "My life won't be worth living if I'm late for work. People have been sacked for being late… although… that's not a bad thought!" As she spoke the fire door out of her son's class opened and the teacher, still talking over her shoulder to someone at the back of the classroom, came out to get the children, unaware that her lateness would mean a telling off for Sophie.

The teacher encouraged the children to line up, listening to their stories about the weekend and patiently responding to each one in turn.

Oh just let them in, Sophie thought as she restlessly checked her watch again. She made a big point of looking at the watch and then sighing loudly, as if that were going to make any difference, the teacher remained oblivious to her performance. After what seemed like an eternity the children started to shuffle into their classroom and Oliver turned around for his last wave just before he disappeared into the building, Sophie smiled and waved enthusiastically until she could no longer see him then she said goodbye to her friends and hurried off to her car aware that the fifteen extra minutes wait at the school would make her later than her quarter past nine expected arrival time.

Most other workplaces wouldn't mind if you were a tiny bit late once in a while, she thought miserably. As she ran to where her car was parked a mum that she knew vaguely called to her cheerfully.

"You should work from home!" she called.

Sophie smiled back and laughed and replied that yes she should, what a good idea.

We don't *all* have rich husbands who'll buy us our own online kids clothing business she thought bitterly, not being in the mood for humour now that she was guaranteed a ticking off from Enid.

It seemed like every conceivable object had been put in Sophie's way to delay her journey to work. The roads were busy, traffic lights were red and every zebra crossing was occupied by incredibly slow pedestrians. Sophie restlessly tapped at her steering wheel and sighed, cursing the frail old lady who was making painful progress crossing. She switched the radio off as the chirpy breakfast DJ began to irritate her even more than she felt already.

I'm not going to make it, Sophie thought and cursed again. She decided to call the school and ask if she could park in the car par. Better that than being late, she thought. If she could just park in the carpark then she would be on time.

The Elm Tree School did have a car park to the front of the building which could take about fifty cars. It was empty for most of the day except for a short time in the morning and afternoon when the children in the school were dropped off and picked up. It was the school's policy though that no staff should park there as it was solely for the use of parents and visitors. The policy frustrated Sophie as her car was so small that she could tuck it away in the corner where nobody else ever parked as there was a trellis which prevented the larger cars parking there.

This is so stupid; she thought and indicated to the left to park for a moment while she called the school. She dialled the number and waited, hoping that it wouldn't be Mrs Wright herself who answered the phone. To her relief it was Tim.

"Good morning The Elm Tree Preparatory School and Nursery, Tim speaking."

"Tim! Hi!" Sophie said hurriedly. "Listen- I'm on my way but I'm going to be late because Ollie was late going into school so I'm calling to ask if I can park in the car park, just on this one occasion."

"Hi, Sophie," he replied then paused, battling with his conscience. "If it were up to me then of course I'd say that it was fine. You *know* that you're not supposed to though…" His voice trailed away.

Sophie was aware of his dilemma. "Can you just ask someone for me please? If I can't then I'm going to be really late!"

The line went quiet for a while and then she heard Tim coming back to the phone saying to someone that he was just asking. When he picked the phone back up his demeanour was different, that of professional yes man and not friend.

He cleared his voice. "I'm afraid, as you know, it is forbidden for staff to park their cars in the car park as this is solely for the use of parents and visitors. If *you* were to park there then *all* the staff would want to park there," he said officially before adding, "sorry."

Sophie instantly felt her stress level rocket through the roof of her miniscule car.

"Yes I know that but I thought, on this one occasion when I'm running a little bit late due to unforeseen circumstances, I thought that just once they might bend the rules a little but whatever. It was just a crazy thought. Can you mention then that I'm probably going to be late then? Thanks!" Great, she thought. What a surprise. That bloody place.

She threw her phone back into her bag in the passenger seat foot well and indicated to pull out and carry on her journey. Toying with the idea of just parking in the school car park anyway she drove past her usual space about a mile from the school and carried on up the steep hill that she usually ran, cursing her place of work for being completely inflexible. At the top of the road she turned left and approached the school and saw that unusually, there was the smallest of spaces at the end of a line of parked cars. Glancing at her clock she saw with that if she could park there then she might be just on time for work, not the fifteen expected minutes early but not late. She hastily pulled in and then slowly edged her way towards the car parked on the end, aware that she would have to park pretty snugly to be fully in the space. As she felt her car gently nudge the one that was parked she grimaced and moved back a fraction and stopped. She grabbed her bag and jumped out and sped towards the school which was now only meters away.

Bursting into the school office and looking up at the clock on the wall Sophie saw with amazement that she was two minutes early by their time keeping and so after signing in she made haste up the stairs so that Enid could get the benefit of her not being late. She didn't bother with her usual stop at the top of the stairs; instead she carried on through to the office so that she could at least be at her desk by half past nine.

Enid was already standing when she made her entrance, clearly waiting for her.

"My office," she said bluntly and walked out of the room.

What? Sophie thought with frustration. I'm not late! She rolled her eyes and turned on her heel, following Enid into the next door office making faces behind her back and dragging her heels comically making Ruth smirk behind her monitor and Laura purse her lips with disapproval.

You can go to hell too, Sophie thought petulantly.

She pulled up a chair opposite Enid who sat at the desk getting her paperwork ready and slumped down into it dropping her bags on the floor.

Later than the expected fifteen minutes but not actually late for work form, Sophie thought sarcastically.

"So, here we are again," Enid started and looked at Sophie as if she had committed the worst crime imaginable. "Why do you think that we keep meeting like this?"

Sophie stared silently, unsure of whether this was a rhetorical question and expecting Enid to answer it herself. She wondered if she could stare Enid out rather than replying. Enid was clearly not going to add anything more until Sophie had answered the question and raised her eyebrows so much that Sophie thought her eyes might actually pop out of her face. Usually Sophie was an articulate individual but meetings with Enid seemed to sap any confidence that she had. She muttered that she didn't know.

"You don't know…" Enid repeated. "Let me rephrase that slightly then. Why do you think that we are here on this *particular occasion?*"

Sophie shrugged and shook her head, making a face to say 'I have no idea.' She decided to try and get away with not talking in proper sentences as the less she said the less she could be picked up on.

"This morning's meeting," Enid deciding that asking her interviewee was going to be fruitless at that moment, "is for *three* separate reasons which raises the question- how committed are you *really* to the school?"

I can tell you that I'm not committed to the school, Sophie thought, well, maybe a little bit but only because you pay me every month.

"Firstly we have to discuss your adherence to the dress code. *Secondly*," She continued, "I heard that you called the school this morning and asked if you could use the car park when you clearly know the car park *policy* and in addition to that you did not arrive by quarter past nine and *thirdly* it would appear that you are wearing make-up when it clearly states in the uniform policy that make-up shall not be worn! I'm not sure how we are expected to encourage the girls not to wear make-up when members of the management team come to work with their face painted with tribal markings!"

I've put on a tiny bit of lip gloss, Sophie thought getting more fed up by the second.

"It says in the uniform policy that management make-up can be subtle…" Sophie bravely stated.

"Subtle, yes!" Enid cried. "Subtle would mean that we can't tell that you're wearing any. You appear to have plastered an entire *array* of make-up to your face. Go and wash it off before we can continue this discussion."

"What? Really?" Sophie felt like she was back at school and getting a telling off from the Head Teacher, the tone of voice that Enid used making even the most confident grown up feel like they'd stepped back many years in time. She shuddered.

"Yes, really," Enid replied.

Sophie got up pushing the chair back as she did and left the room markedly, bumping into Ruth on her way out who was making a cup of tea.

"I've got to wash my lip gloss off," she stated.

"What? *Really?*" Ruth said with disbelief.

"Yes, really," Sophie replied.

"It's wasted on her anyway," Ruth said more brightly.

"I feel like I did when I was a teenager and got told off by my House Master for having crimped hair!" Sophie whispered back to Ruth. "She's *worse* than he was- I'd rather have the cane."

She continued on to the small toilet that was on the landing a flight of stairs down from the fire door, a place that she often hid and waited for Enid to leave the office. Sophie took her time to remove the lip gloss aware that every second was one less sitting with Enid. I hate her, Sophie thought as she wiped the last traces of pink off her lips. This job wouldn't be so bad if it wasn't for Enid breathing down our necks. She returned upstairs joining Enid who looked up at her and continued her monologue.

"That looks much better. Now where were we? Make-up..." She pondered, "Now... dress code... Here is the Uniform Policy- I expect it to be copied out a hundred times by tomorrow. Finally..." she continued, ignoring the look of disbelief on Sophie's face, "... the last item on my agenda *for now* is the fact that you *insist* on trying to bend the rules to suit yourself. You are aware both that you are expected to arrive for work fifteen minutes before your start time and that staff are not permitted to park in the car park. I am confused as to why you thought that you would ask to do that this morning?"

Sophie sighed audibly having given up now trying to hide her frustration. She took a moment to compose her thoughts.

"Ollie's class went in late this morning which made me run late for work. I called the school because I thought that they might be flexible and that if I could park in the car park then I would be here on time. Sometimes things happen in life which means that not every day runs like clockwork. In the end though I *wasn't* late and I *didn't* park in the car park so I'm not sure why I'm being told off!"

Occasionally at work Enid's manner got the better of Sophie. Usually she managed to remain calm and professional. She knew that at work you're not going to get along with *everyone* in the office but sometimes Enid was *so* frustrating that it made Sophie's mild manner snap. Twice previously Enid had made her cry and Sophie had hated herself for letting it affect her like that and was even more cross that she had cried in front of everyone in the office. She often cried at home, in the evening when Ollie was tucked up in bed and she felt the hopelessness of her situation. She'd sometimes call her mother and try and work out the best thing to do but she always felt trapped in the end- she owned her house and Ollie was settled at school, Sophie had a job where she was able to work in between school hours and on a Wednesday when she had to work late she had a trusted babysitter. Even though she spent her life rushing from one thing to the next everything seemed to be set up just perfectly and the fact that Sophie hated her job wasn't high up the list of reasons to upset the balance. Today though, right now she wanted to leave that school. She wanted to put her house on the market and move far away with Ollie and start again.

"You're not being *told off* Sophie. We are starting to *question* your commitment to the school. You are aware of the *expectations* that we have of you. You already start work at half past nine allowing you to drop your child off at school. If even *that* time is too early, well…" her voice trailed off and she shook her head and looked at Sophie patronizingly.

"But I wasn't even late!" Sophie could feel that her face was flushed and she took a deep breath to try and alleviate the stress that she felt building up in her body.

"You arrived at nine twenty-nine."

"I start work at nine thirty!"

"You are *expected* to be here for quarter past so that you are ready to start at half past!"

Sophie wondered how long this conversation could be drawn out and if she could waste a whole day's work this way. Enid on the other hand suddenly got up, buttoned her jacket and walked out of the room. Sophie waited and listened hearing her go through to the office and then out again, through the fire door and down the stairs.

She just likes the sound of her own voice, Sophie thought. She was sure that although she hated it and was always in trouble for something, it was the safest job in the world as staff generally left soon after starting. The fact that she had managed to stick it out for six months really meant that she was a longstanding member of the team. Each month Sophie had to compile a list of new staff and staff who were leaving so that the training team could assess their training needs and make up a new timetable for courses. Often staff left during the same month that they started which meant that Sophie had a constant job updating the training schedule.

She returned to the office and slumped down at her desk, switching on the computer with her foot. As she waited glumly for it to start up she gazed wistfully over Ruth's shoulder out of the window where she could see blue cloudless skies. Immediately Sophie felt hot and uncomfortable in the small airless office and got back up again and wandered over to see what was happening out in the real world. She could see folk sitting at outside tables covered with sun umbrellas at the hotel next door, enjoying a cool drink in the morning sun, relaxing and chatting happily unaware that they were sitting about twenty meters away from a complete mad house.

"Does anyone mind if I open the window?" Sophie asked, turning round to address her colleagues.

Laura shifted her large mass in her chair where she had sat since 8am and looked at Pam.

"Are you feeling it cold again today Pam? I'm feeling *cold* but let's have a vote."

There are some people who have worked here too long, Sophie thought ruefully. She looked at Pam who had been in the same spot also since 8am and was wearing a cardigan buttoned up to the top with a hot water bottle tucked inside.

"Oh I'm *always* cold!" Pam said. "I always need my hot water bottle. Open it if you want to, I'll just get a refill." She got up and shuffled through to the kitchen to boil the kettle.

Laura looked crushed that Pam had not voted with her and continued her work with a look of irritation. Ruth looked round and smiled and said that it would be good to get some fresh air. Sophie slid the heavy wooden window upwards and propped it open with a piece of wood that was there for that purpose. It was only possible to open it by about five inches. Sophie bent down and pushed her nose out of the small gap and deeply breathed in the fresh air. Oh to be outside right now, sitting and chatting to normal people at one of those tables and having a drink or going for a long walk in the fresh morning air. She breathed in deeply then stood up straight and returned to her desk, collecting her lunch from the kitchen before doing so.

She sat down and logged onto the computer, switched on her monitor and took the lid off her Tupperware lunch box.

"Is it lunchtime already?" Laura declared. "Sophie you eat all the time, it's not fair that you're so *thin!*"

"I'm not *thin!*" Sophie retorted. *"I'm slim* because I work hard and run it all off! I don't eat all the time though either!"

"Some of us don't have time to go for a run…"

Don't make me feel guilty because you didn't get to work part time too, Sophie thought.

"I'm just really hungry today. I'm trying to eat healthily because I've got a date on Friday and so for breakfast I just had fruit but now I'm *starving!*"

Interest levels suddenly shot up in the office. All ears were on Sophie.

"A *date?*" Laura said. "Anyone nice?"

"Oh well I'm not that sure really, it's kind of a blind date! Crazy I know but he's a friend of a friend and by all accounts he's really lovely. Anyway it's my first date in a while and so I just thought I'd try and look my best!" You never know, she thought, he might be the one for me and then I'll never have to come into this stupid place and see your irritating face ever again. She smiled at Laura. "I'm on a healthy eating kick for the week, not that I really eat that *unhealthily* but I'm just trying to make sure I get enough fruit and veg."

"So, what have you got then?" Pam asked, peering over to Sophie's desk and into her Tupperware.

This was something that annoyed Sophie about working in such a small office- the daily lunch inspection. *Every day* without fail they had to talk about what they had for lunch. It was impossible to quietly sit pigging out on a piece of chocolate brownie cheesecake. *Every day* everyone had to declare their lunch. Sophie listed the contents of her Tupperware in a monotone voice, completely bored of this procedure and munched away on a carrot stick ignoring the eyes watching her every mouthful. She didn't care much what anyone else was having for lunch except maybe when Enid was having one of her potent home-made spaghetti bolognaise. In those instances Sophie would have to leave the office and get on with some photocopying in the room next door, the sight of Enid slurping the slippery spaghetti being too much for her to bear after already spending the morning opposite her.

"I like my veg." Laura stated. "I'm not too keen on mushrooms I'll be honest with you and cabbage…" she shook her head, "but anything else I'll have it. What is it they say, that you should eat five fruit and veg a day? Well, *apparently* pizza counts- the tomato on the top counts as one."

Sophie rolled her eyes at Ruth and started to mark some work as she ate a chunk of watermelon with the plastic fork that she got from the kitchen. She could hear Laura's voice droning on still but zoned out of the conversation. Laura could be the friendliest person in the world sometimes and then turn into a double crossing nuisance at the drop of a hat. She seemed to be in good spirits today but Sophie wasn't in the mood for small talk. Her mind drifted off to Friday evening when she was meeting Paul. The more she thought about him the closer he got to a handsome prince. Every sentence from their conversation last night had been replayed many times over in Sophie's head, talking to a member of the opposite sex and one who seemed keen to meet her had given her a boost, she couldn't remember feeling optimistic like this. She finished her lunch and still felt hollow with hunger, craving chocolate or cake, but was determined to persevere at least until her date.

***

After a week of facial scrubs and masks, a little more sleep than usual, mostly healthy food, a few runs and her Thursday night gym visit Sophie felt ready for her big date. Ben called just as she had waved off Kerry. When she saw his name on her mobile Sophie felt annoyance.

What does he want? She picked it up and answered 'Hi' brightly.

"Hi Soph, how's it going? How's me boy?"

Everything about his opening lines irritated her. She wished that he wouldn't call her 'Soph' any more as it had been an affectionate term and she didn't want him being affectionate with her any more. She hated it that he had to be involved in their lives at all. He had shattered them and now it was as if it had never happened.

"Oliver's fine thanks," she said bluntly. "What time are you coming round tomorrow?"

"Well that's why I'm calling actually," he cleared his throat, something he did when he knew that he was going to be a pest but was going to do it anyway, "something's come up, you know, that I have to deal with and so I thought maybe I could pick Ollie up on Saturday? I'll be there first thing! I can have him next weekend too if you like, you know, to make up for it." Silence.

The *one night* that I want to go out! Sophie thought. I've not wanted to go out at all for *three years* and now you're cancelling. Usually when this happened she didn't have any plans and so she'd say, oh yes OK that's fine pick him up whenever. This weekend though she actually had a plan that she wanted to keep and felt annoyed that her life had to still revolve around her ex's. She must have paused for some time.

"Oh what's up Soph? Have you got a date or something?"

Sophie's silence spoke volumes.

"Hey wow you've got a date! I don't know how I feel about that!" Ben joked. Sophie winced. Do we need to discuss this, she thought?

"Hey what's he like? What does Ollie think about him- has he met him yet? Is he, you know, a good role model and all that?"

Sophie felt her body tense. I don't need to talk about this with you, she thought. She felt awkward telling Ben that she had a blind date, they'd always spoken about how hideous they both thought that would be and Ben had promised Sophie that she would never need to go on one.

"He's nice but Ollie's not met him yet, of course- those two things are completely separate. I wouldn't let anyone meet Ollie unless I was completely sure myself that we were going to stay together- he's had enough upset in his life." Why am I even explaining this, she thought?

Ben was oblivious to the dig at him.

"Yeah good idea, you don't want him to meet any old guy. Anyway, they've got to be gold top don't they- only the best for me boy."

Like you, you mean, Sophie thought bitterly. She hated it when he gave her advice generally but this was even worse.

"It'll be nice anyway, for you, to have a weekend to yourself?" Ben added.

"Not really," Sophie replied flatly. "Anyway, what are you doing tomorrow night? You know, it's not good for Ollie when you change your plans. I've been telling him all week that Daddy's picking him up and now you're not coming when you said you are. He said the other day that Daddy only sees him when he's not busy."

"Oh did he? Aw man that's not good. It was just some extra work. Let me see what I can do, yeah? I'll text you." With that he hung up leaving Sophie none the wiser as to what day he was coming and so not sure if she would be going out on her date after all.

Sophie's date had become the talking point of the week even though she was now unsure if it was happening at all.

"Good luck tonight!" Ruth had said with a smile as Sophie hurried out of the office on Friday, "I can't wait to hear *all* about it!" And the rest of Sophie's friends had said the same later on at school.

"Have you got your sexy underwear ready?" Lou had asked.

"What? No!" Sophie had said. "He's not going to see my underwear!"

"You never know!" Lou had said with a mischievous smile. "You should *always* have on sexy underwear, just in case."

"I don't think I have any sexy underwear anyway..!" Sophie had said making a mental note to get some.

She had told the girls that she was still waiting for Ben to let her know what time he was coming round.

"The whole thing might still be off!"

"I know it's not ideal but if you're really stuck then you can drop Ollie off with me for a while. It would mean that you could still go out. I'd offer to babysit but Steve is out tonight- some pre match drinking session, there's a big game tomorrow apparently which means he's going out on Saturday night as well!"

"What?" Sophie had replied. "And then he'll be in bed all of Sunday with a hangover? When do *you* get to go out? Honestly Jules I don't know how you can put up with that *all* the time! I can't remember in all the time I've known you, your husband *ever* being around with his family at the weekend. And when he's around in the week he just sleeps!"

"Oh I don't want to go out anyway," Jules had said, "Don't worry, I'll make sure the boys wake him up on Sunday morning- I'm booking in a long lie for then," she said with a twinkle in her eye.

As they spoke Sophie heard that she had a text and checked her phone.

"Oh that's Ben. He's coming round at seven. That's late… he *always* seems to get stuck in traffic but I suppose that's just Friday's for you."

"You're very patient with him," Lou had said, "I'd want him round at five o'clock and no later. I couldn't be doing with hanging around waiting for someone."

Sophie suddenly felt a surge of excitement that she was actually going out on a date, "I'd better get home and get ready!"

"What are you wearing?" Lou asked. "Something low cut? Maybe off the shoulder? A mini-skirt perhaps?"

"Um, I don't know! I actually hadn't thought that far ahead…" Sophie replied, "I'd better go and see what I have in my wardrobe that isn't too ancient." The look on her face suddenly turned to one of concern. "Oh God. I've not been out for more than three years. What am I going to wear?" She looked at her friends who were all different proportions to her. "I'd better go right now and see- I bet I'll be up at the supermarket in half an hour getting something naff."

"Sophie!" Lou exclaimed. "That's one of the *first* things I'd have thought about!"

"I did say I was out of practice!"

The door to the classroom opened and children started to trickle out, excited that it was the weekend.

"Well, we'll get all the details tomorrow night anyway, won't we?" Tina added. "Unless, of course, you cancel us when it becomes a weekend shag-a-thon."

"Tina! I don't think so! We've already established that I don't have any sexy underwear anyway so don't worry, I'll see you all tomorrow night."

She greeted Oliver as he sped out of the classroom waving a piece of paper for his Mummy to read.

"What's this? Oh dear! *Another* inset day? Mummy will have to think about that later because now it's the weekend and you *and* I need to get ready! You are going to see Daddy and I'm going to see my friends."

When they returned home Oliver was put in charge of his own packing while Sophie started to get ready for what had become a date with a capital D. She went through to her bedroom to see what she could wear cursing herself for not thinking about that sooner. The thought had crossed her mind last night but after talking to Ben the mood had passed and she had been so tired that bed seemed like the more attractive option. I must have something to wear, she thought.

Sophie opened her wardrobe and rifled through all the garments hanging there; it was so true that you could have so many clothes and yet not a thing to wear. There were countless items that she had mentally labelled as 'holiday' clothes, always surviving the clear outs in the hope that one day she really would be lounging at that poolside she always imagined. Turning to her chest of drawers she pulled out the drawer that contained tops and went through every bundle, trying to find one thing that, firstly, just fitted her and secondly, looked decent. Why didn't I think about this sooner, she thought getting more exasperated by the minute? She turned her attention to the bottom of her cupboard where she kept her many pairs of shoes.

Shoes were Sophie's weakness and she had numerous pairs of them- all with very high heels except for her work shoes. They were all kept in their original boxes, bundled up neatly with a photograph of the shoe or boot on the side of each box. It was an area of her life that was unusually organised. She loved her shoes but never got to wear them, up until now. She knelt down and passed her finger down each bundle of boxes studying the contents closely. There were shoes of all different colours and styles; patent or with ruffles, tasselled or plain, some with closed toes some with peep toes, shoes with flowers on the buckles and boots with mirrors on the heels, shoes that were so high she wasn't sure that she could walk in them and shoes with three straps that felt secure. She had shoes labelled 'Italy heels' as that's where she pictured herself wearing them and knee length boots that didn't quite fit but that looked so good she'd decided to keep them anyway.

Oliver came into the room with some Lego that he needed help with separating and she turned to him to help.

"I'm *hungry!*" he complained, looking like he might keel over through weakness.

"Let's have some tea and get you ready for your weekend and then I can get ready to see my friends," Sophie told him and left her clothes search until later.

The two went downstairs and Oliver sat in the kitchen reading his school book while Sophie made tea. Once he'd finished his reading he went to fetch some paper and his colouring pencils and sat busily drawing until Sophie asked him to put it away until after he'd eaten. She wasn't sure if she was eating with Paul later and so took an apple from the fruit bowl and sat down with Ollie and munched on that as he ate some pasta. She picked up the paper that he was drawing on.

"That's a very lovely picture!" she told him in between mouthfuls, "What a beautiful princess! And who's that little boy there?"

"That's me!" Oliver stated, "And that's you and you're getting married!"

Sophie was taken aback by his picture but didn't let it show. Sometimes he said things that just made her want to cry. All the planning for her sister's wedding must have sparked his imagination, she thought.

"Do you want Mummy to get married?" she asked.

"Well, everyone at school has a Mummy and Daddy at home," he said in explanation.

"You have a Mummy and Daddy too; just they live in different houses," she knew that her explanation wasn't satisfactory but didn't have any other one right then. "They might think that *you're* lucky because you have two houses, two bedrooms, two sets of everything and when it's your birthday and Christmas you get two sets of presents!" Her words sounded hollow to her, Sophie didn't think that two sets of everything was compensation at all. Oliver seemed happy for the moment with that explanation and the two sat and finished their food. Sophie quickly cleared away the dishes and looked at the clock. Half past five. Plenty of time to get them both ready.

By the time she had got Oliver ready for his weekend away it was quarter past six and Sophie began to feel slightly panicked. She had gone into his room and found his suitcase packed full of what the boy had considered to be weekend essentials; Mr Ted, who already took up half of the suitcase, some little plastic road signs, a small globe, some gem stones that her mother had given him, a bouncy ball, a plastic spider and a green plastic crater with an alien popping out of the top.

You've got all bases covered there, Sophie had thought.

"Oh I really meant clothes!" she said out loud and proceeded to tip out all of his carefully packed toys and replace them with enough pyjamas, tops, trousers and underwear to see him through until Sunday evening.

"No! Mummy! I *need* them!" the boy wailed and frantically collected up all his discarded treasures.

They managed to fit them all in on top of his clothes, apart from Mr Ted who he held.

"There you go mister, all ready. Go and get your toothbrush and toothpaste for Mummy that would be a big help. Then you could watch a cartoon while I *try* to find something to wear?" Sophie hoped that this suggestion was agreeable as the time she had to get herself ready was slipping away. Gone was her idea of having a long soak in the bath or plenty of time to make sure her new make-up was applied just right. Another rush job, she thought.

By seven o'clock she had managed to find something to wear and applied some make up. She had made a pretty good attempt at the smoky eyes that the girl had shown her during her make-over and she admired her reflection in the mirror. She hadn't had time to wash her hair and so she tied it up into a simple chignon, allowing some strands to fall out around her face giving the style a softer look. It made her look quite sophisticated, she thought, but it was just the only way that she knew how to put her hair up. Twisting her head from side to side she inspected her appearance in the mirror. She applied another coat of lip gloss as the doorbell rang.

"That'll be Daddy!" she called to Ollie who was playing quietly in his bedroom.

She rushed down the stairs to open the door and called up to Ollie again. She unlocked the door and swung it open, Ben was standing there. Sophie was fairly impressed that he was actually on time. He was visibly taken aback.

"Wow Soph you look *great*!" he said with genuine surprise.

"Don't sound so shocked," Sophie replied, as if she always looked awful.

"I didn't mean it like that," he said. "I mean, I think that you look great all the time it's just that tonight you look *really* great! Who's the lucky man?"

Sophie struggled to know how to respond to his compliments. He was often complimentary to her, saying the she was a good Mum or that she looked nice or that she managed with everything very well. She usually deflected them. This time she flatly ignored it. It annoyed her that after everything that had happened he could be so *attentive* sometimes, she didn't understand.

"I'm not going on a date anyway," she lied, "I'm just meeting some friends in the pub."

"Well, you look great. Everyone will be checking you out. I bet you pull! Aw man I feel a bit jealous now!"

"I'm not going out to *pull!*" she replied crossly, annoyed that everything with Ben seemed to be on such a superficial level. "I'm just going for a sociable drink, that's all. It is possible to go to the pub and just have a drink with your friends; you don't *need* to always be looking to *pull* someone."

She felt irritated with the conversation and awkward that he ex was giving her compliments, as if he were toying with her emotions, and called up to Ollie again.

"Come on darling! Daddy's waiting and Mummy needs to go!" She had a look into the living room to see what time it said on the clock on the fireplace. "I have to go soon!"

"I'll go and get him," she said to Ben. "He's obviously deep in thought about something."

"It's OK. I'll go up. No worries. You get on with what you're doing."

With that Ben stepped into the house and bounded up the stairs before Sophie had a chance to protest. She watched in dismay as he went up two at a time leaving a trail of mud in his path. Great, she thought, resenting still having to clear up after him, why couldn't you just have stayed outside. She stomped up the stairs after him now feeling cross with everyone and headed for Ollie's room. She stopped at the door taking in the sight of the boy sitting on the carpet playing cars with his Dad and felt a pang of sadness in her heart.

That's all I wanted, she thought to herself, my own little happy family. For a moment she drank in the image and wondered briefly what life would be like if everything had gone to plan and she had married this man and didn't have to think again about going out on dates and meeting someone else. Ben sensed her standing in the doorway and turned around to look at her.

"You really do look beautiful," he said and turned to Ollie. "Mummy looks pretty doesn't she?"

Sophie gazed back at him for what seemed like minutes but was only a second and felt like she had when they had first met at her friend's party and they had caught each other's eye across the crowded room, much like the cliché, and Ben's cheeky smile and handsome features had instantly won her over.

"Lucky man, whoever he is."

She snapped herself out of her daydream, his comment confusing her again and making her want to shout that if she looked so beautiful why on earth did he not marry her and why did he run off with someone else?

"Right anyway I've really got to get ready now," she said flatly.

"OK we're off anyway," Ben replied getting up from the floor and picking up Oliver's case. "Come on son, time for stories at Dad's."

By the time Oliver had made sure he had brought all the toys he needed and had found the DVD that he'd wanted to take, the only one that didn't seem to be in its own box meaning that Sophie had had to hunt through all their other DVDs to find it before the boy had appeared with it having found it in his CD player, it was getting on for half past seven, when she was supposed to meet Paul. She sent him a text to say that she was on her way and rushed into the bathroom to check her appearance and apply final coats of lip gloss and mascara, not feeling much like going on a date anymore. She looked at herself in the mirror and forced a practiced a few smiles in readiness for greeting Paul. It felt funny that she was going to go and spend an evening with someone she'd never met before. Her phone beeped. She looked and saw it was Paul replying.

"Stop checking yourself out now," it said. "You look lovely. See you soon. X"

Sophie smiled at the message and felt her optimism return.

Chapter Four

Sophie had arrived at the pub shortly after half seven and met Paul outside as arranged, sitting at a table in the beer garden. She didn't want to look too conspicuous meeting someone she didn't actually know in public and thought that it would be quieter there than inside. She was right. Paul was the only sole braving the slightly damp evening and sat alone with his pint. He saw her as she parked having arrived early and chosen a spot where he could see the car park and having been told by Jules exactly what car she had. Sophie checked her reflection one last time, smoothed her hair and got out of the car. From the distance she wouldn't have known that it was him, he didn't look like the photos she had been poring over for the past two weeks. The gravel made it difficult for her to walk in her heels and she gingerly made her way towards her date concentrating, with each step, on not losing her balance. In the end she had decided to wear her skinny jeans and a black halter neck and to brighten it up a bit she had chosen her highest, shiniest, yellowest heels. They looked amazing which made up for the fact that they were very difficult to walk normally in and were hurting her toes immensely. Sophie cursed her choice only steps away from the car as she crunched and wobbled her way over the gravel. She fully expected to have bleeding toes by the end of the evening. She fixed her eyes on her destination and engaged full concentration so as not to topple over.

If I don't crash over because of these damn shoes, she thought, I'll faint through lack of food. She felt slightly light-headed after her week eating mostly fruit.

As she approached the beer garden Paul stood up and she noticed that he was considerably shorter than she had expected, to the point that she wished that she hadn't worn such high heels as she was now in danger of towering above him. The mental image that she had built up of him seemed to have strayed somewhat from the photos she had had. Getting closer still she saw that he was wearing glasses which she hadn't noticed either. In fact, the fairy tale prince image that had been building in her head for the past few days had been wildly optimistic and began to rapidly dissipate. He blinked through the thick round glass like one of the three blind mice and grinned goofily at her as she approached, still clutching his pint in one hand and with the other in his pocket. If she hadn't arranged to meet him there she might have mistook him for someone collecting for the RSPB. The image of Ben sitting playing with Ollie popped back into her mind and right then for a moment she wanted all that back.

Just without the heartache, she thought and shook the thought from her head. She put on her best smile. It's what's inside that counts, she said to herself, it's what's inside that counts.

She looked at Paul and smiled. He grinned back.

"Wowzers."

Wowzers. Sophie wasn't prepared for this opening line and was momentarily lost for words. She'd practiced her response to his 'Hi' or 'Hello' a hundred times that week but nowhere in her bank of first words was 'Wowzers'.

Wowzers, she thought, who says *Wowzers*? Apart from maybe children's television presenters in the very early 80s but she was pretty sure Paul wasn't one of them.

She recovered her composure and opted for a goofy smile herself and got ready to respond but Paul saved her from speaking by repeating his greeting.

"Wowzers," as if the first time hadn't made enough of an impact he repeated it just in case. "Jules didn't tell me that her friend was so *hot.*" His goofy smile broadened and he looked her up and down.

"Wowzers," Sophie replied and then shook her head and laughed. "Hi!" she corrected herself and extended her hand. I am going to kill Jules, she thought.

"Very official," Paul said good-humouredly and shook her hand, "Good evening."

There was a short pause while both took in the vision before them. Paul belched and indicated to his pint.

"First pint of the evening never sits well. Oh well, better out than in!" His eyes looked like they were about to pop out of his head as he smelt the air that had just been expelled from his mouth. "Phew!" He indicated to a crumpled up packet of crisps in the ash tray. "I knew cheese and onion was a bad idea!"

Kissing's out of the question then, Sophie thought.

Her eyes fixed themselves on the empty packet of crisps and she wondered if he'd finished them all or if there were any tiny crumbs still in the packet, the mention of food suddenly making her feel ravenous after her week-long detox. She wondered how early she could leave without seeming rude and hoped that it was after the first drink, the thought of a night in front of the telly in her pyjamas eating toasties suddenly feeling like a very attractive option. She couldn't think why she had ever wanted to go out on a date.

"Did you know that if you rub garlic on your feet it makes your breath smell?" He chuckled at the thought. "Pretty gross huh?" Silence. "D'you wanna drink? I thought I'd get a swift pint inside me before you arrived to calm the old nerves but I'm sure you could twist my arm to have another one."

Sophie wished that she had had enough time to walk down to the pub as the only way that she could imagine enduring this evening now was to get hammered. She hadn't thought that Jules would set her up with one of Steve's footy mates.

"I'll just have a Diet Cola please; I've got the car."

"You can jump in my taxi later, if you want a drink. I promise not to take advantage of you!" Paul chuckled then looked serious. "I'm only joking."

He belched again. Sophie wasn't sure how long she could put up with his wind problem before saying something. As they walked into the pub to go to the bar she excused herself to go to the ladies.

"I've just remembered I have to text my sister something," she mumbled.

"What is it with women and toilets?" Paul replied. "My ex used to spend *hours* in the loo- probably to get away from me!" He laughed.

Sophie laughed and shook her head. "Oh I'm sure she didn't! I won't be a sec."

"I'll line the drinks up!" Paul called after her causing a group of men at a nearby table to look over. Sophie glanced at them, noticing one in particular who she thought was extremely attractive. She caught his eye and he smiled causing her to blush. She smiled back regretful that she couldn't spend the evening in his company instead.

He looks more like my handsome prince, she thought, on a purely superficial level. She made it to the Ladies, happy that the pub was carpeted making it much easier for her to walk in a stable fashion. She immediately got out her phone and called Jules who answered straight away, concerned that there was a problem.

"I thought you were on a date with Paul?" Jules asked. "Is everything OK?"

"Never *ever* set me up with someone that you wouldn't be prepared to date yourself," Sophie said only half-jokingly. "Jules, what were you *thinking?* I've been with him for five minutes and it's already plain that he has a serious wind problem!"

"Aw give him a chance," Jules pleaded, "Steve said that he was really looking forward to going out, especially after everything he's been through. I'm sure he's sweet really."

"You sound like you don't know that! I thought that you said he was one of your friends!"

"He's more a friend of Steve really," Jules admitted.

"Jules! I didn't know you'd set me up with one of Steve's footy mates! Oh God. I'd better go. I will continue this conversation with you tomorrow, if you're brave enough to come round!" Sophie paused. "Actually, can you come down here in a bit and save me? Oh please!"

"I've got the boys," Jules said regretfully. "I would love to come down; I've not seen Paul for ages."

"Jules you said that he had you in stitches all the time!" Sophie was losing enthusiasm for the date rapidly.

"Well, I meant that he's a friend *online* and sometimes his status updates are so funny! Oh dear Sophie you sound a little bit cross. Give him a chance!"

"I've got no choice now do I? I'm giving him and hour and if he continues to break wind them I'm making my excuses early. Thank God at the moment it's just coming out of his mouth. See you tomorrow. Our friendship is officially under review," Sophie hung up aware that she'd been in the toilets for quite a few minutes. She smoothed her hair down and applied a coat of lip gloss, mainly for the benefit of the good looking guy who had just smiled at her, and went back to find Paul. She saw him sitting in a booth on the other side of the pub and as he saw her he patted the seat next to him marking the spot where she would be stuck for the rest of the evening. She carefully made her way over to him noticing that the group of men had gone leaving the table empty. She used it to steady herself as she tottered past. She vowed not to wear these yellow heels again, not until I have someone to hold onto, she thought.

She smiled at Paul as she sat down with him and apologised for being in the toilet for such a long time but he wasn't that concerned.

"I don't know what you girls do in there!" he said, "Us blokes are in, have a slash, out. That's it." He slurped his pint. Sophie noticed that there were no other drinks on the table.

"Shall I get us a drink?" she offered.

"I was wondering when you were going to ask! I'll have a pint please; strongest lager they've got."

Sophie got back up from the table and went to the bar. A young, male came over to serve her and smiled warmly asking what she'd like to drink. Sophie ordered and idly glanced around the pub as she waited. There were lots of groups laughing and drinking, not many couples she thought.

"Is that everything?" the bar man interrupted her thoughts.

Sophie nodded and said that it was.

"Five pounds sixty then please," the man smiled at her again making eye contact as if to distract her from the prices.

"*Five pounds sixty?*" she asked horrified by the amount and then recovered herself aware that she would give herself away for being old, "Five pounds sixty. There you go!" she handed him a ten pound note and waited for her change. I could have got a twelve pack in the supermarket for that, she thought, it *is* a long time since I've been out. She took the drinks back to the table and sat down with Paul who had been checking her out while she stood at the bar.

"You've got a great bum," he told her matter of factly, "Cheers."

"Do I?" she asked, genuinely not knowing if that was true.

"Oh yeah, best one in this pub for sure. It looks good in those jeans too."

Are men allowed to be so blatantly sexist these days, Sophie thought? A young woman walked past from a table in the far corner towards the toilets. Paul's gaze followed her behind for a few moments.

"So," Sophie said curtly, slightly annoyed that her date, whatever she thought of him, was looking at other women's bottoms, "I don't think I asked you what you do for a living?" A very dull question, she thought. Paul looked pleased that she'd asked though, there was no hint on his face that he thought that it was a dull question.

"Have you seen those vans?" he asked, "You know the ones with animals on them?"

Sophie shook her head, vans not being on her radar.

"Oh you must have done. You know the ones; they've got animals on them."

She continued to shake her head unaware of such vehicles. Paul remained certain that she did know what he was talking about.

"I think you do but anyway, they're self-hire vans. Actually, I've got cars, vans and trucks. The cars have a hamster on the side, the vans a hippo and the trucks have a giraffe. Clever, huh?"

Sophie had no idea why but decided not to ask.

"So anyway, it's a company that hires out cars and vans to people."

"Ah OK," Sophie nodded thoughtfully, "So, was that your idea- the animals?"

"No actually, I just work in the office, not *actually* my own company! I love it though, great job. Company car too."

Sophie nodded again, glad that Paul liked his job so much but not sure what else to ask about it. She decided to change tact.

"So, how do you know Jules?"

"Well, I don't really know Jules," Paul admitted, "Steve is a friend so I have met her but only once, I think. Lovely lady! If I'd have known that she had such attractive friends though I'd have hung around her a bit more! Me and my mate Dave go clubbing sometimes. Well, pretty much every weekend if I'm not working. If we'd have seen you in the club I'd have looked at him and said, Dave, I'd give her one, would you?" Paul looked at her, pleased with his compliment. Sophie smelt something that was unmistakably wind from his other end.

Thankfully before she had to respond to this last remark a woman appeared at the table clutching a sheet of paper and an ash tray with a 50p coin in it.

"Quiz?" she said. A more unenthusiastic person Sophie had never seen before.

"Pardon?" Sophie replied.

The woman visibly sighed. To speak again appeared to be a massive effort.

"Quiz? Are you doing the quiz?"

"Quiz! Wow yeah!" Paul suddenly sprung into life, "I am King of the Quiz in The Plough! What's the minimum you can have in a team?"

The woman looked like she might collapse through utter boredom and braced herself to speak again, sighing loudly.

"Any number."

"OK great! Shall we be a team of two then Sophie? Great stuff. I had no idea there was a quiz here on a Friday night otherwise I'd have told Dave and Phil to come along too!"

Sophie didn't have much say in the matter but decided that doing the quiz might make the time pass more quickly. Paul paid the pound to cover them both and went up to the bar to get a piece of paper and a pen, the journey being too much for the woman to be bothered to make. She waited at their table for their team name so that she could write it on her paper.

"What's our team name?" he asked sitting back down at the table.

Sophie looked thoughtful.

"I'm never very good at thinking of names," she said.

"How about "The Blind Daters'?" Paul looked pleased with himself.

"Oh maybe not!" Sophie said almost hysterically, "What about 'Two's Company'?" she suggested not wanting to draw attention to the fact she was on a blind date, "All the other teams seem to have at least four people."

"Oh yeah OK that's good," Paul agreed. He turned back to the woman. "We're 'Two's Company'"

The woman wrote the name on her paper and left the two to continue her round of the pub. Sophie heard her say, "Quiz?" to the next table and stifled a giggle.

"There's someone who's obviously getting job satisfaction!" she laughed, "She sounds like she hates her job more than I do!" Her tummy growled, protesting that all it had been given since lunchtime was an apple and she put her hands on it in an attempt to muffle the noise. "Did you want something to eat before the quiz starts?" she asked Paul.

"Nah you're alright. Might have a kebab later, on my way home, well…" he looked at her hopefully and raised his eyebrows, "unless…" he let the words hang there as an invitation.

Sophie sat speechlessly for a moment thinking that she really should say something to the effect that she would not be getting in the way of his kebab plan but wasn't sure how to put it without being rude so she let the words hang there unanswered, a bad idea she thought as this would no doubt raise his hopes further.

"I think I'll quickly order some chips," she told him and without waiting for his reply got up and went back to the bar.

The chips arrived just before the quiz was due to start. Sophie was about to smother them in tomato ketchup when Paul held his hand over them.

"Whoa there missus!" he said urgently, "Steady on the ketchup! I'm more a brown sauce man," he got up and went to the bar to ask if they had any.

Get your own bloody chips, Sophie thought. She smiled at him as he sat back down with a brown sauce bottle, took off the lid and started to cover half the chips with it.

"What's yours is mine!" he joked, "Oops I've probably got more than half there…"

Sophie smiled again patiently, much as she would do with Ollie, when he was being silly, and moved a couple of brown sauced chips onto his side of the bowl. She put ketchup on hers and started to tuck in; ignoring the fact that Paul was watching her in admiration. She was so famished that she polished off her side of the bowl before Paul had made a start on his, his attention seeming to have been caught by Sophie's apparent love of food.

"I *love* it when a woman loves her food," he said as she munched away on her last chip. "So many girls nowadays pick away at a salad leaf, it's just not *attractive.*"

Sophie wiped the ketchup from her chin.

Twenty minutes later the quiz was ready to go and Paul pulled his chair in to the table eagerly and sat poised, pen in hand, for the first question. They heard the taps of the quizmaster testing out the microphone and an ear piercing whistle caused by the feedback. After a loud sigh her monotone voice resonated around the pub.

"One… two… one… two," she tapped the microphone again although it seemed to be working fine. Her voice could be heard as she asked a colleague if she could hear that OK. "One… two… one… two… "her colleague snapped back that she should just get on with it, probably fearing that her shift would go over if they didn't get a move on, Sophie thought. "OK," she paused, "question one," she paused again and sighed, "question one is… general knowledge," another long pause. "On a Monopoly board… what colour… is… Coventry Street?"

Sophie giggled. This is going to be a long evening she thought.

Two and a half hours later and the quiz was still going on. Sophie sat slumped at the table having very nearly lost the will to live. Paul even was beginning to look a little impatient and was doodling on his beer mat. He insisted that they stay until the end though seeing as they'd got so far. Sophie looked at her watch. Just after half past ten. Usually when Ollie went away for the weekend she was tucked up by now either reading a book or watching the telly in bed. She liked to get up early in the morning and go for a long run before breakfast. She felt so tired and restless after sitting in one place for the whole evening and she desperately wanted to go home.

"Last round," the miserable voice spoke again breaking her thoughts. The mood in the pub suddenly seemed to lift as everyone breathed a collective sigh of relief. "Last round… is a picture round… this week's picture round is all about… pasta. Name the pasta shape from the picture."

The mood in the pub deflated again and those taking part in the quiz braced themselves for the final push.

"Oh God," Sophie said resignedly as a piece of paper showing various types of pasta was placed in front of her on the table. She sat upright and, picking up the paper, considered the pictures. She pointed to each one. "Tagliatelli. Macaroni. Lasagne. Conchigle. Farfalle. Spaghetti. Tortellini. Penne. Rigatoni. Fusilli." She placed the paper back down on the table and looked at Paul squarely. "What I don't know about pasta isn't worth knowing."

Paul looked at her in total admiration. "Wow you're awesome," he said as he frantically scribbled the words down on their quiz sheet. "You're *amazing*. I need to get Dave and Phil down here and we can be a team of four.

Dave's our sports man, I'm general knowledge and Phil knows everything there is to know about flags so with your food knowledge we'd have it all covered."

Sophie nodded thoughtfully but decided not to speak. Phil sounds like an interesting guy, she thought.

They left as soon as the results had been announced. Paul was visibly upset that they hadn't won, coming third to the Bright Sparks and Three Degrees and an A Level although he had been impressed by their names. "Brilliant," he had said shaking his head, disappointed in their own effort. "Just brilliant." Sophie had felt that she had failed him but he took the blame himself.

"No it wasn't you. You got *all* the pasta! That was a-*mazing!* It was my music round. Useless. *Useless!* Really bad. God don't tell Jules that I didn't get them all because she'll tell Steve and I'll get ribbed about it until Christmas. Sorry, we could have won if I'd not messed it up."

"Don't worry," Sophie consoled him, "I think that we can live without the nine pounds fifty prize money!"

They got to the car park where Paul's taxi was waiting. He walked her up to her car and took her hand.

"I've *really* enjoyed tonight," he said, "I've not had such a good time for ages."

Sophie stood with her hand in his, wondering if it would be rude to pull it away from him but finding the situation rather awkward and standing dumbly instead. She had no idea what the dating etiquette was at the end of an evening when you've had an OK time but not found the other person attractive at all. He gazed at her, blinking as if she were an angel who was dazzling him with light. She sensed that he was waiting for her to ask if she could jump in his taxi with him or offer him a lift home but she just wanted to get away now, back to her quiet house all by herself, the quiz lady's voice still echoing in her head, to make a hot chocolate and tuck herself up in her cosy bed. They stood in silence for a brief time and then Paul lurched forward as if to kiss her but at that moment she finally lost balance, something that had been threatening all evening and she wobbled on her heels and had to steady herself on her car, breaking the moment. She smiled at Paul and stifled a yawn.

"Oh I'm *sorry*! Really busy week for me at work," she yawned again just to hammer the point home that she was tired and good for nothing. Paul looked at her like he didn't care that she was tired. She hadn't realised that he'd been tipping the pints back and he now looked at her with a slightly drunk smile, his glasses sitting wonkily on his nose. She needed a line to draw the evening to an end. "Maybe we can do it again sometime."

***

"That was the *wrong* thing to say! Uh-uh!" Lou made the sound of a quiz show buzzer and shook her head. "A hundred people were asked what not to say at the end of an unsuccessful date and a hundred people said," She put on a high pitched voice, "Maybe we can do it again sometime!"

"Oh God," Sophie said looking troubled, "I didn't want to offend him! He's a nice guy, apart from his wind problem… and roaming eyes… and he didn't really look like I thought he was going to look… and I'm not sure we had that much in common…"

"You're suddenly very picky!" Lou laughed.

"I don't think so..!" Sophie defended herself, "He just wasn't really my *type*."

"So you have a type now then do you?"

Sophie smiled. "There was a guy in the pub when we arrived who was really, *really* cute. He smiled at me and it made me get butterflies in my tummy but he left not long after we arrived."

"Doesn't that tell you something?" Tina asked mischievously.

"I found the whole thing of meeting someone I didn't know a bit *weird* though and then the pub quiz made it a bit *weirder.*"

"What, you didn't want to sit answering general knowledge questions all night on a first date?" Lou asked incredulously. "It sounds very romantic to me."

"It gave us a focus for the evening. I'm not sure I could have sustained a conversation with him for the *whole* night and I can now tell you that the national currency of Egypt is the pound and that the polish flag is red and white."

"Oh *everyone* knows *that!"* Lou scoffed.

Jules who had been sitting quietly sipping a diet coke joined in the conversation.

"Oh it's such a shame though. Steve text me earlier and said that Paul *really likes* you!"

"Jules you hardly even know who he is so stop being disappointed! I'm struggling to know how I ever let you set me up with him! Why would you ever have thought that I'd be perfectly matched for one of Steve's drinking buddies?"

"Opposites attract," Jules had said hopefully.

Lou and Tina nodded in agreement.

"It is true," Lou stated. "If you're too similar you might run out of things to talk about."

"He said 'Wowzers'! And he burped and farted his way through our date. Honestly it was disgusting! There wasn't anything about him that I liked. He's not the best looking man in the world, he has *very* bad skin probably due to all the lager he drinks and his teeth looked like they needed a *really* good clean. I could put up with all that though if he had a sparkling personality but he really didn't and he was *constantly* checking out other women which is probably just about the *worst* thing someone can do on a first date. I thought he was good with children; I didn't know he was one! How do you know he's good with children anyway when you've only met him once?"

Tina and Lou looked at Jules, amused at the sound of her choice of partner for their friend.

"Well, I just thought that he was because for Christmas he gave the boys a selection box. Steve brought it home from the match before the holidays. I just thought that it was really sweet- he must know what children *like.*"

"Any numpty knows that children like sweets!" Sophie laughed. "That was a whole evening of my life that I'll never get back. No offense ladies but I think I'll take matters into my own hands, just because we're friends it doesn't mean that you have any idea about who I'd like. Thanks for your help but I think I might get on better at this alone- I have a better idea of what I'm looking for now." She remembered the good looking guy in the pub. "I'll keep you informed of my progress but if I'm going to look for a Plus One I think I'll do it myself!"

"What are you going to do then?" Tina asked.

"Well, I've had a few random encounters with the opposite sex now. I think I might go for your idea and create my own profile on one of those dating sites. It's the little things about someone that attracts you in the first place, like his sparkling eyes or gorgeous smile, and only I'm going to know that when I see it so I think I'll take over proceedings now, if it's all the same with you."

Tina clapped her hands and bounced up and down where she sat on the sofa.

"Good idea!" she cried. "I can give you some pointers if you like?"

"No thanks!" Sophie declined her offer. "Lou and Joules have put me right off friendly help! I'll call you if I need any guidance but I think I'll be OK. You might need to help me describe myself as I can't think what I'd say about that but otherwise I shall probably be fine. I'll keep you informed."

On Monday morning Sophie sat at her desk searching the internet for dating sites, Enid being out of the office for the day at a regional meeting. Usually she was left a detailed list, with timings, to complete but for some reason today there was nothing. She did have her regular Monday jobs to do but those generally could be done in half an hour so she decided to use the rest of her time positively rather than waste it by randomly surfing the web.

Tina was right, she thought, as she scrolled down the numerous different dating sites that came up on her search, there was a dating site for literally everyone. There were sites for professionals, the over 60s, sites where you had to get your friends to do your profile. Sites for rich people, time poor people, Christians, single parents, *ugly* people, *farmers* as well as sites to find a *long term* partner or just have a fling, local ones, national ones and even ones abroad.

That's going to get expensive, she thought.

She couldn't believe that some of the sites were so *specific*. Who *specifically* knew that the one for them was from Poland or happened to be a policeman? Why did *divorcees* need their own dating site? And what was *that* one? Sophie clicked on a link which took her to a page showing a picture of a woman brandishing a whip and quickly minimised the page.

She furtively glanced around the office to check that everyone was still hard at work and not noticed the X-rated content of her browsing. Satisfied that everyone was too busy with their own workloads she turned her attention back to her computer and went back to her search. There seemed to be literally hundreds of dating sites making it very difficult to know which one to choose. She decided first to try one that she had seen an advert for on the telly.

It must be OK, she decided, because it was on during Ant and Dec's Saturday Night Takeaway. She followed the link to the website.

The door to the office opened and Chris the I.T. man appeared, looking more serious than normal. Sophie couldn't think of a time that she'd ever seen him smile. He had a workload enough for ten people and was always getting more and more things added to his seemingly endless list. She minimised her page again.

"Hi, Chris!" Pam piped up first. Sophie and Ruth looked up and smiled and said 'Hi'. Laura moved her head slightly, acknowledging his entrance but didn't waste any energy by vocalising a greeting. Chris mumbled something and looked round at Laura's computer screen. Satisfied that there was nothing to see there he casually wandered round to Ruth, saying that he was just looking for something. Ruth's computer also seemed to hold nothing of interest and he moved round to the other side of the desks where Pam and Sophie sat. He glided past Pam, hardly casting a glance in her direction and stopped by Sophie and bent over her, holding onto her desk.

"It's OK everyone, back to work. There's nothing to see. There's just a bit of a glitch on the system." The rest of the office dutifully got back to what they were doing while he focussed his attention on Sophie's computer. She groaned inwardly as Chris clicked on the internet explorer icon and up her dating site popped.

"*Sophie!*" Chris hissed under his breath. "Haven't you *read* the I.C.T. policy?"

"What? Oh no probably not. There are so many policies I can't keep up. Remind me…?"

"The ICT Policy states that no employee is to access any materials that are not directly related to work at any time and all use of resources will be monitored!" Chris whispered loudly. "I'm sure that you *have* read it as it was part of your induction *and* when I gave you your log in I asked you to sign it to say that you'd read it…?"

"Oh. Oh yeah…" Sophie mumbled vaguely.

"I can see *exactly* what you're looking at downstairs!"

Laura stirred at her desk on the opposite side of the room, realising that Sophie had been doing something she shouldn't have. Sophie looked sheepishly at Chris who shook his head, like a disappointed father.

"It's just as well I was by myself in the office. Mrs Wright usually sits next to me you know. Do you know how to do this?" he asked her and clicked on an icon at the top of the page which made a list of options drop down. He went to 'delete browsing history'. Sophie looked dumbly at her screen.

"No… no I didn't know that… Mrs Wright sometimes sits and works at my computer once I've gone…" she trailed off thinking about all the times she'd got into work and found the principals nail varnish bottle and empty cup of peppermint tea on her desk.

Chris looked the most amused that Sophie had ever seen, his expression softening a little.

"Just do that and remember to log out," he told her, "and remember, I can see *everything*… unless you're doing in private browsing… *" he winked at her and left the room, holding his hand up to say bye to everyone. Sophie pulled a face at Ruth who was grinning at her over her screen.

She decided to continue her online dating investigations later at home seeing as her surfing habits were being so closely scrutinised at work. Once Ollie was safely in bed she went to hers, bundling the four pillows against the headboard and sat up with her lap top balanced on her knees.

I could happily live in a bedsit, she thought. The only time they seemed to need to go downstairs was for the kitchen. She went back to the website that she had chosen to try first to find her prospective Plus One- a national and by all accounts popular and successful dating site. The home page showed lots of little pictures of attractive smiling people who were supposedly looking for a date but looking at them all Sophie couldn't believe that any of them really were. Her initial reaction to online dating was that it would be a little bit desperate and seedy and definitely something to keep quiet about. The site proclaimed that a fifth of couples said that they had met online and they had some photos of such happy couples, grinning into the camera, rather smugly Sophie thought.

They're probably all models anyway, she decided cynically. She was slightly disappointed that she had to create a profile before she could have a nosey through prospective dates and, more to the point, her competition. The only way to see who was out there was to sign up so she opted for the free trial. She started to fill in the required fields stating that she was a woman seeking a man and taking a couple of years off her date of birth. The next question asked what age of man was she looking for. She didn't want to limit her chances of finding someone by setting the age range too narrow but then decided that an 18-year-old or 70-year-old would be a bit weird and so set the range from 30-45. She felt a bit odd signing up to an online dating site; it wasn't something that she would have ever imagined that she'd have to do having been completely and blissfully happy. But that was a long time ago now, she reminded herself.

As she filled in each field another list dropped down underneath asking her seemingly endless questions. All fairly basic and sensible at first she thought, her postcode, her town, her email address. She then had to choose a user name. She tried her first name but someone was already using that. She sat pondering the subject, not having any inspiration beyond her own real name and not able yet to look at what user names other people had for ideas. This is ridiculous, she sighed, and randomly punched in some numbers and letters which the system then accepted. She took a piece of paper and pen out of her bedside table drawer to write it down, a sequence of characters she would never remember. Just in time, she thought, I was about to ditch the whole idea. She verified her email address and was taken to her profile page where she was greeted by *more* questions. There were questions upon questions under different headings, breaking her down into different sections. Her resolve wavered again. She didn't have to dissect herself like this when she met Ben.

What am I doing, she thought, what the hell am I doing? Her eyes gazed blindly at the screen for a second while her mind drifted off, thinking of her life as it was now rushing from one thing to another to another, to school and to work and to school and to the shops and back home to do homework and make tea and pack lunches and put on washing and do housework and then stories and baths and then bed… waking up exhausted for another day of the same. Then another day… and another day… And arriving at the weekend tired but determined to spend time with her son, their quality time being limited during the week, but then her feeling of aloneness usually being highlighted by the people they saw at the places that Oliver wanted to go and not having any family close by to drop round and see and not any friends who weren't already busy with their own lives. Suddenly all she wanted was a man there next to her to put his arms around her and make her feel loved and not alone anymore.

That's what I'm doing; she thought with a new resolve and continued with the signing up process. She looked at her next set of questions. As she did this her mobile rang and she looked at the screen to see if she wanted to answer or not. Joules. She answered it.

"Hi, Joules! Are you alright?"

"Hi Soph. Yeah we're fine. Same old stuff really. Steve saw Paul today though *randomly*. I think he popped by his work *on purpose* to ask him about you! Oh Sophie, he *really* likes you. He doesn't know if he should try and call you again because he said he's not heard from you."

"Oh god I'd completely forgotten about that. I should have text him or something just to say… um… I'm not sure what to say actually."

"He *really* likes you."

"Does he? Well, that doesn't mean that I'm going to really like him!" Sophie felt a sudden guilt that she didn't fancy the man that her friend had set her up with, "He's just not my type," she continued, a phrase that was beginning to trip off her tongue quite easily, "He's lovely I'm sure but not my type. I'll have to call him or something." There was a pause. "I'm actually, don't tell anyone, just signing up for a dating agency," there was another pause, "Joules?"

"Oh dear, he'll be so upset! He was dumped by his last girlfriend…"

"Oh God, don't tell me that! Now I feel *really* bad! He was the first man I've been on a date with for about three years-it was *quite* unlikely that we were going to fall in love with each other and live happily ever after?" her voice pleaded with her friend to understand. Jules sighed audibly.

"Oh well, yes you're right. I just thought that maybe…" her voice trailed off. "I guess it was a bit of a shot in the dark."

"Maybe a little one. I'll call him and make sure that he's let down very gently. I'm sure he'll be happy enough if I tell him I'll still do pub quizzes with him though," she laughed. "He was *quite* impressed by my knowledge of pasta. Anyway, seeing as you're on the phone. I don't suppose you have a spare moment to help me with this?"

"Yeah I'm free. The boys are in bed and Steve is out with Paul. They decided that they needed to catch up over a beer. What do you need help with?"

"Well it's just this dating site. I might need some help. I'm going through the signing up page…" she looked again at the questions on the screen, "actually these ones are OK but I might need some help in a bit."

"One of my friends at work has just signed up to a dating site," Jules said, "she had to write a description of herself that grabbed everyone's attention. I wrote it for her so fire away!"

"OK cool well the first bits easy. 'Current marital status'. There are a lot of options! That's *terrible!* One of them is 'married'!" She shook her head. "There, 'never married'. They should have a 'nearly married' option. Is 'never married' there just to put people's minds at rest that you don't have a crazy ex? Well they'll be in for a surprise because I've never been married but *still do* have a crazy ex!"

"Well, he's not *unstable,"* Jules said.

"Don't be nice about him. One of the questions is 'How many times have you been married'! I'd lie about that one really if I'd been married more than once, wouldn't you? Anyway, do I want more children?" Sophie's resolve waned again. "I've not met anyone yet and they want to know if I want children with him."

Jules offered the voice of reason. "Well, you know, would you like more children *generally*? Or are you happy with just the one?"

Sophie considered this for a second.

"More than one is a flipping nightmare," Jules added.

"Aw you can't say that Jules! Your boys are lovely."

"Try having them for 24 hours," Jules challenged.

Sophie thought.

"I think, that if I met someone who *did* want children, then I'd love to have another but if they *didn't* want to have any then that would be fine too. I think… That's difficult," she looked at her options, "fantastic, not sure."

"Next!" Jules called, getting into the spirit of it.

"OK next is 'Qualifications'."

"*Qualifications*? What like *academic* qualifications or just like what makes you a generally fabulous person?"

Sophie looked at the options.

"They want to know how well you've done at school. It's suddenly like a job application."

"Well some people might feel intimidated by brains or not want to go out with a dummy…" Jules said. "You're *very* qualified aren't you?"

"Well yes for my job but maybe not for this! Let's see… I can say I have an honours degree. I *could* say I'm a professor thought! I don't suppose anyone is going to check that out! I always wanted to be a professor…"

"Sophie we really need to get you out more. I don't think people will be that bothered."

"Not bothered? I worked hard for that degree! OK anyway, next questions," she clicked 'Next' at the bottom of the page then groaned. "Oh God there are *tons* of them. These ones are describing me though so I might need your help. Are you really sure you can talk this long?"

"Oh yeah its fine, Steve is out blowing our money on booze so I think I'm allowed to make a call!" Jules said cheerfully. Sophie wondered if she felt as happy about it as she sounded.

"Are you alright Joules? He always seems to be out…"

"Oh it's fine. I'm used to it. Really. Don't worry about me! I'm waiting for your next question."

"OK here goes. There are a lot though. First ones are easy, eye colour, hair colour, length of hair… I can do them! Next ones require a bit more thought- dress sense. Am I 'bargain basement', 'casual', 'simply stylish', 'snappily dressed', 'trendy', 'sporty' or 'haute couture'?" She paused. "Wow that's *difficult."*

There was a pause on the line while they considered the choices.

"I'm *all* of them at some point! I'm snappily dressed for work, sporty for my runs, casual at the weekend…" her voice trailed off as she considered some more. "What do you think?"

Jules thought some more. "'Simply stylish' I think. That doesn't say much, doesn't commit you to anything but makes you sound quite with it."

"I hope they're not all like this," Sophie said, "otherwise we'll be here all night. OK 'Simply stylish' it is. Next. Do I look 'plain', 'above average', 'pretty', 'attractive' or 'wow you're gorgeous'?" she laughed. "*Then* they want to know if I'm 'skinny', 'athletic', 'petite', 'overweight' or 'sexy'? Some of these really don't make sense. I'm sure I can be overweight *and* sexy! This is exactly why I didn't want to do this. You can't put yourself into boxes like this. If you met someone in the flesh you'd know *exactly* what they were like just by looking at them. This is impossible."

"This is just a way to meet some people," Jules reassured her friend. "I say just try this and then if you don't get on with it then there's no harm done and you can think of another way to find your man. I don't think that you need to be too exact really. Say that you're athletic of course and attractive, because nobody likes a big head."

"I'm not enjoying this. How important is it to me that my new partner is attractive? Well my attractive is different to someone else's attractive- there are a few flaws in this system."

"I think that you might be taking it way too seriously," Jules stated.

"Depends how seriously everyone else is taking it."

"Say it's important," Jules directed, "then you might just get the 'Wow you're gorgeous' ones." They both laughed and Sophie ticked the box.

"OK next. 'About you'. Oh my God it's like one of those psychometric tests that you have to do when you do a course at work. Am I a time waster?" Her thoughts drifted to work when she made her photocopying jobs last for five hours rather than go back to sitting opposite Enid. "Can I handle a lot of information?" She thought of Enid's lists that were waiting on her desk in the morning. "Do I stand up for myself? This is really making me think about my line manager a bit too much!"

"They're getting bit weird," Jules agreed. "Stacy didn't have to answer stuff like that. She just had to say what she looked like, what sorts of things she liked doing in her spare time and then write a little bit about herself, penned by yours truly. Maybe you should find out what site *she's* using because I know that she's been out with a couple of *really* nice guys?"

"I feel like I've made the commitment to this one now thought Jules and, no offense, but I know what your 'nice guys' are like!" Sophie laughed. "I'm just joking! I'm sure they're all just as ridiculous." She randomly ticked boxes down the extensive list provided. "There, I've done that one." She clicked 'next' and groaned as she saw the next table of choices. "OK I spoke too soon; this has got to be the most ridiculous dating site ever! More 'self-description'." She ticked 'Always' to everything good and 'Never' to everything bad down the table of random self-descriptive words- stable, fun, fickle, loyal, honest, excitable, old-fashioned, modern, accepting, calm, caring, hot tempered, violent...

"I'm hardly going to tick 'Violent' am I?" Four pages of the same and she was offered another heading. "Oh here we go Jules, this is for you! 'Friends Description'". She read out the list of words that seemed similar to the ones that she had just answered for herself.

"Just tick all of the good ones," Jules told her.

"What, all of them? Aren't there any that stick out in particular?"

"No just tick them all, honestly."

"If I ever go on a date through this," Sophie said, "I am going to have to remember how utterly amazing I've made myself sound. OK here's one from the next list. Thinking caps on. 'I am usually satisfied with my current levels of emotional and spiritual development.' What the flipping heck does *that* mean? I'll say yes, yes I am. 'Every day I see humour in the situations that I find myself in'," she thought about work. "Not really… 'Every day, no matter what my agenda is, I always take time out to smell the flowers and look out over the land and think how wonderful it is to be alive'? Is this person on drugs?"

"They are getting quite *deep,*" Jules agreed.

"They don't seem to have one that says, 'Every day I thank my lucky stars that I've made it to the end of the day without causing my line managed serious harm' or 'I barely manage to keep my life ticking over so meeting a man might just tip me over the edge," both ladies laughed. "It's only funny because it's true!" Sophie said. "'I have a high sex drive'."

"Do you?" Jules's interest suddenly rose as she expected some outrageous revelations.

"No I mean that's the next question! I don't even know what that means. What's sex? I'll put 'sometimes'".

Sophie clicked to the next page and was dismayed to see that the progress report told her that she was 45% complete.

"Oh dear Jules we're not even half way with this! It says that I'm 45% complete. What a nightmare. Maybe I should go and get on with it. You must be getting bored!"

"No not really," Jules said. Sophie wasn't' sure if she was being polite. "There's something that I want to watch on the telly though at half nine so maybe I will go." Sophie heard the smile in her friend's voice.

"Good idea. We could be here all night. If I don't catch you at school then I'll see you on Friday?"

"Yes definitely. Nothing will get in the way of my Friday night and I won't be able to *wait* to hear about this! By Friday you'll be positively *inundated* with offers!"

"I hardly think so," Sophie said modestly. "I will know myself a whole lot better though! See you Friday. Give me a call before then if you feel like a chat."

The ladies said goodbye to each other and Sophie thought for a moment about her friend and her husband who seemed to be away for more and more of the time these days. I just wouldn't want that, she thought, I would rather be single for ever than spend my life with someone who made me unhappy for *any* reason. She turned her attention back to the questions with a new resolve. If there's a question 'Do you like football', she thought, then my answer will most definitely be 'No'.

It took Sophie a further two hours to complete the questions on the dating site, most of them sending her into deep thought, and she felt exhausted by the end. She couldn't remember ever having to think so hard since her University days when her tutor had asked her 'Why do we have something rather than nothing' during an early morning Philosophy lecture. She put her laptop down on the bed next to her, flopped her head back against the headboard and sighed. She thought over some of her answers and wondered if 'friendliness' really was the most important quality in a new partner especially after her date with Paul who had been incredibly friendly.

Most of the questions had made her chuckle about work- 'Did she ever feel plotted against', 'Did she ever dislike people', 'Does she ever waste time', 'Is she ever tempted to make fun of people behind their backs'? She decided that under normal circumstances she would behave differently. She had left 'Things that you are most grateful for' blank so as not to tempt fate and decided that the three things that she was best at was 'raising her son', 'keeping fit' and 'earning money'- not very exciting or sexy but the way it is, she had thought and some of the other options were rather random, like 'car maintenance'. 'Running' was the interest that she put top of her list to share with a new partner and she decided that 'This Country' would be a suitable distance to find love, not wanting to limit her chances of finding someone but also being slightly realistic and not ticking 'Anywhere in the world' as meeting up in Paris or New York or Australia might be a bit tricky.

Once all of the questions had been answered she was given the option to post a photo as well, being told that most people prefer a profile with a photo, but she didn't have any on her computer and she didn't feel much like taking a photo of herself so she left it without, despite warnings from the website that she was destined to fail without one. I'm sure the guys can wait for a few days to see what I look like, she thought. She clicked on 'Post Profile'. Shit, she thought, I've gone live. Now to sit back and wait.

'Congratulations!' A banner appeared across her screen. 'You are now one step closer to finding your perfect partner'.

We'll see, Sophie thought cynically.

The site offered a free limited membership which she decided was fine for now, the monthly subscription for a 'Premier Account' being about the same as her car insurance which she thought was a bit much. She was frustrated that she couldn't access a lot of the features though as she browsed the site and thought that she might upgrade at a later date depending on how she got on with it like this. One thing that she could do though was snoop on her competition and so she went to 'Online Now' to see who was around. The first woman that she saw looked considerably older than her, to her relief. Sophie read her introductory descriptive paragraph about herself to get a heads up of who she was up against. It read, 'Hey guys my name's Marcia, coming from the name of the planet. I can give you loving that is out of this world. I'm a nurturer. I'm a feeler. I'm a toucher. I'm a kisser. If you've had a bad day at work baby I will reach over and rub your back and anywhere else that feels tense.' Sophie stared at her computer dumbstruck. Suddenly the bit about Adult Education and enjoying running in her spare time didn't seem that attention grabbing.

Sophie quickly forgot about Marcia though when she saw her Inbox filling up with messages within minutes of her posting her profile.

Almost like they're just sitting there waiting for a newbie, she thought.

Chapter Five

"So?" Jules looked expectantly at Sophie, raising her wine glass to be filled. "I've missed you all week at school. Have you had any luck?"

"Yes do tell!" Lou piped in. "We're gagging to know! Jules *told* us that you were taking the plunge! I've been so busy though, I've not managed to catch you in the morning."

"Found any hunks yet?" Tina took a gulp of her wine. "What site have you gone with- Uniform Dating?" her eyes sparkled with anticipation.

"This was supposed to be a secret!" Sophie scolded Jules. "I didn't really want anyone to know, it's kind of embarrassing isn't it? And no I've not gone with 'Uniform Dating'- how shallow!"

"There's nothing wrong with a man in uniform," Tina smiled broadly.

Sophie laughed. "I wouldn't have thought that a man would be any more attractive just because he wears a uniform!"

The four ladies pondered on this last statement and then broke out into laughter.

"Well... OK maybe you have a point there. Anyway, that's my secret blown!"

"Well, it's not really. I've not told anyone else... just us three. So come on tell us! Have you any hot dates lined up yet?"

Three sets of eyes fixed themselves on Sophie, eager to hear the latest gossip about her man hunt. She wished that her initial efforts had been as exciting as they seemed to think it would be.

"No dates, not yet. Yes, I have registered with…" she looked around comically then whispered, "an *online dating agency* but to date I am still single. Signing up was a *nightmare!* I've never answered so many questions about myself before- I didn't even know the answers to some they were so deep! It took me over two hours to complete their questionnaire. But anyway, I'm on a free trail right now, just to see how it goes. It was funny though, when I completed my profile, within minutes I had 149 matches! 149! I've not managed to plough my way through them all yet. The first lot did look a bit like a line-up of suspects though. I'm ditching the ones that I don't like the look of because there are just too many- I think that I might have to narrow my search down a bit. At the moment it's set to the whole country."

"So out of 149 there must be one or two that look alright?"

"Well not that many to be honest. There was one that looked quite nice but his icebreaker, as we call it, said something along the lines of, 'I'm passionate about Life Long Learning and the journey's that we take to satisfy our own personal fulfilment'. I mean, it's bollocks isn't it? I think I might have mentioned in my profile that I was in Adult Education- I might consider revising that bit."

"Anyone nice close by? Why don't you try and meet someone local?" Lou asked.

"There were a couple who looked alright but one of them, Clint, sent me some fairly heavy questions so I might just leave him."

"Clint is quite a sexy name?" Tina suggested.

"Do you think? Sounds a bit creepy to me! But it's just a name isn't it? He keeps asking to see my photo- I've not uploaded one yet. I can't find any nice ones of just me! Anyway, Clint sent me some questions to get to know me a bit better and one of them was, 'Do you believe in global warming'. It's not really a belief system is it, global warming? I just thought though, what a stupid question, so I probably won't contact him."

"Wow you're being *very* ruthless!" Tina sounded impressed.

"I think that you have to be! There are hundreds and hundreds of men on this site. I couldn't possibly reply to all the ones who have sent me a message but I think that some of them literally send a message to anyone because I had messages within *seconds* of posting my profile. So, yeah, anyone that I don't like the look of is ditched I'm afraid purely for the fact I just don't have the *time*. How would I ever manage to meet up with them all anyway? I'm going to choose very carefully."

"What about the other one?" Tina prompted Sophie. "You said that there were a couple."

Sophie smiled.

"Oh look, she's blushing! You *have* found someone nice already!" Lou sounded thrilled.

"No I've not! Don't be silly!" Sophie deflected the comment. "There *is* one guy who just looks quite nice and he sent a funny little message so I will probably reply to him."

"What did he say? What did he say?" he girls were eager to hear.

"Well it wasn't much. It'll sound silly now probably," Sophie wished that they could talk about something else, "he just sent a little message saying something about the fact I've not put a picture on there yet. He just said that either I must be pug ugly or just modest and that he'd love to see what I look like," she looked at the three disappointed faces whose attentions were fixed on her.

"Is that it?" Lou said. "I was expecting something a little racier than that!"

"Well, I thought that it just sounded quite sweet and he does look really nice in his photo. Like, *really* nice. But then I always think- why is he on a dating site if he's that good looking? There must be some serious flaw in his personality if he's had to resort to online dating?"

"There's nothing wrong with online dating!" Tina told Sophie. "I think that you're going to have to embrace it a bit more! You're good looking too but you're so busy that online dating is quite a good way of meeting people. He might have a really busy life too. Don't be too cynical about it all, you might just meet someone nice."

"Where's Ruth by the way?" Jules asked. "Has she been locked in again?"

Sophie was glad of the change of subject.

"Ha yeah she's been chained to the photocopier for the weekend! Actually she's not feeling that good. Quite good timing really as it makes my recent absence from their conference look a bit more genuine. Just a summer cold she thinks but she sounded really rough- lucky for her I took her call this morning. Enid had asked her to call back to confirm to her that she had made a doctor's appointment. Honestly we're treated like children in that place!"

"So, are you going to ask this guy out for a drink then?" Lou asked bringing the conversation back round to Sophie's dating plans.

"Oh God no! I'll wait for him to ask me, I'm terribly old fashioned. Top up anyone?"

Sophie got up to fetch the wine from the kitchen. Jules called through.

"You might meet someone at my birthday night out too, that's only a couple of weeks away!"

Sophie returned to the living room, wine in hand, and went round the ladies topping up their glasses.

"Oh what date is that again? Did I say that I didn't have Oliver that weekend?"

Jules looked upset.

"It's two weeks today! You did say that Ben was having Ollie that night. Oh I do hope that you can make it! That new place is going to be open in town so I thought that we could go there first. Oh I do hope that you can come out Sophie, I hardly ever get to go out and it wouldn't be the same without you. Check with Ben and let me know. If you can't then we might have to reschedule my birthday."

"Oh dear I don't want to disrupt your plans! If I said that it was OK then I'm sure that it is, I've just got so much going on right now," she suddenly randomly remembered the note that Oliver had given her from school last week. "Oh shit when is that inset day? I'd *totally* forgotten about that! It's not this Monday is it?" She looked hopefully at her friends. Lou shook her head.

"You *really* need a diary Sophie! Especially now you're going to have lots of men after your time as well. The inset day is this Monday- Simon's taken the day off because I was asked to up my hours. I'm not sure he could cope with another one!"

"I'll have Ollie, my boys will love to have him round and he's *so good!* I kind of thought that you might have forgotten!"

"I didn't forget- the thought didn't have a chance to register in the first place! Thanks Jules, what would I do without you? There would have been no chance of me getting the day off work anyway; they need at least three months' notice. All this talk about trying to meet a man has taken my attention off the important things in my life, maybe I really don't have time for anyone else!"

"Of course you have time. There are more important things to life than work you know," Lou said.

"So, what are you going to do about a photo- for your online profile?" Tina brought the subject back round again to Sophie's dating endeavours. "I don't think I'd bother to contact anyone of they didn't have a photo. Why don't I take one now?"

Sophie shook her head. "Oh not now I look terrible."

"No you don't but anyway, look my super smart phone can do editing so if you're a bit tired I can get rid of the dark circles or spots or any other imperfections. You'll need a picture at some point so you may as well!"

Sophie detested her picture being taken at the best of times and had very few of herself. She had hundreds of Ollie and some of her with Ollie but photos of her alone were few and far between.

"Oh go on then. I guess then you know that the people who get in touch probably like your face."

"Or are just *very* desperate!" Tina chuckled. "Just joking."

"Let me just go and sort my hair out," Sophie said, "I might as well make an effort." Just then her phone rang. She cursed herself when she saw it was her mother.

"Oh damn I meant to call her earlier. I'll just have a quick chat, it's my mum," she left the ladies and the bottle of wine in the living room and took the phone into the kitchen.

"Hi Mum!" she said. "Sorry I forgot to call earlier. Well I didn't *forget*. I've just been so busy."

"Hello darling. You're *always* so busy! You really must slow down. Dad is worried that you're working too hard."

"I don't really have a choice at the moment mother. How are you? I've got the girls round..."

"I'm not on for long anyway darling so don't worry, there's a program on at 9 that I'd like to watch. It's an adaptation of that book I read recently, you know, the thriller about the prostitutes. It has Leonard Conway in it, have you seen him? He's that actor that everyone's talking about just now because his clothes seem to fall off all the time! He has, by all accounts, a rather muscular body."

"Mum! Is Dad there? He won't want to hear you say that! I've not heard of Leonard whatshisname anyway nor the programme, I'm much too busy to keep up with popular culture. Is everything OK? How's Dad?"

"Your father is fine. He's asleep on the sofa just now. I'm calling to remind you that you have to organise your sister's hen weekend. You've not said much about it. I think she'll be expecting something special so you might need to start thinking about it now."

"Oh yeah. I'd forgotten. I'll have a think."

"Well I think you might need to book something soon so that we're not disappointed."

"What- are *you* coming too?" Sophie asked with some alarm in her voice.

"Well don't sound too pleased darling! Of course I'm coming! I'm mother of the bride. It will do me some good to let my hair down. Now, your sister did say that she didn't want a stripper but... you know... she probably really would and I think it's fairly traditional these days. Mrs Coutts had one for her 50th- a fireman. Really I've never seen anything like it, quite fantastic. Anyway darling that was all. I think that you should get onto that as soon as possible. A fireman would be fine, I could ask around my circle for a phone number, but I'm sure that you can think of something a little more original, like, oh I don't know, a *vicar*. Oh look that's nearly 9. Bye darling, Oliver could call on Sunday? Bye."

Sophie put down the phone and went back to sit with her friends.

"Has anyone else's mother changed drastically since you were little?" she asked nobody in particular. She got up again. "I'll just go and do my hair."

Later on when the girls had drunk all the wine and retired to their own homes Sophie inspected the pictures that Tina had taken. They were alright, she thought, although she looked rather plain in them without any make up. She chose one to upload and put it onto her online profile. I'll really need to get some different ones too, she thought. She idly scrolled down through the messages that she had received since she was last online but nobody looked that appealing. A yellow envelope started to flash at the top of her list of messages showing that there was a new one to read. She felt a flutter of excitement in her tummy when she saw that the message was from Dan, the man she had told the girls about earlier. He had three pictures on his profile and came under the 'Wow you're gorgeous' category although he had labelled himself as 'attractive'. There was a photo of him on a yacht looking rather cool in some aviator shades, another with a birthday cake in his hands that had sparklers on the top making an over-the-top face of surprise and then Sophie's favourite, one that she had gazed at for a while when she had first received his message, of him just sitting in a pub, leaning back in his chair relaxing with a beer in one hand and looking at the camera with a very incredibly sexy look, a smile playing on his lips and his hypnotic eyes looking directly at her. Sophie imagined that if he was sitting there in front of her looking at her like that she might just actually melt; it was a look that said he wanted you to get closer.

'Well hello gorgeous' his message read. 'What is a stunning lady like you doing on a crummy website like this? I happen to be down your way with work on Monday-would you like to keep me company in the evening? Let me know. Dan.'

Sophie's tummy fluttered with a mixture of excitement and panic and she wondered who could possibly have Oliver on a Monday night. Ben, she thought, I'll ask him first thing in the morning.

✳✳✳

"Ah yeah I'd love to help Soph but I'm busy on Monday. Why are you going out on a Monday night anyway? You're always out these days! I hope that you're still spending time with our son!"

Sophie took a deep breath and let the remark pass over her.

"It's a one off thing and I thought I'd ask you, as Ollie's dad, because you're always saying that you want to spend more time with him. He has an inset day on Monday too so I don't suppose you're around in the day instead?"

"I'd love to help Soph, I really would, but I'm working all day then Sarah's taking me out after that so no can do. Another time, yeah?"

"Well actually I need to ask you about the holidays too. Ollie will be off school for six weeks in the summer and I was just wondering if you were going to spend any time with him then? I don't have much time left to take off."

"This is all a bit last minute Soph, we need more notice than this. Sarah has our year all planned up- we're away in the summer, flights all booked and everything."

"It's not really last minute! There are still about three months or something until the holidays. Are you away for six weeks?" she asked, not being able to believe that he was sounding so reluctant to have Oliver.

"Well no we're away for two but then I'm working. We can't all work part time you know."

Sophie inhaled deeply. She felt the feeling of anger and frustration brewing inside. Talking to Ben often made her feel like this. She took another breath.

"I work the hours that I do so that I can drop Oliver off at school every morning but I have to work over the holidays too. Oliver will be off for six consecutive weeks- how do you think I'm going to manage that? I can't take six weeks off work either! I can't remember the last time you helped out with his holidays."

"I give you money to pay for that sort of stuff Sophie. That money is for Oliver not you."

"You give me £30 a week Ben! That covers his packed lunches for the week and some meals. I don't think you have any idea how much money I actually spend on his upkeep. But I don't care about the money, I just need help with his holidays because I can't take all that time off work either!" She felt like Ben was being purposefully obtrusive. She wished that she didn't need his help at all.

"Yeah well I don't think I'll get the time off work now. I'll ask. Sarah's not got so much work on right now so we can't really afford for me not to be working too. I'm self-employed now remember, I have to pay for my own holidays."

"Right OK fine so you can't have Oliver in the holidays. Forget it. Are you still having him in a couple of weekends?"

Ben thought at the other end of the phone. "Yeah! Yeah I think that'll be OK!"

"You said that it would. I really think that we need to set up regular visits for Oliver, so that we all know what's going on. We don't know from week to week if he's seeing you or not- it's not good for him you know for it all to be so uncertain and it means that I can't plan to do anything more than a week ahead!"

"Yeah it's just that I need to work sometimes Soph, so I'm not always around at the weekend and then if I've been working then Sarah likes to spend time with me too."

Sometimes I wonder why you ever came back, Sophie thought.

"I really need to know for definite if you can have Oliver the weekend after next because it's Jules's birthday and she's planned a night out."

"Out on the piss are you?" Ben asked.

"No Ben, I'm not. I'm a grown up now with a child. I'll manage to go out to a bar and not get drunk. Listen, if you don't want to be involved with Ollie anymore then let me know because to be honest, it was easier when you weren't around at all. But if you want to see him then I want a regular plan set up, even if it's once a month, because he needs to know when he's seeing you and I need to know. I'll assume you're having him the weekend after next, because you said that you could the last time we spoke and so you can confirm that you are once you've checked with *Sarah.* Maybe Ollie can join in with whatever both of you are doing."

She hung up and breathed deeply, her body shaking and her cheeks feeling flushed with anger. He was useless, he came back to see his son but spent so little time with him it hardly seemed worth it. At the same time his close presence seemed to disrupt their lives completely. Sophie sent her babysitter a text to see if she could come round for a couple of hours.

Sophie's babysitter was free and so despite Ollie having to go to Jules's for the day she also arranged for him to have a sitter for the evening on Monday. She felt guilty about the situation but it was a one off, she decided. She never went out in the week; unless she was forced back in to work so once won't hurt. She replied to Dan's message saying that she was free for a couple of hours in the evening and where did he want to meet. He sounded pleased that she was free and suggested a new bar by the marina where, he told her, he now kept his boat. Sophie tried not to get too excited.

***

Monday morning was the usual flurry of activity but slightly less hectic as Ollie was being dropped with Jules and not at school. She told Sophie that he could have his breakfast with her and to bring him down in his pyjamas and she would sort him out.

"One more boy won't make a difference!" she convinced a worried Sophie who already felt terrible that Jules was having him for the day.

"You're going to play with Luke and Freddie!" Sophie told Ollie in the morning. "Did you remember? You're so lucky because you have a day off school. Poor Mummy still has to go to work!"

"Why can't you look after me today? Your work is silly."

"Mummy's job's not silly darling," Sophie lied, not wanting to give the boy a work complex, "it's just that you are getting an extra day off school and Jules doesn't go to work on a Monday. Maybe next time Mummy will have a day off too," she said hopefully. "Anyway, you'll get to play with Luke *and* Freddie! That'll be nice won't it pumpkin?"

Oliver looked at Sophie suddenly as if she were the most embarrassing thing that he had ever encountered in his short life.

"Don't call me names Mummy."

"I don't call you names darling!"

Ollie looked like he might burst.

"You did just then. You *always* call me darling. You're going to call me 'darling' in front of Luke aren't you?"

"Of course I'm not darling, I mean, *Oliver*. I won't do it anymore. Mummy's just used to it and we *are* at home- that should be alright shouldn't it? Nobody can hear just now. Mummies are allowed to call their son's sweet names though; I think?" she asked hopefully. Oliver shook his head from side to side sternly.

"Please don't call me 'darling' in front of my friends."

"What about 'pumpkin'?" Sophie asked.

The boy shook his head.

"Sweetheart?"

He continued to shake his head in a vigorous manner.

Sophie tried not to smirk. "What about 'Monkey'?"

Oliver continued to shake his head.

"Can I still call you 'Ollie' though?"

He thought for a second and then continued to shake his head.

"I'd just like you to call me 'Oliver'. In front of my friends."

"Ok darling, sorry, I mean *Oliver*. I will try not to call you embarrassing names in front of your friends. What about 'Mr Man'?"

"Definitely not!" the boy looked horrified. "Harry said that the Mr Men are for babies."

"Well, *Oliver*, everyone likes different things and we still like the Mr Men don't we? So don't listen to what *anyone* else says. Oh! I forgot to tell you. Mummy got an email from your Aunty Jo and she told me that she has a *very special job* for you to do at her wedding! But you have to be very good and grown up in your special Scottish outfit."

The boy looked at her suspiciously.

"What job is it?" He asked.

"Aunty Jo was *wondering* if you were *careful* enough to look after the wedding rings in your sporran. It would be a very important job- only really for big boys?"

"I'm a big boy! I can do it!"

"It's probably the most important job of the whole day-looking after the rings? Are you sure?"

The boy considered this for a moment.

"Will the rings be gold?"

"Oh I'm not sure darling. Probably."

The boy looked thoughtful once more and then nodded his head.

"Can you do that for Aunty Jo?"

The boy nodded his head again.

"I'll look after the rings in my Scottish purse and then I can swap them for some cash."

"What?"

"I can swap gold for cash."

"Where did you learn that from?"

"I saw it on the television one day at Daddy's. You can get cash for gold."

"Well that is why we watch children's DVDs! Aunty Jo will need the rings back I'm afraid. You would have to keep them safe until she needed them."

The boy looked disappointed that there wasn't anything in it for him.

"Maybe if you could do that special job then we could also put some sweeties in your sporran," Sophie cringed at her blatant use of bribery but Oliver looked much happier with the situation.

"Did you have a wedding ring?" he asked innocently. Sophie felt the sadness that she hid return.

"No darling, Mummy and Daddy didn't get married. Mummy's never had a wedding ring," she made a sad face at the boy. "Maybe one day, eh? Anyway *Oliver.* We better go otherwise Mummy will get into trouble for being late."

Minutes later they were at Jules's, her house being just down the road.

"I am under *strict* instructions this morning not to call Oliver *anything* that would cause him embarrassment in front of his friends, especially Luke because he's a big boy," she told Jules. "My little boy is growing up. I'm not sure if I'm allowed to kiss him goodbye either. Thanks *so much* for having him," she handed her a bottle of wine that had been left over from one of their girl's nights. "There, you might need this later. Better rush! Bye darling!" she called through to Jules's living room and a very cross looking boy emerged.

"Oh sorry darling, Mummy's just used to it! Listen, be very *very* good and I'll see you later at about afternoon snack time. Are you too old for kisses?"

The boy looked around furtively to check that his friends weren't looking, put his hand up to his mouth and signalled for a secret kiss to take place. Sophie quickly planted a peck on his nose and then one on his forehead.

"Bye bye *Oliver,* Mummy loves you more than anything in the whole wide world. Bye Jules!" she called through to her friend who had gone through to the living room to sort out a scuffle between her two sons. "Call my work and say I'm needed immediately if it all gets too much. I'll have to catch up in the week because I might have some juicy gossip!"

Her friend rushed back into the porch.

"Gossip?"

"No time! I need to go!" she said smirking secretly, "See you later though. I'll text you to check Ollie's being good."

Having dropped Oliver off at Jules's, Sophie was able to get into work earlier and checked the clock in the office when she arrived.

"Ten past nine," she thought, "Brownie points for me!" and she rushed straight up stairs to make a point to Enid of being early for once.

Entering the upstairs office she encountered Enid, looking like she'd just finished filming for a cold remedy advert. If

Sophie had imagined what someone would look like with a heavy cold then Enid was it. Her nose was actually red and when Sophie walked in she was noisily blowing it into a tissue which she then discarded into the bin with what looked like a hundred others. Her eyes were blood shot and this became more noticeable when she took off her glasses to apply some drops to them. Blowing her nose seemed to set off a coughing fit and Sophie watched her imagining the tiny germs being expelled into their tiny airless office.

"Morning," she croaked, her voice sounding contagious, "Summer cold."

Yuk, Sophie thought, I don't want to catch *your* cold. She wanted to pull her shirt up over her nose so as to offer at least some protection from Enid's lurgie and regretted rushing to get in.

Sophie glanced at Ruth who was sitting at her desk looking pale after her bout of illness. She had moved her chair away from Enid sitting as far away from her as she could so as still to see her monitor. Sophie smiled sympathetically at her.

"Are you OK now Ruth?" she asked.

"Some of us have made it in despite being ill," Enid interrupted.

I think we wished that you hadn't bothered, Sophie thought. The room fell silent, Sophie deciding to catch up with Ruth in the cupboard later and Ruth not wanting to draw attention to herself after her absence. Enid started to speak but this set her cough off again and the office held their breath. She coughed for what seemed like minutes before it subsided and she cleared the phlegm from her throat.

"I have a funding form for you to complete for our new candidate," she managed to say. "It's on your desk. Do that first," she started coughing again and fumbled around in her jacket pockets for another tissue but she had used them all up and so she stood up, still coughing and left the office to get some more. Everyone waited until she was definitely clear of the room.

"Why couldn't she just stay at home?" Sophie said to nobody in particular. "I really don't want to catch *that.*"

"I don't want to catch it *again*, especially from her," Ruth said, making a face to show her distaste.

"You do look quite pale," Sophie told her. "I bet you wish now you'd had another day off."

"Yeah well apart from not getting paid..." Ruth replied.

"Oh yeah..." Sophie remembered the sickness policy. Staff were usually hounded and bullied so much when they were off that it was easier just to come in. Enid had been known to phone people up and even go round to their homes just to check up that they really were ill, the sick police Sophie called her.

"Enid is obviously dedicated to her work and has shown that by coming in today when she is feeling so unwell," Laura piped up showing solidarity to her senior.

"According to the Sickness Policy," Sophie said in a rare moment of actually remembering the contents of a school policy, "staff shouldn't come in when they're contagious. Shall I print it off and put it on her desk?" she asked mischievously with a wicked smile playing on her lips. Ruth smirked. The office fell silent as they heard the fire door opening. Sophie located the form that Enid had told her to fill in and snatched a pen out of her drawer and started to scribble down the information. Enid came back into the office and glanced around each desk to make sure that everyone was working. She sat down at her own desk and started to cough again, holding her fist up to her mouth.

Sophie wondered how long she could hold her breath before she passed out. She filled in the details that the form required and passed it over to Enid's desk, balancing it on the top of an existing bundle, not wanting to get too close in case she should catch any germs.

"There you go Enid, that's the form you asked me to fill in."

She watched as Enid picked up the form and scanned over what she had written.

"What's this?" she asked Sophie. "This is an institute of education, not the local state comprehensive."

"Sorry?" Sophie had no idea what she was talking about but was sure that she was in for a telling off.

"Since when have we used capitals to complete a funding form?" she asked Sophie, still managing to sound haughty even with a heavy cold.

"I thought it would be clear in capitals," Sophie replied, suddenly feeling stupid. That didn't take much time, she though, and looked at the office clock to see how long she'd been in the office.

"We write in Elm Tree script. I would have expected you to know that by now. Print off another one and do it again," Enid said hoarsely and cleared her throat. She coughed again.

Sophie sighed inwardly and started to search for the form. I am so bored of this, she though. A strand of hair fell out of her pony tail and she tucked it behind her ear while she scanned through the numerous documents on the system. It fell from behind her ear again and she pushed it back. It refused to stay however and she started to feel increasingly irritated so she reached to get her hairbrush out of her bag and took the band out of her hair to retie her ponytail. She brushed her hair through before doing this.

"That's disgusting," Enid said. "We have a toilet with a mirror that you can do that sort of thing in."

Oh God, Sophie thought, we've put up with you coughing your germs over us and now I'm getting told off for *brushing my hair*! It's not as if I've got lice or anything. She looked over to Ruth for a morale boost as she got up to go to the toilet to sort out her hair resigned to the fact that she was always going to be in trouble for something.

Returning to the office with her neatly tied pony tail she caught the end of the conversation that Enid was having on the phone. It sounded to Sophie that she was being put in her place by the school principal, something that everyone in the office loved to hear. Enid put down the phone and swung her chair back round to her desk where she silently fixed her stare at her monitor for a while. Sophie sidled back to her desk and sat down trying not to draw attention to herself in case of another telling off and the office fell silent. Eventually Enid spoke.

"Our principal requires ten copies of the new curriculum and guidance materials for a meeting that she has this afternoon at 3. Also ten copies of the national standards for education and ten copies of the theories of education document that I've just printed out for you." She looked at Sophie over her monitor. "That should keep you busy," she said in a dead pan tone.

The documents that she asked Sophie to print and photocopy were all extremely lengthy and she found herself standing at the photocopier for the rest of the day. She was hard pushed to get it all done before she left but she just managed to, determined not to have to stay behind.

She was so busy at work and then when she eventually picked up Oliver that she hardly had a chance to think about her last minute date that evening. It had been arranged so swiftly that she hadn't had a chance to build it up like the last one with Paul. Maybe that was better, she thought, as he didn't quite live up to my expectations. She wished that she'd managed to prepare for this one like the one with Paul though as Dan did look rather gorgeous.

"Do you want a snack before tea, Ollie?" she asked looking in the fridge to see what they had.

"What have you got?" he asked.

"Well, I've got ham or chicken or wraps or sandwiches or cheese or cucumber or grapes or a biscuit or crisps or a cereal bar or some breadsticks or some raisins or some carrots and humus that you said you liked the other day?" she reeled off all the snack food she could think of, impressed that for once they had full cupboards.

The boy thought.

"All of those," he replied.

"*All* of them? Wow you're hungry! I'd better just make you tea then."

She took some eggs out of the fridge to make an omelette and glanced up at the clock. It was nearly 5. Sophie wished that she hadn't stood chatting to Jules now for so long. If I do tea now then I'll still have plenty of time for a shower and to get ready, she thought. As if on cue her mobile rang. Maybe not, she thought.

"Hi, Jo!" she said. "You OK?"

"Hi, Sophie! Busy! Have you heard from Mum?"

"Yeah she called me the other day, briefly. She was reminding me of my bridesmaidly duties of arranging your Hen Do. I hadn't forgotten, I just thought that it was maybe a little early to start planning that?"

"Well, I think that we should know what we're doing. But that's not why I'm phoning. Did she mention a stripper? I don't want a stripper! I thought that we could all go to a health spa or something but when I spoke to her at the weekend she started talking about strippers! I'd hate a stripper please tell her we're not having one!"

"Why can't you tell her?" Sophie asked, not really wanting to have the conversation with her Mum.

"Well, Mum and Dad *are* being very generous by helping out with the wedding costs so… I just don't want to offend her but… I mean… Mum wanting a stripper! It's just wrong Sophie but I think that it would be better coming from you."

"Why me?" Sophie protested. She sighed. "Oh OK I'll say something next time I talk to her. I'll just say that we're doing something else or that Andrew would be very upset. I've no idea what's got into her at the moment. Do you mind if I call you back tomorrow? I randomly have a date later, bit last minute, not advertising it like last time and I need to make Ollie's tea and get him all ready for bed before his babysitter comes *and* get myself ready too. Can I call later in the week?" she asked, cutting off her sister as she was about to quiz Sophie on her date. "Great. Speak then."

She hung up and put the phone down on the kitchen surface and got on with making Ollie his tea- with that and homework to do and baths to run and the boy to get ready for bed Sophie didn't have the luxury of taking her time to get ready for her date. She began to wish that she hadn't agreed to it after all.

Kerry arrived at 7 on the dot and Ollie was pleased to see her, being his regular babysitter. He liked her, Sophie thought, as she was someone who gave him undivided attention without having to make tea or do the washing or send emails. She usually brought him round a new book to read or a toy to play with and they often watched a DVD before Ollie went to bed pushing her up his 'Popular' list. Sophie didn't know what she would do without her; she rarely couldn't make it when Sophie asked and was there regularly on a Wednesday evening while she went back into work. Sophie gave Ollie an extra strong cuddle and promised him lots more tomorrow night.

"Mummy won't be going out tomorrow," she told him.

"You never go out on a Monday," the boy had complained, making her feel guiltier than she did already.

"You'll have lots of fun with Kerry I'm sure, have you chosen a DVD yet?"

The boy rushed up the stairs to choose one and Sophie said goodbye to Kerry, promising that she'd be back by half ten. That seemed late enough to be out on a Monday night.

Chapter Six

She had arranged to meet Dan at 8 o'clock outside a trendy wine bar situated in the marina in town. Sophie had never drunk there before, just walked past it a few times on the way to the cinema and always thought that it was far too hip for her. The evening was warm and clear, she brought her denim jacket but took it off as she walked towards the bar and draped it over her arm. Wearing a plain t-shirt dress and knee high boots with a brown suede tasselled bag, her look was simple and she hoped that it was appropriate for a Monday night, not having been out on a Monday night for quite some time. She had left her hair down having managed to get it to sit right and it blew gently in the evening breeze. She cast her glance around the marina to see if she could spot anyone who looked like the three photos that Dan had on his profile. Looking at her watch she saw that she was slightly early for once and so she casually leaned against a wall just along from the bar and waited, idly playing with her mobile to pass the time.

"Hello gorgeous," a man said, his well-spoken and slightly gravelly voice making her jump and drop her phone on the ground, causing it to fall apart in pieces at her feet. Instantly she felt clumsy and oafish next to this sharply dressed and very handsome man. The man looked amused, standing there in a crisp grey suit, with his collar open and tie hanging loosely with his hands in his pockets. His hair was cut smartly but left longer on the top and it flopped to one side, he ran his hand through it as he smiled at Sophie, his boyish good looks and public school accent making her heart beat a little faster.

"Sorry," he said, "I didn't mean to make you jump." He bent down to pick up the various pieces of her phone and expertly clicked them all back together and handed it back to her with a grin. "Excuse the suit. I've just finished work. It's Dan, by the way, how do you do?" he extended his hand towards Sophie, who took it and smiled. "My office is over there," he pointed to the other side of the marina where there was a new development of office blocks and apartments. "If you look you can see mine actually, it's at the top, the one with the balcony. Awesome view over the city and out to sea. I'm based in London but we have operations down here that require my attention now and again, allowing me to breathe some fresh air and get out on the boat," he pulled at his tie, "I wish I'd changed before coming out though, damn thing. Working late," he pulled a face to show his disapproval. He turned his attention back to Sophie who had composed herself and was listening intently, not quite believing that her date was so good-looking, "You look gorgeous. What can I get you to drink?"

This is more like it, Sophie thought, and asked for a soda water and lime. Dan raised an eyebrow in reply.

"I have the car," Sophie stated. "I can't really stay out for that long…"

"On a school night," Dan finished her sentence and grinned again. "Better get to it then." And with that he guided her into the bar, gently resting his hand on the low of her back. It was busy, Sophie thought, for a Monday night and full of very fashionable people drinking. The air was full of voices and laughter, raised above the background music that was playing.

Dan ordered her soda water and lime, asking for it in a way that made it sound like he'd never heard of it before and a pint of lager for himself and he suggested a table outside away from the noise and crowds. Sophie felt the eyes of envious women watching her as she followed him outside. They sat down at a table looking out over the yachts and speed boats that were moored in the marina. A tall slim blonde woman walked outside after them and positioned herself in Dan's view, lighting a cigarette and blatantly trying to catch his attention as he sat with Sophie. Dan turned away from her though, apparently unaware of her advances and focussed his attention on Sophie.

"So," he smiled, "it's good to meet you. What is an utterly *gorgeous* woman like you doing on a dodgy dating site?"

Sophie looked embarrassed.

"Don't worry, I'm on it too," Dan grinned again showing his perfect white teeth. "You have a kid don't you? I'm assuming that's why you have to be home early. So, what happened there then? Your ex must be a bit of a nob for letting you go?"

Sophie laughed at Dan's forwardness. "I thought that that was on the list of 'Five Things Not to Talk About on Your First Date?' she asked. Dan scoffed at this.

"That's all bollocks isn't it? Everyone wants to know that don't they? You don't need to tell me anyway if you don't want to, I'm just interested. This might sound crap but I don't really use that site, I just dip in to it now and again, to see if there's anyone decent round. Usually there's not, you don't have to worry about your competition because there is none. How come you're single then?"

Sophie shrugged. "Not sure. It's just happened this way," she smiled. "It's not the way I had hoped that my life would turn out. I thought that my ex was the man that I was going to spend my life with but then he did a runner just before our wedding," she looked at Dan feeling like she'd said too much already and not wanting to scare him off. The look on his face was one of genuine shock.

"What, when you had his kid as well? What a prick," Sophie laughed, finding his honesty refreshing. He continued. "What an idiot. You deserve a whole lot more than that."

Sophie was trying not to let her imagination run away with itself. Sitting in front of this funny and self-assured and *gorgeous* man she was finding it difficult not to put him in the place of her handsome prince and go walking up the aisle with him.

"I've never been like that though," he carried on his train of thought. "You know, thinking that I'd meet 'The One'. I'm not sure if that's the way for me. Undoubtedly it works for some people, many of my friends are pairing off now and tying the knot, having sprogs and buying houses and they all seem *very* happy. Who's to say that's the right way though? What do you think now? Are you still holding out for Mr Right?"

Sophie began to feel disappointment looming. Yes, I bloody was, she thought, and for a brief second there I thought it could be you.

"I'm not really sure," she said vaguely, "I've not thought about it that much." Like hell you've not, she thought. "I guess I did *hope* that I would…" her voice trailed off.

"Well, I might be Mr Right for now but you might change your mind in ten years' time or twenty years in favour of someone else."

No I wouldn't, Sophie thought.

Dan laughed. "Sorry I'm getting a bit deep and we've only known each other for…" he looked at his watch, "ooh about ten minutes." He leaned back in his chair like the photo on his profile and looked at Sophie with his mesmerising dark eyes. "I can't understand it. How long have you been single?"

"Oh… about… three years now actually!" suddenly it sounded like a very long time.

"Three years! Christ! Why?" Dan seemed genuinely surprised. He sat upright waiting intently for her reply. Sophie didn't know why so found it difficult to know what to say. She tired of this dissection of her life.

"No reason I guess, I'm just always kind of busy with work and my son. He's five," she added.

"But still, three years! You must be gagging for it!" he laughed good-humouredly. "Sorry, just joking. Listen, here's the deal. I'm here to have some fun. That's all, just safe and honest fun. No strings. It's hard to find anyone willing to have fun these days," he lowered his voice and leaned in towards Sophie so close that she could feel his breath on her cheek and smell the faint aroma of lager. "I have a lot of fantasies that I want to fulfil and I need someone to help me fulfil them and they don't have anything to do with buying houses or having babies." There was a pause. "What do you say?" he grinned at her; she began to feel annoyed with herself that she found him quite so attractive.

There was silence. Sophie didn't know what to say but her face must have spoken a thousand words. Dan looked sheepish.

"There's nothing wrong with it. You're single, I'm single. It's just some fun."

"Maybe *you've* just not met the right person yet either," Sophie said in an attempt to change his way of thinking.

"Maybe I think that *you're* the right person, for now," Dan smiled, "you're very good looking you know. Have you ever had a threesome?"

***

"And *then* he asked me if I've ever had a threesome!" Sophie retold the story in hushed tones to the girls the next morning at school. She'd made a big attempt to get up earlier so that she would catch them before she had to rush off to work. "It turns out that he just wants *sex!*" She whispered the last word. "It's such a shame because he is *utterly* gorgeous."

Her three friends looked at her, expecting more.

"Is that it?" Lou asked, "There's nothing wrong with sex, Sophie, especially if he is a hunk."

"No I know that but a *threesome*!" she looked at Jules helplessly. "*You* wouldn't want a threesome would you?"

"What, with you and Dan?" Jules asked.

"No! I'm talking generally now! I don't just want to have sex. I've managed for three years without sex thank you very much. I have a million better things to be doing though than helping someone to live out their porn dream. What Dan was suggesting just sounds like *prostitution*! Except that if I said yes, he wouldn't have to pay. I really want to meet someone who's got more going on in their head than that. Although, he does have a pretty high powered job… but still…"

"Well I'm not sure what the problem is," Tina said. "If you fancy him then why not just go for it and see what happens. Maybe not the threesome bit, but just say that you're up for some fun. There is actually nothing wrong with having sex. He might change his tune and decide that you *are* the one for him."

"A relationship started with sex is going nowhere…" Sophie replied.

"Not necessarily. How old was he?"

"It said on his profile that he was 36."

"And he's never been married nor has any children?"

"No I don't think so, why?"

"Well, you never know, he might decide that he wants all that after all and then you'll be there to make it happen!"

"It would just feel a bit weird that's all. He suggested that we go for a drive but I said I had to get back for Ollie. He's been texting me since. I think that he's the most handsome man I've ever spoken to," Sophie said wistfully.

"You might meet someone nice when we go out for my birthday too!" Jules said, changing the subject, "we'll have to sort that out. You can all make it can't you? That's going to be the highlight of my year so far."

The bell rang. Ollie, who had been playing happily with Jules's boys ran back over to Sophie to collect his book bag and packed lunch. She gave him a last kiss and a cuddle and watched him run over to his class who were already lined up at the door.

"Bye then," she said to her friends, "off I go to the mad house!"

When she arrived at the school after her morning sprint up the road the staff entrance was locked and so she rang the bell and waited. Usually this door was open and the staff in the office could normally see whoever was leaving or entering that way through their window. As nobody came to open the door and seeing that it was going to make her late she ran along to the main entrance and rang that bell too. Somebody's got to let me in, she thought. Still nobody came and so she ran back to the staff entrance and tried again wondering if the bell had stopped working. She looked at her watch restlessly and cursed whoever was in there, annoyed that she had arrived in time but now would be late anyway. Through the main entrance she caught sight of a parent leaving having dropped off their child and Sophie darted back over to that door and breathlessly thanked them for letting her in, the suited man holding the door for her.

She rushed through into the office to sign in, hoping to do that and get up the stairs as quickly as possible. Tim was standing in the way of the signing in book. He looked surprised to see her.

"Oh hi, Sophie. Where did you come from?" he asked. Here we go, Sophie thought.

"Morning," she replied, "I just came in through the door, like I normally do."

"Which one?" he asked with a puzzled look on his face, "I didn't see you coming in the staff entrance."

"Um no that's because it was locked. I stood there for ages ringing the bell but nobody answered so I came in the other door, one of the parents let me in," she said this almost defiantly, annoyed that the door had been locked and made her late. They probably locked it after everyone started at 8 and forgot to leave it open for me, she thought.

Tim looked troubled. "It's not really appropriate to come in the main door, Sophie. You shouldn't really let the parents let you in either. If Mrs Wright had seen you you'd probably have got the sack, there and then."

Sophie rolled her eyes. "Well nobody else was going to let me in," she said petulantly. "I could have been standing there all morning. Everyone forgets that I start later."

Tim shook his head. "No we don't Sophie. We remember it every day when you get to go at half two and we all have to stay until 6."

Well go and renegotiate your contract, she thought.

"I'd better get up there otherwise I'll be even later," she said and walked briskly out of the office and up the stairs.

Ruth was standing at the photocopier when Sophie arrived upstairs. Through the door to the office she could hear a chorus of coughing.

"Hi, Ruth! Oh great is she still insisting on coming in and infecting the office?"

Ruth grimaced. "It's not just Enid now, Laura's got it too. It's like a competition in there to see who's the sickest. I'm out here getting some fresh air. How are you? You're late by the way," she teased.

Sophie grinned. "Well if they'd have bloody well let me in downstairs then I'd have been on time!"

Ruth laughed. "Hurry up then or Enid will give you lines. I must not be late; I must not be late."

Sophie checked her watch. "Oh shit I'd better go!" and with that she hastily walked through to the office where Enid and Laura were coughing in unison. She ignored them and said 'Hi' to Pam.

Enid cast her glance up at the clock on the wall and looked like she might comment.

"I was standing outside for ten minutes before anyone let me in," Sophie said shortly and switched on her computer. "For some reason the staff door was locked."

"The staff door should *always* be locked at 8am after all the staff have entered the building," Enid said quietly and steadily so as not to make herself cough again. "Those arriving later should come through the main entrance of the building."

Oh well, Sophie thought, I've obviously missed something. Who knows what you're meant to do in this place. She focussed her attention on the list that was on her desk and started to decipher Enid's illegible spidery handwriting. Photocopying, more photocopying and a bit more *photocopying,* she thought. Enid interrupted her thoughts.

"Here are the starters and leavers, Sophie. I need that first, by half ten," she looked up at the clock again which was heading towards ten and passed a sheet of paper over, "so that's quite a tight schedule, you'd better get on with that now."

Sophie hated the way that she was treated, as if completely unable to manage her own workload. She was even less motivated this morning with thoughts of sexy Dan playing in her head. She took the paper from Enid and looked at the list of names- new staff starting employment this month at the school and those who were leaving. She sighed. This was a never ending job- the staff list- as staff turnover was unbelievably high. Some staff started employment and left in the same month.

"Have you read this Sophie?" Pam passed yet another piece of paper over her way, "The day sheet."

The day sheet came around to the office daily, as the name would suggest, and contained information regarding the next seven days at the school that all staff were supposed to read and then sign to show that they had done this. Reading the day sheet was just another way to kill some time. Sophie put down her work and took the day sheet from Pam. Detailed on the day sheet were staff absences and holidays, children's absences and holidays, any meetings that were to take place, lost property and other general news and information about what was going on at the school. On days when there was nothing to do Sophie would find herself reading the lost property list with great interest.

"Three pink socks. That raises a lot of questions," she said to nobody in particular. "What were pink socks doing in the school in the first place when everyone knows that Elm Tree grey should be worn? I bet they're stupidly expensive socks from Harrods or somewhere, knowing the parents at this school, and they've insisted that it should appear on the day sheet even though pink socks are banned or they'll withdraw their children. They must have one sock at home… I see the life size teddy is still in lost property. If

Ollie had a teddy that big and he *lost* it then I would notice and I'd know that it was at school... these parents are so rich that they probably have no idea what toys their children have... How can you lose a life size teddy? One red Elm Tree handkerchief. I do love it that they have Elm Tree issue handkerchiefs..."

Enid cleared her throat markedly causing Sophie to jump; unaware that she had become so engrossed in the day sheet. She rapidly scanned the rest and put her initials at the top to show that she'd read it and passed it over to Ruth who looked like she needed something to do.

Sophie turned her attention back to the work that she had been doing. She opened up a new document and started to re-do her staff list.

"There are two members of staff who started this month and who are also *leaving* this month!" Sophie said incredulously. "I'm not surprised though. There are... one, two, three, four, five, six... *six* people leaving who started last month and..." she counted. "*Twelve* people are leaving this month! Twelve!"

Nobody commented.

"It's quite a lot, for one month," she mused.

Enid looked like she had had enough. "Sophie, are you going to provide a commentary on today's events or can we get on with our work in peace?" she asked. "It doesn't matter who is starting and who is leaving- I just need the training schedule done."

Sophie continued to work in silence. She willed Enid to leave the office so that she could relax and read her emails and she wanted to text Dan. She didn't want to take him up on his offer of a threesome but she hoped that she could see him again and maybe, in her daydreamy head, change his mind about meeting The One.

"What arrangements have you made for your son this summer holiday?" Enid asked in a rare moment of camaraderie, it seemed to Sophie. She never just 'chatted'.

"Oh I'm not sure yet," she admitted, "I need to ask his Dad if he'll have him for some of the time but I *doubt* that'll happen. I'll probably just end up having to fork out a small fortune for holiday clubs of some sort… my parents might also come down and stay for a bit. I should really get that sorted…"

***

Later that evening Sophie called Ben to see if he would help out over the holidays, but she didn't hold out much hope. He often didn't answer the phone if he wasn't expecting a call; his girlfriend didn't like him talking to Sophie. Sophie knew this as Ollie had told her after one of his weekends with his Dad. She tried anyway.

"Hi Soph. Everything OK?"

She was surprised that he answered.

"Hi. Yes, fine thanks. Ollie's fine. I'm just calling about the holidays."

"Holiday's?" Ben asked. "What holidays?" As if schools didn't have holidays and Sophie just put them there to be awkward.

"You must remember- we spoke about it the other day. Every year we have this season called 'summer' and the schools go on holiday for most of it. I know you said that you've got to work- we've all got to work- but could you have Ollie for just a short time? Just one week would be a help and if you can't do that then I really need you to help with the cost of childcare for that time."

"OK well there's no need to be sarcastic," Ben replied sounding hurt. "I've been thinking about it actually and I'd like to have Ollie for a week in the summer. We could go camping or something."

Sophie felt a sadness creep over her, she had loved camping with Ben.

"And I've spoken to Sarah and I'll have him regularly from now on. Like every other weekend. Starting next weekend."

"Next weekend- is that the tenth?" Sophie asked just to confirm, the tenth being Jules's birthday night out. She couldn't quite believe that he had changed his tune since the last time they spoke.

Ben checked his calendar. "Yeah the tenth is next weekend. I'll have a look into the summer. Probably a week in August would be good as I've not got much work on then and Sarah's going away, so I could have a nice week with just Ollie. In fact, you know, I thought that it would be nice for Ollie to come out with us- you and me. It would be good for him, you know, to see his Mum and Dad getting on."

Sophie wasn't sure how she felt about that and gave a non-committal answer. The last thing she wanted to do was go out on happy family days with Ben. He wants the best of both worlds, she thought. She told him that she needed to know soon about the holiday's and they arranged that he'd collect Oliver the next Friday. They said goodbye and she text Jules to say that she was on for her birthday. She got a reply fairly soon after with lots of happy faces and 'Here come the girls!' with lots of exclamation marks. Sophie smiled. It would be good to have a night out with her friends.

She switched on her computer to see if she had any messages from Dan. She logged in to the dating site and saw that she had another Inbox full of messages. Three of those were from Dan, her tummy fluttered with excitement. The first one was polite, saying that it was lovely to meet her and he was sorry if he'd shocked her with his proposition. He must think I'm a right old prude, she thought. The second said that he was going to be down her way again in August and so maybe they could meet up then. The last one had been sent that evening and asked if she wasn't talking to him now. She laughed. Give me a chance, she thought, I've been at work all day. Going to the home page she decided to search who was online right then and scrolled down photos of men after men after men. It's so difficult to choose people this way, she thought, static pictures being entirely different to seeing someone in the flesh. Three photos caught her eye out of about a hundred and she bravely clicked on the 'flirt' icon. So far she had only communicated with those who had contacted her but she was finding it increasingly easy to be brave behind her computer screen.

***

Having no definite plans that weekend Sophie asked Oliver what he'd like to do.

"Charity shop! Charity shop!" he chanted with glee.

Easily pleased, Sophie thought with amusement. He loved the charity shops in the local village because he was allowed to buy lots of toys at once. His favourite being the one with the 10p box that was always slotted under the lowest shelf where he could crouch for quite some time rummaging. Saturday mornings were often spent browsing through the odd assortment of nick nacks that the charity shops had on offer.

It was a pleasantly warm Saturday morning at the end of May. Sophie walked through the village holding Ollie's hand, smiling at the sunlight and feeling the brightness causing the same feeling within her. She had even felt that it was hot enough to bring out her summer clothes and wore a cropped t-shirt with her favourite comfy jeans, feeling rather self-conscious at first about baring her white skin but glad to have the soft breeze gently touching her midriff, keeping her cool. Ollie held a tiny plastic bike that he had acquired at the first charity shop. Today they were going to go to them all. They ambled along the high street in no particular hurry, Sophie looking in all the windows as they walked past; the greengrocer, butcher, card shop, hairdresser, estate agent...

She stopped at the latter and casually looked at the properties for sale. She owned a three-bedroom house in a village outside the town. This had been bought with Ben but when he had left she had had no option but to take over the payments herself and when he returned, with the help of her parents, she had bought him out. This had seemed like the easiest option at the time, the thought of putting the house on the market and moving being too much to think about with everything else. As Sophie had a lump sum in the house anyway after selling her first flat in the centre of town for twice as much as she had bought it for, just at the end of the property boom, to buy Ben out wasn't as costly as she would have thought. The house now though seemed far too big for Sophie and Ollie, the two of them spending most of their time upstairs and the whole of the downstairs becoming like a show room, only used as a way through to the kitchen. With the summer sun in the perfectly blue sky shining, the flowers in the hanging baskets above each shop blooming and the gentle breeze blowing playfully Sophie felt with optimism that it might be time for a change. Her ventures out into the dating scene this morning feeling like the start of something good. She pushed a strand of hair from her cheek as she looked in the estate agents window at the properties that were well within her budget and much smaller. That could be the answer to all my problems, she thought.

A one-bedroom house and a two bedroom ground floor flat caught her eye, both within a few miles of their house and still within the catchment of Ollie's school, she thought. She peered through the window between the house adverts and saw a suited man sitting at a desk twirling a pen between his fingers.

There is someone who needs something to do, Sophie thought.

"Come on darling," she said. "We're just going in here for a minute."

Oliver, who had been happily driving his new bike along the estate agent window ledge, stopped and looked at the shop front that he was being asked to enter. His demeanour changed.

"You said we were just going to the charity shops!" he cried obstinately. "You *always* go into shops. And *stop calling me that!*"

"Right Mister. Do you want to go *straight* back to the charity shop and tell them that we don't need the little motorbike anymore?"

The boy shook his head.

"Mummy sometimes does need to go into shops that we had not previously discussed; I can't always give you a detailed itinerary. This is Mummy's prerogative."

The boy looked at her blankly completely unaware of what she was talking about.

"Ok?" she asked him bluntly, feeling rather cross that minutes ago she was flavour of the month because she had forked out 10p for a little plastic bike and now she was the object of his sulk. She took him by the hand and with the other pushed the heavy glass door that took them into the estate agent. The man sitting at the desk jumped up as soon as he heard the sound of the door and bounded over to help open it.

"Allow me," he smiled at Sophie and pulled the door wide open for them, saying "Hi" to Oliver who came in miserably behind. "Very heavy door," he confirmed. "Can I help at all?"

Sophie cast her eyes around the vast array of property particulars.

"I was just coming in for a little look really," she said, smiling back at the sandy haired man. She noticed his piercing blue eyes, vivid against his pale skin.

"Look away!" he replied, "I'm here if you need me," and with that he went back to his desk and sat down, leaning back and twisting himself from side to side in a way that suggested that he was bored. Sophie started to look around at the properties but felt conscious that he was watching her, all be it because he had nothing better to be getting on with. She turned towards him, his suit looked slightly too big to fit his frame as he lounged in his revolving chair.

"Actually," she said, "I could do with some help. I have a three-bedroom house in Highfield. A semi-detached. I was just wondering how much it was worth because it's too big for us," she looked towards Oliver, "and we'd be better off in something smaller, like a one-bedroom house or a little flat."

The man looked more hopeful and sat up in his chair. He gestured for Sophie to sit down opposite.

"Down-sizing?" he replied.

"Um yeah something like that," she replied.

The man pulled the keyboard on his desk towards him and started to tap away. He inspected his computer screen momentarily, tapped a bit more then pushed his chair back and made his way over to a photocopier at the back of the room to retrieve some paper that it was now turning out. He brought them back to the desk and put them in front of Sophie who had become inadvertently transfixed by this man's movements. She snapped herself out of it and focussed on the paper in front of her.

"These might be of some interest," the man sat back down in his chair and fixed his clear blue eyes on Sophie.

"So, just a little pad for yourself and the young man?" he asked. Sophie nodded. "I can come and value your house if you like, that's no problem," he smiled at Sophie causing the skin around his twinkling eyes to crease a little. "I'm Christian by the way."

He extended his hand across the table and Sophie took it.

"How do you do?" he smiled and fixed his stare on Sophie.

For a second they sat there, holding hands across the table, Sophie hypnotised by this man's charm. On first glance she hadn't noticed his strong physique, finely chiselled features and the way his smile spread to his eyes causing them to sparkle. For a moment she felt completely engulfed in this man's beauty.

"So, erm, is it your house?" Christian asked, eventually moving his hand and taking a form from one of the drawers under his desk. He patted his coat pockets looking for a pen and then located one in his chest pocket.

Sophie nodded. "Yes. Yes, it is. My house."

Christian started writing on his form.

"What's the address?"

She gave him the details that he required and he gave her one of his business cards.

"You'll probably want to look around at other estate agents but here's my card if you decide to come with us. Just give me a call if you want me to come round and put a value on your house, I've set up a file for you in case you do."

Sophie slotted the card into her purse, noticing the one she'd got from Mike the washing machine man still in their too. The start of a collection, she thought. She stood up and told Ollie that they were ready to go and thanked Christian.

"I'll give you a call then, if I decide to put my house on the market," she told him.

"Yes, do," Christian replied and smiled at her, holding her gaze again for a few moments too long. Sophie would have happily stood there all day but Oliver had other plans and started to drive his little bike across her shoes and up her leg.

"Ok that's enough now. Ollie that's enough!" she looked at Christian apologetically but he was watching Ollie with a mixture of amusement and indulgence. The boy stopped driving his bike and looked up at his audience.

"Mummy, Joshua said that ladies don't have willy's. He said that they have a vajenga instead."

Sophie looked at her son in horror, exasperated that he should choose exactly this moment to impart his ill-informed information. Christian laughed.

"You've got a little bit of work to do there," he said to Sophie, smiling broadly.

Sophie was momentarily lost for words.

"Do they Mummy? Do you have a vajenga?"

Sophie was sure that he was doing this on purpose just to embarrass her and told him to 'Shush'.

"I'm not having this conversation with you right now Mister. There is no such word; Joshua needs to check his sources," she looked at Christian. "Excuse my son."

Christian shook his head, still amused by Oliver's question and more so by the look on Sophie's face. "He's fine," he said, "he might even have invented a new game there," he laughed again.

A smile spread onto Sophie's serious face and she laughed too. It crossed her mind that laughing wasn't something she did that often anymore, not real laughing anyway. She smiled at things and her mouth moved as if in laughter but she didn't feel it in her heart. Oliver looked at her and joined in despite having no idea what the joke was about.

"Right, anyway, I'd better take this one away," she told Christian, "I'll have a think about it anyway and give you a call. I'm pretty sure I'd like to downsize."

"Great. Yeah give me a call and I'll pop round. Take care. Nice meeting you," he smiled and held her gaze.

Sophie wanted to talk to this man all day. Oliver pulled her arm.

"Come *on*! You said we were just going to be a minute," he complained.

Sophie smiled apologetically. "The charity shops are calling. Nice meeting you too."

The words 'Take care' hung in her mind all day. 'Take care'… She didn't think it was the usual thing that an estate agent would say. 'Take care'… She laughed at herself for overthinking things.

Chapter Seven

Working at The Elm Tree School was bad enough during the day without having to go back at night. But go back in they did every Wednesday evening. Enid and her training team undertook different courses and workshops mainly with their own staff but sometimes with external students. Sophie was always amused by the reaction of the people coming in from outside to the fine china they were served their break tea on and to the troop of suited bodies who greeted them at the door. She wondered if they could sense the oppressive atmosphere and misery of the Elm Tree staff when the two groups were trained together.

It was always such a rush for Sophie to get back into school for six. She would collect Oliver from school, take him home to do his homework and reading, give him tea and then Kerry would arrive allowing her to go back in to work. She flatly ignored the expectation of being back in fifteen minutes before six, it being enough of a nightmare trying to get into town anyway for that time. There was the tutting and cursory glances at the clock by Enid and Laura, as in the morning, but nobody ever did anything when she was late and so Sophie took it upon herself to arrive just in time. Officially they worked until eight. Unofficially they were usually there until well after ten by which time Sophie felt like she needed to hold her eye lids open, so tired was she after her long day. This evening was the start of their First Aid training.

Laura normally ran the First Aid courses but nobody knew why. She had apparently done a First Aid certificate years ago but it was badly out-of-date and she hadn't had any experience of actually doing first aid. Sophie's certificate was more recent than Laura's and she wondered how she had the authority to train others. Nobody took any notice of her concerns. That afternoon Laura had told Sophie that she would be helping her with her class that night. Ruth had told her later while she was photocopying that she normally got other people to assess the practical exercises because she was too lazy.

"I'm not competent to do that though," Sophie had said to Ruth. Ruth replied that nobody seemed bothered about that.

Kerry arrived a few minutes early and profusely apologised to Sophie that she would need to leave by half eight that night because she was going to take over the care of her gran and spend the rest of the evening with her. Her Mum was with her now but couldn't stay.

"I'm really sorry!" she proclaimed, "it usually doesn't matter at all what time you get back."

"That's fine," Sophie said, reassuring her, "of course you've got to go. They'll just have to do without me for once; God knows I'm usually there until all hours! It doesn't sound like I'm doing much tonight anyway so that will be fine. Don't worry!" she smiled at Kerry. Shit shit shit, she thought to herself, that's going to go down like a lead balloon.

She arrived at the school a couple of minutes after six having had difficulty finding a parking space and having a lethargic feeling that was unusual for her, in no hurry at all to get back in. She just couldn't be *bothered*.

She encountered Laura standing in the hallway waiting, looking at her watch with a patronizing look on her face, raising one eye brow and pursing her lips like Enid usually did. She tapped at her wrist.

"You were *expected* to be here by quarter two," Laura said, "Enid's gone out of town to present a workshop and has left *me* in charge."

"Oh right," Sophie replied not that impressed by Laura's promotion for the night but relieved that Enid was out. "Laura, my babysitter needs to leave by half eight and so I need to leave by, well, about eight really. Training *should* finish by then anyway," she said this as she went into the office to sign herself back in. Tim and Mark were still sitting at their computers where they were now expected to be until training was finished.

"Getting away early *again*?" Mark joked.

Sophie smiled and whispered, 'trying' and returned to where Laura was standing.

Laura pulled herself up to her full height, sucking her tummy in and pushing her shoulders back- here was a woman who was going to take full advantage of her all-be-it brief time in charge.

"I can't allow that Sophie. Enid has given me *strict* instructions not to let you go before everything is tidied up."

Because that's all I'm good for, Sophie thought bitterly, tidying up the dishes at the end.

"She's leaving my house at half past eight, Laura. Are you suggesting I leave a five-year-old boy at home by himself? I won't be doing anything tonight anyway! This is your training- I'll just be standing around like a loose part!" she felt her frustration rising at the situation.

Laura shook her head and smiled smarmily at Sophie making her want to punch her on the nose.

"I really need you tonight Sophie. You are going to be assessing the CPR."

"I'm not competent to assess the CPR!" Sophie snapped back.

"Well I will be there in the background but Enid thought that it would be good for you to have some responsibility."

"So, these girls are going to get their First Aid qualification because I said that they were doing the CPR properly? I've only got a basic First Aid certificate!"

"I will be there too Sophie, checking."

Well why don't you just do it then, Sophie though. She decided quickly that she was going to get nowhere like this. She hated herself for it but she changed her tact and tried to grovel instead.

"Laura, as a Mum, you must understand the predicament I'm in? I can't stay here knowing that my babysitter is going at half eight. You *know* I'm hardly needed. Please, I'll tidy up the cups and plates after the break at half seven so that everything will be away. *Please* let me go at eight!"

She could see that there was a battle going on in Laura's head, between her conscience and her desire to crawl to management. Her resolve wavered slightly.

"Well, we'll see how I get on. We do have a *lot* to fit in tonight. If we can finish in time to let you go then we will but I can't promise anything…"

"*Please!*" Sophie pleaded.

"I've said I will try. Now, have you set up the dolls?"

"Um, no sorry. What dolls?"

"The dolls that you were checking earlier. The resuscitation dolls?"

Sophie knew what dolls she meant but hadn't been aware that she was supposed to have done anything with them. She decided to go for the mute approach. Laura raised her eye brows causing her forehead to wrinkle up like an accordion. She shook her head.

"You were *supposed* to be getting them ready for tonight Sophie! They're upstairs in Enid's office. You should have had a practice with them!" she paused. "*I'll* get them!" she paused again and went over to open the door to the hall where they would be doing the training. "It's not been set out. *It's not been set out!* Sophie this is why we come in early!" she sighed. "*You* stay here and welcome people," with that she scuttled off to collect her mannequins.

Sophie positioned herself outside the main door and waited to welcome those who were coming to the training event.

Standing there in her black trousers, jacket and stiff white shirt she felt like a nightclub bouncer. They had to put on such a show for external students. Sophie joked to Ruth earlier that this must be to make up for the fact that the training was shit.

***

At half seven Sophie began to feel edgy. She hadn't been involved in the training at all and had sat at the side with the students listening to Laura's take on First Aid. Most of it seemed to be based on when her own children had got bumps and how she had dealt with situations wrongly. There were things that she missed out too, Sophie noticed, as she had done her certificate much more recently than Laura. Sophie sat and hoped that none of the people doing the training tonight would ever be in a situation where they would need to administer First Aid. She tried to make eye contact with Laura to remind her that she needed to go home but Laura seemed to be making it her mission not to have her eye caught.

I need to go soon, Sophie thought feeling increasingly panicked. Kerry was such a star and she would be lost without her. She usually stayed until all hours on a Wednesday so Sophie wanted to be home in time on this one occasion as it was something that was so important for Kerry to do. She began to get restless and shifted in her seat. The class had had their break and so the table at the back of the hall was ready to be cleared but Sophie had wanted Laura to give her the go ahead before she started otherwise she would get into trouble for disturbing the proceedings. She looked at her watch for the umpteenth time. I'll give it five more minutes, she thought, and then I'll just have to do it. Five minutes passed and Laura was still ignoring Sophie's attempts to catch her attention. She *knows* I need to go, Sophie thought getting more and more anxious that she wasn't going to be allowed to go in time for Kerry. It would be quite like this place if they had locked all the doors, she thought, just so that I can't leave. She was no longer listening to the detail of Laura's training, instead she sat and tried to work up the courage to just get up and walk through the circle of chairs and go and tidy up the cups and saucers. Whatever she did, she thought, she was in for a bollocking in the morning. Unless…

From the hall the office staff heard gasps and shouts. Laura's voice could be heard over the commotion telling everyone not to panic, here was a real life first aid situation for them to deal with. Tim's head appeared round the door to witness the scene of mild chaos. Sophie's lifeless body was slumped in the middle of the group.

"Stand back everyone!" Laura initially took over the situation with confidence. "That's it, give her some air. Now…"

She looked to the skies as If for some divine guidance. All eyes were on her.

"So… here we have a casualty. What would we do next?"

Everyone looked confused.

"Is she really unconscious?" a voice piped up.

"What, is this part of the course?"

"Is she an *actor*?"

"No I saw her keel over!" another added their thoughts. "She did look *really* pale."

"Yeah she looked *awful.*" The lady who had been sitting next to Sophie said.

"I thought it when I arrived," a third voice joined in, "I thought, that woman looks *haggard.*"

Thanks very much, Sophie thought as she lay fully conscious on the floor having taken a deliberate dive in an attempt to be noticed and get away early, you try working in this place.

Tim pushed his way through the group and bent down to look at Sophie, lifting her head slightly.

"Laura as our First Aider I would ask that you deal with this situation while I take the rest of the group through to sit in the lobby."

Laura fumbled over her words as she tried to remember what the appropriate response would be. She tried to take a crafty peek at her power point notes. All the while a stern looking woman had been observing the proceedings and not being able to take any more she also pushed her way forward while taking an ID badge out of her pocket.

"Hilary Ramsden. Qualification Authority and trained in paediatric first aid. We need to put this casualty into the recovery position."

Sophie was aware that she now had about ten minutes to leave and so didn't actually want to be rushed to casualty. She had been heaved into the recovery position rather rudely and was also conscious of the fact that her knickers were on show. Lucky I've not got any sexy ones on Lou, she thought. She began to make groaning noises and lifted her hand up to her head.

"What happened?" she mumbled almost inaudibly. She slowly lifted her head and then let it fall back to the ground and then decided to leave it there, not trusting her acting skills enough to carry on the performance.

"Take it easy," Hilary said. "You're fine. You just fainted. It is *very* hot in this room." She looked up to Laura who was standing uselessly at the side.

Sophie pushed her body up with her hands and sat on the spot where she had fallen. She rubbed her head as it now really hurt, her dramatic tumble causing her to actually bash it on the floor. This was good for her cause.

"Yes…" she said feebly, "Yes I did feel *really* hot."

Tim arrived with a glass of water and offered it to Sophie, inspecting her face with a mixture of suspicion and faint admiration remembering the conversation about getting home early.

"Thank you," she said weakly and took the glass. She had a tiny sip and looked up to the various faces that were peering down on her.

"I'm fine now. Really. I feel fine. I might like some fresh air though…"

Hilary Ramsden nodded and helped Sophie get up from the floor.

"Good idea," she said and turned towards Laura. "I'm going to help this young lady outside where she can get some air. I think that she should then be accompanied home. I will then be back to discuss your future delivery of this qualification. And would someone turn the heating down! It's nearly the summer and the radiators are *boiling*!"

With that she led Sophie, who managed to grab her coat and bag on the way, outside.

***

"That little performance of yours last night has lost our ticket to deliver First Aid qualifications," Enid told Sophie flatly the next morning, as if it were her fault. "Hilary Ramsden is an external verifier and she was doing a spot check."

Sophie didn't reply as had no answer to that. Laura should have known what she was doing then, she thought, she was the one who was supposedly qualified to do the training. She sat down at her desk and went to switch on her computer.

"I wouldn't bother turning that on," Enid told her, "today you will be recycling," she looked towards piles of lever arch files that were messily bundled up under the window on the far side of the room.

"Those are years' worth of sent and received emails. Each sheet is in a plastic pocket. You'll be finished when I have the empty pockets on my desk, the paper has been shredded and the files are neatly returned to the cupboard."

Sophie felt like adding to her head injury and bashing her head on her desk. Five hours of plastic pocket recycling. Suddenly photocopying seemed like an alright job. At least I've got some things to occupy my mind this time, she thought as she removed page after page from their plastic envelope. Sexy Dan, as the girls had christened him, was continuing to bother her by text message and she couldn't get Christian out of her head, despite the hilarity caused by telling her friends that he was an estate agent. She hadn't decided yet on whether she should try and sell her house or not but was tempted to try just so that she could see more of him. Everything about being in a smaller house would be better, she knew, but the process of getting there would cause so much upheaval that she wasn't sure if she could cope with it right now, what with all the other juggling balls she had in the air. She thought that she might ask Christian to come round and value the house at least and then go from there and then she could see him another time, just to check and see if he really was as tummy flipping gorgeous as he had become in her mind over the previous few days. Maybe she could drop into the conversation that she'd be in town on Friday night, if she was feeling very brave.

Chapter Eight

Joules birthday night out had been built up to being the night out of the year, by Joules mainly. The girls met at Sophie's on Friday night and got a taxi from there. Everyone was excited to be going out for once and Joules was convinced that Sophie was going to meet her 'Plus One', it being their main talking point at the moment. Sophie wasn't that bothered anymore, unable to forget about Christian and being in almost constant communications with Dan, playing along with his suggestive texts but stopping short of saying yes to anything. He was due to come down again soon and was keen to meet up.

Joules arrived armed with a bottle of Bailey's, 'to line our stomachs with' she announced and Tina and Lou had shared a bottle of wine while they were waiting for Simon to get home from work, Tina passing Lou's on her way.

"Friday night traffic," Lou explained, "maybe Ben has a point. Bottoms up!"

The four knocked back a shot. Sophie screwed up her face and stuck out her tongue.

"Oh god, yuk. I've not had that for years! That might have to be my last drink of the night," she laughed and nipped upstairs to collect her shoes and bag.

"Ooh let's see what shoes you're wearing tonight!" Joules asked excitedly, loving Sophie's huge collection of heels. She held up her own foot and twisted it round for all to see. "These are my new birthday plimsolls," she told the others as she showed them her black satin pumps that were covered with tiny coloured jewels, "no heel though I'm afraid, I couldn't *walk* in the shoes that you wear Sophie."

"Sometimes I can't either! I've got these ones tonight- I can walk in them unaided and might even be able to dance in them, but we'll have to see about that! Taxi's booked for half past so he should be here in a minute, shall we wait outside?" she checked that the back door was locked and switched the lights off before joining the others at the front of her house.

The taxi arrived on time and they bundled in, Joules sitting in the front to direct the driver as she was the only one who knew the bar that they were going to.

"We went there for a works night out last year- it was so great. It's a *really* trendy restaurant with a bar."

"Did Ollie get away OK?" Lou asked Sophie.

"Yes he did, for once Ben was on time. He was asking me all sorts of questions about babies tonight. Apparently Joshua's Mummy's had a baby- is he in the other Primary One class? Ollie asked if *we* could have a baby. It makes me feel so sad; I remember when he was born just wanting another one! I wish I'd had two… before Ben left," she laughed, "I tried to put him off by telling him that babies would cry all night and would break his toys but he said that he'd just booby trap his room to keep them out."

"Is Ben having him for some of the holidays?" Lou asked.

"Yeah I think he is now- just one week though. It's better than nothing I suppose. I'll have to use the holiday club for the rest of the time."

"He can come round to us if we're around," Joules said over her shoulder from the front of the taxi.

"Thanks Joules. What would I do without you? I feel awkward when Ben picks up Ollie now when I'm dressed up to go out because he always tells me how nice I'm looking- I mean; why does he tell me that? It's so confusing."

"Ooh do you think he wants to get back together?" Tina asked. "You wouldn't take him back though, would you?"

"No!" Sophie shuddered. "Definitely not. Let's not even go there. Is this it Joules?"

The taxi had stopped in a side street in town somewhere that Sophie had never been before and Joules was rummaging in her bag for her purse to pay him. Lou stretched over from the back and handed her a twenty pound note to cover the fare.

"It's your birthday, darling. You shouldn't need to pay for anything! Depending on how much you're planning on drinking anyway."

The ladies got out of the taxi and followed Joules who strode ahead down the road clearly on a mission to get started with her night out. She had taken them to what looked to Sophie like a very trendy part of town.

"Am I going to feel old in here?" she asked, casting a worried glance at the collection of very young and hip looking smokers who were gathered just outside.

"You're not *old!* Come on!" and with that Joules pushed the door open and led them into an already buzzing restaurant. As they went in there were tables of various sizes, some occupied and some set out waiting for their diners. Past the tables there was a bar that stretched round the corner to a dance floor with luxurious looking leather sofas around and booths to sit in.

"Ooh grab us a seat and I'll get the drinks in!" Tina said above the noise of music and chatter and she headed over to the bar leaving the others to find somewhere to sit. They chose the last free booth on the far side of the dance floor where they had a good view to the bar and tables.

"Just so that we can check out the talent," Joules had told the others.

Sophie shuffled along the seat and put her bag on the table. She looked across the empty dance floor to the bar and tables. She saw a group of young women coming in and loudly greeting their friends who were already seated, inspecting their menus and sipping on wine. Lots of air kissing and compliments followed. Four smartly dressed men came in after and headed straight for the bar and ordered four lagers. Couples dotted around, at tables and at the bar, all drinking. Is this the kind of place I'm going to meet someone, Sophie thought? She hadn't been anywhere like this in years so busy had she been getting on with things since Ben had left. She couldn't imagine ever meeting someone that he had things in common with in a place like this, everyone looked so *cool*.

"Any more dates lined up then Sophie?" Lou asked, breaking her train of thought as Tina came back from the bar and placed four bottles of beer on the table.

"Happy birthday, Joules!" she said and took a swig out of her own bottle.

"Ooh thanks!" Joules said, her face animated and smiling. Sophie looked at her friend and realised that she hadn't seen her happy like this for a long time. She was so pretty and looked lovely tonight wearing glittery eye shadow, lip gloss and a bright red top. Wasted on her inattentive husband, Sophie thought. Steve had even complained about having to stay in and look after their boys tonight, time with his son's seemingly being well down his agenda.

"So?" Joules persisted. "How many dates have you got lined up?"

"Oh, none at the moment. There was quite a nice looking guy online and he sent me a message and seemed really keen for us to meet up but he can't come up with a date yet. Apparently he plays badminton on Monday and Thursday, Tuesday is bridge night, Wednesday night and Saturday afternoon is five-a-side football with the boys and then Saturday night is boys night out which leaves Friday night but he's been busy then too so far… Not sure what he does on Sunday, probably recovers from his busy week."

"Oh *God*!" Lou exclaimed. "Are you sure he's not *gay?* Bridge and *Badminton?* Who plays bridge anyway- how *old* is he?"

Sophie giggled at her friend. "He's a bit older than me. 40. He looks quite dashing, a little bit George Clooney with his specks of grey hair," she smiled wickedly at Lou and took a drink from her bottle. "Apart from him there are a few others online who look alright but it's *really* difficult to know what they're like just from pictures and I don't know when I'm going to have the time to meet up with them all!"

"Didn't you say that Ben was having Ollie for a week soon?" Tina asked. "You could have a whole week of dating!"

"Yeah... I could do I suppose... I'd rather just have some peace and quiet though! I was going to give that guy from the estate agents a phone..."

"Nothing about those words- estate agents- sounds attractive," Tina said.

"He doesn't *look* like your average estate agent..." Sophie pondered, not really being sure about what an average estate agent looked like, "he's very well spoken and seemed so genuinely friendly and down to earth. I'd love to see him again... I'm not that bothered at the moment about meeting anyone else, I'd just like to get to know him. He's just so... *dreamy.*"

Lou rolled her eyes.

"Sophie did you used to read Bunty magazine?"

Sophie laughed, used to being teased by her friends for being so square.

"So, what did you think of the homework this week? A daily food diary! As if I have time to write down every single flipping thing that Ollie eats! And the fat content! I'm sure that Mrs Newman is just trying to prove that we're all terrible mothers."

"I just made it all up last night," Joules admitted, "otherwise she *would* be able to prove that! My boys are addicted to pizza and sometimes I just can't be *arsed* to convince them to try something else! So this week we've had tuna pasta bake, chicken casserole, spaghetti bolognaise, stir-fry, Shepherd's pie… all made up for the homework of course!" she giggled and took a drink out of her bottle, casting her eyes around the restaurant.

"Sometimes they get *so much* homework!" Sophie complained. "They've already spent hours working at school and then we have to spend another hour at home doing homework. Although it usually ends up as being hours spread through the week of tears and tantrums and in the end *bribery* to get them to do it. Next weeks is even worse though- a weekly diary of the weather that we're having *here* and the weather in *Barbados.* How can I get the weather for Barbados? And it's not just if it's sunny or not, they want rainfall figures, wind speed and direction, temperature and *pollution levels…*"

"Don't look now!" Joules hissed suddenly, very conspicuously diverting her eyes from the bar to Sophie," ten o'clock!"

The other three ladies looked at Joules in complete bewilderment.

"Joules, darling, did you have some pre- drinks at home?" Lou asked.

"I'm not drunk!" Joules whispered rather loudly. "Ten o'clock!"

"What are you talking about? It's coming up to half past eight. Well, quarter past," Tina said looking up at the clock above their seats.

"No! Ten o'clock. Oh no, I mean ten past two," she shook her head, trying to figure out the time she meant to get her friends to look over to the bar, "no scrub that. Five to six."

"What *are* you talking about?" Lou asked again. "Speak in proper sentences!"

Sophie glanced over her shoulder to the bar where Joules had been looking.

"Sophie! I told you not to look!"

"Look where?" Sophie asked, looking over to the bar again.

"*There! The bar!* There's a guy standing there. See- the one over there with a beer in his hand."

"Everyone has a beer in their hand!" Lou said beginning to lose patience with her friend.

Joules lowered her voice even further. "He's tall and broad and has *ginger hair,*" she whispered, "and he's been staring at *you* since we've sat down!" she said to Sophie, "he looks like a *rugby* player or something. There, look, he looked again. The one with the white rugby top on."

The mention of rugby players grabbed Tina's attention and she too craned her neck to see the object of their conversation. A man of Joules description stood leaning against the bar, now with the four ladies all staring directly at him. He stood up straight, as if coming round from a trance, and turned towards two other men who stood alongside.

"He was *definitely* watching you Sophie! See, I *knew* that tonight would be your lucky night!"

"Don't be silly Joules! He was probably looking at the time or something! I'll go to the bar next and you'll see that he's not looking at me!" her phone beeped on the table and lit up showing that she had a text message. When Ollie was away she liked to keep her phone in sight just in case there was any emergency at Ben's. She looked at the screen and saw that it was Dan.

"Ooh Sexy Dan! What does he want?" Tina asked with great interest.

"Probably sex of some kind," Sophie said with a little irritation in her voice. "It's all he talks about. He's obsessed. It's actually getting quite boring."

"It's boring to keep talking about it!" Tina said. "Why don't you just do it and get it over with. You know you want to."

"I don't!" Sophie replied. "I'm just looking for a bit more than just sex," she said and casually looked back over to the bar but the man who Joules had identified wasn't there anymore and Sophie felt slightly disappointed. "Oh he's gone now anyway," she said to Joules.

"No, look, he's sat down over there with his two friends. Shame there's not four of them; we could have had one each!"

Sophie laughed and shook her head at her friends- if their husbands knew how keen they all sounded to meet someone else... She hoped that she would meet someone who would make her forget about all the other men in the world, even her friends just *talking* about other men seemed wrong to her.

"Let me go and get another drink," Sophie said noticing that Joules bottle was empty and standing up at the table. "Who wants another?" she squeezed past Lou sitting next to her and walked over the dance floor to the bar. She had decided to wear her favourite jeans as they were so comfy and fitted her like a glove. They were perfectly faded and had the beginning of a tiny hole in her right knee. With them she wore a cropped t-shirt that hung off her left shoulder and a pair of neon yellow and black strappy shoes with a heel that tapered down to a point and were about five inches tall. They were surprisingly easy to walk in despite the pointy heel and she click clicked her way across the floor. Her three friends watched her with great interest to see if she was being checked out. They all seemed to get some kind of satisfaction in taking part in her quest for a man.

Sophie felt self-conscious that someone might be watching her and she tried to look nonchalant as she made her way to the bar. She leaned up against it and put one foot on the silver pole that ran along the bottom edge. As she stood waiting to be served she was aware of a figure joining her and adopting the same leaning position next to her. Without moving her head, she tried to glance to the side and see who it was. A new member of the bar staff appeared and asked the person next to Sophie what they would like to drink.

"The lady was here first," a man's voice spoke. Sophie turned as he gestured towards her so that she should be served first. It was the man that Joules had pointed out to her earlier. Sophie started to protest that she didn't mind but the man insisted. "It will give me a few moments to admire your wonderful shoes."

Sophie thought it odd that a man would be interested in her shoes. Maybe *he* was gay, she thought, that was usually Lou's answer to these sorts of things. She thanked him and ordered her drinks.

"If you're at a loose end later maybe you could come and keep us company over there," the man said to Sophie, gesturing to a table with a group of men, "we've been here playing rugby today and literally have no idea about where anything is. We could do with a group of attractive women to keep us right," he smirked at Sophie looking at her directly with his clear blue eyes. His hair was messy and deep red and he had handsome if craggy features. He towered above Sophie who was diminutive by comparison, he being of broad build as well as being tall.

"OK! We'll see!" Sophie said.

Back at the table this response did not go down well.

"Sophie when you get propositioned by a *rugby team* you don't say, 'we'll see'!" Tina said exasperated.

"I wasn't propositioned by a *rugby team*!" Sophie retorted. "It was a rugby *player* but he wasn't propositioning me! I think he's gay anyway because he seemed to have a great interest in my shoes…"

"He's not gay," Lou stated confidently.

"Well whatever, I've come out to have a good time with you lot and especially Joules because it's her birthday. I don't want to go and talk to a load of people that I don't know."

"A group of extremely attractive and fit rugby players that you don't know, there is a difference," Tina said, half joking. "Well if you're not going to join them *I* will!" she said defiantly and downed the last of her lager. "Who wants another?"

"You're on a mission! Go on then," Lou replied, "Sophie?"

"Not for me thanks, I'm still on my first! I'll get my own later."

Tina managed to take a detour to the bar so that she could stop to talk to the rugby players first.

"She's encourageable!" Sophie said. "She's *desperate* to meet someone else."

"I know how she feels," Joules replied.

"What's she saying to them?" Sophie said with a slight panic in her voice. "Oh *God* I wished I'd kept my mouth shut about needing a Plus One. I don't *really* need one, do I? I'm a bridesmaid anyway; I can just go with Ollie," she looked over at Tina intently trying to read her lips as she spoke to the group of rugby players. "They're all quite big, aren't they..?" she thought out loud. "They *look* like a team of rugby players…"

"I think that's what Tina's finding irresistible," Lou said with resignation. "As soon as she has a few drinks inside her… honestly she's as bad as her husband!"

"She's just talking to them…" Sophie said.

"Yeah, because none of them would be interested in a 40-year-old mother of two!" Lou laughed. "Tina would agree. She's jump into bed with any of them given half a chance though, she's desperate to be all square with her husband."

"I don't think she would, not really. She's just all talk," Joules said. "We might have lost her for the evening though!"

It was about twenty minutes later when Tina returned from her flirting trip looking slightly rosy and animated, holding a fresh bottle of beer that she had been bought by one of the rugby team. She sat down next to Lou with her back to the men.

"He *does* fancy you Sophie," she hissed rather too loudly.

Sophie shushed her friend. "Not so *loudly*!"

"He does though. And he's *really* lush."

"What have you been saying...?" Sophie asked with dread.

"I just kind of mentioned you and he said that he noticed you as soon as he came in. He *really* wants to talk to you."

"Oh God this is like school!" Sophie said to her slightly tipsy friend. "I don't need or want to be set up with anyone, especially in a way that I would have been in sixth form. If I have an opportunity to talk to him later then I will, just to keep you happy, but I'm definitely not going to make a special effort."

"Good evening, ladies," the flame haired man who had spoken to Sophie at the bar appeared at their table holding four fresh bottles of beer. "These are compliments of the team," he grinned and placed the bottles down on the table. Lou looked amused and winked at Sophie who suddenly felt awkward and uncomfortable and just like she did in sixth form about meeting the opposite sex.

Sophie had been a late starter when it came to dating and had been more interested in reading about her handsome prince than going out and trying to meet him. Ben had just appeared out of the blue one day. Although intelligent and articulate she wouldn't have had the first clue about how to initiate a conversation with a *man*. She suddenly felt like that again and stared at her bottle, wishing that the spotlight of attention wasn't on her.

"I'm Phil, anyway," the man said, sensing that there was some awkwardness at the table but on a mission himself to speak to the woman that he desired, "nice to meet you all."

There was a pause. Sophie felt like everyone was waiting for her to spring to life and take control of the situation but she had no intention of doing anything of the sort, hoping that this rugby player would quickly tire of her and move on to pastures new. He, however, had no intention of doing that either. Joules suddenly stood up.

"Why don't you sit down, Phil? I've just spotted one of my work friend's; I'll be back in a minute. Keep my seat warm for me!" with that she hurried over to a group of women who had got up from their table and were about to leave the restaurant. Joules called her friend's name as she rushed over and waved; her friend heard her and waved back, smiling broadly. Sophie watched them embracing and start to talk animatedly. I doubt any of my work colleagues would greet me so warmly, she thought. She looked up at Phil who was still standing at the table, as if waiting for Sophie's approval before sitting down. There was nothing that she could do but smile at him and he awkwardly sat down at the table.

"I hope you don't mind me joining you like this?" he said, "the guys might come over too in a bit, once they've all finished eating. We haven't been formally introduced," he said to Sophie as she sat stiffly next to him. He extended his hand.

"Sophie," she said, "it's Sophie. Hi," she smiled again.

Lou and Tina were looking at each other and seemed to be communicating by eyebrow. They both turned to Sophie.

"We'll be back in a minute," Lou said. "I, *we,* are just going to the loo."

Sophie groaned inwardly. What a stitch up. She shifted uncomfortably as she sat as far into the corner of their booth that anyone could be.

"Your friends are great," Phil said. "Tina's such a laugh. She said you'd take us clubbing later."

Oh great, thought Sophie who couldn't think of anything worse right now than making the night last any longer that it needed to having suddenly lost her appetite for socialising.

"So, do you come here often?" Phil asked and then cringed at himself for asking her the most classic pick up line.

Sophie laughed, realising that he didn't mean to sound so cheesy.

"No," she replied, "I really don't. I've never been here before in my life."

"You live here though?"

"Yeah I live just out of town," she said and then stopped herself, not sure how much information she should give away to this stranger.

"Special occasion then, your friend's birthday?"

"Yeah," Sophie replied.

"Well, I'm glad that you came out tonight," Phil said with a genuineness that touched Sophie and made her think that maybe he wasn't so bad after all. She relaxed slightly and slowly uncrossed her arms that she had tightly folded in front of her when he had sat down. They chatted amicably for a while.

"You have to most amazing heels in this place!" Phil eventually said and looked at her feet under the table. "I mean, man, they are *awesome*! Look at them!"

I am aware of my shoes, Sophie thought.

Phil took a huge gulp from his pint of lager. Sophie thought by the look of him that he had probably already had quite a few. His skin was slightly glowing and he had the beginning of perspiration on his forehead and upper lip. His broad stature made his pint glass look small in his hands. He probably drinks those in a couple of mouthfuls, Sophie thought.

"I was looking at them earlier. There's only one way that those shoes could look *any better*," he declared and looked at her as if waiting for her ideas. Sophie had none so he continued, "the only way those heels could be improved," he continued, "is if they were on my naked body."

So unprepared for this remark was Sophie that she choked on the mouthful of lager that she was in the process of swallowing. She grabbed a napkin that had found its way onto their table and held it to her mouth, coughing. Phil looked concerned but was unaware that his thought had shocked her, instead taking her reaction as one of extreme pleasure. He grinned at her and raised his eyebrows.

"Good thought, huh?" he leaned towards Sophie and gently stroked his right hand against her left thigh. He lowered his voice. "No woman has ever made this man come through intercourse alone," He paused and looked into her startled eyes, "maybe you could, with a little help from these bad boys."

Sophie was frozen to her spot, her mouth slightly open and completely lost for words. Phil the now fairly sweaty and leering rugby player sat closely next to her with his hand resting on her thigh. Another man appeared at the table wearing a white t-shirt and jeans. Sophie instantly noticed his strong-looking forearms covered with slightly sandy coloured hair.

"Hey Sophie, I thought it was you. Just thought I'd come and say 'hi' but you look like you're busy," Christian said with what seemed like a little disappointment in his voice.

***

Christian didn't hang around for long after he had come over to say 'hello', Phil's apparent closeness to Sophie making it look as if they were an item and nothing like the reality of their meeting moments before. The two men had nodded at each other and said, 'Alright', Phil keeping his hand clasped firmly on Sophie's thigh like he was marking her for his own. Christian had made a hasty get-a-way when he realised the situation and Sophie helplessly watched him disappearing out of the restaurant. She had hoped for the rest of the evening that they would be lucky a second time around, on their travels around the various night spots in town, and bump into him again but it didn't happen.

Back at work now she recalled every last detail in her head, cringing at the memory. Enid had told her to check through some audio files that they had on the system and delete any that were no longer needed. Sophie assumed she meant the questioning sessions that they did with staff to cover aspects of their qualifications and not the secret recordings that Enid did in the office in case anyone should be complaining. As she sat at her desk with her headphones on, not listening to anything yet but looking like she was hard at work, she wondered how long Christian had been in the restaurant and cursed Phil for ruining her chance of talking to him again. Phil had seemed on the surface to be a rather nice man- ruggedly handsome, very funny and with quite a sweet genuineness about him. He had spoken fondly about his upbringing in Wales and how his dad had taken him to the rugby as a young boy and, when he heard that Sophie's sister was getting married, how he had been best man recently and what a responsibility it was. If it had stopped there then he would have been perfect but unfortunately he had, what Sophie thought, a very unhealthy obsession with her shoes.

"So, anyway," Phil had said when Christian had left, "I bet I could get those shoes shiny like they've never shined before," he lowered his voice. "How do you think I could get them all shiny?"

Sophie wasn't in the least bit interested, her thoughts still lingering on the moment before, cursing herself for not dealing with the situation differently. Phil had had other things on his mind.

"Oh I don't know," she had said distractedly as her eyes had gazed across the restaurant, hoping to see Christian again, "polish them?"

"Not exactly," he had grinned as if Sophie was making a joke, as if she really knew what he was thinking but was coyly skirting around the subject, "how else could I make them shiny and *smooth*?"

Sophie had shaken her head, rather bored now of the subject and thinking worriedly that he was moments away from actually drooling. She let out a puff of air and shook her head. "Dunno."

Phil had looked pleased that he could finally tell her what was on his mind. "I could lick them," he looked at her with expectant eyes, eager for her response.

"*Lick them?*" Sophie had repeated rather more loudly than intended causing a group of women standing nearby to glance round with great interest on their faces. "Why would you want to *lick them*? *Lick them?*" she asked again incredulously.

Why would anyone want to lick my heels, she had thought again, she couldn't think of anything more unhygienic.

A sleazy smile spread across Phil's now reddened and glistening face, the combination of alcohol, heating and sexual arousal making him sweat somewhat.

Sophie didn't find out at that moment why this normal looking man wanted to lick her shoes as her friends arrived back en masse to the table. Lou winked at Sophie when she noticed the position of Phil's hand which caused Tina to notice too and she suggested that the three of them go back and have a dance.

"No, *no* it's fine come and sit back down," Sophie had said firmly, "you've been gone way too long already!"

She straightened her headphones to make herself look busy and repositioned herself in her chair. Christian had looked so much more comfortable in his jeans and T-shirt making her think how awkward he had seemed in his suit. Seeing him again had confirmed to her how much she fancied him. That was a better way to meet someone, she thought, in the flesh. None of this fussing around sending messages and trawling through online profiles. She decided that she would have to call him with the pretence of putting her house on the market and tell him that it was a shame he didn't stick around on Friday night because she could have done with being saved from the advances of Phil. She made a mental note to call the estate agency later and make an appointment.

Eventually, after about half an hour of daydreaming with her headphones on, Sophie sighed and thought that she had better do some work. At that moment the school principal breezed into the office, as she often did when she was bored.

"Enid! Just the person! I need someone to have a thought shower with."

Enid mouthed 'tea' to Sophie and she took her headphones off, laying them on her desk and went through to the kitchen to boil the kettle. She found the work that she did so monotonous that making the tea was sometimes a welcome distraction. She located the principal's special peppermint tea amongst the others that they had and looked around for her tea cup.

Oh crap, where is it, she thought and remembered that she hadn't done her 'Friday job' of washing up the week's tea cups, so keen had she been to get away for Joules night out. The principal normally liked her own bone china tea cup but the only ones that were left were cheap tea-stained white Pyrex. I'm sure it will be fine, Sophie thought, picking one up and dropping two tea bags in the bottom. At least I've got that bit right. The last time she had made her tea she had committed the heinous crime of only putting one tea bag in and was still living it down, it being the office joke in the absence of anything funny ever happening. She poured the freshly boiled water on top of the tea bags and hummed a little tune as she went back into the office holding the cup of fresh tea.

The principal, who was sitting on Enid's chair and had turned it around to talk to Enid who sat at the phone desk behind, swung herself round at the sound of the door, swishing her hair extensions as she did so. She visibly started as her eyes stopped upon the cup that Sophie held. The whole office stopped and looked. Sophie wondered why she had ever thought that it would be OK to use cheap china.

Enid shook her head patronizingly at Sophie.

"Sophie, Sophie, Sophie. What are we going to do with you? Last time you couldn't get the tea right; this time you haven't got the cup. Four years at university and you can't even get the simplest of things right," she continued to shake her head and exchanged a look with the principal who smiled indulgently at Enid.

"It's fine," she said in a way that sounded like it wasn't fine at all but of massive inconvenience. She nodded her head towards the space on the desk that she wanted her drink placed and Sophie did this, "*you* make it next time seeing as your staff are incapable. Where were we?" and with that she swung back round to face Enid, without as much as a 'thank you'.

Sophie was getting used to this by now and thought nothing of it, returning to her desk. She put her headphones back on and scrolled down the list of audio files that they had on the system. There were some staff names that she had never seen before and she turned to Pam to ask which ones were still employed at the school, lifting up her left headphone. Pam was engrossed in whatever she was doing and stared at her monitor. Sophie tried to get her attention by just looking at her but Pam was so transfixed that she didn't notice.

"Pam!" Sophie whispered. Pam didn't react. "Pam!" Still nothing. Enid was aware of Sophie's voice. "Pam!"

Pam turned her head by a fraction and smiled awkwardly, not like her usual friendly self, Sophie thought. She continued to whisper.

"Do you know if they've left?" she asked and twisted her monitor round so that Pam could see the screen, pointing to a name on her list. Pam shook her head and quickly focussed her attention back onto her own screen.

"What about that one?" Sophie asked and pointed to another name," and her, I've never *heard* of most of these people!"

"Ladies *please!*" Enid's voice snapped. Sophie looked over at her dumbly. What have I done *now,* she thought?

"It is of the *upmost* rudeness to *interrupt* someone when they are speaking! *Especially* when it is our own principal!"

"I was asking Pam a question," Sophie said bravely.

"You were *talking* when you should have been *listening,*" Enid spat the words out with contempt.

"Sorry I didn't know I was meant to be listening," Sophie replied, "you told me to listen to the audio files…"

"When our *principal* is speaking," Enid said, "we are *all listening.*"

The words hung in the stuffy office air for all to contemplate. The principal rolled her eyes and tutted at the uselessness of Enid's staff. Frances shook her head at Sophie, getting great satisfaction from the situation that was unfolding following on from the first aid fiasco the other evening.

"Can I continue?" the principal asked Enid primly.

Sophie sat and wondered how she could listen to the audio files, for she would no doubt get into trouble for slacking *and* to the principal at the same time. She positioned the headphones at an angle so that only one ear was covered and looked over at her employer, whose back was turned to her, and tried to look interested despite not being able to hear what she was talking to Enid about. Pam cast a quick regretful glance at Sophie and Sophie mouthed back, 'Sorry' feeling awful for getting Pam into trouble too.

***

I now know, she thought the next morning as she bounded up the stairs to the office, that any time the principal is in our room I must keep my big mouth shut, stop what I'm doing and listen. Or at least, get on with what I'm doing and pretend to listen. She burst through the door to the office, being so deep in thought that she forgot to stop and check who was in.

The principal sat at Sophie's desk and stopped mid-sentence, looking up with her mouth still open to speak. Sophie stopped in her tracks, frozen to the spot. Everyone was sitting in the wrong seats and all looked over to Sophie who had clearly interrupted some kind of meeting. The office often had meetings without her before she started. She once mentioned that she'd not been to a meeting before, concerned that she might need to know what they were talking about, and Laura had said she's never been to a meeting because they had them at 8am and she started at half 9. Why not make one of your meetings later, Sophie had though. The only free space was at Laura desk and so as not to cause any further disturbance, although she needed to go to the loo before starting work and hang up her coat and bag, she sidled across and lowered herself onto the empty chair, putting her bags on her knees and an interested look on her face. Ruth looked like she might burst, so hard was she trying not to laugh. The principal shut her gawping mouth and turned her attention back to Enid and smiled thinly.

"What was I saying?"

Sophie sat there for the next hour in her outside coat with her bags on her knees, bursting for the loo but not able to move in fear of being told off for interrupting. She was relieved when the meeting was eventually halted when the principal received a call from the downstairs office that she had to go and attend to and everyone's mood lifted when she was clear of the training office. Enid stood up and walked past Sophie, also on her way out.

"When our principal is here," she said to Sophie, "hang up your coat and bags. Outdoor wear that is not strict uniform is to be kept *out* of her sight. And book me a car for my appointments next week!"

Sophie waited for her to be clear of the office before moving. Everyone silently shuffled back to their desks and Sophie went to hang up her coat in the kitchen area. She came back into the office repeating, "Book a car, book a car" to herself and looked at Enid's timetable for the following week which was displayed on the wall.

The school had three cars that staff had to use if they were required to go out during the day and the keys were all named and hanging up in a key safe in the main office. Each car had a respective mobile and the three phones were always on charge in a tangle of wires on the office floor. The policy was that you were to book cars a week in advance but there was always some mix up and Sophie often witnessed great arguments about who had what car and where and why was 'car 2' out when 'mobile 2' was in. Cars had to be signed out and signed back in and an estimated arrival time back at the school had to be identified, even if you weren't exactly sure, and questions were asked if you were later than this. Sophie knew the procedure but as yet had not been allowed out of the school at all since she started, her training in the way they do things obviously not yet complete.

"We do things The Elm Tree way," Enid had told her on her first day of work. "When we are outside the school we must uphold the *excellent* reputation of the school *at all times,"* making Sophie feel like she was some kind of loutish oaf who randomly swore and picked her nose in public.

"I'd better do that first then," she said to nobody in particular, "book a car." Just to keep her ladyship happy, she thought.

"She likes the red one," Laura said, in a rare moment of helpfulness.

"Really?" Sophie asked. "I thought she'd like one of the big black Audi's?"

"Oh no she doesn't like driving *those,* she says that they're too difficult to park sometimes. School car parks car be *very* busy," Laura looked over to Sophie smiling patronisingly, her eyes closed and a haughty look on her face, as if Sophie had no idea about the outside world because she'd not been 'let out' yet. "The Nissan is *so easy* to park."

Sophie couldn't imagine Enid enjoying driving the tiny clapped out Micra rather than one of the luxurious black Audi's but that was the thing about this place, she thought, you never know and the small car did seem to be more practical. She emailed the main office to book the red Nissan for all of Enid's appointments the following week.

***

Later that evening as Sophie was browsing health spas, hotels and cottages, all possible venues for her sister's hen do, her mind wandered to the men that she had recently met, all of whom were keeping in touch despite the lack of interest on her part. The only one whom she hadn't heard from was the one that she liked a lot, but she knew that there was no reason for Christian to get in touch especially as she had had Phil clamped onto her leg when he saw her last.

Paul kept in touch on the social networking site and they exchanged messages, although Sophie was taking longer and longer to reply to each one. He was especially keen for her to join him, Dave and Phil for a quiz at the Plough soon but as they were on a Wednesday night she was able to give a genuine excuse, for once being pleased that she had to work on Wednesdays. Sexy Dan text her frequently, mostly detailing what he'd like to do to her and what he'd like her to do to him. She found it quite tiring and time consuming at first responding to these messages but soon realised that she could be quite creative herself and send her own suggestive texts back with no thought that one day she might actually have to live them out. He thought that he would be down with work soon and sounded keen to meet up with her again. His texts were ever hopeful that she had encountered someone else keen to join them for some 'fun', as if it were something that she asked people in normal conversation.

Phil had added Sophie onto his social network after they had met on Joules night out and she had accepted his friend request hoping that if he wasn't the one for her maybe one of his rugby friends was. Tina was impressed with her thinking. Sophie was finding his constant comments about her shoes, though, slightly disturbing and worried that it would put anyone else off. He had clearly read through the content of her wall and had commented on most things, inappropriately she thought. Her status had mentioned shopping with her sister and he had commented, 'Bet you went to the shoe shop too, he he he'. Her status had mentioned a long run that she had done and how much her legs hurt and he had commented, 'Bet they still look good in heels, he he he'. She had said that she was finding it difficult choosing from the vast array of bridesmaid shoes and he had commented, 'Let me know if you need any help with that, he he he.' He managed to make it sound like he was practically drooling at the thought and she could imagine the slavering look on his face.

The online dating site was beginning to be a bit more fruitful and there were a few possible dates lining themselves up. Ben had confirmed that he would have Ollie for a week at the beginning of August and so she decided that if she could keep them hanging on for a while longer she would take her friends advice and try and cram a few dates in then. She was sure that she should have a few more days to take off in the holidays too.

At the forefront of her mind though was Christian. She couldn't get the image of his disappointed face out of her head after Joules night out. She checked in her purse to see if she still had his card and deciding that the only thing to do was to get him to come round and value her house she left the card out to do the next day.

Chapter Nine

On her way home the next day Sophie randomly decided to drop in past the estate agency and arrange for Christian to come round and see the house rather than phoning him up. Seeing him in the restaurant during their night out had given her an aching desire to see him again, even if it was just to make an appointment. She parked in the visitor car park behind the shop and checked her appearance, a day at work usually dulling it somewhat. She slapped her cheeks gently to bring some colour back into them and ran her hand through her hair. Suddenly she felt rather silly for making the detour and going out of her way like this when she could have just called. She hesitated for a moment with her hand still in her hair, wondering if she should carry on home and phone him, the last thing that she wanted was for him to think that she was stalking him. A tapping sound made her jump, interrupting her thoughts and she whirled around to see who was there. Christian stooped down to look at her through the window and waved.

"Hi!" Sophie said and then realising that he couldn't hear she wound down her window. "Hi!"

"Hi!" he said and smiled. Nobody spoke for a moment. "How are you?"

"Oh, yeah, good!" Sophie replied trying not to let on that the sight of him was making her heart race and causing her to find it suddenly difficult to talk in a normal manner. She felt her cheeks start to redden and cursed her body for blushing too easily.

Christian smiled broadly. "Are you getting out?" he asked and put his hand on the door handle to open it for her. There was a pause while Sophie summoned up enough courage to speak again, her body having started to shake as if she were shivering causing her voice to sound somewhat wobbly. She took a breath.

"Yeah!" she replied, "I am. Well, I was…"

Christian pulled the door open and stood back slightly so that she could get out, extending his hand for her to hold. As had happened before when they had met for the first time they held hands for a little too long, Christian looking at her face as if searching for some kind of reaction from her. Sophie was so nervous that she stood as stiff as a board, her heart pounding inside her chest.

"Did you have a good night on Friday?" he asked her, keen to know about the man who had been gripping her leg so tightly. Sophie laughed dismissively.

"Yeah! I guess," her mind was racing trying to think of what to say about Phil, "I was with some friends."

"Really?" Christian asked, "You looked quite cosy. I thought you must have been with your boyfriend."

"No!" Sophie exclaimed, a little too loudly she thought on later reflection, "No, I don't have a boyfriend!" she took another deep breath and tried to compose her thoughts. "It was my friend's birthday. I don't know who the man was who had his hand on my leg," she paused suddenly thinking that sounded wrong. "Um, he was quite drunk!" that's no better, she thought.

"Ah," Christian said as if it all made perfect sense, "I thought he was your boyfriend. He did look *really* close!"

"He wasn't that close…" Sophie said hopefully.

"Oh well that's a shame, I might have stuck around if I'd have known that. What brings you here? I'm just off home," Sophie suddenly felt silly that she hadn't just phoned.

"Oh well I was just passing… I could have just called actually… I'd just decided that I'd like you to come and value my house, I mean, you know, your estate agency not you in particular…" a voice inside Sophie's head started to shout at her to stop talking utter nonsense. Christian didn't seem to notice that she wasn't talking with as much composure as she normally did.

"Great!" Christian said with feeling. "Toby's inside still if you want to go and make an appointment now?" He looked at his watch. "Oh bugger I've really got to go!" He looked at Sophie and there was another moment of silence. If this was a film, Sophie thought, he'd slowly move closer to me, we'd close our eyes and our lips would meet… "Great seeing you; get Toby to put it in the diary for Thursday. Late Thursday, when I'm working. Hopefully see you then," he put his hand on her forearm and gave it a gentle squeeze. She stood and watched him bound over to his little sporty MG then snapped herself out of her daydream and gathered her thoughts. She shut her car door and strode across the car park and under the archway that led around to the front of the building, waving at him as he sped out of the car park. She cringed and cursed herself for not being able to just talk normally to him.

The man in the estate agency was much older than Christian but bore a striking resemblance to him. He was very smartly dressed in a pinstripe suite and yellow silk tie and smiled at her as she entered the shop with the same crinkly eyes that Christian had. He stood up and extended his hand to her.

"Hi, nice to see you," he said, as if he was expecting her.

***

"Ooh do you think that he *likes* you?" Joules beamed at the excitement of it all. The two ladies stood outside the classroom door waiting for the children to come out.

"I'm not really sure," Sophie pondered. "I think there's *something* there. I can't explain. I just have a *feeling...*" she shook her head and smiled. "I'm probably being silly. Anyway, he's coming round at six."

"What's this?" Lou asked, hearing the last part of the conversation, "Another date?"

"It's not *another* date!" Sophie protested. "I've only had two so far!"

"Did you say *another* date?" Tina joined the group and looked eagerly towards Sophie for more information.

"No it's not *another* date!" she repeated, "as I was *saying,* I've only had two! Christian, the one that makes me go actually weak at the knees, is coming round later to value my house," she looked sheepish, "half so that I know how much it's worth and half so that I can see him again... Oh God, what's happening to me? How old am I?"

She rushed home with Ollie and got changed out of her black work suit and into a plain grey mini dress with black knee length boots. Too dressed up, she thought and removed the boots. No good without the boots, she thought and put on her jeans instead. She rummaged through her drawers for a top to wear and took out her cropped t-shirt. That's what I had on when I saw him in the restaurant, she thought, and put it back, continuing to rummage. Eventually she plumped for another cropped t-shirt, remembering Lou's comment, 'Then they'll know how fit you are'. As if a little bit of skin is going to make someone like me, Sophie thought.

***

She began to hover at the window just before six having done her hair and powdered her nose. Bang on six Christian's little car sped up the drive and came to a sharp halt. Sophie dived behind the curtain so that he couldn't see that she was waiting. She heard the car door shut and footsteps before the doorbell rang, she paused for several moments before answering and took a deep breath to try to abate the nervous shaking that was threatening to start again. She felt her heart starting to pound. This is crazy, she thought, why can't I just talk to him normally like I can with everyone else? She called up the stairs to Ollie to tell him that there was someone at the door that she needed to talk to, hoping that he wouldn't embarrass her this time.

Sophie opened the door and smiled at Christian who stood there clutching a clip board with some paperwork attached. He was still wearing his ill-fitting suit. His eyes flickered to her bare midriff.

"Hi!" she said.

"Hi!" Christian replied looking back into her eyes, stepping into the house and wiping his shoes on the mat although they didn't look dirty at all. He smiled too and extended his hand for her to shake which she did. He suddenly looked awkward at the formality and kissed her on the cheek causing her stomach to feel like she was being dropped from a great height. She felt lost in a haze of desire for him.

"Shall I take my shoes off?" he asked, looking into her immaculate living room and at the polished floor.

"Oh, no!" Sophie laughed, wanting to give the impression that she would be very easy to live with. "It's fine," she shook her head and dismissed the thought, happy to clear up any mess that Christian should make. He wiped his feet some more and stepped into the living room.

"Nice house," he observed looking around. "You've got a lot of space," he looked through to the dining room and conservatory at the back and then the garden beyond.

"So, I won't take any photos today as this is just a valuation," he said and lay his clip board down on the dining room table and went into the kitchen, "I'll just let you know how much it's worth and then you can have a think about it."

Sophie followed him into the kitchen like a faithful puppy, hanging on his every word.

"Nice kitchen."

Sophie felt pleased that Christian seemed to like her house and stood waiting for his next comment. He had a look out of the back door.

"Nice garage. Can I open this door?" he asked and Sophie dived for the key that was hanging above the toaster and opened it for him. He leant his head out and listened. "Quiet." A motorbike roared past on the busy road beyond Sophie's fence followed by the sound of a car horn and a screech of breaks. "Well, that's what I'll tell people anyway," he smirked.

He cast his eyes around inside some more.

"Nice units," he stopped looking around the kitchen and rested his eyes on Sophie, meeting her gaze. For a moment neither of them moved, standing in touching distance of each other. He opened his mouth as if to speak but then stopped and no words came out. Sophie willed him to pull her towards her and kiss her and a feeling of desire passed all over her body; she felt like she might actually melt from the inside out. For what seemed like minutes but was just a passing moment they stood, Christian unconsciously licking the corner of his lips as their eyes locked causing the feelings within Sophie to completely engulf her.

Crashing and clattering and squeals of delight coming from elsewhere in the house broke the silence and Christian looked shocked and concerned. Seconds ago Sophie was sure that he had been waiting for something to happen between them.

"What was *that*?" he asked.

Sophie sighed. Ollie. All I ask for is *five* minutes without a disturbance of some kind, she thought.

"That will be my son," she said with resignation in her voice and headed off to find the source of the noise, Christian following on her heels.

It didn't take them long to find the reason for all the commotion at the bottom of the stairs with Oliver holding one end of the bannister which had been pulled off the wall and Mr Ted strapped to a chair, goggles on and what Sophie thought was a startled look on his face.

"Oliver what *are* you doing?" Sophie asked, feeling slightly less patient with him than she normally was. "What have you *done* to the bannister?"

"What's a *bannister* mummy?" the boy asked.

"A *bannister,* darling, is the thing that you are holding in your hand!"

Christian took the bannister from Oliver and had a look at the way it was connected to the wall.

"It was just held on with screws," he said, "it should be quite simple to fix, I could do it easily. Bit of a botched job by the looks of it though," he said passing his hand over one of the holes that was now on the wall where the stonework had been pulled away. "It could have come away at any time," he looked at Oliver's teddy that was still attached to the chair with a belt that Sophie didn't recognise. "He's quite an adventurous bear then?" he asked Oliver, "seems like he's into his extreme sports?"

"He's Mr Ted," Oliver stated.

"Hello Mr Ted," Christian said. "What was he doing? Abseiling?"

Oliver shook his head and giggled as if this was the most ridiculous suggestion ever. "No! He was on a death slide!"

Christian nodded seriously. "Ah," he looked at Sophie and grinned, "lucky the boy wasn't hurt anyway, eh? Shall we go upstairs?"

Oh yes please, let's go upstairs, Sophie thought dreamily and followed Christian casting a disapproving eye at Oliver as she passed and mouthing, 'No more'. Christian popped his head into all the rooms.

"Bathroom. Nice and white," he looked into Oliver's room. "Bedroom two," he crossed the hall. "Bedroom three, not a bad size," he stopped outside Sophie's room. "Bedroom one."

Suddenly the fact that there was a double bed in her room seemed like it was there as an invitation to him. They both looked at it and again there was a moment of silence.

"Well," Christian eventually spoke. "You've got a really nice house. We've got houses like this on the market for just under two hundred thousand but with the garage and conservatory you should get a bit more than that," his phone in his pocket beeped and he took it out and looked at the screen. "Oh damn it I didn't realise the time," he looked at her regretfully, "I'm sorry I'm going to have to rush off. Do you still have my number?"

Sophie was disappointed that he had to go. "Yes. Yes, I've got it on your card, I think, the estate agency number anyway," she cringed at herself for suggesting that there should be another number that she had for him but he didn't notice.

"What's your number?" he asked almost causing Sophie to keel over, "I'll give you a call in the next few days, once you've had a chance to think about it."

Sophie recited her number as casually as she could while Christian keyed it into his phone, trying not to get too excited that he was taking it.

"Got that," he phoned her phone and they heard it ringing from downstairs. "There, now you've got my number too," he grinned and put the phone back in his pocket. "I'd better get going."

Sophie followed him down the stairs to where Ollie was trying to unfasten Mr Ted after his death slide experience.

"If I ever do a bungee or parachute jump," Christian said to the boy, "Mr Ted can come too, yeah?"

Oliver looked at Christian in complete awe and nodded his head.

"Cool," Christian responded to Ollie's nod. Sophie handed him his paperwork that she had collected from the dining room table and he took it, smiling. Their eyes met again. "Thanks."

"That's OK," Sophie said, mesmerised by his looks and charm. Another moment of silence passed.

"Anyway, I'd better go. Nice seeing you," he turned to address Oliver, "and you and Mr Ted. Take care," he said, shaking the bear's hand. Oliver giggled and Sophie swooned. He turned back to Sophie. "Take care."

***

Sophie was unable to think of much else at work the next day apart from Christian and his gorgeous blue eyes and seductive smile. The various times that they'd met merged into one happy daydream. The way that his mouth moved when he spoke and smiled and laughed had her hook, line and sinker. Each time she thought about him the daydream ended as he pulled her towards him and kissed her, gently at first and then passionately making her heart beat faster despite it all being in her head. Even Enid slurping down her spaghetti bolognaise at lunchtime didn't bother her that much as Sophie idly worked through a massive bundle of paper that she had been instructed to individually fold.

When she collected Oliver from school she announced to him that she thought that it was about time that he started to get pocket money and agreed to five pounds a week and gave him a bonus pound for saying 'Thank You'. She suggested that from now on Friday's should be known as 'Pizza Friday' and as soon as they got home she looked up pizza shops in the area to see if any delivered. She also agreed to the boy setting up a rather elaborate pulley system in his room to lift Mr Ted up in his chair to perform another death defying stunt. The feelings that Christian was giving her had definitely put her in a good mood and this carried her through to the next week, the prospect of him calling her even being enough to give her hope that one day they would be together. After he'd been round to the house he sent her a friend request on her social network site which she had accepted immediately. He didn't seem to use it much, there not being much activity on his wall, but there were a few gorgeous photos of him including one of him leaning against a wall with a little boy next to him in the same position. His nephew maybe, Sophie thought, and started to fall in love.

The following Friday Ben collected Oliver for the weekend as agreed. When he picked him up he showed Sophie his new calendar and asked her to let him know all the dates that he was to have the boy that year.

"It's every two weeks, Ben," she said flatly, wishing that he didn't need to make such a fuss about everything, like he was doing her some massive favour all the time.

Her mood was beginning to deflate somewhat after the week had passed with no phone call from Christian and that evening, when Ben had taken Ollie away, she got into her pyjamas, made a hot chocolate and got into bed with her lap top to have a look and see who her matches had been over the past days. Her friends all had various other commitments that night and so their drinks night had been postponed until the next week.

Her matches didn't give her any reason to cheer up, a stranger group of men Sophie had never seen before. There were some messages but mostly just winks, nudges and questions to answer. She suspected that what she could do was greatly limited by the fact that she wasn't willing to pay up yet. She had a look at all the questions that her matches had sent for her response, as if they would give them an accurate picture of me, she thought cynically. The questions were just plain weird and scary, some odd and some just boring. Joseph asked if she thought that leashes were a good idea on children. Wayne was a Safety Expert and asked her if she thought that risk assessment was necessary before foreplay. Clint was persisting with his questioning although she never responded and asked her if she thought that shops should charge for plastic bags. She did have an opinion about this but decided that the online dating site was not the place to discuss such matters. He then asked her if she preferred Weetabix or Coco Pops. Ah now you're talking, she thought. She stopped looking through the questions when she reached 'How often do you visit the doctor' and 'Do you lie to your dentist about your flossing habits', both which she thought were nobody else's business. Clint's list of questions was endless and Sophie snapped her computer shut thinking that he ought to get a life. She switched on the telly instead and propped herself up against her pillows, watching it until she inadvertently dropped off to sleep.

She woke up with a start at the sound of the door bell ringing. Looking at her phone for the time she saw that it was nearly 2am. She froze, still sitting up in bed with the telly on, listening with fright for it to ring again. Finding the remote control in between the folds of her duvet she switched the telly off so that she was in silence, able to hear the slightest sound. The only person she could imagine that was ringing her bell at 2am was an axe murderer and she pulled the duvet up to her chin as protection. The bell rung again and she gasped, clutching the duvet even closer. Oh God, she wailed in her head, this is one of the reasons that I *hate* being alone. She was too scared to go and see who it was and she continued to sit as still as a statue, willing for whoever it was to go away and bother someone else, working out her escape if they should happen to hack down the door. I'll climb out of my window and jump off the roof, she decided, if they follow me then I'll run up the middle of the road to the 24-hour garage at the top of the hill. Her phone was in her hand, poised to call her neighbours, as if they would be any match for a man with an axe.

Whoever was outside showed persistence as they held the bell down causing it to ring repeatedly for about half a minute. Oh God, Sophie wailed again, go away! Surely Pat and Peter next door could hear this too and would be round to save her soon.

The bell eventually fell silent and Sophie sat completely still and waited for a further sound. Nothing was heard. She sat and listened. Still nothing. Sitting in petrified silence she held her breath so as not to make any sound at all and listened. She jumped as her mobile phone rang in her hand. She hesitantly looked at the screen, half expecting the words 'Axe Murderer' to be showing as the caller ID. Instead it said, 'Christian'.

"Christian?" she said out loud, "*Christian?* What does he want?"

Such was her surprise that he was calling that she forgot to answer and the phone stopped ringing.

"Damn," she said and continued to look at the screen, waiting for it to ring again. It did seconds later and she answered.

"Hello?" she said gingerly, half expecting it to be someone else on the other end other than Christian.

"Hi! Sophie! It's Christian!" he whispered loudly. "You know, Christian from the estate agency."

Sophie decided not to even pretend that she didn't know which Christian it was.

"Hi!" she said brightly as if it wasn't unexpected that he should be calling at such an early hour. "How are you?" Why am I exchanging formalities at this time in the morning, she thought?

"Yeah, alright!" Christian answered. "Listen, can I come in? Are you home? I'm standing outside your house!"

Oh my God, Sophie thought, of all the times for him to come round why did he choose now when I've been snoozing and have a puffy face and crazy bed head? She felt rather dull to have gone to bed on a Friday night rather than hitting the town. Why has he come round, she wondered?

"Erm, yeah! I was in bed actually... I've just woken up..." her voice trailed off, wondering how she could improve her appearance on her way to the front door. "I'll be down in a sec."

She grimaced as she remembered that the green knickers she was wearing under her pyjamas had a pattern of little red apples on them. Why would that ever be an OK pattern on grown up pants, she thought, what *was* I thinking that day? Lou was clearly right about needing sexy underwear. She quickly opened the top drawer of her chest of drawers and rummaged around for a pair of less embarrassing knickers, finding a black pair with lace edging. That's better, she thought, if not very exciting. She took her pyjama's and apple pants off in favour of the black knickers and then put a more grown up t-shirt on and hurried down the stairs to open the front door, running her hand through her hair to try and detangle it. At least it's dark, she thought, deciding not to put the lights on.

Christian stood outside looking slightly the worst for wear with his shoulders hunched and his hands thrust deep in his jeans pockets. He was wearing a thin V-neck sweater over a white t-shirt and looked cold in the night time chill. He grinned sheepishly at Sophie when she opened the door.

"Hi," he said, "Sorry it's late… Can I come in?"

Sophie laughed and said that it was fine, as if it was a normal occurrence for her to have gentleman callers in the early hours of the morning. She stood back indicating for him to come in.

Christian stepped into the house and kissed her on the cheek politely. Before the door was shut he was tenderly kissing her, his hands gently cupping her face and stroking her hair. Sophie was taken aback, not quite believing that it was happening, the thing that she had daydreamed about for days. As the week had passed she had become more and more fed up waiting for him to call and by that evening she had given up hope completely, deciding that she must have got the wrong end of the stick about the whole thing. Why would he fancy me anyway, she thought, some dowdy old single mum?

"I've been waiting for this to happen," he said softly in between kisses. He looked at her with drunken puppy dog eyes, his lips glistening in the street light that came through the frosted glass window at the top of her front door, "since I met you I've been waiting for this. I want you so much."

***

Sophie traced her finger over the strong curves of Christian's chest as they lay naked together in her bed. His arm was around her and she gazed lovingly at his face as he stared up to the ceiling thoughtfully. She never lay naked in bed but with him it felt just right. All she wanted to ask him was what he was thinking but she had read somewhere that that was one of the questions you shouldn't ask a man after making love. He looked down to her adoring eyes and kissed the top of her head.

"I wish that this had happened a long time ago," he said as if in answer to her question.

"It's happened now?" she replied, not quite sure what he meant.

"Yes. Yes, it's happened now," he kissed the top of her head again.

***

"Shit!" Christian exclaimed as he picked up his watch which had been cast aside on the bed. "Shit, is that the time?"

Sophie woke up and was instantly aware that her face was pressed up against his chest, her hair having drastically messed itself up in the night and her mouth open. She quickly shut her mouth, passing her fingers round her lips and chin to check for dribble. Why do I go to sleep with normal straight hair and wake up with a *haystack,* she thought, as if I've had electric shock treatment in the night? She breathed in the smell of Christian's skin and kissed his chest, smiling at him as she remembered the events of the early hours of the morning.

"Morning," she smiled again, willing him to stay in bed for a little longer so that she could enjoy the feeling of his strong arms around her and the warmth of his body next to hers. He didn't look like that was his plan.

"Hi. My alarm didn't go off!" he said, rubbing his forehead with the flat of his hand, "I can't *believe* I forgot to set it! Today of all days."

I can believe it, Sophie thought and grinned remembering the way that Christian had kissed her just hours before. She sighed deeply, I can believe it, she thought again. He put his watch back on and got out of bed, walking over to where his clothes had been abandoned at various points of their route from the bottom of the stairs to the bed. She watched him as he went, admiring his muscular body. He didn't look much like an estate agent.

"Have you got to go?" she asked him sadly, pulling the duvet up to cover herself.

Christian stood in the middle of the floor naked, holding his clothes. He dropped the bundle apart from his boxers and pulled them on.

"Yeah I've got work; we can't all laze around in bed all day," he laughed, "I'll see you soon though?"

Sophie nodded. She wanted to jump up and down on the bed and shout out, yes see me soon, but decided that it was too soon to show such enthusiasm.

He hurriedly got dressed and sat down on the edge of the bed where Sophie lay. He pushed a strand of hair away from her face and lent down and kissed her fondly, holding her chin in his hand. He pulled back and looked at her, stroking his finger around her lips before kissing her again.

"Last night was amazing," he said, "I wanted that for so long. *You* are amazing," he looked at her fondly, "I thought something was going to happen last time I came round, I had to come back and see you. I'm so sorry I have to go," and with that he kissed on the end of her nose, got up and hurried off down the stairs. She lay back in bed and heard the door shutting downstairs. Shutting her eyes she could still smell him and taste his kisses. I could live on this feeling forever, she thought.

***

Lethargy crept over Sophie that morning causing her to delay her usual run. She lay in bed until nearly midday lost in thoughts about Christian and his incredible body and the kisses that she could still feel on her lips, clutching her mobile in her hand in case he should send her a message as he worked. He hadn't said anything but she assumed that she might see him later, once he'd finished. When she eventually got up she made herself go out for a while and ran down to the country park, passing the group who ran there. Their numbers were smaller than normal today but she recognised the leader as she passed and smiled, feeling like she was floating on air. I won't need to go there to find a man, she thought as she passed the group.

At around four o'clock Sophie had a bath and got herself ready as if she were going out on a date. The feeling of excitement and desire was still strong inside her. She was ready by five and sat idly on the sofa under the window, waiting in hope that Christian would appear unannounced once again, her mind drifting back to earlier that morning when they had kissed so passionately and slept entwined all night. For a while she sat, jumping at the sound of each car that drove into her close and then feeling the huge disappointment when each car drove away. Eventually she decided that she should do something to pass the time and so she fetched her computer from her room and switched it on with the intention of searching for a suitable Hen Do venue. Tina had also suggested badges, hats and other accessories that they might need and so she searched various party sites to see what they had, every so often checking her watch. By six o'clock she had ordered what she thought would be a perfect Hen Do kit and just had the venue to book. After a conversation with her sister earlier in the week she made a shortlist of three cottages that would sleep them all and emailed them to her. They had decided that if they booked somewhere to stay for the weekend then they could decide the details nearer the time.

It was fairly late by the time Sophie decided that Christian was not going to show and that she should just go to bed. He might turn up at 2am again, she thought hopefully as she made herself comfy on the bed to watch some telly. She gazed at it blindly though, unable to concentrate on anything else apart from her memories from the night before and she closed her eyes to remember; the feeling of his warm body next to hers, his arms around her, his hands moving all over her body, the way that he smelt and tasted, the way it felt to be kissed by him. She eventually dozed off. About 11pm she was woken by a text and got a lovely feeling that it was Christian, apologising for being so late but offering some genuine reason. She picked up her phone and saw that it was her sister instead. She sighed deeply and opened the message to see what it said. Jo had looked at Sophie's suggested venues and liked one in particular and thought that Sophie should enquire about and book it, Mum will pay, she said, it can go on the bill.

Sophie sighed again. She might as well do that now. She reached for her lap top and switched it on despondently. She felt so sad that Christian hadn't come round or even bothered to text. She had an urge to look at a photo of him and logged into her social networking site for a quick fix. She went to her home page first to see if anything interesting had been happening. At the top there was a picture of Debbie and her boys at the park. No Steve again, Sophie thought. Lou had also posted a picture, this one of her children with Simon on a family day out to the zoo.

Sophie idly scrolled down the news feed but wasn't interested in what was happening to other people today. She was just about to go to Christian's page to look at his photos when a news story caught her eye. She saw his name. She felt the butterflies fluttering in her tummy as she began to read the update. He had been tagged in some photos. Oh, Sophie thought, that's why he's not called, he's been at a wedding. She looked more closely and suddenly felt a sick feeling replace the one of pure lovely joy that had been with her that day.

"What?" she said out loud, "What?" she repeated as a feeling of confusion took over. Her breathing quickened and she felt the tears stinging her eyes; on her face a look of complete bewilderment took over. Christian had been tagged in someone's photos. Sophie stared at him, dressed up in a grey suit with a yellow cummerbund around his waist and cravat neatly tied around his neck, a flower in his lapel and a look of adoration on his face as he held the hands of a brunette who wore a wedding dress. They were standing at what looked unmistakably like an altar. He had been tagged in his own wedding photos.

***

"What does she have that I don't?" Sophie whispered to Joules, trying to be quiet so as not to wake her boys' despite being at the other end of the phone. Her text to Joules, "What a shit how could he do that to me?" sounding so desperate that her friend had called her almost immediately.

"How about an engagement ring? Or, I should say, a wedding ring. I hope he didn't say his vows in a church, he doesn't *exactly* live up to his name does he?" Joules had said slightly harshly after hearing the whole story, having no patience for cheating men before realising that Sophie was genuinely upset. "Oh Sophie, it's nothing to do with what you have or don't have, he's just a man. A stupid, idiotic man. He probably doesn't even know what he's doing because his thoughts are controlled by his dick and no doubt he was plastered when he turned up at yours. I feel sorry for his wife too- how would you feel if you're new husband had slept with someone during the early hours of his own *wedding day?*"

"Oh don't say that, Joules, I feel terrible enough as it is. I had no idea! Every time I saw him I felt this electricity between us, like something was going to happen. He didn't give me *any* indication that he was *engaged,*" she sighed deeply, "he was *so* lovely…"

"Oi!" Joules snapped, "not that lovely! I don't think cheating on his new wife and messing you around like this is very *lovely!*"

"I know…" Sophie agreed, "It's just, you know… if he wasn't such a shit…"

"Yes well he is so don't even give it a second thought. I'd put it on his social network wall about what a shit he is. He must be one of those idiots who has more than one profile- one for his wife and family to see and one for all of his bits on the side."

Sophie sighed again. All of this was news to her; she had no idea that not everyone was just genuine.

"Sorry if I woke you up, Joules. I had to talk to someone."

"That's OK. Steve is out clubbing with his friends or something anyway, I was watching a late night film and stuffing my face with popcorn. I need to come running with you one day, I've been promising myself that I'll go on a diet for years- I don't have anyone to look good for though so what's the point," she laughed hollowly.

"Me neither. Next time I'll come round to yours and help you eat the popcorn."

Chapter Ten

Enid was standing waiting in the office as Sophie arrived for work on Monday morning after spending the rest of the weekend feeling love sick over Christian, and helpless which suddenly made her feel very alone. She had spent a considerable amount of time thinking about each and every occasion she had seen Christian and was *sure* that she hadn't imagined the attraction between them. She definitely hadn't imagined the way that he had kissed her when he had turned up at her house during the early hours of the morning. She couldn't work out what had really gone on but the thought that her feelings had just been so blatantly trampled on by someone that she cared for a lot was too much for her to think about and so she tried to adopt Tina's 'all men are bastards' approach and put on a brave face while feeling worthless, unlovable and used. This particular Monday morning was the first that she wasn't actually dreading work, deciding that she couldn't feel any worse than she did anyway and that the distraction would probably do her some good- better that than sitting at the computer poring over the wedding pictures. The sight of Enid didn't even give her the usual mixed feelings of dread, hatred, boredom and sickness, so low was her mood. Enid stood in her blue trouser suit with her arms folded, seemingly waiting for Sophie to arrive.

"You might as well not sign in because we're going out," she said, without as much as a 'Good Morning'.

"She has to sign in," Tim hesitantly piped up from the far corner of the communal desks, a worried look on his face but determined to put Enid right on the signing in and out policy, "staff must sign in in *that* book," he said pointing to the signing in book, "but then sign out for a visit in *that* book."

Silence came over the office.

Enid fixed her stare on Tim as if stunned that anyone should have the gall to contradict her then she bustled out of the office snapping, "Keys and phone", which Sophie assumed was to her. She looked at Tim helplessly, never having gone out in a work car before. Enid appeared again buttoning up a blue outdoor coat.

"Come *on* Sophie, hurry up! We don't have all day. Get the keys and phone. The car keys for the car that you booked me last week and the phone that goes with it," she sighed loudly, "do I need to spell out *everything* for you? And you won't need that," she said indicating to Sophie's coat, "or *that,*" pointing to her bag, "only Elm Tree coats and bags are taken outside the school, as I'm sure you are aware. Yours are on order but in the meantime you will just have to come as you are."

Sophie instantly felt panicked. She always carried her mobile in case someone needed to contact her about Ollie. She thought of the procedure that his school secretary would have to go through if there was an emergency at his school or if he had an accident. If anyone had to get in touch with Sophie through the Elm Tree office if she wasn't in the building then it would take so long that they would give up, she was sure. They would no doubt have to prove their identity over the phone for Tim to give out information regarding Sophie's location, a message would be taken and he would tell them that he would call back. He would then probably try to call the work mobile but Enid would have it switched off anyway because nobody would ever need to contact *her* and the first Sophie would know about it would be when Ollie didn't come out of school with the rest of the class at the end of the day and the teacher would look at her with shock and concern and say he'd been taken to hospital four hours ago and they had tried to call her work. She needed to bring her own phone.

"I'm sure Tim will look after your bag," Enid continued, "I don't think we have any *thief's* in school. Now come on we are expected at ten thirty."

"Where will I put these then?" Sophie asked, holding up a couple of tampons for all to see, feeling pleased at her quick thinking skills. Enid stared at them for a moment as did everyone else in the office, including a parent who was signing in some medicine for their child and a window cleaner who had just appeared to do the inside of the office windows. Sophie didn't care who was watching, she just needed to bring her phone so she kept her arm aloft, tampons on show until she got the reply she wanted.

"Oh just bring your bag then."

A small victory, Sophie thought and grinned at a fumbling Tim, clearly the sort of man who couldn't cope with 'women's problems'.

She found the car key in the key safe and with some help from Tim the mobile that went with the Nissan and rushed out after Enid to the car park. The fresh air was preferable to the stuffy office and Sophie breathed it in gratefully. Enid turned to her and extended her hand to take the key.

"Which one have we got today then?" she asked almost playfully, Sophie thought, as if leaving the office raised her spirits as it did for everyone else. Enid stopped in her tracks when she saw the Nissan key ring that was being given to her. Sophie instantly knew that she'd made the wrong car decision.

"What's this?" Enid asked, holding up the key and looking at Sophie with the same withering look that she was used to, the cheerful playfulness having instantly gone. It didn't last for long, Sophie thought. She decided that the answer to the question was too obvious to articulate and so kept her mouth shut. Enid clearly wanted an answer though and continued to stare at Sophie, one eyebrow raised and lips pursed in disapproval. Not a day passed when Sophie wasn't asked a question that was so simple and yet impossible to respond to and so, as she often did, she opted for the silent approach.

"I asked you to book me a *car* not a *tin can!*" Enid snapped. "Did you think that it would be *appropriate* to turn up at Saint Andrew's School, our nearest competition, in *that*?"

"But Laura told me..." Sophie started but Enid pushed past her to go back into the school before she could finish.

Sophie stayed stuck to the spot, not sure if she was required to follow Enid or not. She saw her through the office window shouting at someone, no doubt Tim, and pointing outside to the car park. Poor Tim, she thought and felt terrible that he always seemed to get into trouble for Sophie's mistakes. She carried on watching as Enid stopped and listened with the same look on her face that was usually reserved for Sophie, with her hands on her hips, leaning forward slightly, intimidatingly. Enid eventually shook her head, rolling her eyes to the ceiling and disappeared from view, appearing again out of the staff door and straight past Sophie with a look of thunder on her face. Sophie scuttled after her, now dreading the car journey even more, the thought of being in a confined space with Enid not being an attractive one at the best of times. Nice one Laura, Sophie thought ruefully despite being slightly impressed by her sneaky trick, thanks for landing me in it again. No sooner had she thought this she heard the main door to the school open and out breezed Laura with a satisfied look on her face, straight past Enid and Sophie to one of the black Audi's. She pressed her key fob and the car lights flashed to indicate that it was open.

"Bye ladies!" she called back and got into the car. She closed the door and it made an expensive thud.

Enid muttered something under her breath that sounded to Sophie like, 'annoying cow' but she couldn't be sure as the noise of the Audi reversing over the gravel drowned her out. She pressed her own key fob to open the Nissan but it didn't work so, muttering some more, she stomped over to open it manually.

"Get in," she barked.

Sophie did as she was told and gingerly got into the passenger side, clipping her seat belt shut. She sat hugging her bag on her knees and then decided to put it on the floor between her feet, out of view, so as not to incur Enid's wrath any more than she had done already. The floral satchel suddenly looked rather scruffy, even in this clapped out second hand car. Sophie wasn't exactly sure where Saint Andrews school was, private schools not ever having been on her radar, but she hoped the journey would be short; the atmosphere being awkward to say the least. The two sat in silence for some time, elbow to elbow, Sophie leaning her legs towards the passenger door to avoid Enid touching them every time she went into first gear.

"So, we're going to Saint Andrew's School," Enid eventually spoke, "they have asked us, as a *private* establishment, to undertake some training for them. It could be a very lucrative contract. They asked *specifically* for the training manager to give a presentation to show them what we can offer. Mrs Wright suggested that you should come too, I'm not sure why," Enid mumbled as an afterthought. "If they like what they hear then we could have work with them for many years to come, while the bulk of their staff complete their qualifications. They seem to have had a new influx of staff. Today's presentation is *very* important and I have been working hard to make sure that it's just right. In the private sector as you are now, we have to *work* for our money, it's not just *handed* to us like you will be used to in the public sector."

Sophie sat in unimpressed silence. Here we go, she thought, here's the public/private sector debate.

"You're in the private sector now, although, it is still questionable as to whether you are actually cut out for it," Enid continued. "In the public sector nobody cares about standards, it's just 'funding' and 'get them through'. Well, here in the *private* sector we have to *impress* people for them to choose us and if we don't get contracts then we don't have work and if we don't have work then we don't have jobs. We have to have the highest *standards,*" Enid smiled smugly. "When we go out of the school we must always uphold the high standards that we have set for ourselves."

I'll try not to randomly swear then or pick my nose, Sophie thought and continued to hold her silence. She had nothing to say to Enid as she completely disagreed with her but trying to have another point of view was more trouble than Sophie had found it was worth. My standards were always very high when I was in the public sector and so was everyone else's, she reminded herself.

"Saint Andrew's is one of the most expensive schools in the south of England," Enid went on, "it has had *millions* spent on it- on the building though, not the teachers. Their outcomes are not very good, well, by our standards. They need us and we need them. And here's a little test for you- Mrs Wright would like to know what you think of the place," Enid challenged her and looked over at Sophie, "although why your opinion should count I have *no* idea."

Oh great, Sophie thought, not liking the word 'test' as it made it sound like her employment depended it. She smiled wanly at Enid and then turned to look out of the passenger side window.

They drove out of the town and carried on for some time through the suburbs and then along country roads, through quaint English villages and past fields shining bright yellow with rape seed. Enid eventually slowed down and indicated and turned the car down a leafy driveway and they carried on down this under a tunnel of trees until they stopped at an imposing wrought iron gate. Enid looked around her dash board, trying to find the button to open the windows but couldn't locate one and so started to wind it down instead, with the handle on the inside of the door, so that she could talk to the intercom that was on the stone gate post. A voice crackled through the speaker and Enid leant her head out of her window to reply, at which point the Nissan stalled. Sophie cringed, sure that Enid was on the verge of a total meltdown about the car situation.

Enid paused, composed herself and brought her head back into the car starting the engine again. The gates slowly started to open.

"They are expecting us," Enid said in explanation, "what they're going to think when they see us in *this* I have no idea. First impressions are so important…"

Sophie wasn't sure if she was supposed to respond to this but decided to remain silent as she felt she had caused enough upset for one day. They drove through as the gates opened and continued along the drive until a 19th Century mansion house came into view, set as it was in the tranquil countryside, surrounded by trees.

"Wow," Sophie said, impressed by the beautiful old building.

"Yes well as I said they have spent a lot of money on the *exterior*. We're not here to judge the outside."

Enid continued to drive past the building and found a space around the back, no doubt tucked away so that nobody would notice the car they had arrived in, Sophie thought. She smoothed her hands over her suit as she got out of the car, directing Sophie to smarten herself up too.

"First impressions…" Enid reminded her.

As they walked back round to the front of the school Sophie cast her eyes over the cars in this car park but didn't see many expensive looking ones- some looked to be more clapped out than their Micra. Such a fuss about nothing, she thought.

Enid rang the bell and the two stood there like the heavy mob, in their dark suits and sour faces. Enid held her black brief case as if she were a door-to-door sales person ready to show off her wares. A moment later they heard footsteps and the door was pulled open.

"Ah, good morning, good morning!" a well-spoken, middle-aged man greeted them warmly, smiling broadly and extending his arms, "how lovely to meet you! Just *lovely!* Enid!" he continued to gush turning towards her and clutching her arms by the sides, "after so many emails and telephone calls it is a pleasure! And who have you brought with you?" he released Enid and swung round to view Sophie. "This must be Sophie, the lady with the degree!" he threw his arms up in wonder and twinkled his eyes at

Sophie as if she were the second coming. Sophie smiled and shook his hand. "Donald. It is a *pleasure* to meet such a pretty thing."

"Hi," she said simply and smiled finding Donald to be an extremely likeable man. She was amused that he knew who she was and that she had a degree, 'degree' usually being a dirty word at work and she couldn't begin to imagine Enid telling someone about it in a positive way.

"The lovely Enid has told me *all* about you!" Donald continued as he led them through the grand carpeted entrance hall to a small office overlooking the grounds. "But she didn't tell me how attractive you were," his eyes flashed mischievously at Sophie causing her to giggle. Enid smiled indulgently but Sophie was sure that she wouldn't be so indulgent later. "I hope that you found a space in our car park?" Donald said lightly. "Some of our staff sometimes pop their cars on to the grass as it gets so busy! Did you? I usually walk, though, or cycle, can't stand driving. Can't stand cars actually, especially those damn big things. Anyway, take a seat. I say," he said to Sophie, "I like your bag, what fun!"

***

"Reflections?" Enid asked Sophie on leaving Saint Andrews, after five awkward minutes of silence travelling back to the Elm Tree school.

Sophie wasn't sure what she meant, wishing she would just speak in proper sentences sometimes.

"Do you have any reflections on our visit?" Enid asked with impatience. "It's always good to reflect upon the things that we do and identify ways that we can improve our own practice."

Sophie's mood deflated again. She had had rather a pleasant morning in the company of Donald who turned out to be the principal of Saint Andrews and a very jolly man. Such a jolly man she had never met and he had taken a definite shine to her, addressing her for most of the meeting and telling Enid not to be such a bore when she tried to talk about money. Sophie's main reflection, though, was the complete personality change that she had witnessed in Enid that morning- from evil dragon to twittery girl in minutes- the effect that Donald had had on her was quite remarkable. She had tucked her hair behind her ear girlishly and even fluttered her eye lashes at one point, Sophie couldn't believe the sweet smile that was fixed on her face as she tilted her head to the side and listened to Donald, lapping up every word that he said.

"Everyone was really nice," she said feebly.

Donald had explained what his staff training requirements were and from what Sophie had gathered, as Enid's proposal was the cheapest, that was why he had chosen them.

"It's OK," he had said to Enid towards the end of their meeting, "you can stop crawling to me now. I've already decided to use you," and he flashed another smile at Sophie, as if they were sharing a private joke.

Sophie had been responsible for printing out all the paperwork for the day which Donald had taken and put in a drawer in his mahogany desk. From what she had seen Sophie imagined that that is where the paperwork would stay, Donald had been more interested in the people involved and how the training would take place rather than the paperwork.

"He seemed keen for us to do the training," Sophie continued bravely.

"Bullshit baffles brains," Enid said and chuckled.

What an odd morning, Sophie thought. She started to roll down the window, feeling hot in her black wool jacket. Enid made a face of displeasure.

"Hot are we?"

"Oh I just like fresh air…" Sophie trailed off, everything she did or said was wrong.

"I like fresh air too… when it's outside."

Sophie wound the window back up- anything for a quiet life.

***

For once Sophie was relieved to be back at the Elm Tree- the return journey in the tiny red car squashed up close to Enid being uncomfortable to say the least. It had taken some time for them to get back as Enid had stopped for petrol, a sandwich and what Sophie was sure was a packet of cigarettes, all of which she thought must be against the Driving Back to School Policy which she was sure existed somewhere. She mentally put 'checking policies' on her To-Do-List for the afternoon.

"Put the keys and phone back," Enid ordered as they made their way back into the school, "and then I'd like you to send Mr Ogilvie, *Donald,* an email saying what a pleasure it was etcetera and if there's *anything* else he'd like to know. Then Mrs Wright asked for that…"

She stopped mid-sentence as they heard raised voices coming from the direction that they were heading. Sophie slowed down, wanting to avoid any disturbances. Raised voices were common in the downstairs office as bolder members of the teaching staff took issue with Mrs Wright over various procedures that they were expected to follow but that were usually downright bonkers. Sophie could never quite believe that such heated arguments were conducted in the communal office and not behind closed doors as everyone could hear them from there, including parents and visitors, but Mrs Wright's attitude seemed to be 'This is my school and I will shout if I want to'.

Enid carried on through to the hallway but Sophie stopped in her tracks, deciding to watch proceedings from behind the door rather than get involved. The voices belonged to the principal, as ever, and Laura. They both stood just inside the office for all to see and hear, their voices echoing down the corridors and up the stairs. The principal was shaking her clenched fist in Laura face and in the other was a crumpled piece of paper. Laura seemed to be stuck to the spot she was standing and was leaning back in order to avoid a strike, a startled look on her face. Sophie had witnessed a lot of unbelievable things within these walls since the beginning of her employment but not yet actual violence.

"And *what is it* that I'm paying you for?" the principal spat in Laura face, her body actually shaking with rage. "How long have you wasted on this piece of utter crap? I wanted an eye catching, *original* and informative pamphlet showing *at a glance* what qualifications we offered. This is a…" she spotted Sophie hovering just inside the staff entrance and swooped on her, ignoring Enid completely, "Miss Bridges, just the person I was looking for. We need an educated opinion. Tell me what you think of *this!*"

Sophie casually sauntered out of her hiding place as if it were perfectly natural that she should be behind the door and hesitantly made her way towards Mrs Wright and Laura with a feeling of impending doom. One way or the other she was about to offend someone. She glanced apologetically at Laura and looked with interest at Mrs Wright, suddenly keen to keep her job. The principal thrust the ball of paper towards Sophie who took it and gingerly flattened it out with her hands.

"Tell me first, does it make any sense?" Mrs Wright looked at Sophie expectantly. Sophie fixed her eyes on the paper and wondered if there was any way she could get out of answering the question. "Sometime today would be preferable."

Sophie always felt a huge pressure to make some highly intellectual observation, her university degree making everyone expect nothing less. She studied the leaflet that Laura had made and couldn't make sense of it at all. She knew that it showed the values of each qualification that they offered and the different paths that learners could take to obtain them, because they had discussed it in the office just last week, but the way that Laura had set it out was very confusing and didn't visually explain anything at all. The logo and graphics that she had used were also all misaligned making the whole thing look unprofessional. Sophie didn't want to be too critical of Laura though as, to be fair, nobody else had wanted to do it.

"Can you tell me what it says to you?" the principal asked, now with some impatience in her voice. Sophie steeled herself.

"I'm not really sure what its saying..." she said as she kept her eyes firmly on the paper, not wanting to catch either woman's eye. "although…" she started to change her mind, "you can see that these are all the different qualifications…"

"Mm, just as I thought. And what about the logo, what do you think about that?"

"Um…" Sophie took a deep breath," It looks fine… well… that bit… might be a bit wonky…"

The principal let out a breathy laugh. "Wonky? Is that what they say at university these days? Yes, you are right though, it is all 'a bit wonky'. Thank you Sophie you may go."

Sophie hurried up the stairs to their office as fast as she could without breaking into a run cursing under her breath for not coming out with a slightly better observation than 'it's a bit wonky'. She could hear Mrs Wright's voice yelling at Laura, who Sophie now felt extremely sorry for, and just before she reached the top she heard a scream and what sounded like a scuffle. She imagined the two women scrapping, Laura trying to pull at Mrs Wright's hair extensions and Mrs Wright kicking at Laura to let go. She laughed at the absurdity of it all.

Sophie burst into the office where Ruth and Pam were completely unaware of the raised voices downstairs, both deeply engrossed in their work. They both looked up and smiled as she came into the office, Ruth taking off her headphones and shaking out her hair.

"Have you had a good morning?" she asked with a smile.

Sophie shuddered. "Have *you* ever been in a car with Enid?" she asked and shuddered again. "Hideous. Laura is getting a massive telling off downstairs by the way. Didn't you hear? It looked like Mrs Wright was about to take a swing at her- because the little flowers logo was out of line."

"Oh those flowers are *terrible!*" Pam replied, "I've tried to do something with them before and they just move! Oh poor Laura…"

As she said this the office door opened and Laura came in looking decidedly rattled, her hair all dishevelled and the colour completely gone from her face. She ignored her three colleagues and went to sit at her desk and switched on her computer looking blankly at the screen with an almost ethereal expression. Enid followed her in shortly afterwards and in a rare moment of what seemed like compassion she asked Laura if she was alright. Laura rubbed her temple where Sophie now noticed there was quite a red mark.

"I blame myself," Laura said to no one in particular, "it wasn't the *best* piece of work I've ever done, Mrs Wright was *right.* I just couldn't get the logo to stay in the right place." She shook her head and brought her hand up to her temple to feel the lump that had appeared, "I deserved it really. I should have tried much harder to get it right."

"Deserved what?" Sophie asked, feeling hugely guilty, feeling that her 'wonky' remark was partly to blame for what had just happened.

Nobody answered.

"What did you deserve, Laura?" Pam asked gently. "It looks like you have a nasty bruise on your head…"

Enid made her way over to her desk, making no comment on the situation.

"Oh my God, Laura, did someone *hit you*?" Pam continued, showing real concern. "What, did Mrs *Wright* hit you? Whatever your leaflet was like, it's not a reason for someone to *hit you!*"

Laura shook her head and continued to look at her computer screen.

"It's nothing," she said, shut her eyes and clamped her lips firmly shut, offering no more information on the matter.

***

Sophie sat with Ollie in the kitchen listening to him read, her mind drifting back to Laura and her head injury. The massive lump that had developed on her temple had an imprint that looked very much like the mark a ring would make and Mrs Wright did wear a sizeable diamond on her wedding ring finger. All evidence pointed to the conclusion that she had taken a swing at Laura and made a firm contact to her left temple with her left fist. Quite impressive for such a small woman, Sophie had initially thought, and with a left hook too. The consensus of opinion between herself, Pam and Ruth was that Mrs Wright could be charged with assault but Laura would hear none of it and Enid had stopped the conversation accusing it of being slanderous.

Just another day in the mad house, Sophie though. Nothing surprised her about the place these days and she turned her attention to Ollie, dismissing all thoughts about work and concentrating on what he was reading.

"What's it called again?" Sophie asked, focussing on the job in hand.

"My Grandma," Ollie replied and carried on.

"Ah. OK," she said and listened patiently to the rather dull story about going to the green grocer with Grandma, trying not to butt in and help when Ollie slowly sounded out his words.

A text alert sounded on her phone distracting her attention and she looked around the kitchen, trying to locate the sound.

"That was good reading mister," she said to Ollie as she opened the fridge to check she hadn't left her phone in there, "do you want to go and play while I make your tea?" the boy rushed off, happy that his homework was done for the evening. The phone beeped again with a second text helping Sophie to find it under a bundle of crushed letters that Ollie seemed to have been saving in his school bag.

You're Mrs Popular, Sophie said to herself looking at her phone to see who the messages were from. She smiled despite herself, Phil and sexy Dan. She laughed at the name that the girls had christened him.

"Ooh which one first?" she said.

Deciding to go for Phil she braced herself for some inappropriate shoe remarks. It simply said, 'Hello gorgeous, how are you?' The 'Hello gorgeous' part gave her self-esteem a much needed boost. On opening the second text she smiled as it also started with 'Hello gorgeous'.

Am I really gorgeous, she thought, or do they just not have anything else going on right now? She text back, 'Fine thanks how are you?' wondering if she could have a whole conversation with both men using the same reply.

Phil's message came first, 'Always good when I'm talking to you', followed by Dan's, 'Not bad, could be improved by a hot date'. Sophie laughed.

"Phil, one. Dan, nil." She said to herself, thinking that Phil sounded less sleazy.

'Lol,' she replied to both, 'what have you been up to?'

The texts flew back and forth from then, she had barely replied to one when the other sent their response.

'Thinking about your shoes,' Phil replied. Sophie rolled her eyes. Here we go, she thought.

'Work mainly… and planning our threesome,' Dan's reply came. She shook her head thinking, one track minds.

She replied light-heartedly at first but then began to tire of the banter having other things to do and started to pay less attention to who was saying what and eventually slipped up and sent a text asking about rugby matches to Dan. His reply was swift.

'Whoa there tiger who else are you talking to? Maybe it's someone to join us for some fun?'

Sophie immediately felt like an idiot and lost all interest in both conversations.

Why does everything always have to end up being about sex, she thought craving for a normal chat.

'No of course not,' she lied.

'Shame,' Dan replied.

Sophie sighed and put her phone down on the kitchen side, deciding she'd wasted enough time on that conversation. He might be gorgeous, she thought, but he is turning out to be a bit of a pest. She went upstairs to check that Ollie was alright and found him sitting up on his bed reading an encyclopaedia. She watched him for a moment.

"What are you reading about darling?" she asked moving over to where he sat to look at the page he was on, "I bet it's something *really* interesting!" she climbed up onto his cabin bed and sat herself right next to him, putting her arm around his shoulders.

The boy looked slightly irritated that his mother had interrupted him.

"I'm just reading about black holes," he replied without looking up at her.

"Wow, black holes! That sounds good! What can you tell me about black holes? Mummy doesn't know that much about them."

Ollie moved his body away slightly and put his arm around his book, much like Sophie remembered doing in High School Maths lessons on the odd occasions that she had actually got the correct answer and didn't want anyone to copy her.

"It's just like a vacuum that uses the power of gravity to pull things towards it," he answered politely and continued to read. "Actually, Mummy, you're disturbing me. I'm trying to read."

Sophie's initial reaction was to tell him not to be rude but she decided to let it pass, admiring his directness but regretting that he was growing up so fast.

"At least I know where I stand with you darling man," she said as she jumped down off his bed, "you'll have to stop reading in about twenty minutes though when I've made your tea- just for a little bit."

"Oh! Mummy!" the boy protested, "I don't want to put my book away! I *hate* you!" he said throwing his encyclopaedia down on his pillows and making a very angry face.

"There's no need for that mister. I didn't say right now, I said in twenty minutes and then you can read again after tea! Don't spoil things by being rude."

The boy continued to look at her with a sulky mouth and furrowed brow.

"Don't look at Mummy like that please darling. Anyway, I'm making you your favourite scrambled eggs for tea," Sophie said lightly. His face instantly changed to one of joy.

"Scrambled eggs I *love* you! You're the best Mummy in the whole wide world!" he smiled happily and picked up his book and continued to read.

Make up your mind which one it is; although, you're stuck with me either way, she thought, smiling indulgently at the boy who was once again engrossed in his reading and went back downstairs to carry on with tea, children are so fickle.

She wasn't surprised to see that her phone was flashing on the kitchen side. She sighed and left it for a while, humming to herself as she made Ollie's tea. They can wait, she thought, until the phone beeped again, then again, then again and so she gave in and took a look to see who it was.

'No offence intended!' the first one read, 'I actually wanted to say I'm down your way this Friday- you free for a drink?'

'Are you still there sexy?' the second read, and then a third, 'Did I say something?' and then a fourth, 'I'm taking it your busy. Text me later. I thought I could take you and your heels out on Saturday?'

"Oh God!" Sophie put her phone back down and continued with her tea preparations, muttering under her breath. "Shut the crap up about my bloody shoes for one fucking second. Jesus! What an idiot. Shit for brains you wa…" she stopped herself and whirled around, aware of a presence behind her. Ollie stood in the doorway his mouth hanging open and his little eyes popping out of his head.

"And those, darling, are all the words we're *not* allowed to say. Jump up for tea then."

Chapter Eleven

Now that they had settled down into a routine of Ollie going to Ben's every two weeks it was much easier for Sophie to plan ahead and it felt good to be able to arrange some more dates. Both Dan and Phil were very keen to see her and she decided that she really should see them again, just in case one of them was actually Mr Right. Yes, Dan did seem a little preoccupied with the idea of a threesome and Phil definitely had a thing about shoes but both had many more positive things about them than negatives and in the absence of a certain Christian they were next best. Both were attractive and funny, had good jobs and exciting sounding pass times and so Sophie pushed their little eccentricities to the back of her mind.

Dan was working on Friday and said that he could meet her after work. He would have to go back on the late train but that wasn't until after eleven o'clock giving him plenty of time to see Sophie. Phil had rugby practice on Saturday and said that he was going to go to the gym as well, a new venture to get rid of his beer belly and get into shape- apparently motivated by Sophie. That would be fine, she thought, she would still have time to run and do what she needed to in the day- at least she would get out and socialise for a while rather than sit at home in her pyjama's wishing that Christian wasn't married to somebody else.

***

Sophie sat outside Dan's work building on the Friday night waiting expectantly for him to appear, her eyes fixed on the revolving doors that he said he would come out. He finished work at six but his train home was much later, he had told her in a text that morning, and so he had plenty of time for a drink or two before he had to head off and as he was 'down her way' it would be great if they could meet up. He had asked her if she was going to bring the car again that evening and when she said that she was he suggested that she pick him up from his office so that they could go for a drive to a pub out of town, then they could talk rather than go to the packed city centre pubs where you could 'hardly hear yourself think'. What a good idea, she had thought, pleasantly surprised by his thoughtfulness. He had been persistently texting her since they had first met and she had decided that she should either arrange another date or stop encouraging him by replying. She didn't really want to do the latter quite yet though as wasn't 100% sure that he wasn't 'The One'.

Nobody had come out of the building since she arrived at ten to. She thought that it was quite late for him to be working on a Friday evening, seeming to her like the sort who would want to knock off early and head into town, especially as it was so warm and sunny. Ollie had been picked up just after five and then she had a very quick turn-a-round to get into town for this time. She felt quite underprepared and pulled at her grey t-shirt dress which had worked its way up to her thighs and tied her hair up, getting annoyed with it in the evening heat. She turned her car engine on so that she could be cooled by the air conditioning, not wanting to be too rosy by the time he made it out. She cast her eyes idly around the marina where his office building was, just on the other side of the water from the bar where they had originally met. As she looking across the water her eyes were dazzled by the bright shining white yachts and speed boats that were moored, all bobbing gently in the summer breeze, and she saw that crowds were beginning to gather outside the bar, drinkers taking to the pavements to bask in the evening heat. She was glad that they weren't going there tonight, remembering the attention that he attracted last time. The thought of going to a quiet country pub with him all to herself was a far more preferable option and the fact that he had suggested it made her feel a little bit special.

Eventually the revolving door started to turn and Sophie sat up expectantly, watching for Dan. She slumped back down in her seat when she saw that it wasn't him, instead a blonde woman appeared leaving the building, buttoning up her grey suit jacket and running her hand through her hair which shone in the sunlight. Sophie checked her watch. Ten past six. She looked over to the door impatiently thinking that if she'd have known he was going to be late she would have taken more time in getting ready. A text message came to her phone and she read it.

'On my way out sexy. Sorry something came up. Two minutes.'

Sophie straightened her dress out again and checked her reflection, her tummy fluttering slightly at the thought of seeing this handsome man again.

He appeared out of the revolving door of the impressive glass and metal building as if in a scene from a film, wearing a very dapper grey suit and putting on a pair of aviator shades. He checked his watch and looked around for Sophie's car looking extremely cool and serious then waved and smiled when he spotted her, his demeanour changing instantly. He came bounding over to where she was waiting.

"Hi, gorgeous!" he said getting into her car and leaning over to kiss her on the cheek. Sophie felt thrilled, as if they were already going out and she always picked him up from work.

"Hi!" she said, slightly self-consciously, aware that this wasn't the case and that this was in fact only the second time they had met. She suddenly didn't know what to say.

Dan didn't seem to notice her hesitation and carried on talking. He looked rather flushed, as Sophie felt, and had a dishevelled look about him. No doubt he had been very busy Sophie thought, working late on a Friday to close some deals with multinational bankers before the weekend or something.

"How are you?" he asked and not waiting for a reply, "It turns out I'll have to get the earlier train at eight so there's not much time for a drink. Fancy a drive?" he flashed his gorgeous smile at her.

"Oh um, yeah OK," Sophie replied feeling slightly disappointed that their evening was to be cut so short. She had no idea where to drive.

As if in answer to her thoughts Dan replied, "We could just head out of town for a while, see if we can find somewhere quiet to stop."

Sophie assumed he meant a pub after all and started the car, deciding to head along the coastal road where she knew there were some lovely ones right on the water.

"You're looking great, as usual," Dan said, "it's a shame about my train. My brother needs my assistance in the morning to choose a new car and so I thought I'd better head off on the earlier one. I didn't think you'd mind giving me a lift."

Sophie suddenly felt like she was being used as a taxi service, as if she didn't have anything better to do that give Dan a lift to the station. He realised what he had said and corrected himself.

"I mean, I thought it would be OK to go a bit earlier as you might have to head off for the babysitter anyway."

"No, not tonight," Sophie explained simply, "Ollie's not with me this weekend."

"Oh now that is a damn shame," Dan responded, slightly to Sophie's annoyance, as if Ollie was something to get out of the way. Dan however was oblivious to any offense that he may have caused and continued to chat about work and sailing and then about a wedding he was at the previous weekend.

"Another one of my friends has given in to society's wishes and gone and got hitched. I don't blame him though; his new wife is something of a beauty. I'd keep hold of her if I were him," he reached inside his jacket and took out his wallet and what looked like a photograph, "she did look exquisite. He's a bit of a cad though; I don't know how long it will last… I'm not sure if it was some kind of joke but they had sat me at a table with four of my previous conquests! With another four at the next table and two at the top table it wasn't bad for one wedding! Look!" he held up the photograph so that Sophie could see. She glanced over and saw that it was of a line of women, some bridesmaids, all done up immaculately with perfect smiles and hair. She noticed that they were all blonde and felt instantly dowdy. "That is a photo of all my conquests from the year 2009 in chronological order!" he said proudly.

Sophie made no comment and kept driving, not really sure what to say.

"You could be one of them if you wanted to…" Dan looked at Sophie and raised his eyebrows smiling. He pulled out a condom from his wallet and ripped it open with his teeth, "how about it?"

Sophie remained speechless. Dan carried on before she had a chance to respond, lowering his voice even though they were in the confinement of her car. "You know, the thought of having a threesome with you has been turning me on a *lot*, in fact, I'm pretty hard right now," he unzipped his trousers to reveal his erection and started to expertly roll the condom onto himself, watching Sophie as he did.

Sophie fixed her eyes determinedly on the road ahead, the light suddenly dawning about what this was probably all about. She felt her face flush as a mixture of anger and awkwardness bubbled up inside her, feeling stupid that she had ever thought that Dan might change his mind and want to settle down. "I'll just drop you off at the station, if that's alright with you," she muttered and pulled in to the side of the road to turn her car around. That's probably all you wanted anyway, she thought, Sophie's taxi service with extras. She glanced at Dan's opened trousers and felt slightly repulsed, her main thought being that she had recently had the car valeted. She glanced around at the other cars stuck in the tea time traffic hoping that nobody could see.

"We won't need this then!" Dan said and comically threw the condom over his shoulder into the back of the car. "You can't blame a man for trying though. No hard feelings?" His face pleaded for Sophie to forgive him. She shook her head.

"I can't believe you showed me that photo!" she said crossly, "why would I want to see all the women you've slept with?"

"Not all the women," he corrected her, "just one year's worth. Probably less than that…"

"Well whatever! I still can't believe you showed me that photo!"

"I thought maybe you'd like to choose one for our threesome, I know some of them would be up for it."

"I doubt that they would and I don't want a threesome!" Sophie snapped suddenly, completely fed up with that particular subject. "I actually want what you think is so unrealistic and boring. I want to meet someone you might call Mr Right and spend my whole life with him and just him. I actually really like you, a lot, but I want you to feel like that about me too. I want to feel special."

"I reckon I could make you feel special," Dan said, a smile playing on his lips.

"Not the kind of special that I mean."

"Oh well, take me to the station then," Dan shrugged, "I've already had my lot for today anyway. You would have just been a bonus extra."

Sophie cast her mind back to the blonde woman she had seen leaving Dan's office building shortly before him and put two and two together. Her feelings towards him instantly changed to one of faint disgust. It was proof of her kind nature that she drove him all the way in to the station and didn't make him get out there and then.

***

Come on Phil don't let me down you big gorgeous ginger hunk of a man, Sophie thought as she waited for her next date to arrive on Saturday. She was beginning to perfect her 'getting ready for a date' routine, having put it into action so often of late.

Dan was history. She was over him. She couldn't believe the nerve of the man. Yes, he was amazingly handsome, had a flash job and an exciting life but Sophie couldn't imagine ever feeling secure and special knowing what she did now. He clearly knew what he wanted but Sophie realised that what she wanted was at the other end of the scale and she was sure that one day he'd end up in a sex addiction clinic.

There had been texts from Phil during the day that did make Sophie wonder what she was doing even entertaining ideas about going on a date with him either but then in between he had sent some quite sweet ones and so she decided to stick with it- she could always go home early as she had the night before. I'll just have to try and avoid the subject of 'shoes', she thought, as he did seem quite preoccupied by her high-heeled footwear.

'How's it going sexy', he had text that morning, what shoes are you wearing tonight?'

'Not sure!' Sophie had replied not wanting to encourage him.

'I'm sure you'll look lovely whatever you're wearing' the reply had come. Better.

'Although those heels you had on the other night were really hot'. Worse.

'It'll just be nice to see you'. Better.

'Naked in your heels'. Much worse. Sophie decided to wait until he got there before choosing her footwear, wanting to gauge his mood and not wear anything that screamed, "I love it that you have a weird shoe fetish, strip me naked and take me to bed in them now!"

He lived in the next village and they had agreed that he would drive round to hers and walk from there to the local pub. Sophie had warned her next door neighbours that a man was coming round to pick her up and they should contact the police if she didn't answer the text message that she had asked them to send her at quarter past eight, just in case he was actually a dangerous criminal. They had agreed to this, showing great interest that Sophie had started dating again having lived next door to her since she had moved in to the house with Ben eight years before. They had seen the couple's relationship develop before their eyes and Sophie and Pat had talked regularly over the garden fence at the front of their adjoining homes. They brought Ollie round Christmas and birthday presents and they always chatted whenever they saw each other, giving each other snapshots of their lives as they went about their daily business.

Phil drove into Sophie's drive bang on eight o'clock. He emerged with some difficulty from his VW Polo, his great mass not suiting such a small car. Sophie stifled a giggle at the sight. He pulled himself up to his full height and put the sunglasses he was wearing on top of his head and made his way to Sophie's front door, looking around as if to check he was at the right house. Sophie was pleasantly reminded what a striking man he was and felt positive about the evening ahead, for once, getting more used to spending her spare time in the company of the opposite sex. As long as I can keep him off the subject of shoes, she thought, we'll be fine. She padded her way to the front door in her bare feet, bright pink pedicure on show.

He noticed her toe nails as soon as she opened the door. Sophie was ready to exchange pleasantries but his eyes were looking elsewhere.

"Naked feet! I like it!" he said and then stepped into the house before Sophie had a chance to gather her thoughts, "couldn't decide which pair of your sexy shoes to wear?" he asked finally looking at her face, "do you need a hand?"

"Hi!" Sophie said, bringing the conversation back to formalities as they seemed to have been missed out, "how are you?"

"Oh yeah, good thanks. Did you need some help? Choosing shoes, I mean. I bet you've got shoe boxes full of some pretty orgasmic heels up there, eh?" he raised his eye brows questioningly, "damn I love your shoes, from what I've seen of them already!"

Sophie hadn't expected him to be quite so randy from the off and decided that she needed to wear the lowest and least sexy shoes that she had, maybe even her trainers. She wished that they had met out somewhere, wanting to get out of the house now as soon as possible.

"I'll be fine thanks! I'm just not quite ready!" she replied, "I'll just go and get some shoes…"

Before she could finish the sentence Phil had picked her up and carried her to the sofa where he sat down with her on his knee.

"Wow you're so tiny I can pick you up and move you round wherever I want!"

Sophie leapt up from his knee.

"I'll just get my shoes then we can go, yeah?" she didn't feel threatened; he seemed harmless enough, just rather frisky. He stood up and lurched at her again, this time to kiss her. He pouted and moved his head around, all mouth and tongue reminding Sophie of the actors she used to watch on American soap operas. She pulled away again and laughed.

"You've only just got here!" she said lightly, "I was looking forward to going out!"

Phil laughed too and looked sheepish.

"Going out, yeah… I thought we could stay in…?"

"Oh but… I was really looking forward to wearing my heels out! I hardly ever get the opportunity and I have so many pairs, it would be a shame not to!" Sophie said in an attempt to enthuse Phil into going to the pub.

The mention of shoes made Phil's eyes glaze over and a broad grin spread over his face.

"You can have the opportunity to wear *all* your heels tonight if you like…" he drooled, "just in the comfort of your own home…"

"It would be nice to go out…" Sophie said again, "I could run my foot up the inside of your leg under the table…" What are you doing, her voice screamed in her head, don't encourage him? Phil looked like he might burst with pleasure that she was joining in with his kinky scenarios.

"I thought, if you fancied it, that I could take you shoe shopping one day soon…"

Sophie was slightly taken aback by the suggestion as they hadn't met that long ago. Phil continued.

"You could choose *any pair* you liked," the smile spread further, "and anything else that suited you for that matter. The only condition would be…" Sophie saw the beads of perspiration forming on his upper lip, "that you would wear them for me… I have a vision of you in some sexy black lingerie, lacy, maybe leather, stockings, suspender belt, maybe with a whip in your hand pinning me down to the ground with one sexy heel… I could watch you in the changing room…" he brought himself back to reality and looked at her expectantly.

There was a pause while they both contemplated the image.

"OK! Let me go and get some shoes on anyway!"

Sophie rushed up the stairs before Phil had a chance to reply, cursing herself for bringing up her shoes in the conversation and even suggesting that she might play along with his fantasies. She heard her phone beeping downstairs but decided to leave it, so eager to get out of the house.

"Do you need any help?" the voice came from downstairs.

"No thanks!" Sophie called back. "I'm fine!"

She rummaged in the bottom of her wardrobe for a pair of work shoes. Work shoes didn't live in their own box like her other pairs. Instead they were chucked into the bottom of the wardrobe in a pile with her trainers, not worthy of being boxed or labelled. The shoe policy at work stated so strictly what kind of shoe should be worn that it had left very little scope to get anything vaguely nice and Sophie had been forced to buy a very plain pair of black court shoes. They were slightly higher than the policy stipulated but by her standards they were flat and dull and made her legs look dumpy. Perfect. She slipped them on and made her way back down stairs.

The sight that greeted her in the living room was enough to stop her in her tracks. Phil was completely naked and reclining on the sofa, one wrist handcuffed to the standard lamp next to him and lay there with what Sophie thought was an erection but as he had something of a beer belly it was difficult to tell. She gawped at him for a second unable to talk. A knock on the door saved her from having to come up with a suitable response to the scene.

"Oh! Who's that?" she said brightly and made her way to open it, as if there was no great surprise that there was a naked man lying on the sofa- men baring themselves to her becoming more of a regular occurrence.

"Tell them we're busy," Phil said, resting his hand on his groin.

Oh God, Sophie thought as she pulled the door open, thinking now that she had been very wrong in ignoring the obvious signs that this man had something of a shoe fetish. She was momentarily startled for a second time when she saw a police officer standing on her door step but then remembered the instructions that she had given Pat next door- if I don't reply to my text by eight fifteen…

"Good evening madam. We were in the area had a call from your neighbour expressing concern at your whereabouts."

Sophie heard a clatter and looked to her right and saw Phil scrambling around for his clothes, still hand cuffed to the standard lamp which then crashed to the floor taking him with it.

"The car in your driveway belongs to a man that we would like to speak to in connection with an incident during the early hours of this morning outside World of Shoes…"

Another crash.

The police officer was joined by another.

"May we come in madam?"

Sophie decided to let the situation unfold without her input and stepped to the side letting the police officers enter the house. Phil had managed to get his trousers back onto his legs but had not managed to pull them up and appeared to have given up and was back on the sofa this time without the erection.

"Do you mind coming with us sir? Once you've pulled your trousers up."

***

"It's definitely back to the drawing board!" Sophie told her friends as they took their regular seats in her living room the following Friday after being called together for an emergency meeting, Sophie craving the company of normal human beings again.

"So you've had a couple of bad experiences…" Lou started to say,

"A couple!" Sophie exclaimed, "I've only been back out there on the dating scene for a few weeks and I'm already wondering if there's anyone normal out there… or anyone who's not *obsessed* with sex! Or shoes for that matter. There's been Paul, cheese and onion breath fart pants who couldn't keep his eyes off other women's bottoms, Christian who just wanted a quick shag before he tied the knot, Dan who I believe has had more partners than hot dinners and I don't think that's an attractive quality by the way, and Phil, caught pleasuring himself outside a cheap shoe shop," Sophie shuddered.

"Well, maybe a few bad experiences… but there are hundreds of men out there!"

"And don't I know it- I get messages from them every day! It's so hard to tell what people are like from photos and emails though… I'm just going to have to be extra careful about who I select. I don't know what signals I'm giving off here but everyone seems to think I'm some kind of hussy! There must be one man out there who would be happy going to the cinema or watching a DVD and talking about normal stuff!"

"Ben's having Ollie in the holidays isn't he?" Joules asked.

"Yes, quite soon actually- the holidays are only a few weeks away! Why?"

"It'll be good for you to have a break," Joules continued looking at her friend with a little concern in her eyes, "you seem a bit stressed out."

"I feel a bit stressed out!" Sophie replied, "I had enough going on with just work and Ollie- I feel like I've got no spare time at the moment because any spare time I had I'm now spending on dates. I have Ollie's birthday to think about too!"

"Well, it might be all worth it in the end… when you find your handsome prince," Lou reminded her. "So tell us about these men! All these men who are sending you messages. There must be one or two who take your fancy?" Sophie laughed at her friend.

"Hmm maybe a few," she thought for a moment, "I'd say there are four who I'd like to meet up with. Mick, another Paul, Will and Edward. Edward! Sophie and Ed- quite royal isn't it?" she grinned.

"Ooh Sophie and Edward!" Joules exclaimed clapping her hands. "That sounds perfect! When are you meeting him?"

"I'm not sure yet, I've not made any plans. I feel like I've been flat out lately and I'm also annoyed that I've not booked any time off for myself to spend with Ollie. It's so difficult booking time off work, though. Sometimes I think it's just easier not to! Everyone else has got a week off."

"Just write it on the calendar," Ruth suggested, "I bet nobody would notice and you're entitled to a holiday for goodness sake! Do it on Monday when Enid's not around- I was doing her diary for next week, she's going to some conference or something. She'll be out until one anyway. If anyone notices, say Mrs Wright said it was fine."

***

Sophie had written down on a post-it note and stuck it next to the kettle that she was to remember to write her holidays on the wall planner in the office, even though these had not been sanctioned by Enid. She felt like she desperately needed a break from the place but also wanted to get away with Ollie and spend some proper quality time with him. He had been full of stories of the camping trip that his Daddy was planning and she felt like she wanted to take him away too. She also wanted to plan the best birthday ever for him in a few weeks' time.

On her way into work she stopped to buy some lunch not having had time to make anything but got distracted by a huge bar of chocolate that was at the end of an aisle and half price.

"Half price is my favourite price," she said and picked it up. She became aware of a presence behind her and looked over her shoulder, suddenly realising that she might actually be talking to herself out loud.

"Oh sorry!" she said, moving to the side as a man was standing there also looking at the chocolate.

"No problem," he said and smiled, looking faintly amused.

How embarrassing, she thought to herself as she walked away toward the checkouts, but wow he was *gorgeous*. She tried to subtly look back at him but managed to catch his attention much to her embarrassment and she turned her head back quickly and made her way to pay, feeling slightly foolish. You've become obsessed, she chided herself. She stood in the queue at the checkout and rummaged in her bag to find her wallet. Moments later she felt a tap on her shoulder.

"I think you've dropped something...?" the man was there again behind her and bent down, picking up something from the floor and handing it to Sophie. It was the yellow post-it note that she had shoved in her bag as she rushed out to school that morning. Now beginning to blush somewhat she said 'Thank You' and turned back to face the tills.

Great now he thinks I'm definitely senile, she thought, talking to myself *and* not able to remember the simplest of things.

She remembered what Joules had told her about Supermarket Dating and she started to imagine the handsome stranger running out after her as she walked to the car and grabbing her arm, desperate not to let this woman go now he'd found her.

"Hi, darling," a glossy brunette attached herself onto his arm having appeared from the ends of one of the aisles holding up an avocado for him to see. "Found it!" she said in a gravelly posh accent and smiled a perfect white smile, adjusting the Gucci sunglasses on her head then entwined her arms around his, her wrists laden with expensive looking jewellery and a huge diamond ring on her engagement finger. She even smells expensive, Sophie thought as she awkwardly held her bumper bar of chocolate; I bet *she* doesn't write stuff down on post-its. Sophie didn't look back as she paid for her chocolate and hastily left the shop telling herself that she really must stop eyeing men up.

I guess it *would* be easier using the rosette system, she thought.

"Look what I found at half price!" Sophie declared as she entered her office, aware that Enid was away that morning. She revealed the massive bar of chocolate from her shoulder bag, hiding it in there in case she came across Mrs Wright on the way, not sure but pretty certain that she would turn her nose up at such things.

"Excellent!" Ruth said, smiling. "A quarter each?"

"Absolutely!" Pam said, showing uncharacteristic cheerfulness. "Enid can get her own bloody chocolate."

"There's definitely enough there for four," Laura piped in then got up from her desk and made her way to the door, "I would hide it if I were you though Sophie, you know what this place is like."

Laura left the room and was heard opening the fire door and walking down the stairs.

"She's changed since Mrs Wright allegedly hit her," Sophie whispered, "I'll put this away for later," she went through to the kitchen to leave the chocolate then returned to the office. "It's next to the kettle if anyone wants a piece."

"Here, Sophie!" Ruth grinned and waved a sheet of stickers at her. "These are the holiday stickers. I got them out of Enid's drawer. Quick, mark your week off!"

"What's that…?" Pam asked.

"Sophie's marking a week off in the summer," Ruth told her, "because there's one spare, she needs a holiday and if she asks Enid is bound to say 'no'! Or at least, make a huge song and dance about it."

The ladies giggled like children as Sophie hastily moved round to Enid's desk, peeled off a long sticker and reached up to stick it on the year planner. She smoothed it down to cover the week at the end of August that was still free then quickly made her way back to her desk before Laura came back.

"I hope Enid doesn't realise!" she whispered once the giggling had subsided. "Otherwise I definitely won't be getting any holidays! Shh!"

The three made themselves look busy as footsteps were heard coming up the last few stairs followed by the creak of the door and then the office door opening, pushed by Enid who trundled in laden down with bags and bundles of paperwork.

"Would someone take these?" she barked at nobody in particular. Ruth stood up and caught a pile of books that were slipping off the top of the pile. "Damn thing was cancelled. Apparently they sent an email- check it for me please Sophie."

Sophie dutifully checked the emails, keen to be good for the rest of the day.

"There doesn't seem to be an email…"

"Well that doesn't surprise me," Enid stated, "what a *waste* of a morning. How have you all been getting on?"

The three ladies murmured that they were all fine, none of them being quite sure what they had had to do that morning. Enid seemed satisfied and turned round to check the diary. Steps were heard again and Laura came back into the office. She did a double take seeing Enid was back so early.

"Don't ask!" Enid demanded and continued to study the diary. Laura meekly sat down at her desk.

The office worked in silence until more steps were heard. These seemed to go elsewhere as they reached the top and the office door remained still. A loud sigh was eventually heard and the door was finally pushed open by Mrs Wright who was holding Sophie's jumbo bar of chocolate.

"Who on *earth* would *think* of bringing something like *this* into school?" she said smiling patronizingly, holding up the bar of chocolate which obscured her own face. "I mean, look at the size of it- *disgusting!*" she laughed. "This is a *healthy eating* school!" Sophie thought of everyone sitting at their desks all day and not being allowed out at lunchtime for a walk and some fresh air, but decided to keep these thoughts to herself. "Who did you confiscate it from? One of the girls' downstairs no doubt, they're not very clever."

Sophie sat stiffly as all eyes fell on her and, for the umpteenth time at work felt stupid. Enid, who had been out when she arrived looked at Sophie enquiringly as did Mrs Wright.

"Miss Bridges, do you know anything about this?" Enid asked.

There was silence in the office as everyone waited for her response, thankful that the chocolate that *they* had brought in on previous weeks had been undetected.

"It's my lunch," Sophie said as if challenging anyone to comment. "I'll run it off later anyway." she couldn't quite believe that she was explaining why she brought in some chocolate. OK so it was an extremely *large* bar but she was going to *share* it.

"I don't think when the girls come up here to borrow your resources that it is really *appropriate* to have this sort of thing lying around," Sophie listened intently but thought that it was a bit harsh; it wasn't as if she had left a sex toy lying around. "As a training advisor, part of the management team, you are expected to be a good role model for the other staff and I hardly think that a kilogram bar of chocolate for lunch is setting a good example! I will take it down and *hide* it in the office and then you can remove it from the premises at two thirty or whatever time it is you go home," she turned to leave the office then turned back and looked over to Enid.

"Sophie's holiday was fine by the way Enid- you could have sanctioned it as her line manager. She's your staff and therefore your responsibility."

Enid cast her eyes over the wall planner, looking rather irked that she had just had a telling off in front of everyone, and took it to mean the week off that Sophie had just put up herself and not the one day off for the wedding that the principal had actually meant. Ruth grinned at Sophie broadly over her monitor and the office got back to work, Sophie feeling elated that in a few weeks she could have a break from the place. Enid got up and left the room with a sour look on her face.

Laura spent all morning trying to produce another pamphlet for Mrs Wright to replace the one that had caused her so much anger the previous week. The flower logo was causing her some distress as she couldn't get them symmetrically on the page and they seemed to keep moving around.

"It has to be perfect," Sophie heard her mutter to herself, "it must be perfect."

There is too much stress in this place over nothing, Sophie thought. Laura eventually got a format that she was happy with and saved it in different colours.

"Come and take a look at this for me girls, before I take it down to show her. What do you think?"

Ruth, Pam and Sophie gathered round her computer to give her their opinions.

"Oh I like that one!" Pam said, pointing to the one with pink and green flowers.

"I like that one," Ruth said pointing to one that used shades of blue.

"Yeah that one's my favourite too," Sophie agreed, "the logo is a bit naff though isn't it? It looks really rubbish."

"Ours is not to question why..." Laura started. She looked up at the clock. "Oh I was meant to take it down ten minutes ago... I'm not that keen on showing it to her though, not after last time..."

"I'll go!" Sophie offered feeling like a break from the office. She wasn't that worried by how Mrs Wright might react to the artwork as it wasn't hers.

"Oh would you Sophie? That would be lovely. Are you sure you don't mind?" Laura looked visibly relieved that she might manage to avoid her employer.

"No it's fine I could do with a walk anyway. Give it here," she took the paper and collected her jacket from the back of her chair and headed down to find Mrs Wright.

She went past the main office as her first port of call but the principal wasn't there.

"Try her office," Mark suggested, "she said she was going to make some phone calls. She said that she didn't want to be disturbed but that must have been about an hour ago...?"

Sophie turned on her heel and continued along the corridor to where the principal's office was. She stopped outside and listened for a few moments, not being in any rush to get back upstairs. There was no noise coming from within so Sophie assumed that she was off the phone. Tim appeared from round the corner and walked past heading back to the office.

"Just go in," he said in passing, "she's not busy. If she didn't want to be disturbed she'd have a sign on the door."

"Uh, OK," Sophie said dubiously but reached for the door handle to let herself in. Pushing the door open she froze as her eyes met Mrs Wright's and she saw that although she wasn't on the phone she was still very busy- stuffing her face with the chocolate that she had removed from the office earlier. Her cheeks bulged with the stuff and there was a brown line around her lips like a confectionary lip liner. She looked like she might say something but then thought better of it, the quantity of chocolate in her mouth preventing her from doing so without making a mess.

"Oh!" Sophie exclaimed and retreated back into the corridor shutting the door. She stood there for a moment wondering if she should try again but knock this time. Bloody Tim getting me back, she thought but couldn't blame him having got him into trouble on numerous occasions. She decided to go back up to the office and let Laura deal with her pamphlet after all.

When she got back upstairs the office was empty apart from Laura.

"Enid's left you some filing to do," she said without looking up, "I think she's written it down so you don't forget... she wants you to put the emails that she's printed into the email folder."

Sophie carried onto her desk.

"They're on her desk," Laura stated, "it would be easier to do it over there... there are quite a few!"

Sophie looked over to Enid's desk and saw a huge pile of paper that she assumed was the printed emails. Why they had to print out emails she didn't know, she thought that their email Inbox was storage enough. Resigned to the fact that she would be doing this for the rest of the day she miserably made her way round to Enid's side, got the bundle of emails and sat herself down at the telephone table where the folders were kept.

Not long after sitting down the telephone had rung.

"See if it's internal," Laura had said sounding bored with the whole situation of Sophie not being allowed to answer the phone and looking unwilling to move herself across the room to answer it.

Sophie looked at the phone display. "It's the office," she told Laura.

"Oh just answer it then," Laura had told her. "You've been *making* calls to them- I don't see why you can't *answer* them. Just get it."

Uh OK, Sophie had thought, not entirely sure if she should. She snatched up the receiver.

"Sophie speaking."

"Sophie, how nice to hear it's you. This is Enid. Get me Laura. *Now!*" Immaculate timing, Sophie had thought.

"It's Enid," she told Laura who moved more quickly to the phone now than Sophie had ever seen her move before.

Laura made an apologetic face, took the phone and started to grovel.

When Enid retuned upstairs she told Sophie that she would prefer it, for now, if she didn't answer the phone. Someone might ask her for information that Sophie wasn't party to yet.

"I could pass them on to you?" Sophie had suggested, keen to be allowed some extra responsibilities.

Enid replied that this would be unprofessional and Sophie couldn't be bothered arguing the point and got on with her job of filing, ignoring the constant ringing of the telephone but getting some satisfaction when Enid had to constantly stop what she was doing to answer it.

With a week off to look forward to Sophie's mood lifted and she toyed with ideas about what to do with it as she slotted each piece of paper into a plastic pocket. It had been years since she had been on holiday. The last one that she had booked had been her and Ben's honeymoon that was subsequently cancelled. She had secretly text her mother to tell her the news and for ideas of places that would suit her budget. Her mother had text back suggesting that they all go to Italy.

"I'd love to go there!" Sophie had replied, "If we could book somewhere cheap?"

"You can't do 'cheap' in Italy darling. Leave it to me," was her Mother's final response.

Chapter Twelve

The week that Ollie was to go to Ben's came round too quickly for Sophie's liking. She had started to dread it from the moment it had been agreed, Ollie never having been away from her for more than a weekend. Even during the weekends, she always knew that at least he was only down the road- this time Ben had decide to take him to a camping site about sixty miles away on the coast and the kinds of things that could go wrong when she wasn't there had started to play on her mind. With worries in her mind she had bought Ollie a cheap mobile phone so she could keep in touch with him by text and sat in his room now packing the brightest clothes that she could find- items that had been languishing at the bottom of his drawers as the stubborn boy had refused to wear them- a red sun hat, his luminous orange arm bands, t-shirts of every neon colour in the spectrum and a yellow hoodie. It took her all her willpower not to nip out to the shops and get him a fluorescent tabard.

"Daddy says we can have sweeties every day!" Ollie told her as Sophie zipped closed his suitcase. He was reading on his bed as she packed and he spoke without looking up from his book.

"Look at people when you're talking to them please darling. Remember to eat your proper food too," she replied then wished she didn't always sound like the boring parent.

"*And* we can go on my bike every day."

"That will be nice. Will you sometimes text Mummy. Do you remember how I showed you?"

The boy nodded. "*And* we can go to the disco at the campsite every night. Daddy said that we could because it's a holiday. Daddy said that we can go swimming every day if I want to."

"Lucky you."

"Daddy said…"

The doorbell rang saving Sophie from more detail of why Ben was the best thing since sliced bread and got up to answer the door.

"Mummy will be planning your birthday party while you're away- won't that be fun! Don't forget Mr Ted!" she said to Ollie as she left the room. He continued to read. She was startled to hear a key being tried in the lock and then turning and the front door opening to reveal Ben, looking pleased.

"Ah! It *is* my old key!" he exclaimed happily. "That's cool. I can use it if we forget something."

"What?" Sophie said as she carried on down the stairs, "you can't just come in just because you used to live here! It's my key now!"

"I can keep a spare can't I?" he asked looking surprised that she should suggest otherwise.

"Well, no not really. It's my house now. I need a spare key actually for Kerry in case she needs to pick up Ollie and I'm not home."

"What, the babysitter needs a key but I can't. I'm his *father.*"

"Yeah, it doesn't mean you need a key to my house though Ben!"

"So what if you've forgotten to pack something."

"I've not. And if I have them you can knock on the door. Or call me!"

"What if you're at work?"

"Well you can wait until I'm home from work!"

"I'm not waiting around for you to get home from work."

"You can't just let yourself in to my house Ben," Sophie said and snatched the key from him, "I need my key."

"Mummy it's not nice to snatch," Ollie's voice came from the top of the stairs as he stood watching the heated exchange of words between his parents.

"See Sophie it's not nice to snatch," Ben repeated his son's words.

Sophie felt like crying. She inhaled deeply.

"No it's not nice to snatch. Please Ben can I have my key back, thanks," she smiled sweetly at Ben. "Ollie darling have you packed everything you need?"

The boy trotted back off to his room.

"Do I need a key to your house Ben? Would Sarah like it if I let myself into your house? Like last weekend when you forgot to bring back his school jumper- should I just pop round and get it? I don't think so. I've packed Ollie's case. He has a new mobile now which is in there too- I'd like him to send me a text when you get to the camp site and keep in touch during the week."

Ollie appeared at the top of the stairs again dragging his small case and started to bump it down the stairs. Sophie rushed up to take it from him. She didn't want him to go.

"What are we doing about his birthday this year?" Ben asked.

Sophie felt her body stiffen not wanting to share the day with her ex.

"I'm not sure that *we're* doing anything..? I'm not sure that we *need* to do something together? He'd love it if he had *two* parties!" Ollie nodded his head at the suggestion.

"What's wrong with me coming along to what you're doing?" Ben asked sulkily, "What's *your* problem all of a sudden?"

"Nothing Ben," Sophie replied curtly, "I'm just not sure if we need to do everything like that *together* anymore, if you'd wanted to do everything *together* then maybe you shouldn't have *left us*?" her eyes looked at him challengingly and she took a deep breath to release the tension that was building in her body. "Anyway," she said turning towards Ollie and smiling, "Darling, what else do you need?"

"Where's his bike?" Ben asked.

"It's in the garage," Sophie replied, "you'll have to move my car to get it out," she went to retrieve her keys from the kitchen and handed them to Ben. "You can move my car," she said suddenly feeling less than helpful.

Ben went to move her car and get the bike out of the garage and Sophie sat down on the bottom stair with Ollie and gave him a cuddle. She felt the tears welling up in her eyes.

"Have a nice week darling. Mummy will miss you such a lot. I can't wait to see you when you get back," she suddenly felt how empty her week would be without him.

"I'll miss you too," Ollie said and suddenly cuddled her back, holding onto his mum tightly. They sat there for a moment cuddling, Sophie kissing the top of his head again and again.

"I will try and think of the best birthday party ever!"

"Can Daddy come too?" Ollie asked.

Sophie sighed. "Oh maybe, if you want him to…" She wished she hadn't started this tradition of the man who left them being allowed to come along to all the special occasions and spoil them for her. She tried to put the bad feelings to the back of her mind.

"I love you," she said to him.

"I love you too," he replied, snuggling into her body.

"How much do you love me today?" Sophie asked.

"Name it," the boy replied.

"Name it? Hmm do you love me as much as if I were to blow up a balloon until it was so full of air it nearly popped?"

"More!" the boy giggled.

"Hmm OK do you love me as much as if I filled the bath up with water but didn't turn the tap off and so the water started to spill over the sides and flood the whole house?"

"The boy laughed. "Much more than that!"

"More?" Sophie said. "Wow! Let's think… Do you love me..?"

The front door opened abruptly, having been left slightly ajar, and Ben came into the house again shaking his head at Sophie. She made a face at him as if to say, 'what now'?

"Right say goodbye to your Mum," Ben said, "and jump in the car. Daddy will get your case."

"I'll put him in the car," Sophie said, not liking Ollie being in the car by himself. She took him out to his Dad's car and helped him get into the passenger seat, wondering what had got into Ben all of a sudden.

She hugged and kissed Ollie and said her 'Goodbye's' numerous times before closing the door. Ben put the case in the back of his car and came round to where Sophie stood.

"I didn't think you were like that," he said to her, "I thought that you were a nice girl. Guess what I found in your car? Some role model you are for our son. Maybe Ollie should come and live with me."

"What?" Sophie said. "What are you talking about?"

"Don't tell me you don't know," Ben replied, shaking his head. "What would your family think of you?"

"What are you talking about Ben? I don't like your tone of voice. I get enough of this at work."

"This," he held up the ripped open condom packet that Dan had discarded the other night. "I saw the condom in the back. Nice. Often have a shag in the back of your car do ya? Where my son sits?"

"Don't be ridiculous!" she replied crossly, feeling angry with Dan for having dropped it and Ben for thinking he could tell her what to do but more so with herself for not having remembered to pick it up. She started to try and explain what had happened but it just sounded worse than it was and so she gave up. Why am I explaining myself to him anyway, she thought? She looked at Ollie's little face watching them through the car window.

"I'm not standing her arguing with you in front of Ollie. You can think what you like. The days of my having to explain myself to you stopped the moment you walked out of the door to run off with another woman. I've brought up Ollie… oh I'm not even going to explain. Don't even go there," she breathed to release the tension that was engulfing her body, "Don't even *start.*"

***

Ben had taken Ollie away on the first Saturday morning of his school holidays. On her mother's advice she had booked a hairdressers' appointment that afternoon to have something to do to take her mind off things. Going to the hairdressers was one of the boy's least favourite activities so it would also be more relaxing to go without him. Sophie felt upset by the situation that had unfolded when Ben had collected him and busied herself; tidying the house to try and make the time pass. She went into Ollie's room to make his bed and saw Mr Ted sitting up there next to the book that the boy had been reading. She imagined the outcry that there would be when Ollie realised that his favourite teddy had been left behind and felt slightly pleased that Ben's week could be spoiled by that one simple thing.

Sophie's hairdresser was positioned opposite Christian's estate agency and despite herself she hoped that she might bump into him.

What are you expecting to happen, she scolded herself as she casually glanced across the road and through the window and saw a man she didn't recognise sitting in his place, that he's realised he married the wrong woman and will run out into my arms pleading for forgiveness? She sighed and pushed the door open into her salon.

Later on she emerged, her hair having been dried with a slight wave as an experiment for the wedding, feeling like a new woman. So amazed did she feel by the transformation that when she got home, for once, she wanted to go out and be sociable, so that someone else could appreciate how nice she looked when she tried.

She thought through her recent dates and ruled them all out immediately. The girls were all busy as often happened on a Saturday evening leaving Sophie wondering about prospective dates on her online site; many lived nearby or within driving distance at least. She looked at the clock; still time to put a bit of make up on and get changed.

Edward came to mind, a man she had initiated communication with on her dating website and next on her list of favourites following the fall from grace of Phil and Dan. He had mentioned meeting up at some point apparently looking for excuses to give his new car a run. She sent him a text saying she was unexpectedly free and did he fancy a drink- casual lies were beginning to trip off her tongue but he didn't need to know that her original date was with a hot chocolate. So far they had exchanged pleasant messages telling each other about their lives so far and generally chatting about stuff- work, keeping fit, food and the theatre. She omitted the fact that the only times she'd ever really go to the theatre was to see the pantomime at Christmas because it was so expensive. This part- having to give everyone a brief life history- did get a bit tiresome when new people sent messages every day, Sophie thought, and didn't imagine that anyone would find her life that interesting. Edward hadn't mentioned sex at all though so far which was a massive tick in a box for Sophie having had quite enough of that subject for the time being and he looked nice in his photos.

Edward replied surprisingly quickly and said that he was free; maybe he had had a similarly tame evening planned Sophie thought. They arranged to meet on the country road up to London at a pub he knew which was situated in one of the pretty villages scattered along the way.

Her hair looked perfect as it was so she added a bit of make-up, chose her outfit and set off on her journey feeling positive and optimistic. She repeated 'Sophie and Ed' over in her head, liking the royal sound of it. Mother will be pleased, she thought imagining that Edward would live up to his royal name; he did look fairly regal in his photographs. As she travelled she got herself lost in daydreams about how this man might just be perfect, based on a few photos and what he had told her about himself.

He had directed her to park in the train station which was a short walk from the pub he had suggested, initially saying that she could meet him there but Sophie had never been to the village before and didn't know where the pub was. It had taken several texts and a phone call to persuade him to meet her at the car park instead, a little to his annoyance she had thought. To her horror as she drove in she saw the cobbles that paved the historic looking street that was signposted as being the way to the village centre and regretted her shoe choice again.

Edward's sparklingly new black Porsche was the first thing that Sophie spotted as she drove into the car park and she tried to smile and wave nonchalantly like it was no big deal to her. He didn't wave back. She stopped waving as her car abruptly came to a halt having been driven into the log that was marking out the parking space and she grimaced at the sound of metal meeting wood. She looked back over to where he sat watching her and made a 'silly me' face. If he hadn't described his car she didn't think that she would have recognised him so different did he look to the photos that he had on his online profile. She felt slightly disappointed as she had quite liked the way that he'd looked and those were the photos she'd based her daydreams on. She could see that it was him, just about, but his pictures were *very* flattering. He didn't seem to be in any rush to get out of his flash car either which was a little upsetting- in her thoughts he would have jumped out to rush over and hold the door open for her to get out. She picked up her clutch bag from the passenger seat and opened the door for herself. I'm an independent woman after all, she thought, I don't need men opening doors for me. As she had time she went round to the front of her car to inspect the bumper. There was no visible damage. She passed her hand over the bonnet and then used it to steady herself as she bent down to look underneath where the bumper had gone over the log. The bumper curved round under the car and she saw the underside was all scratched up.

"Bugger."

"I can see right up your skirt."

Sophie swung round instantly pulling the back of her dress down unaware that her bottom had been on display. She had thought that it was quite short when she'd put it on but then decided that as it was such a cool dress that it would be fine if she didn't bend over…

"Hi!" she said cheerily. "Silly me; bumped my car…"

"I saw. Shall we head down then?" Edward glanced at Sophie's dress then strode off without so much as a 'You look nice' or 'I like your hair'. The look that he had given her was almost one of contempt and made her suddenly feel cheap and tarty, like she didn't have enough class to be seen with him. She felt gutted. It was such a beautiful summers evening and she had felt so pretty with her hair done and quirky dress. The shortness of the dress and high heels also gave her legs more length and she felt better than she remembered feeling for a long time. Edward successfully quashed those feelings.

"Where's he going?" she said slightly desperately and tottered after him as fast as she could go in her heels. "Why did I wear this dress? Stupid short dress! Stupid high heels!"

"Do you always talk to yourself?" Edward called back after her.

What's his problem, Sophie thought almost in tears now he had stridden so far away and her heels making her struggle on the cobbles. This wasn't how she had imagined their initial meeting to be. Eventually she saw him stopping at the bottom of the hill and waiting for her, at last showing some gentlemanly qualities. She had rather hoped that he would walk with her arm in arm but clearly that wasn't going to happen. With as much grace as possible- as he was now watching her every step- she continued down the steep cobbled street to where he stood. Other people in more sensible shoes walked past her as she gingerly made her way forward at a pace more common to a snail. She ignored Edward's look of impatience as she reached the bottom.

"So where's this pub then?" she asked rather feeling like a seat.

"It's a *wine bar* actually," Edward replied and started off along the road again. "They also do food. Thankfully we're nearly there!" he called back over his shoulder.

He reached his destination and stopped, looking at his watch. Sophie finally caught up with him and straightened her dress out, finding that as she walked the static made it stick to her tights and ride up her legs. What a disaster already, she thought. Edward looked unimpressed and made his way into the wine bar letting the door go so that it shut before Sophie had a chance to go through. It crossed her mind that maybe Edward was related to Enid and for the first time that evening she smiled.

Edward chose a table at the back of the wine bar which was deserted except from a young man polishing glasses at the bar. Sophie clip clopped her way across the wooden floor to where he had already sat down and was now inspecting the menu. She idly looked around at the empty tables and then cast her eyes back towards the window at the front. She could see there was a pub across the road which already had people spilling out onto the pavement, laughing, talking and drinking, some shouting but all looking like they were having fun.

"Binge drinkers," Edward stated following her stare.

Sophie pulled a chair out from under the table and sat with her back to them. I might rather be over there in the packed pub binge drinking that here with you, she thought. She looked up and smiled at Edward, determined to make the most of being out. Maybe this was just his way and once they got to know each other the ice would start melting. He looked back down at his menu.

They sat in silence until the waiter came over and asked them what they'd like to drink. Edward ordered a gin and tonic and then looked at Sophie for her order.

Gin and tonic's a bit of a girl's drink, Sophie thought and didn't approve of anyone drinking at all if they were driving. This man was rapidly losing brownie points.

"I'll just have a soda water and lime… as I'm *driving*," Sophie said and smiled sweetly at the waiter who smiled back and scribbled her order down on his note pad. Her comment was lost on Edward who continued to pour over the menu. Sophie noticed his hands which looked incredibly soft and smooth, like a girl's hands Sophie thought again and tried not to smirk.

"Are you eating?" Edward asked without looking up from his menu.

"I'm fine," she said, "I had something earlier." Her appetite for the date was also rapidly dissipating.

Edward raised his eyebrows and nodded and continued to read. Sophie started to inspect the wine bar décor.

The waiter returned to their table carrying their drinks on a tray. With a flourish he placed Sophie's soda water and lime down in front of her and gestured towards the glass showing her the decorations he had added- a green cocktail stick, umbrella and a little plastic sword balanced across the top of the glass spearing a lime.

"For madam," he said and looked at Edward, "to spice up your evening a little," he winked at Sophie and she smirked. I have more chemistry going on with the waiter, she thought.

"Are we ready to order?" the waiter asked and looked at Sophie.

"Oh I'm not eating, it's just *him.* "

The waiter turned his attention to Edward who finally put down his menu.

"Is the salmon fresh?" he asked.

"Is that from the starter selection or the main course sir?" the waiter asked politely.

Edward sighed irritably.

"Well clearly the starter as I'd order that first!" he snapped.

"You might have decided to skip to the main," the waiter said determined to have the last word, "some people often do these days," he patted his tummy and winked at Sophie again who tried not to smirk. "The salmon starter is a pate sir," he explained.

Edward ignored the suggestion that he might be a little thick around the waist.

"Yes but is it *fresh*?" he asked again impatiently.

The waiter paused and looked at Sophie who smiled but ultimately wasn't going to get involved.

"Yes. Yes, the pate is *fresh,* " the waiter spat the last word out as if Edward had insulted him deeply.

Edward briefly looked at the menu once more and then looked up at the waiter. "I will have the celeriac, goat's cheese and toasted almonds to start," he said, clearly deciding that the salmon wasn't as fresh as he'd like, "but only if the celeriac is *thinly* sliced and the almonds just *lightly* toasted. I would have preferred a ewe's cheese so maybe you could feed that back to the chef. Then I'll have the sirloin steak and sautéed mushrooms. Don't put the peppered sauce *on* the steak- put it on the side- and I don't want it at all if the mushrooms are soggy. I'll have a green salad instead of the chips. Then for desert I'll have the iced mojito parfait with sweet cucumber salsa. I'll have a bottle of sparkling mineral water for the table and your wine list please," he looked at Sophie. "So you're going to sit and watch me eat then?"

"Pretty much," she replied jokingly but Edward didn't laugh.

Sophie was convinced that they would have sat in silence for the whole evening had she not initiated a conversation. Edward had inspected the wine list for some time and after many questions to the waiter had chosen a glass of the house red. He had then looked at his perfectly buffed finger nails for a while and played around with his mobile phone before focussing his attention on the picture that hung above their table.

"So," she had eventually said, "what do you do for a living?" she cringed at the boringness of the question but Edward didn't seem to mind.

He sat back in his chair and puffed out his chest with what looked like self-importance, idly stirring his drink with the cocktail stick that had come in it, their waiter seeming to be a fan of adorning drinks with accessories. He had appeared to be so rude up until then that Sophie had lost all interest in him as a date but she decided that it would be preferable to try and chat than to sit in awkward silence.

"So, as I might have said before, I own my own business," Edward started casually, perking up considerably at the mention of work, "my company is called Global Input Technology and is a premier e-business and integration service provider *worldwide* specialising in IT consultation and product development. I spend my time between London and New York mainly, sometimes Milan, sometimes Paris, sometimes the middle-east… We manage solutions and remote diagnostics to deliver hi-tech transactional services to a global market but with a local ambience. We're a single source provider in quality transcription services."

Sophie wanted to tell him that he was talking utter bollocks but managed to bite her lip. She tilted her head to the side and nodded as if listening with deep interest but he may as well have been talking Taiwanese. The only thing that made any sense was that the acronym of his company name was GIT. She stifled a yawn and casually glanced at her watch.

"I really hardly have time for anything other than work. My job requires twenty-four seven attention. At the moment I'm employing twelve people in London. We have our own offices in Canary Wharf. It's a great responsibility employing staff, you know, their future is in my hands."

Twelve people, Sophie thought, the way you're explaining it sounds like you employ twelve *hundred*! Edward's world sounded like a million miles away from Sophie's though.

"So there's a great buzz in the office but if I wake up on a Monday and think, God dammit I can't be bothered going into work today I can just take the day off or work from home, because I'm the boss," he smiled smugly.

"That would be good if you had children," Sophie added although she was sure that children were not on Edward's radar.

"I can't think of anything worse than having children," he replied confirming her thoughts. There was another long pause while Sophie wondered why on earth he had said 'yes' to a date. She waited to see if he was going to return the favour and ask her about *her* job. He didn't so she decided to tell him anyway.

"My job's not quite as exciting as running my own business…" she started but Edward's interest was already elsewhere, watching the waiter arrive with his food.

The celeriac, goat's cheese and toasted almond starter was placed in front of Edward and Sophie braced herself for a very long evening. As he chomped on his food he looked around inspecting the interior of the wine bar- anything but make eye contact with her. She wished that she had at least ordered a starter, him eating making her hungry but not seeming like the kind of bloke who would appreciate it if you pinched some food off his plate. She considered making more casual conversation but then decided she couldn't actually be bothered and he didn't seem bothered either appearing to be happy for them to sit in silence. Sophie sat leaning on the table with her arms folded and looked around and they continued like this through to desert.

By the time desert came Sophie was ready to bang her head against the table and was using extreme will power to stop herself from doing this. She heaved an audible sigh of relief when Edward's iced mojito parfait with sweet cucumber salsa arrived and looked at her watch. Nearly ten o'clock. She felt irritated that she had wasted a whole evening like this wishing that she had made her excuses hours ago. The unexpected sound of the main door opening broke her thoughts and she twisted round to see a group of men coming in, the first customers since Sophie and Edward. They looked around the empty wine bar and had a discussion. One of them shrugged and went up to order some drinks. Sophie gazed at him indifferently as he shoved his hands deep into his pockets to reach for some change. She frowned slightly as his face seemed familiar. He became aware that she was staring at him and looked back, also now slightly puzzled as Sophie seemed familiar to him. They momentarily held each other's gaze and then the penny dropped.

"Mike!" Sophie cried and waved. "Mike!" she got up from her chair and rushed over to where the little round man stood at the bar, never having been so pleased to see anyone in her life. Mike looked shocked initially, not being used to attractive women practically throwing themselves at him in this way. "Mike, it's *so good* to see you!"

Mike pulled himself together, remembering he was with his friends, and acted like this was a normal occurrence for him.

"Hi!" he beamed, "It's Sophie isn't it?"

"Hi! Yes, it is! Mike! Hi! You tried to hit on me when I called you out when my washing machine broke down!" Sophie held out her arms and hugged him. Mike looked over-the-moon.

"Oh yeah sorry about that," he mumbled and glanced sideways to see if his friends had heard that bit, "I had nothing to lose…"

"It's fine! It's so good to see you!" she said again, "It's still not working properly. Well, what a surprise!"

Mike looked past her to Edward who was watching with little interest from their table.

"So I hope we're not disturbing a romantic evening…?" Mike asked, indicating towards Edward, "You seem to have the place all to yourselves!"

"You're not disturbing us at all!" Sophie said and then under her breath, "Actually I could do with your help!"

Mike recognised a damsel in distress when he saw one and tilted his head towards Sophie's to listen to her plea.

"That man over there is the rudest man I've ever met," she whispered to Mike, "We're on a blind date… hideous."

Mike nodded understandingly and looked over to Edward and smiled.

"Need some company?"

Sophie smiled at him and nodded. "If you like..?" She turned towards her table.

"Anyway, Mike, would you like to join us? Edward! Edward this is my, erm, brother. Do you mind if he…"

Mike was already on his way to sit down with Edward followed by his two mates. They pulled some chairs around the table and signalled for the waiter to come over and take their order. Edward looked at Mike as if searching for the family resemblance.

"No food for us thanks!" Mike said cheerily. "Just drinks. Lager please, three of. So, Ed," he said extending his chubby hand across the table, "Ed. Eddy. Nice to meet you."

Edward gingerly shook Mike's hand. He looked uncomfortable to be sitting at the same table as someone who was not posh.

"I had a mate called Eddy once," Mike continued, building his part somewhat Sophie thought but glad to have the company, "Eddy... nice bloke. Got done for assault though in the end, was quite handy with his fists. Learnt all he knew from me of course!" Mike punched his fist into his palm and grinned wildly, "South-east featherweight champion 1998. Put on a few pounds since then," he said patting his midriff. "So, anyway sis," he turned his attention back to Sophie who was listening to his ramblings with wide eyed wonder. "How's my nephew doing? How's the little man?"

Sophie pulled her thoughts together and was about to answer when Edward held up his hands to signal everyone to stop talking. This was the most animated that Sophie had seen him all night.

"Sorry hold on!" he said to Mike. "I'm sure you won't mind if I talk to your... sister... for a moment?"

Mike sat back in his chair and folded his arms making it clear that he wasn't moving. "Be my guest."

Edward paused for a moment and then turned back to Sophie.

"Do you have a child?" he asked, saying the word 'child' as he might say 'rabid dog'.

Sophie realised that she might have neglected to tell Edward about Ollie but then again it hadn't ever come up in any of their conversations. She suddenly felt guilty that she did.

"Oh um yeah, I must have said that? Didn't I? I have a five-year-old boy."

Edward was already up and out of his chair and putting his jacket on that had been draped over the back of it.

"I'm not interested in that kind of commitment," he said addressing Mike, as if a man would understand. Sophie thought he was being a bit over the top, as if she'd asked him to have Ollie for the weekend. "I didn't know you had a kid. That kind of changes everything."

Sophie wasn't sure what would change exactly as the evening had been awkward already, without the mention of children. Maybe he did like me after all, she thought as she watched him carefully buttoning up his jacket, maybe he's just a bit abrupt.

"Bit of a wasted journey really, if you'd had told me you had a child I wouldn't have bothered. Nice meeting you anyway," he smiled thinly and extended his hand for Sophie to shake. She did so and smiled apologetically. She was going to say, 'if I ever need an I.T. solution…' but decided that any light-heartedness would have been lost on Edward having seen no evidence of a sense of humour so far.

Sophie, Mike and his two friends watched as Edward left the building and walked past the window hunched forward with a slightly pissed off look on his face.

Sophie turned back to her new companions and smiled, shrugging her shoulders. The waiter came with the three lagers and placed one in front of each of the men. He asked Sophie if she would like anything else to drink. She said no, not planning on sticking around for long.

"Where did you find *that* one?" Mike asked. "If I *was* your brother I'd have given him a piece of my mind! I can't believe the way he spoke to you. What an idiot."

"I only met him a few hours ago. I, um, I met him *online*..." she said with embarrassment, expecting the men to burst out laughing feeling rather silly now about the whole thing. Mike nodded his head knowingly.

"Ah yeah, been there, done that, got the t-shirt. I gave up after date number, oh what was it, about eighty-two?" he made a weary face and Sophie giggled.

"Well, my friends suggested it in the first place... I was quite happy being single! I've got a wedding to go to next year, my sister's, and I thought it was about time I found someone to go with... I'm beginning to wonder if I should bother though, and I've only been on a few dates!"

"I gave up after a date with a woman who burped the national anthem. It's not only men who are weird. That's why I thought I'd have one last stab in the dark and ask you out that day. I thought you looked nice and the worst that would have happened is that you'd said 'no'... and the best, well..." he smiled making the skin around his eyes crinkle.

Sophie instantly felt bad that she had judged Mike so harshly appearing now to be the nicest man she'd met.

"I'm sorry; I just wasn't really expecting to be asked out..."

Mike shook his head and put his hand up for Sophie to stop.

"It's fine. Don't worry about it. I shouldn't have, clearly I was in the wrong. As I said, it was my last ditch attempt. I've now accepted things as they are and, you know, I'm happy. I feel happier than I ever have felt before, now I've stopped trying to meet someone. You know, if you ever want to talk then you have my number… I promise not to ask you out."

Chapter Thirteen

It was the Friday night two weeks after Ollie's week away. Sophie was filling bowls with crisps and putting bought dips into her own terracotta pots, as if she'd made them herself, getting ready for the girls to come round. She felt relieved to have a night when she didn't need to get dressed up or make herself look pretty after her many dates the week before. Lou came into the kitchen offering help.

"It's fine. I'm done thanks. You could take these through though?" Sophie indicated to the crisps and dips.

Lou lifted up Sophie's left hand and inspected her fingers.

"No ring yet then?" she said with mock disappointment. Sophie laughed.

"No not yet! I'm still trying though. I fact, I've been on *heaps* of dates since last time!" she followed Lou through to the living room where Tina and Joules were exchanging stories of why their husbands were never around.

"Remind me why I want to meet a man...?" Sophie said when she heard their conversation.

"Oh not all men are like that," Joules replied, "we've just been really unlucky. So! Tell us about your dates! Paul is still hanging out for the day that you give up looking."

"Oh dear... well... Where should I start?"

"Start at the beginning," Lou replied.

Sophie took a deep breath as if she had plans to talk for a long time. "Well, you know about Edward... or Mr Rude as we'll call him. That was the Saturday that Ollie went to Ben's. Next one was Jon!"

"Ooh Jon! I've not heard about *him*!" Joules said with some excitement in her voice as her face lit up in anticipation.

"You kept him secret," Lou added.

"That was really not my intention- I've just been busy. Jon was nice. Well, nice looking. I met him in the Plough on the Sunday night; you know that pub down on the water?"

Her friends nodded.

"Sunday night, Sophie- you went out on a school night?" Lou said with surprise.

"Yes well, as you'll hear, I've been getting busy in the dating department. It was so strange to be able to go out again, whenever I felt like it, but I was missing Ollie so much that I thought I'd try and fill my week up. Jon had been suggesting that we meet up so I just thought I'd have nothing to lose if I asked him out and I wasn't doing anything else."

"Wow Sophie that's very modern of you," Lou teased.

"Yes well, I do prefer to be asked… Anyway, where was I? Oh yes, he lives in town so he was cool to meet up last minute. He was on the dating site- all my recent disastrous dates have been from the dating site..." Her friends sat listening intently. "I set my hometown so that I could meet more local men- I'm not traipsing up to London every weekend! So anyway, that's where I found Jon…"

"So what did he look like?" Lou interjected.

"Quite cute," a smile spread across Sophie's lips, "*really* cute actually!" she grinned at her friends.

"Tell us!" Tina said impatiently.

"OK, well, he has kind of mousy brown hair, just normal hair."

"What's normal hair?" Lou asked.

"Well you know- just short hair. He had just the most gorgeous blue eyes though. I thought Christian had gorgeous eyes…"

"Yes well we don't like him anymore do we?" Tina reminded Sophie.

"No we don't like him anymore…" Sophie said reluctantly then shook the thought of him out of her head. "Jon! Jon had amazing eyes and such an infectious smile- a *gorgeous* smile. I reckon he could actually get you into bed just by smiling and staring at you with those eyes…" she smiled sheepishly at her friends for even suggesting such a thing. "… however he spoilt the date somewhat by claiming to be the second coming of Jesus."

"What! Are you *kidding*?" Lou spluttered her wine all over the floor as she struggled not to laugh, *"That's* got to be on the list of 'Things not to talk about on your first date?' Was he being *serious?"*

"Oh yes, deadly serious. He suddenly changed completely. You know, we'd been having a really nice chat up until then. He seemed really normal. Everything he said just seemed to be exactly what I'd think about things and we had the same kind of silly sense of humour. I told him about Ollie and he seemed cool with that and he thought my job sounded crazy. We were having *such* a nice time and he kept kind of pausing sometimes and just *looking* at me with those eyes…"

"Maybe he was trying to convert you," Tina suggested.

"Maybe he was looking into your *soul*!" Joules offered.

"Nah he was probably trying to get you into bed, like you said," Lou said decisively.

"Well, whatever, he was just so… well, perfect and then he casually threw that into the conversation and I didn't know what to *say*! I thought maybe he was joking at first but he looked completely serious."

"So what did you do?" Tina asked.

"Well, he got a bit weird after that- quoting the bible and telling me about why he had returned to earth and the end of the world… He showed me his hands and where he had been nailed to the cross," she opened her eyes wide as she said this and put a look of mock horror on her face, "and he *really believed* he was Jesus! He started asking a lot of questions about me and about Ollie and I suddenly felt really uncomfortable telling him anything- he just got really creepy! So… Well… I got really freaked out and said I was going to the loo. It was right across the pub and you could see it from our table but was also *right next* to the door to the pub kitchen. I went into the loo and felt so scared that I thought; I just can't go back. So, there was a window in the door to the loos and I watched him through it for a few minutes waiting until I could make a move. He sat just gazing over and I thought he was just going to look at the loo door until I came out but then someone came up to our table- a pregnant woman- and asked him something and it must have been for a chair because he got up and carried one of the spare chairs at our table over to a table behind. As soon as he turned his back I was out that loo and into the pub kitchen in a flash and I told them I needed to get out of the pub *now.* I said I was on a date and it was just really bad and they thought that it was kind of funny and let me out of their staff door at the back of the pub. I have never moved so fast, honestly, I got so scared!"

"Sophie you really have been watching too much telly," Lou said, "What did you think he was going to *do*?"

"I don't know!" Sophie said defensively, "He just seemed suddenly quite scary!"

"He wouldn't have *done* anything to you though, not in a packed pub!"

"Well, no but he might have followed me home or something…" she shivered, "He just gave me the creeps. It would have been difficult to continue the evening, anyway, with him proclaiming what he was- I wouldn't have been able to take him seriously."

"OK next! Who's next on your hit list you ruthless woman?" Lou joked.

"Next was Paul- another Paul. I met him on *Tuesday* night. I thought I could space them out in the week, so I had a night in and then a night out. You know- early to bed then late, early to bed then late," she grinned at her own sensibleness, "he had been making dates with me for *ages* but then always cancelled them so again I suggested it."

"Wow you're brave," Joules said, "I'd *never* be able to ask someone out on a date…"

"Well I should hope not- you're a married woman!" Tina responded.

"Well, yeah, I mean, if I wasn't married…" Joules replied.

"He had one photo on his profile which was just *utterly* gorgeous," Sophie continued.

"Sophie is this how you're choosing men now, by how *good looking* they are?" Tina asked, remembering a conversation they'd had about being superficial.

"No! Well, not really! But when the first you know of these guys is a photo of them it's pretty hard not to instantly judge them on the way that they look. But I've now learnt not to do that because he looked *completely* different! Like so different you'd have thought it was a different person! But apparently the photo was taken when he was serving in Afghanistan…"

"*Afghanistan!*" this time Tina nearly spilt her wine, "You didn't tell me you had met any men in *uniforms!*"

"He's not a man in uniform!" Sophie assured, "He *used* to be a man in uniform but now teaches children in Vietnam, or somewhere!"

"Well, still…" Tina started.

"No! Don't even think that! He was as dull as dishwater and so full of his own importance that I'm surprised he had space in there for any internal organs. It was all just 'me, me, me!'"

The ladies nodded, Tina still looking devastated that she'd missed out on seeing him in person.

"I'd have come to the same pub you were meeting him in, you know, just for a peek," she said sulkily.

"Perv," Lou stated.

"Well you'd have wasted your time then," Sophie said, sounding less than impressed, "he was a bore although he thought he was the cat's pyjamas! I thought I was looking nice again that night too, I always make such an effort for these idiots and it's always for nothing. He spent the first half of the date telling me how utterly brilliant he is and the second half of the evening telling me how I need to change my style if I'm *ever* going to find a boyfriend. I mean, why would I take fashion advice from some ex squaddie? Apparently I should try a different hairstyle, get rid of the wooden beads I had on and try out some different clothes, 'grungier' I think he suggested."

"What a wanker," Lou said and the other ladies laughed, "I hope you said the same to him!"

"No, that's the thing that's annoying me now- apart from the fact I've wasted a week by myself going out on useless dates- I'm annoyed that he left thinking that I'd actually listened to his shitty advice. Anyway… The next was OK actually, they weren't *all* useless. I'm not sure what's happening with him yet! Mick, his name's Mick. I met him on the Thursday night. I was pretty knackered by that time actually, what with work as well that week and I'm just not *used* to being out all the time anymore. So actually that night I don't think I was looking like anything special. But we got on really well…" Sophie smiled and raised her eyebrows, "Yeah, really well…"

"Wow!" Joules said excitedly, "So when are you seeing him next?"

"Well, I did see him the next day… that was a complete nightmare. I got home from work about three and there was Ben's car sat outside the house. It had rained on the first night of their camping trip and then Ollie had wet the bed twice and he'd run out of clothes- also, by all accounts, without Mr Ted the week had been a bit of a nightmare," Sophie smiled with satisfaction, "He was pissed off though by the time I got there because he said he'd been there since half two and that's why he needed my spare key."

"Do you have *his* spare key?" Tina asked, "Why didn't he just go and buy some other clothes?"

"Well exactly, but that would have meant him spending money. Everything's got to be such an issue. Anyway, it was so nice to see Ollie, I'd been missing him *so* much and I got a massive cuddle from him- he clung onto me like he'd really missed me too. I was standing on my front grass holding Ollie and basically arguing with Ben about why he still wets the bed- which he doesn't at home anyway- when *another* car turned up and it was Mick!"

"Good timing," Lou said.

"Yeah bloody great timing! So he sees us arguing and was right over to my side asking 'what's going on' and 'is there anything that he could do to help' and 'OK mate there's no need for that attitude'- basically making things worse! And Ben was like, 'who do you think you are anyway' and 'don't talk to me like that in front of my son'- you can imagine."

The ladies nodded.

"And the two of them just started arguing about nothing and started to push each other around and before I know it they're on the grass having a full-on fight!" she looked at her friends listening with great interest and then they all spontaneously laughed.

"Men!" Lou said, "Nothing like a good fight."

"Why was he round anyway?" Joules asked.

"What, Ben?" Sophie replied.

"No! Why did Mick come round?"

Sophie paused then smiled. "Because after our first meeting the night before he'd made a compilation CD for me with all the songs that made him think of me," there was a long pause.

"A *compilation* CD?" Tina asked incredulously, "What? Like the compilation tapes we used to make by recording the songs off the radio? Remember that? You always missed the last bit of the song because the DJ would start talking and you'd quickly switch the tape off. Is that the sort of thing you should do after a first date?" she looked enquiringly at Sophie who looked back shrugged.

"After the run of date's I'd had it was a welcome gesture," she smiled, "and besides, he's got really good taste in music! I didn't like the fighting though... that was s bit weird... and because Ollie had seen me he wanted to come home and the fighting had freaked him out too so in the end Ben decided to just cut his holiday short and leave him with me! Which was lovely... but I did have another date planned on the Saturday. Ollie was due back on the Sunday so I thought I might as well pack them all in but with him coming home early... well... he had to come too!"

"What- to the pub?" Tina looked shocked.

"No not to the pub! I'm not going to take Ollie to the pub with me am I? No, I'd arranged to meet up with him in the afternoon- Will- and we *were* going to go to the cinema. I've been really careful to keep my dates away from Ollie but Will's in the navy..." Sophie looked at Tina and giggled, "...and he was only back for a few days before he was off somewhere else so I had to take my chances. He didn't mind at all- I told him that Ollie had come back early and he was cool about it, he suggested that we all go to the fair instead. I just told Ollie that we were going with one of my friends and that seemed fine. Ollie *loved* him! Will called him 'little buddy' which Ollie liked a lot, he bought him balloons and candy floss…"

"Shouldn't you be very careful of strange men buying children sweets and balloons?" Lou asked mischievously.

"Yes you should, but this was different… I had been kind of chatting through messages for quite a while…" Sophie said defensively, "I wasn't going to *leave* Ollie with him! Anyway, they got on fine, he was really good with him and Ollie seemed to thrive on feeling like we were like a family- like being out with a mummy and daddy…"

"What about you- did you like him?" Tina asked, her eyes sparkling at the thought of Sophie having a boyfriend who was in the navy and the prospect of meeting all of his friends.

"I liked him…" Sophie replied thoughtfully, "… but I didn't *fancy* him."

Tina looked disappointed.

"He was quite overly affectionate and kept trying to kiss me, which was rather awkward with Ollie there but I managed to dodge his advances! He just seemed to instantly really like me, which I think is odd because I'd like to take things really slowly…"

"Really? Well, what about if I say the word 'Christian'?" Lou asked.

Sophie smiled bashfully. "Oh yeah… well I guess you have a point. He was nice enough- we got on really well, no awkward silences, he made me laugh and seemed to like me, he got on great with Ollie and that wasn't an issue for him at all… there was nothing wrong with him at all, I just didn't *feel* anything for him… I'd love him as my nanny though!"

"Ask him!" Tina replied, "We could do a nanny share!"

"I think being in the navy might have better prospects for him…" Sophie said, "Ben thinks I'm a complete tart at the moment."

"And why are we bothered about what he thinks all of a sudden?" Lou asked with raised eyebrows.

"Oh I don't know… I just feel like I have to explain myself to him still and he just always seems to be there. He called when we were out with Will and I made the mistake of answering the phone- I don't know why… but after finding the condom in the back of my car and then bumping into Mick and then calling when I was out with *another* man he doesn't think I'm a good role model for Ollie… when actually all Ollie knows is that we went to the fair with a friend and had a great time!"

"Everyone knows what an amazing Mum you are, Sophie," Joules said, "You don't need to explain yourself to anyone, not even Ben. He left you and didn't contact Ollie for six months- he can't exactly blame you for trying to meet someone else! It's difficult because he lives so close to you still- I wouldn't have thought that his new girlfriend is very happy with the situation either!"

"No and I hope she puts a stop to him coming to the birthday party I've planned for Ollie too! I'm beginning to hate the fact that we always have to *share* those times together! If he had wanted to share those times he shouldn't have left us in the first place… bloody man."

"It does seem a bit… *awkward*…" Jules agreed, "What are you doing this year, for the party?"

"Soft play!" Sophie announced happily, "For the past five birthdays' I've done *everything* myself and had them here but last year I realised that they were just getting too big for the house. The amount of *time* I took over pass the parcel, making up their party bags, making all the food, coming up with games… and pin the tail on the donkey just isn't as popular as it used to be… for a small fortune instead I've booked the Play Barn and for a couple of hours we'll have it all to ourselves… and all I need to do is bring a cake!" she smiled feeling very pleased with the choice.

"Great! Ollie will love that and it is *much* easier…" Joules replied, "Just a shame if Ben has to come too…"

"Oh well there will be plenty of places in there for me to hide from him... But anyway, at least after quite a lot of activity on the dating front I have one 'maybe'."

***

Nobody questioned Sophie's week off that she had written on the calendar herself. Enid spent the week running up to it making judgements on her suitability for the job, however, due to the fact that she was taking time off- even though everyone else had been on their holidays. Her mother had come up trumps and booked a last minute all-inclusive package to Lake Garda and told Sophie that it was to be their treat, enjoying time with their only grandson and daughter as they lived so far away.

"Thank your Dad," she had told Sophie on the phone, "and maybe you'll meet a nice man in Italy! Then we can come and visit you there! Lake Garda has some *very* exclusive resorts."

Going on holiday with her parents at the age of thirty-six wasn't ideal, she thought, but admitted that she was in no position to complain and was eternally grateful them for treating her and Ollie like this.

She remembered what Ruth had told her about staff's leave being cancelled at the last minute and so tried to be the perfect employee the week before hers- not that she was ever *not* the perfect employee, she thought, but she didn't want to do anything to incur Enid's wrath.

"Before anyone goes on annual leave…" Enid had told her on the Monday morning before she was due to go away, "… they need to put a memo round the school so that everyone is *aware* and can contact you before you go- just in case they have any urgent questions. You should get all staff to sign and say that they've read and understood the memo. This is, as I'm sure you're aware, an appendix to our Annual Leave Policy."

Sophie wasn't aware of it and didn't remember anyone else doing this but drew up and printed out several memos to put up at various points in the school and with nothing else to do that morning she decided to take one round herself and get everyone that she could find to sign it. Most of the staff don't even know who I am, she thought, so I don't suppose anyone will object if I have a holiday. As she went around the school collecting signatures she found that most people were happy for her that she was getting out of the place for a while at least and nobody could think of any reason why she shouldn't be allowed. Because I have no responsibilities at all here, she thought, in stark contrast to my life where I am responsible for everything.

By mid-morning she returned to the office with pages full of signatures, to Enid's visible displeasure.

"Did you get all the teaching staff...?" she asked as she glanced over all of the names on the paper.

"Yes I printed out the current staff list," Sophie replied, "Everyone who works here today is on the list. It might change tomorrow of course…"

Enid continued to inspect the memo ignoring Sophie's remark. "And everyone in the office has signed it…? Did you get Chris… oh yes…? What about the health and safety man… yes… the kitchen staff…?"

What is going to happen next week, Sophie thought, that the kitchen staff are going to have to bother me about? She sat down at her desk and looked at Ruth in exasperation. Enid accepted defeat and handed Sophie the memo.

"File it in the memo folder then. All signatures seem to be present."

Sophie took it and went to find the memo folder feeling like she had won another small victory. In this place, she thought, you have to take your victories when you find them. She filed her memo and returned to her desk.

"Did you manage to get all that photocopying done…?" Enid asked casually.

"Mmm hmm," Sophie nodded.

"… What about all the pamphlets that I asked you to fold..?"

Sophie continued to nod. Enid raised her eyebrows and turned back to her computer in defeat and started to type.

"Did you finish that report that Mrs Wright asked you to write...?" she asked without taking her eyes off her monitor, throwing one last spanner into the works.

Sophie looked at her blankly. This was the first she'd heard of any report. She searched her brain for any memories of being asked to do such a task. She frowned at Enid who continued to work, thinking deeply.

"You do remember don't you?" Enid asked.

Sophie searched her face for any kind of clue as to what she was talking about. Enid sighed and pushed her keyboard away, turning her attention towards Sophie.

"Does Saint Andrews ring any bells? Report? Costings? Needs analysis?"

Sophie continued to think. She opened her mouth to speak and then thought better of it and let it fall shut.

"Is there any reason why you are doing goldfish impressions?" Enid asked impatiently, "You *must* remember. Mrs Wright asked you to write a report about the school and then provide a *detailed* account of the needs of each student and, with that in mind, how much it was going to cost. I told you weeks ago Sophie, Mrs Wright wants it by Friday. A week on Monday at the very latest." Sophie groaned inwardly at the suggestion that she would be handing anything in next Monday, her flight to Italy leaving on Friday night. "Mrs Wright needs it so that she then knows what funding we can apply for," Enid looked at Sophie with an 'I'm always right' expression.

Sophie's mood of optimism deflated.

"I thought she just wanted to know what I thought of the school…" she replied hesitantly, "That's all she said…"

"She does want to know that," Enid said, "she also asked… maybe you weren't at the meeting… anyhow, she also wants to know student numbers, their training needs and if anyone's going to cost us extra. It will have been written down in the day book which you should be checking every morning when you arrive at work. By Friday. Here."

Enid dumped a large bundle of paperwork on Sophie's desk, stretching over her own.

"These are the Needs Analysis. They arrived from Saint Andrews this morning."

"So I couldn't have done it before anyway… if they've only just got here…" Sophie's voice trailed off, not wanting to sound at all like she was questioning Enid who made no further comment on the matter.

Sophie looked helplessly at Ruth.

"I'll just go and get a red folder…" she said to no one in particular and made her way to the cupboard, hoping that Ruth would follow her through. She did so and shut the door behind her.

"The look on your face is priceless!" she laughed.

"It's not funny!" Sophie wailed, "What does she mean? I've no idea what she wants me to do! They never show you things or explain things properly."

"Don't worry!" Ruth said, still smiling, "Enid will be getting you to do something for the sake of it. They've got the training contract already and I sorted out the schedule last week. The Needs Analysis are never looked at again anyway so it really won't matter what you write," she opened the filing cabinet and flicked through the folders before finding the one she needed from which she pulled out a sheet of paper and gave it to Sophie. "Just use one of these for each student- all the information is on the system already so you'll just be copying it out. They do so like everything on paper. Enid wrote what's there already so she shouldn't have a problem with it! Then just do a little summary of the school on a document- take it off their website, that's what I'd do. At least you've got something to do this week!"

Sophie instantly hugged her friend. "I love you Ruth! I don't know how I'd survive here without you!" she took the sheet of paper and started to photocopy it.

Sophie had finished her report by the end of the day on Tuesday but she managed to make it look like she was hard at work on it for the rest of the week and handed it in complete to Enid on Friday, neatly presented in a red folder. Everything had to be in a red folder. Before Enid had a chance to comment she was distracted by a telephone call which then took her down to the office to discuss something with Mrs Wright leaving the coast clear for Sophie to leave on time for her holiday. She was out of her seat by twenty-eight minutes past, ignoring the look of horror on Laura's face that she was leaving two minutes early.

"Bye everyone!" she trilled happily, "Have a good week! I will miss you!"

"Don't lie!" Ruth said laughing, "You won't give us a second thought once you're out of that door."

"Yes you're right actually, I won't!" Sophie joked, "See you!"

***

Sophie's plane was taking off from Heathrow where they were meeting her parents at 10pm. She collected Ollie from school and went back home to put the last few bits and pieces in their bags and sort the house out before they left it for a week.

"Mummy is just going to do a little bit of cleaning before we go. Can you play nicely while I do that?" she asked Ollie, "Please don't make a mess."

"I'm going to play at going on holiday," the boy stated and started to make plane noises.

Satisfied that he was meaningfully occupied Sophie got on with her jobs, rushing manically round the house trying to get everything done. She wanted to leave by four to give them plenty of time to get up the motorway in the Friday night traffic and be at the airport to be able to calmly check in and catch their flight. Sophie was on a mission. She dragged the cases down the stairs and called up to Ollie that she was about to load up the car.

"OK Mummy!" the little voice came down the stairs, sounding like he was still happily occupied.

Great, Sophie thought, now if I just get our hand luggage sorted and she retrieved a ruck sack from under her bed.

"Ollie, can you choose some tiny toys to go in our hand luggage please?" she called to the boy as she hurried downstairs to put his packed tea in the bag and then back up to get him a change of clothes, "they can't be big because our bag wouldn't fit on the plane if we took too much stuff but you might want something to play with!"

She zipped the ruck sack up. "There!" she said triumphantly, "just passports and flight itinerary then we'll be off on our holidays!"

***

They arrived at the airport at seven Sophie had plenty of time to find the long stay car park and make her way with Ollie to the bus stop to catch the interlink bus. She sent her

Dad a message to say that they were on their way over to departures and where would they like them to meet. Just as she was putting her phone in her pocket it started to ring and she looked, expecting it to be her Dad's response. To her horror it was the Elm Tree.

"What do *they* want..?" she thought and hesitated, unsure if she should answer it or not. The phone ceased to ring briefly but whoever it was persisted and it immediately rung again. "Here we go…" she said and answered. "Hi," she said flatly.

"Good evening, Sophie." She heard Enid's unmistakeable voice and felt a feeling of dread, despite being miles away.

"Hi!" she replied brightly cursing herself for answering, "are you alright?"

"*I'm* alright," Enid replied. There was a pause as if Enid was expecting Sophie to identify what wasn't alright. Sophie was in no mood now for Enid's games.

"I'm just at the airport Enid, my flight leaves soon. Did I forget something?"

"I'm just going through your report now Sophie. I'm struggling to identify…"

At that moment a plane that had been approaching roared directly over Sophie's head and Enid's sentence was drowned out. She waited for the noise to subside but then the bus to the airport arrived and belched to a stop, the doors whooshing open and the engine chugging as the driver waited for her to get on.

"I'll have to call back!" Sophie shouted down the phone, making the instant decision that she would deal with the aftermath of hanging up on Enid *after* her holiday.

***

As she stood in line some time later to go through to the departure lounge Sophie couldn't quite believe that they'd made it. She smiled to herself as she lifted her hand luggage up onto the conveyer belt to be security checked feeling liberated that she was leaving all her worries behind, for a week at least. As she dumped the bag into one of the black plastic boxes she was suddenly aware of a loud buzzing noise coming from within. She froze and glanced from side to side, seeing if anyone around her reacted to the sound. Her mother, standing behind her poked her firmly in the ribs with her finger.

"They're good aren't they?" she whispered loudly and smiled knowingly, nodding her head towards Sophie's bag. Sophie was horrified.

"No! It's a toothbrush!" she said to her mother, and then louder, as if addressing the whole queue and anyone else who cared to listen. "It's a toothbrush! My electric toothbrush is in my bag. An *electric toothbrush...*" she dived for her bag, apologising to the security guard who was about to push it through the x-ray machine. "I'll just switch off my toothbrush!" she said and unzipped the bag, revealing the offending toothbrush sitting on the top of her badly packed belongings happily buzzing away. She took it out of the bag and held it up just to make sure that everyone who had heard the noise could see and then clipped the end off to remove the batteries. She frowned at her disappointed mother.

***

They arrived at their hotel in the early evening following an uneventful flight and long, stuffy connecting bus journey where the tired tourists had to endure a couple of hours' narrative from the lively young tour rep about her recent promotion. How she kept her enthusiasm up for so long when each one of her jokes was met with a wall of silence as the forty sour faces just off the plane from Heathrow fanned themselves with her leaflets, Sophie didn't know. Bubbly was a word that was invented for this girl and Sophie admired her persistent spirit. The main item of information that Sophie picked up from the tour reps monologue was that, sad that she was that it was her friend who had lost her job to make way for her and had to return to Britain to face a life of rain and unemployment, *her* life had been nothing but cocktails, sun and freebies since she moved up into the space that had been vacated and life was just peachy. She looked at her captive audience with some pity that they didn't have a job like hers. Sophie wondered how long the girl could keep up her chirpy demeanour if she had to sit opposite Enid for a day.

After a long drive the bus started pulling into hotel car parks and releasing handfuls of tourists eventually stopping at the Hotel Da Vinci where Sophie and her family were staying. They made their way into the hotel reception which was bustling with activity. A batch of new residents were checking in while the last intake was checking out. Sophie looked around the fraught scene as they waited in turn. The couple in front of her seemed to be trying to change the room they had booked to one that was away from a road as they had come on holiday for some peace and quiet and not to listen to the sound of traffic. They raised their voices, as they attempted to overcome the language barrier, over the sound of a group of young men laughing raucously at a nearby table which was obscured by empty pint glasses. A small boy helping himself to a fizzy drink at the self-service bar, his cup overflowing, jumped and spilled the liquid as his father shouted at him to behave from the other side of the room, a rather pink looking woman sitting next to him continued to read her British newspaper. Sophie had to practically shout to explain to Oliver that he would have to wait a minute before he could go and help himself to a drink triggering a barrage of complaints of it 'not being fair'.

"I thought that I told you to leave Mr Grumpy behind?" Sophie said lightly, "remember we talked about that at home?"

Oliver scowled at her, feeling hot and bothered in the intense heat and after the long bus ride from the airport.

"I put him in the suitcase," he told her.

Great, Sophie thought and sighed, beginning to feel rather hot and bothered herself.

The reception area led into the dining room which was also busy as rather flustered looking holiday makers stood in line at the huge buffet tables which were covered with metal dishes full of food from every nation it seemed- except the one that they were in. Sophie craned her neck so that she could look through the window out to a pool where the sun still beat down on all those still sunbathing and swimming, enjoying the sunshine to the last, excited cries and chatter rising above the general noise. A sign was propped up against the bar which read, 'English Football-showed here'.

"It's busy…" she said dubiously, thinking that her mother would have booked a more exclusive apartment. Her mother looked crossly at Sophie's father who stood with their passports, blinkers on ignoring his wife, waiting to collect their keys at reception.

"Yes," her mother stated sourly, "busy with English '*Sun*' readers! They are the last people I'd want to share my holiday with! Jerry, what were you thinking?"

"It was rather last minute dear…" Sophie's dad's voice trailed off, "I'm sure Oliver will love it!" he smiled indulgently at his Grandson and ruffled his hair. "You can eat as many ice lollies as you like!" Ollie beamed at his Granddad.

***

They made it out to the pool before dinner and found plenty of spare sun loungers as people started to drift off back to their rooms. Sophie chose two still basking in sunlight and covered them with beach towels from the bathroom, having forgotten to bring her own, and pushed her tote bag underneath one pulling out her headphones, MP3 player and book; ready to settle down for a while. Sophie's mother soon joined her and lay down on the next lounger, covering her face with a huge floppy hat, the same turquoise colour as her patterned sarong. Sophie had quickly dressed Ollie in his all-in-one sun suit, which covered him from his ankles to his wrists and up to his neck, and a hat and herself in one of two bikinis' that she had kept ever hopeful that one day she *would* go on holiday and then covered it up with an oversized white vest top, feeling rather awkward about walking poolside with such white limbs. She wore some heeled sandals to at least make her legs look slim, if not bronzed. A brief feeling of regret passed over her for not having time to do a tan before the holiday but then she made a firm decision that the holiday was for her to spend time with her son and parents and so it didn't matter what she looked like. Her recent activities in the dating department making her feel like she was now constantly being judged on the way she looked.

"I spoke with your sister just before we left, about your situation," her mother spoke from beneath her hat, "you know, if you don't meet someone by the wedding then there will be *plenty* of eligible bachelors there for you to choose from! She told me that there would be at least four single men and maybe more- the best man's relationship seems to be on *very* rocky ground. You'd have to move house, of course, if you met someone at the wedding... as it's so far to travel..."

"Or I could just enjoy the occasion!" Sophie replied. "If I don't meet anyone by then, which is highly likely if recent events are anything to go by, then I'll just go with Ollie and have a nice time. I'm sure I don't *need* to meet anyone! I wish she'd not bothered to put 'Plus One' on my invitation, she *knows* I don't have a plus one."

"Well maybe she just thought that it was about time to find one!" her mother stated unsympathetically.

Sophie firmly pushed her headphones into her ears, covered her eyes with sunglasses and lay back, watching her Dad pulling Ollie round in the swimming pool on an inflatable air bed as she rubbed sun cream onto her body. What's wrong with being single anyway, she wondered. Her gaze drifted over to the bar where a guy with jet black hair and olive skin stood diligently polishing the brass of the beer taps looking smart but cool in his unbuttoned white shirt and black trousers with a little white apron around his waist. He casually looked over to where Sophie laid, his eyes lingering for a moment and then turned his attention back to a customer at the bar. Sophie reached under her sun lounger to retrieve her book and opened it to the first page. She held it up as if reading while peering over the top to the bar. She watched as he served the woman a drink and then got on with his polishing, his eyes wandering around the few people still left around the pool and then resting on Sophie again.

What a result, Sophie thought; being checked out by the Italian bar tender although admittedly checking women out is probably one of the perks of such a job. She smiled despite herself and turned her attention back to her book. Reading felt like an effort though and she soon tired of it. She stretched her body out feeling the heat of the afternoon sun beat down on her bare skin and sighed deeply, letting the unaccustomed but welcome feeling of total relaxation wash over her.

What felt like moments later but was actually an hour Sophie was startled by her Mother prodding her again. She lifted up her glasses and looked with one eye open, the sun now being low in the sky.

"It's nearly six o'clock darling. We're all ready for tea," her Mother had changed into a summer trouser suit and made herself up.

Sophie yawned sheepishly and sat up, looking beyond her to the other side of the pool where Ollie and his Granddad stood, also dressed for dinner.

"OK Mum but we've just got here... I'll meet you later? It's so nice to chill out for a change..."

"Dinner is served between six and seven darling so we're best to go down now and get a table. We're all hungry."

"OK well you go down then. I'll meet you in a bit."

"If you don't eat dinner here then there won't be any food until breakfast!" her Mother said, as if talking to her as a child, "you'll waste away if you don't eat anything!"

"I'll be fine for one night- I'll grab something later from the bar."

"You can't survive on crisps darling!"

"What time's breakfast?" Sophie asked, not particularly feeling like moving from her sunny spot.

"Breakfast is from half seven until nine but your Dad and I like getting there early. Don't we Jerry?" she addressed her husband who had appeared by her side holding Ollie's hand, the boy pulling away from him and saying he wanted to go back in the pool. He nodded dutifully looking less than convinced, as if a lie in was his preferred option. "They have lunch here at twelve and then there's a little bus that goes into the town every day at two so I thought we could do that tomorrow."

"I'm not sure that Ollie will want to go walking round the town in the midday heat..." Sophie's voice trailed off.

"It won't be midday darling it will be two o'clock," her Mother replied.

"Well OK, whatever, we were hoping just to be able to chill out by the pool..."

"Ollie will get bored being in the pool *all* day!"

"No he really won't, he'll love just being able to play."

"Well your Dad and I will be on the bus at two," her Mother said briskly, "I see that the hotel also has crazy golf so I've booked us all to have a game tomorrow."

"Oh Mother..." Sophie replied, "We've not come to Italy to play crazy golf...! Please can we *not* do that, it's one sure fire way to get your grandson into a bad mood- it's frustrating even when not played at this temperature..."

"Well, we'll see…" her mother said, "anyway, hurry up for dinner. We'll see you there," she turned round and took Ollie firmly by the hand and led him away, Sophie could hear her saying that swimming time was done for today and it was tea time now. She slumped back down onto her lounger and looked up to the clear blue sky.

Surely we can forget about clock-watching on *holiday*, she thought and closed her eyes again. The sound of the shutters being pulled down over the bar disturbed her peace again and she looked over to where she saw the handsome bar man locking them shut. He made his way to the end of the pool where he started to unwind the cover. Maybe it is time to get going then, Sophie thought and not wanting to hold him up she gathered up her belongings and made her way over to her balcony. She walked past him and he looked up and smiled.

Sophie smiled back and said, 'Bye' and continued over to her balcony, climbing over the waist height wall as gracefully as she could just in case he was still watching. She pulled the French doors open and stepped inside, depositing her bag and towels on the bed and then returned to the window, behind the curtain, to see if he was still there. She could hear spraying now and saw him holding a hose, watering the hanging baskets and flower beds around the pool, the water spilling over onto the paving slabs where he stood in his flip flops and rolled up trousers. Sophie idly watched him for a moment wondering why Italian men were so much more handsome that English ones and then pulled away from the window to get changed for dinner. I'm here to chill out, she thought, but if I *was* going to have a holiday romance then *he* is the one I'd like it with.

Despite her mother's initial efforts at getting Sophie out of her sun lounger she soon gave up and Sophie managed to spend most of the week firmly on it. They had quickly got into a little routine of Sophie going for an early swim while her parents took Ollie for breakfast, followed by swimming, sunbathing, siesta, sunbathing and swimming. She felt closer to Oliver as the week went on and Sophie enjoyed the time together just playing and not having to worry about the usual daily chores and timings. As the week passed she also got more adventurous with her flirting with the gorgeous guy behind the bar, deciding that she needed some practice anyway and here was an opportunity, and he responded to this with the same. He smiled and said 'Hello' to her in passing, winked at her on one occasion when she ordered some drinks, watched her as she swam up and down the length of the pool each evening as he watered the plants and often waved from the bar if their eyes met fuelling Sophie's imagination where she had already moved to Italy with Ollie to be with him. Ollie was having his own success in the love department and had taken a shine to the kid's club organiser and followed her round at every chance. Her name was Lucia and she seemed to have endless reserves of good humour and energy and could be seen at the crack of dawn taking the Early Bird exercise class and at the end of the evening judging the children's singing competition.

On the last day of the holiday there was to be a children's disco in the evening followed by a quiz and Lucia came over to ask Sophie if they would be there. Sophie stopped her reading and sat up, putting her sunglasses on her head.

"What time is that?" she asked hesitantly, being wary of committing to being anywhere other than poolside especially on the last day of their blissful holiday.

"It's later. At eight o'clock. Your son is very good at dancing," she said. "He shows me yesterday. He will enjoy."

"Oh yes, I'm sure we'll be there!" Sophie replied feeling a little miffed that she knew more about his dancing than she did. Unless I get a better offer which is highly unlikely, she thought.

"I will look out for you!" Lucia said cheerfully.

Sophie settled back in her lounger and put her sunglasses back on. She cast her eyes around the pool area to see where the object of her recent daydreams was. At first she couldn't see him but then he appeared carrying a heavy looking box which he dropped down onto the bar and proceeded to unpack, filling up the fridges with cans of soft drinks. Sophie sighed and returned to her book, no holiday romance for me, she thought, never mind, I guess there's not much point to them anyway.

Ollie was excited about the disco and Sophie gave into his wishes and left her poolside spot for a while to help him gel his hair before dinner, Lucia having said that it would look 'cool' that way. Her parents suggested that they take him down to eat while she had one last swim, their bus taking them to the airport first thing in the morning. The only really bad thing about holidays, she thought as she swam up and down, was that they had to come to an end. Gradually it was only Sophie in the pool, swimming in silence, the only noises that she could her was the gentle swishing of the water and the sprinkling of the hose as the bar man got on with his daily jobs. As he got round to the last flower bed she reluctantly decided that she should really start to think about getting out. She swam back to the shallow end and climbed up the stairs to retrieve her belongings from her home for the week, feeling sad that tomorrow it would be inhabited by somebody else. She gave her hair a quick rub with and then wrapped the beach towel around her dripping wet body deciding to dry off properly in her room and made her way over to her balcony.

"Hi!" the bar man waved and called over to her, more animated than she had seen him all week. "Hi!" he said again, smiling broadly.

"Hi!" she replied.

He stopped what he was doing and walked over to her. Sophie's tummy filled up with butterflies as the object of her recent daydreams approached. She waited awkwardly as he made his way over to where she stood; glancing around her just to make sure it was actually she that he was talking to and not someone else. Up close he was more perfect than she had imagined his perfect olive skin contrasted against the crisp whiteness of his shirt, jet black hair and deep brown eyes. She self-consciously folded her arms trying to cover the redness of her skin where she had neglected to reapply sunscreen and felt very pale. He stopped before her still smiling and fixed his smouldering eyes on hers. They stood in silence for a moment, Sophie not sure now what to say as formalities had already been exchanged.

"Vieni qui spesso?" he eventually said in his thick and seductive accent.

Sophie hadn't studied Italian and had gone on holiday assuming that the Italians would just speak English. She had made an effort in the fact that she had purchased a tiny phrase book and could now ask where the toilets were and how much do ice cream's cost but that was where it ended. She looked blankly for a second.

"Do you speak English?" she eventually replied.

"Inglese?" he said. "Non parlo degli inglesi. Posso parlare solo la mia propria lingua. Lei è molto bello."

Sophie's head swam in the wonderful words but had no idea how to respond. She swiftly took out her phrase book to try a different tact and flicked through the pages eventually finding what she wanted as the bar man stood patiently waiting.

"Par-la An-glai-se?" she replied, putting emphasis on each syllable. She frowned at herself as she tried to say what she saw in the book but realised she might actually now be talking 'O' Level French and then looked at him hopefully, the language barrier immediately taking away the romance of her fantasies.

"La città è buona la fa venerdì sera vuole venire per una bevanda?" he replied. His words flowing from his mouth so quickly that Sophie couldn't even begin to reference them in her book. She put the useless publication back into her bag and looked into his beautiful eyes. Part of her wasn't bothered by the fact that she had no idea what he was saying, just listening to him talk was giving her enough pleasure, apart from the slight awkwardness it was causing by not understanding.

"Are you finished for the night?" she asked hopefully. Again a silence descended on them for a moment.

"Se lei è libero poi mi incontra dopo nel quadrato di città. So un ristorante attraverso l'acqua che serve il realmente buono cibo. Lei può incontrarmi dopo?"

Sophie bit her lip; this was a communication barrier beyond any she had ever experienced before. She decided to have one last stab at it by using the international language of gestures. She tapped her watch.

"Are you finished?" she repeated. The man shrugged and grinned.

"Sarò giù alla sbarra di hotel di raccogliere I miei salari a otto. Incontrarmi lì se lei ama."

"Ah," Sophie nodded, admitting defeat. "OK well nice speaking to you! We're going home tomorrow which is a shame."

They smiled and nodded at each other.

"Spero che la veda dopo. Ho sperato di voi parlare tutti settimana. Penso che lei è molto bello, lei ha un bel sorriso. Amerei vedere il suo sorriso ogni giorno."

Sophie looked at him longingly and sighed. She smiled.

"Really nice talking to you," she held up her hand and waved. "Bye."

"Arrivederci. Spero che la veda dopo."

In her relief that the stilted conversation was at an end Sophie held her thumbs aloft and turned on her heel, the thought of using sign language having got the better of her. What are you *doing*, she thought to herself as she hurried back to her apartment cringing at her own goofiness. *Thumbs up* woman what were you *thinking?* Oh my God he must think I'm a *total* nerd, if there is such a thing in Italy. She shook her head and frowned at her own complete idiocy. *Thumbs up*, she thought again, *thumbs up?*

She returned to her room to get showered and changed for the children's disco trying to put the embarrassing episode behind her. Every so often it popped back into her head-

thumbs up- and made her wonder at her own sanity. The most gorgeous and cool looking Italian waiter and I go and do *thumbs up*, she thought crossly, at least that's one reason to be glad about going home tomorrow. Her parents were still in the dining room with Ollie when she got down stairs. Sophie helped herself to a quick snack from the buffet before they all went outside through the French windows at the front of the hotel to a small stage area set up for the children to dance. They found a seat at the front and Ollie ran over to find Lucia and show her his new dance moves while Sophie's Dad went off to order them all some drinks.

He waited to be served at the hotel bar, nodding at the young man who made way for him as he put some money in his wallet. The man briefly looked around as if looking for someone and then made his way out of the hotel alone.

***

Landing at Heathrow the next day Sophie couldn't remember ever feeling so low. She had left behind an amazing place, a gorgeous man and a lovely time. OK so she couldn't communicate with the gorgeous man but if she had stayed she would have taken Italian lessons and then been able to explain about the 'Thumbs up' mistake.

The passengers all shuffled off the plane and entered the airport building and Sophie switched her phone back on. She hadn't missed it for the week, its silence being a welcome break and dropped it back into her bag. As soon as she had it beeped and then again and again and then she heard its ring tone.

"You've been missed!" her Mum said, "It must be important!"

Sophie thought back to the previous week when she had hung up on Enid and groaned with dread.

"I'll listen to them later," she replied, "I'm sure they're nothing."

She finally had a look at her messages when she got back to the car with Ollie, having collected their bags, said goodbye to her parents, who were catching a connecting flight to Scotland, and made their way out of the airport and onto the bus to take them back to the long stay car park. There were texts from Paul, Dan, Phil and Mick. Sophie clicked her tongue. No, no, no, maybe, she thought. She read Mick's message which suggested a date when she got back. Maybe, she thought again. Then dreading the sound of Enid's voice she listened to her voice mailbox.

"Hi Sophie. It's Jon. Remember we met. I'm outside your house. Are you in? I'd like to see you again."

Jon, Sophie thought, *Jon*? She thought for a second and then remembered. Oh my God, *Jesus Jon*? She wished that it had been Enid. She listened to the next message.

"Sophie, are you in? I can see there is a light on. I want to see you again."

At least the timer switch is working, Sophie thought, but oh my *God.* She looked at the message details and saw that they were left last Saturday night. She shuddered to think what state her nerves would have been in had she been at home. Another three messages followed.

"Sophie you left me sitting in the pub. You never said goodbye. I'm waiting to see you."

"Sophie I thought that you were different from the rest. I've been persecuted by everyone. I thought you were different. I want to see you again."

"I'm going to wait here until you answer my messages."

Sophie gasped and clutched at her throat, dropping her phone into her lap.

"What are you doing Mummy?" Ollie asked form the back.

"Oh nothing darling, Mummy just suddenly thought I'd lost my keys but look, found them!" she held up her keys for him to see and looked over her shoulder, smiling. "Off we go, back home," she turned back round her mind racing. She picked up her phone.

"Mummy, are we going yet?" Ollie asked.

"Yes darling I'm just checking something!" Sophie replied and text Joules.

'Hi! Back in the country. Are you busy in an hour or so- Jesus weirdo hanging around my house last week!'

She tied her hair up into a pony tail, admiring her tanned face and found some little boxes of raisins at the bottom of her bag to keep Ollie occupied for a moment. Joules soon replied.

'That's funny- I'm sure there was a story on the news on Tuesday that some guy claiming he was Jesus had been arrested after three men were stabbed on Saturday night'.

Sophie's body went cold and she sat frozen in her seat her mind racing. She returned her attention to her phone and re-read the message from Mick.

'I'd love to' she replied, deciding that she needed a man about the house after all.

***

Sophie didn't feel any enthusiasm about returning home and Ollie spent most of the journey crying because he missed Lucia. When they got back she checked for anyone hanging around before they got out of the car and did a quick sweep of the house just in case anyone had broken in and was waiting for their return- looking in cupboards, under beds and behind doors. Once satisfied that they were alone she miserably got on with the mundane chores of unpacking their bags and putting on the washing before she retreated into bed. She sat up for a while looking at nanny agencies and wondered how feasible it would be to sell the house and move to Italy, sure that she would find a job that Ollie could come with her too, Italians seeming to be more welcoming to children than the English. She loved the way that the locals had reacted to Ollie with joy and happiness although, of course, she hadn't understood a word of what they said. She put her illustrated phrase book into the recycling bin deciding that it had been of no use whatsoever and then downloaded some songs that had been played on a loop through speakers by the pool, she assumed that they were the bar man's choice, and drifted off to sleep listening to them sadly, her thoughts still firmly on holiday.

It was quite some time later that her sleep was disturbed abruptly by the ringing of the doorbell. As she slept so soundly it took a few attempts to get her full attention but when it did she woke up fully and gasped in horror.

Oh my God, she thought, it must be Jon! He must be out of police custody and has come to get me! Her hair flopped messily over her eyes as she grabbed her phone ready to call 999.

"Mummy!" Oliver scampered through to her bedroom and threw himself onto her bed and between the covers before she had a moment to think. "Mummy, who's at the door?"

"I don't know darling," she said lightly, not wanting her feelings of alarm to show. What is it with people ringing my doorbell in the middle of the night anyway, she thought? Her phone in her hand started to ring and she looked at the caller ID. It was Christian. *Christian,* she thought, what does *he* want *now*?

Sophie looked at the clock, it was half past two. She sighed, pushed her hair away from her eyes and sinking back into her pillows groaned loudly, ignoring her phone. She covered her head with her duvet making Ollie laugh at the late night game of hide and seek.

"Here we go!" she said, the duvet muffling the sound of her voice. She sat back up. "Let's go back on holiday," she said to her son flatly.

"Yes!" Ollie clapped his hands and bounced up and down on the bed, his face beaming. "Can we go back to Italy?" Sophie felt guilty for suggesting it.

"Oh, maybe not, not right now anyway. Mummy will just go and get the door."

The bell rang again impatiently.

"Alright, hang on a minute!" she said crossly now, feeling annoyed that Christian always seemed to think that it would be OK to disturb her sleep.

"Who's at the door, Mummy?" Ollie asked again.

"It's just Christian," she replied flatly.

"Who's Christian, Mummy?" Oliver asked.

"Oh, he's the estate agent darling, you know the man who came round to see our house? He must have something important to tell me, something that couldn't wait until the morning," the phone rang again and she put it to her ear. "You snuggle up in bed and I'll be back up in a minute. Christian!" she hissed down the phone. "What are you *doing*?"

"Hi Sophie," Christian's voice was at the other end of the phone, "are you going to let me in or what?"

Sophie made no attempt to tame her wild hair as she stomped downstairs in her floral pyjamas to answer the door, yawning wildly and wondering if anyone could get divorced two weeks after their wedding.

She reached the bottom of the stairs and unlocked the door, pulling it open paying no heed to the state she must have looked. Christian stood there shivering and smiled at her apologetically.

"Can I come in?" he asked, not batting an eyelid at her crazy hair do. He glanced at her pyjamas briefly but made no comment.

"I've just got out of bed," she told him in explanation. He nodded and stepped into the house, closing the door on the evening chill. Sophie stood with her arms folded, rubbing them to keep warm, not having reacclimatised yet to the British summer. Christian thrust his hands in his pockets, not looking like he had much to say.

"So..." Sophie started, "so you're married now then?" she nodded her head and looked thoughtful. "I saw the photos."

She looked at Christian her eyes pleading for an explanation but none was forthcoming.

"You might have seen that I 'Liked' them," she paused briefly, "anyway what a surprise to see you. Are you just back from your honeymoon then? How was it?" she looked at him with challenging eyes.

Christian started to speak and then stopped several times before he managed to construct a complete sentence.

"You look great, have you been on holiday?" his reply caught her off-guard briefly and she was momentarily flattered before she remembered how he had deceived her.

"Yes I've been to Italy. We just got back this evening actually so I'm quite tired from the journey," there was no glimmer of remorse on his face. "So, have you just got back from your honeymoon?"

Christian nodded. He reached out to touch her arm but Sophie flinched and so he returned his hand to his pocket.

"I'm so sorry, Sophie, you've got to believe me," his face pleaded for forgiveness. "The last thing I'd have *ever* wanted to do would be to hurt you. I like you so much…"

Sophie shook her head and opened her mouth to respond but Christian put his finger to her lips. The touch of his skin sent shivers through her entire body.

"Please let me finish. I wish I'd met you a long time ago… I've kind of messed up… I like you so much…" he fixed his clear blue eyes on hers, "I think I've fallen in love with you."

Sophie couldn't believe what she was hearing, the words from a daydream that had played over constantly in her head for weeks before she saw him in his wedding photos. The most perfect daydream that had ended with such hurt, the man that she had wanted so much. She wanted to cry.

"What do you mean? What about your wife?" Was he telling her that he was going to leave his wife even though they only got married two weeks ago? She couldn't believe that he now had 'a wife'.

Christian paused now for a second, seriously considering the question.

"I love my wife," he said in explanation, "I just think that I love you too."

Chapter Fourteen

Ollie watched his mother applying another layer of eyeliner in the bathroom mirror as he sat in the bath. Kerry was coming to babysit so that Sophie could meet up with Mick. She had bravely told Christian that she didn't want to see him again despite the fact that she really did, married or not. She told him how she would feel if she found out that someone was cheating on *her* and how she didn't think that he should be entertaining such thoughts about her when he had a new wife. She told him to resolve that situation first and then come back although she knew that she would never see him again and nor would she want to ever be involved with someone who she knew had not been faithful. Although her heart was breaking when she told him all of this she knew that she didn't want to ever be 'the other woman'- sadly sitting around waiting for someone else's marriage to break up when it clearly never would; eagerly waiting for her lover to turn up to take her out to dinner and then receiving a brief message minutes before to say that something's come up and he can't make it after all. She inspected her reflection in the mirror, I'm surely worth more than that, she thought.

"Mummy, why do ladies put make up on?" Ollie asked with interest. "It makes you look different. You have pink cheeks and black eyes and red lips," he observed, "When you don't have make up people will think they don't know you!"

Sophie considered this for a moment and thought that maybe this was becoming true, that she wasn't herself anymore when she went out on dates. She looked at her made-up face and suddenly realised that she was trying to be what she thought men were looking for.

"I don't know darling, sometimes it makes mummy feel prettier when I have pink cheeks and long eye lashes..?" she suggested hopefully.

"I think you look pretty without make up on," Ollie said.

"Well you are a very special boy for saying that!" Sophie said and kissed him on his forehead, avoiding the bubbles in his hair. "One day you will make someone a very lovely husband."

Ollie looked horrified.

"Yuk," he declared, "girls are annoying."

***

Mick arrived at the pub late, clutching a CD in both hands. He looked around worriedly and then instantly relaxed when he spotted Sophie sitting by herself at the far end of the bar. He smiled pleadingly at her, hoping that she would forgive him for being held up.

"Oh man I'm really sorry!" he said as he approached where she sat, "my boss grabbed me just as I was leaving and got me doing jobs that everyone else should have done! I thought I was going to be there all night!" he looked at her with his big puppy dog eyes as if he might cry if she said it wasn't alright.

"It's fine," she smiled and pulled the seat next to her out from under the table, "I have a boss who sounds *exactly* like that. Sit down," she patted the seat for him to take. She felt a fondness for this boyishly good-looking guy. He pushed the CD towards her and smiled bashfully.

"I've made you another CD," he looked at her with wide eyes, "I hope you don't mind… these songs are all about you. I hope you liked the last one."

Sophie took the CD and glanced down the playlist that he had written on the back of the case. 'Wonderful Tonight', 'Crazy For You', 'Right Here Waiting For You', 'Take My Breath Away', 'You're Beautiful', 'Just Can't Stop Loving You', 'I Will Always Love You'...

Should we be using the 'L' word at this early stage, Sophie wondered. She smiled at Mick who was looking at her anxiously.

"Wow," she said, "Thank you. It's... lovely. The last one was, um, really good. You have great taste in music," she didn't tell him that she was slightly freaked out by the content although it was flattering that someone should think so highly of her.

"You look *amazing,* by the way," Mick continued, "You always look amazing."

"Well, you've only seen me twice!" Sophie joked, "Sometimes I don't!"

Mick looked embarrassed and awkward at his comment, her humour being completely lost on him.

"Oh yeah well, you look nice anyway."

"Thank you," Sophie smiled and took the compliment, remembering reading somewhere that it was rude not to and feeling guilty now that she had deflected it. "So, do you want a drink?"

"I'll get it!" Mick quickly offered, "I'll get you another one?"

"Thanks," Sophie smiled again. She felt like she should pay her own way but was getting used to having drinks bought for her at least, "I'll just nip to the loo, while you're doing that."

She jumped off her tall bar stool and made her way over to the toilets feeling happy that this might be a successful date after her recent stream of dodgy ones. She didn't know when one should use the 'L' word but supposed that for everyone it was different. Oh my goodness, she thought, he might love me already- this could be it! She started to imagine Mick as her wedding date. Her mother would probably think that he was too young but she was sure that everyone would *like* him. He seemed fairly inoffensive, had expressed a keenness to meet Ollie and he was so cute- a bit like the good looking one out of Ant and Dec, Sophie thought. At 26 he was ten years younger than her but she didn't think that that was an issue these days- plenty of people had partners much younger than them. She made her way back to their seats.

As she sat down she was shocked by the look of annoyance that was on Mick's face, no longer adorable.

"Are you alright? What's up?" she asked, looking at the drinks in front of him wondering if the bar man had got his order wrong. Mick scowled, much like Ollie did sometimes Sophie thought, when he didn't get his way.

"Those lads over there were checking you out," he nodded his cross-looking head in the direction of a table where a group of middle-aged men sat. Sophie looked slightly incredulous and laughed it off.

"Don't be silly!" she said as she sat back down, "They're probably here for the quiz! We can move next door when that starts, I'm not sure I could endure it again, I've done it once!"

"Don't call me silly!" Mick said sulkily, "I'm not *silly*. They were watching you when you walked past their table."

"Were they?" Sophie frowned and shook her head, "I don't think so. If they were it was probably because I was making so much noise in my boots! It has been said that I sound like a herd of elephants!" her light-heartedness wasn't rubbing off on Mick who continued making evil eyes at the offenders. "Anyway, what have you been up to?" she carried on trying to jolly him along.

Mick seemed reluctant to take his eyes off the men but gradually relaxed back into their conversation.

"I've just been working mainly. That's it really. And I made your CD. And Kevin came round to play computer games with me last night and the night before... actually Kevin comes round most nights... but he wouldn't if you came round!" Mick quickly pointed out.

"Ah OK. I don't really play computer games..." she said, "I don't want Ollie getting into all that yet so we don't have one... well, just my little lap top," she stopped speaking and there was a pause while she thought of something else to say. Mick looked at her with a drunken puppy dog look, hanging on her every word. "I'm quite hungry actually, do you mind if I get some crisps or something?"

Mick shrugged. "Yes get some crisps," he reached inside his bomber jacket to get his wallet back out again. Sophie stopped him.

"I can get this!" she said and reached to get her own purse out of her bag. She looked over to catch the attention of the guy on shift that night and smiled as she recognised him from the night she was there with Paul. He made his way over to them.

"Hi there, what can I get for you?" he smiled back at Sophie also recognising her and looked at Mick, registered that she was with a different man and winked at her.

"Alright mate!" Mick who had been bristling next to Sophie finally had to speak, "she's with me alright?" He clutched the bar tightly and Sophie was sure that if they had been sitting at a table he would have pushed the thing over in anger. She looked shocked at his response and felt embarrassed.

"It's alright Mick, he's just taking my order!"

"You need to chill out mate," the bar man said and continued to serve Sophie in stony silence. Sophie sat stiffly, her brain now in overdrive, wondering what on earth was going on.

"So!" she said once she'd got her drink and was idly stirring it with the straw as she thought of what to talk about next. Mick's reactions were beginning to worry her slightly. He looked around the pub waiting to confront anyone else who had the cheek to be looking at Sophie but slowly brought his attention back round to her, glancing occasionally from side to side, just to check.

"So, like, what are you doing next weekend? My mate's having a party and he's invited us. I told him all about you."

"Did you? A party? What kind of party?" Sophie asked, slightly worried that she would stick out like a sore thumb at any party that Mick was going to, being so much older than he was. It was a long time since she'd been to a party that wasn't for the under 5's.

"It's just a house party. He still lives at home. His Mam and Pa are going to Spain so he's having a few of us round. We don't need to," Mick said hurriedly, noting the look of doubt on Sophie's face, "I just thought it would be nice."

"I'll have to see… I have Ollie next weekend so… where is it?"

"Near mine," Mick replied, "about an hour from here. He said we can crash over."

Sophie's mind raced trying to think of a suitable excuse, house parties not really being on her radar these days and 'crashing over' not a thing she was keen to do at her age.

"Is it Friday or Saturday?" she asked.

"Friday."

"Ah I can't really do Friday's! My friends always come round on a Friday, it's like a tradition- they'd be really upset if I cancelled them! I could have done Saturday!"

"Friends?" Mick asked, as if this was a new concept to him, that Sophie should have friends. Sophie raised her eyebrows in response, not quite sure what his meaning was. "What friends? See, that's what I have a problem with…" he continued, "friends. What sort of friends?"

"Um… just friends?" Sophie replied, still puzzled by what he meant.

"Yeah but are they male friends or female friends?" Mick asked.

Sophie suddenly wished they were male, just to wind him up. She decided not to cause a scene though. "They're female friends of course. I have four female friends who come round for drinks on a Friday night- is that OK? They're friends from the school- they have children too." What did you think I was doing, she thought, having a wild orgy while your back's turned?

The light dawned and Mick nodded his head without a hint of embarrassment for his manner. "Ah OK. Yeah I don't mind *that*," he considered this for a moment, "Yeah I don't mind if you see your girlfriends… I'd rather you saw me more though!"

Sophie realised that being ten years her junior *and* male meant that Mick was actually very immature. She felt like she would have to negotiate with him like she did with Ollie.

"I'm just going to the loo again anyway," she said and made a point of walking as suggestively as she could, winding round all the tables she could see that had males sitting at them. She wiggled her bottom, pulled her tummy in, puffed her chest out and swished her hair over to one side as she made her way to the toilet, this time smiling and making eye contact with as many men as possible. She could feel the jealous fury bubbling up inside Mick and shook her head in amusement. One child in my life is enough for now, she thought.

Mick had come round the next morning with another CD, full of remorse that he had flown off the handle about the fact that other men were looking at her in the pub. She wasn't really sure what to say to him as the whole thing seemed so ridiculous to her so she had sat and said nothing, as he poured out his heart, which had wound Mick up even more as he then accused her of not caring. Sophie realised then, if she hadn't known before, that she didn't really care because Mick was just a random man she'd met off the internet who didn't really know her at all.

***

Sophie sat idly browsing speed dating sites while Enid was out of the office the next day. She twisted her monitor round slightly to make sure that see the screen couldn't be seen and, looking over at Laura, casually reached down to her bag to retrieve her mobile to put it on her desk, just hidden under a bundle of paper that she was doodling on.

"Got lots of work to do this morning?" Laura asked making Sophie jump and involuntarily shuffle papers round in an attempt to make herself look busy.

"Yes! Yes, quite a lot! I've got all that marking to do," she said, 'marking' being her default response when she had nothing to do and nobody seemed to be bothered to check.

Laura nodded silently and continued to look at her screen. Sophie rested her chin on her left hand and slowly slid her mobile out from under the papers to text her sister.

"Sending text messages?" Laura spoke again and looked over her glasses at Sophie.

Oh my God, Sophie thought, she's psychic. She pretended to type. "No! Not texting no, I was, um… just switching it off as I realised it was still on…"

"You know that texting's not allowed," Laura continued, ignoring Sophie's protestations that she wasn't. "I won't say anything though, on this occasion. I know that we all from time to time need to make contact with the outside world." She got back to her work. "Are you remembering that it's a skirt day tomorrow?" Laura asked as she continued to look at her monitor, "I'm sure that Enid's told you already."

Why is she being so helpful today, Sophie wondered?

"Oh, um, yes she probably did. What time's Enid back anyway?" she asked.

"I think she said she'd be back at lunchtime," Ruth told her.

"It's on the timetable," Laura said.

"Ah OK," Sophie said, nodding. Plenty time to search for speed dating events in the area then, she thought and carried on, every so often moving bits of paper from one side of her desk to the other, randomly typing and looking thoughtfully at her screen to make it appear that she really was very busy.

There was only one company that ran speed dating events in town and they seemed to always be on the first Thursday of the month. She looked at the calendar and noted down Thursday the 6th of October on a piece of paper which she then folded up and put in her bag thinking that she must ask Kerry if she could babysit then. She wondered who would come with her.

***

"I just went by myself," her sister told her on the land line later, having become distracted from her reason for calling- bridesmaid shoes- by Sophie. "I didn't know anyone else who wanted to go and I'd just moved back up here- lots of people just go by themselves. You spend the whole night talking to guys so you don't really need to go with anyone. I don't know how your one does it but when I went all the women got to sit at a table, there was about 20 of us or something, and the men moved round us all one at a time. So we got to sit down for the whole evening! We had a piece of paper with numbers one to twenty or whatever it was and all the men had a sticker with their number. So when each one sat down you got their name and wrote it next to their number and at the end of the two minutes, once they'd moved on, you wrote a quick comment to remember them by- like 'bad breath' or 'really funny' or 'gorgeous blue eyes'- just to trigger your memory because then later on you logged into your speed dating account and put your top three in… and then the men did the same… and once you've put your score in you get to see who has rated you- Andy put me first, I put him second… which is a bit of a sore point!" she laughed, "I told him that it was really first equal but I messed it up. Anyway, do you think you'll go with anyone?"

Sophie thought for a moment.

"No… I don't think so… I can't ask and of my friends because they're all married, happily or otherwise but I'm probably better off just going by myself. I could ask one of the girls from work to come with me but I'm sure that would *not* be appropriate."

"You'll be fine. If you get there just in time, then you won't need to hang around."

Sophie idly picked her mobile up from the bedside table as she spoke to her sister to read a message that had just arrived.

'Do you have a minute?' it read, from Lou.

"Jo, do you mind if I call you again in the week? I have a few things to catch up with," Sophie said. "I need to make another call too and I've got some ironing to do. I'll let you know if I go!"

"Yes and remember to have a look at shoes!" her sister reminded her, "You can get some dyed the same colour as your dress. See if there are any on that website I told you about."

"Oh, OK. Will do! Bye!" she went downstairs to put the phone back and text Lou back as she did.

"Yeah are you OK?"

The phone rang seconds later.

"Hello?" Sophie listened for Lou's voice but just heard sniffs and sobs instead, "Lou? Is that you? Are you OK?" More sniffs could be heard then a huge sigh as Lou tried to compose herself to speak. "Oh my God Lou, are you OK?" Sophie asked in alarm.

"It's Simon," Lou managed to say through her tears.

"Simon? What's wrong? Is he OK?"

More sobbing.

"I don't give a fuck."

"Lou! What's wrong?"

Sophie heard her friend blow her nose noisily and then a door closed before she spoke again. Lou sighed.

"Simon's leaving," she said simply.

"What?" Sophie asked in surprise, "*Leaving*? What do you mean *leaving*?"

"I mean he's leaving," Lou said again.

"Why?" Sophie asked, "Why is he leaving?"

"He's been banging his secretary," Lou broke down again. Sophie couldn't believe it; Lou had seemed to have the perfect husband.

"*What*?" Sophie asked again, "How do you know?"

"Because he left his phone on the kitchen side and he got a text message from her," Lou said through sniffs, "He always carries his phone around with him, *all the time,* and it winds me up. He even takes it into the toilet, he *never* just leaves it lying around. I didn't think anything of it, I was just being nosey and then I saw her name and wondered who it was; I don't ever get any messages from men. I didn't think it would be anything, I just thought it would be something about work and it was, but not what I was expecting!"

Sophie waited for the floods of tears to stop before she tried to speak again. Lou spoke first.

"I mean, with his *secretary!*" she spat, "What a *cliché*! *Everyone* has a flipping affair with their secretary! What a boring, predictable, *obvious* choice. I mean, why not with the 60-year-old tea lady or the cleaner or his male boss? Why did it need to be with *her*? She's so *young* and has such *long hair*. Why couldn't he have had an affair with someone for their *personality* and not their fricking *body?* Why are men so *obsessed* by bodies! *I'd* have a perfect body if I hadn't given birth to his *children!"* she growled down the phone and then broke down again, sobbing uncontrollably.

"Oh, Lou!" Sophie said helplessly, wishing she was sitting with her friend in her kitchen and not at the other end of the phone so that she could give her a hug, "I don't know what to say, I'm so sorry!" Sophie's heart broke for her friend. "Do you want me to come over? I could get Ollie up and pop round...?"

"No. No don't be silly," Lou replied, "You can't drag Ollie out of his bed, " she sighed. "I'm fine. I'm just numb. I don't know what to think anymore. I thought we had it all..." she trailed off.

"Let me know if you need me to look after the children at all or *anything,*" Sophie told her friend, "Anything at all, let me know. What an idiot."

Lou laughed hollowly. "Yes, to put it very mildly. Looks like I'll be joining you on the dating site."

"Oh Lou… maybe not…" Sophie started.

"Yes. I'm not staying with him. I don't know how Tina could have put something like this behind them. I will *never* trust him again. Trust is such a precious and delicate thing- I don't think it can ever be fixed… I took it for granted, that I could trust him- what a fool!" Sophie could hear Lou blowing her nose loudly down the phone. "Anyway," Lou continued, trying to be brave, "what have you been up to, tell me about your exciting life. I've not spoken to you for ages."

"Oh, nothing really. You know my life's not that exciting! Just work… tomorrow's a skirt day. Speed dating maybe…"

"Speed dating!" Lou suddenly sprang to life again, "Book me a ticket."

"Are you sure?" Sophie asked, "It's quite soon…"

"The sooner the better!" Lou declared, "I've wasted enough time already being upset! Bring it on."

***

Sophie walked into work the next day feeling like she'd finally made it. She was wearing a skirt on a skirt day. Of course she hated the place with a vengeance but it felt rather good to know that today she had actually done something right. She smiled at everyone she passed hoping that they would all notice her adherence to the Visitor Policy and almost wanted to bump into someone with trousers on just to say, excuse me but why are you wearing trousers, are you not *aware* that it is a skirt day? She walked confidently into the office; head held high and smoothed down her ironed skirt.

She was greeted by a frosty silence. Ruth half smiled at her but everyone else seemed awkward in her presence. Enid stood up and picked up an empty printer paper box from under her desk and walked towards Sophie with it, holding it out in front of her.

"Phone please," Enid said sharply.

"What?" Sophie was baffled.

"Phone. Please. In the box."

"What?" Sophie repeated again wondering what she'd done this time.

Enid rolled her eyes and inhaled deeply. "Put your mobile phone in the box. As you know they are not to be used on the school premises and yet apparently yesterday you were seen sending a text message from your desk. It is forbidden. I have no option but to ask everyone to relinquish their phones until the end of the day," she held the box out for Sophie to put her phone into. Sophie glanced sideways at Laura who had the look of an innocent angel as she typed. What a grass, she thought. There was no point in trying to plead with Enid to keep her phone in case Ollie's school phoned as Enid would just tell her they could phone the office. Sophie sighed and rummaged in her bag to retrieve her phone and threw it in the box.

"Do you want anything else?" Sophie asked. Ruth stifled a giggle.

"That will be all. Thank you," Enid said and took the box back to her desk. She sat down and put the lid back on it and then put it underneath the desk for safekeeping.

Sophie made her way round to her desk glumly feeling lost without her phone.

"Don't make yourself too comfy," Enid said getting up again, "We're going downstairs to hear all about e-portfolios. Apparently they're the next big thing and Mrs Wright wants us to start using them."

"Now?" Sophie asked.

"Yes now. Why have you got something else to do?" Enid stood up again and buttoned her jacket.

"No, nothing else… apart from marking…"

"Right then off we go," Enid led the troupe of skirt suits out of the office and downstairs to the comfortable study.

The study was set up with a table where the housekeeping staff had laid out the fine bone china tea set and plates of biscuits and sandwiches. Hospitality was second to none for visitors. Sometimes it was a bit much when the visitors weren't used to such formality and only succeeded in making them feel uncomfortable. Usually they were allowed to have first access to the refreshments but the e-portfolio lady seemed to be running late again and so Enid directed everyone else to help themselves and take their seats.

"If she doesn't have the courtesy to be on time then we don't need to show her the courtesy of waiting," Enid said. The training room staff pored their teas and all sat down in a stiff navy line to wait in silence.

Not long after Tim popped his head round the door and then opened it fully.

"Here they are," he said and showed a young woman in. "Sorry Enid we went upstairs first…"

"Why would we have a meeting upstairs?" Enid challenged Tim who couldn't give a reason.

"Hi!" the visitor gushed, clutching a briefcase, "I'm *really* sorry I'm late! There was an accident on the way down- fatal- the M25 can be *horrendous* sometimes! I heard it on the news once I was out of the traffic; it was a really bad smash and, well, awful isn't it?" she looked at the line of five sour faced women, all sitting primly in their matching suits delicately holding their tea cups. Sophie smiled at her sympathetically. She looked pretty in a floral shirt and tight fitting jeans, completely inappropriately dressed for the school. Sophie pulled at her own stiff white collar, wishing that she could wear a floaty floral shirt.

Enid put her cup down on the coffee table and stood up to welcome the visitor.

"Welcome," she said grandly, "welcome to the Elm Tree Preparatory School and Nursery. We hope that you have had a pleasant journey down."

The girl looked at Enid with a bemused look on her face as if trying to work out if she was being serious or not.

"Well yeah, apart from the fatal road crash I guess!" her high pitched laugh resonated around the room.

"Well quite," Enid said stiffly and smoothed her jacket down, "If you would like to help yourself to a drink then maybe we could get started…"

The girl looked over at the hospitality that had been laid on for her benefit and then, out of duty more than anything Sophie thought, asked if she could have a glass of water.

"It's a bit early for biscuits for me," she said, "But you crack on."

The girl's name was Kim and she spoke enthusiastically about her company's e-portfolio system. Sophie listened and wondered if she could catch a quick word with her on her way out and see if they were recruiting. She had used e-portfolios extensively in her last job and Sophie's attention gradually drifted off elsewhere. She thought back to her holiday and yearned to be back there sitting by the pool in the glorious sunshine, having a little swim when the heat got too much and a cold drink from the bar, served by the handsome bar man. Then after lunch going back to the room for a wonderful siesta- what a good idea- to find that the cleaning fairies had been in and the unmade beds that had been lazily abandoned that morning had been crisply made...

The door burst open bringing Sophie back to reality and Mrs Wright joined the group.

"Don't let me interrupt," she said loudly, interrupting Kim who was in the middle of explaining the email system, "What are we learning about?" She smiled expectantly. Kim looked baffled.

"The e-portfolio system..."

"Oh yes of course!" the principal clapped her hands together, "Well carry on; don't let me hold you up!" and she sat upright with her hands clasped in her lap, all ears. Kim opened her mouth to continue. Mrs Wright started to look around the group. "Do we all need to be here?" she asked Enid. Enid looked at who was there. "Who's manning the fort, as it were?" Mrs Wright continued, smiling "someone needs to answer the phone!"

"Well, I thought that we should all know about this..." Enid started to reply.

"What, even *her?*" Mrs Wright nodded towards Sophie.

"Oh well, I suppose she doesn't need to be here…" Enid started to say.

Hello, Sophie thought, I can hear you!

"You probably only needed *senior* management here as this is really just an initial enquiry," Mrs Wright continued, "Enid are you losing your touch?" she laughed smugly. Enid bristled.

"Sophie you can go back to the office now. We'll feedback to you later."

Sophie looked puzzled. "I'm not allowed to answer the phone…"

Kim looked on with some amusement as the power struggle unfolded.

"The phone is diverted so I can deal with anything when I get back. There is a pile of paperwork on the shelf from last Wednesday's training that needs to be filed and then photocopying for next week. Mrs Wright is *right*; we don't all need to be here," Sophie continued to sit, "Off you go then!"

Kim smiled at Sophie who felt like the school dunce now, not needed at the presentation and not able to answer a telephone. Laura asked, having completely missed the point of having an e-portfolio in the first place, if they could still print emails as Sophie made her way out and she felt relieved that she didn't need to endure a whole morning of Enid and Laura ripping the whole idea to shreds. These were two women who resisted change at every opportunity. They'll never buy into someone else's company anyway, Sophie thought, if they want an e-portfolio system they'll just nick all the best bits from other peoples and get the IT man to make it look like theirs.

The office was stuffy and hot when she got back and Sophie opened the window as wide as it would go in an attempt to get some air circulating. She was boiling in her wool jacket and took it off. I hate this place, she thought and retrieved her mobile from the box under Enid's desk. She checked it for messages and slumped down into her chair, I'm not allowed to do anything or be involved with anything and nobody is interested in a thing I have to say. The more time I spend in this job, she decided, the more unemployable I'm going to become and she added 'job websites' to her list of things-to-do, after 'bridesmaid shoes' and 'speed dating'.

Speed dating, up until recent events, had seems like such a random and crazy idea that it wouldn't even have registered on Sophie's radar. Suddenly it seemed like the best idea ever, if her sister could meet her husband that way then why not her and with revived optimism she turned her attention to arranging tickets for the event in town the following month.

***

Sophie wished that she had kept the details of Ollie's party to herself when the day had come. Instead it had become something of a reunion with her parents and sister coming down for the event along with Ben and his mother. Sophie busied herself getting Ollie into his party clothes and retrieved the supermarket cake he had chosen from the top of the kitchen cupboard having decided this year to part from tradition completely and not make it herself. Ollie had spotted the Buzz Lightyear cake anyway when they went shopping and that was the decision made, none of her creations could beat that one. She didn't mind Ben's mum coming to the party at all and made sure Ollie kept in touch with her but resented Ben for leaving them but then still expecting to do some things together. He never contributed to the events financially; he usually arrived late, got Ollie over-excited, made a mess and then left without offering to tidy up.

This year was no different except for once Sophie could also leave the mess behind. At the end of the party she left with Ollie and bags full of presents, the boy's face red and slightly sweaty but smiling wildly.

"Was that good mister?" she he asked him after thanking the soft play staff profusely after her offer of helping them tidy up had been refused. They made their way out to the car. Ben was still making his way to his car and stopped when he saw them and walked back towards them.

"What does he want *now*?" Sophie muttered and immediately felt tense.

"Hey! Good party, *man*!" he said to Ollie. "That was the best party *I've* ever been to!"

"Well it should have been for a hundred and twenty quid!" Sophie said flippantly, not expecting a contribution.

"Yeah, good choice," Ben replied completely oblivious to the comment, "Did you like it dude?" he asked Ollie who nodded his hot little head. "Cool! Listen, Soph, it's cool that we can do this sort of thing together still, you know, it's really important for Ollie…"

Sophie inhaled deeply; don't tell me what's good for Ollie she thought.

"Kind of makes me think sometimes…" he broke off and looked at Sophie as if wanting her to finish his sentence.

Sophie's arms were hurting from the weight of the bags of presents she was carrying and the handles were beginning to dig into her skin. She was in no mood for Ben's remorse.

"Right anyway Ben we've got to go now and open these…" she indicated to the bags.

"Yeah of course, I'd come too but I kind of need to shoot off now…"

"Never mind!" she tried to keep the jubilation in her voice to a minimum, "See you later then. Ollie say goodbye to Daddy, he's going."

She stood while they said their goodbyes and continued onto their car, the tension leaving her body as soon as Ben walked away.

Chapter Fifteen

During the run up to the speed dating event Sophie tied off all other dating business on the internet, sending messages to those she had met and was still to meet that she had actually met someone else now and was no longer available. She painted quite a romantic picture of the meeting with this fictional man, a chance meeting at the park, and spent so much time getting the story just right that she momentarily believed that it was true. If only it were that easy.

The evening that the dating event was taking place came round and Kerry was in place to babysit. Sophie felt slightly put out that she was missing her gym night but full of anticipation that tonight she might meet her future husband. She drove round to collect Lou who still insisted on coming even though her situation was still unresolved with Simon who seemed to be still spending time at the house to look after the children on the days that Lou worked.

"So what's going to happen then?" Lou asked eagerly as she clipped her seat belt shut, "What do we do?"

"Well, I'm not *entirely* sure, but…" Sophie explained what she had understood from the company website as they drove into town. She stopped when Lou started to sob.

"Oh I don't know if I want to do this anymore! I loved Simon! I didn't ever want to meet anyone else!"

Sophie instantly felt guilty, like she was dragging her friend along.

"Well, just sit at the side then, or do you want me to take you home? You don't need to come."

"No, no it's fine. I'll come. Serve the bastard right."

Sophie smiled sympathetically at her friend who was going between still loving her husband and wanting to forgive him to hating him with every inch of her being at regular intervals.

As Sophie was planning for the night she imagined the pub to be in the trendy part of town but as they got closer her satnav took her in the opposite direction and she realised that it was at the harbour instead which was decidedly seedy and just along the road from a dodgy looking lap dancing club. The two ladies looked worriedly at each other.

"Are you *sure* you don't want me to take you home?" Sophie asked, smiling as she pulled up to park the car behind another with no wheels, "Better make sure the windows are wound up."

"I can't leave you here! No it's fine, we'll have a giggle."

The two made their way up the path towards the pub. Sophie pushed the door open and the two walked in, Lou heading straight off to the toilets to sort out the mascara that had started to run down her face following her break down in the car. The pub was spacious with a bar in the middle facing the door and tall tables scattered around. They must have looked out-of-place or lost as the bar tender stopped what he was doing to check that they were alright.

"Oh yeah, fine thanks!" Sophie replied, not really wanting to admit that she was there for speed dating as the bar man was quite attractive but deciding that there was going to be no way of hiding it. She lowered her voice to a whisper, "Is this where the speed dating is?" she hissed. The guy laughed sensing Sophie's concerns.

"It is. The pub should be filling up soon. You'll have a crack! Although…" he looked at Sophie with a twinkle in his eye. "… How come *you* need to come speed dating?"

Sophie was never sure how to respond to this remark, as if she must have done something terrible or have a massive flaw to be single.

"Oh you know, I don't know!" she dismissed the question, "So where do we go?"

"Just stick around here, get a drink. As I say, the place should start getting busy soon. Once everyone's here then Abby will take you all through it. What can I get you?"

"Oh just a soda water and lime please. Lou what do you want to drink?" she asked as Lou reappeared from the toilets minus black rings underneath her eyes.

"I'll have a glass of white wine."

The bar man smiled cheekily at Sophie. "Are you sure you don't need something stronger?"

"No! No I'll be fine with just my soda water thank you."

"Was he trying to get you drunk?" Lou asked once they'd taken their drinks and sat down at one of the tables away from the bar.

"I seem to have a thing with bar men at the moment," Sophie replied, "See *he* looks nice though! Why can't I just randomly meet someone *nice* like him*?"*

"I don't want to be rude darling but isn't he a bit *young*?" Lou asked smiling.

"Is anyone sitting here?" a middle aged heavily made-up woman indicated to the spare seats at the table.

Sophie shook her head. "No. Nobody's sitting there it's just us two. Help yourself."

The woman turned round to two others approaching from the bar, cocktails in hand.

"Over here!" she took her coat off and hung it over the back of the chair signalling to two others to join her. "Thanks," she said, smiling, "I'm Marianne. You're newbies aren't you? I saw you coming in- you looked petrified!" she laughed. "These two are new," she said to the other two women who nodded knowingly.

"So, you've *never* done this before then? I'm Babs by the way. This is Phillipa," she indicated to the third woman who smiled and extended her hand to Sophie. Formalities were exchanged, "We come here all the time!"

"Oh... really?" Sophie looked dubious, "What, *all the time*? That doesn't say much for the quality of the men..."

The women laughed. "Yeah, well... you'll find out for yourself!" more laughter followed, "I was married for thirty years to a man who smelled his pants every morning and clipped his toe nails at the dinner table, I'm in no rush to go back to that! This is just quite a laugh."

"My ex-husband had to talc himself up after any contact with water- I don't miss the permanent layer of white powder in the bathroom..." Marianne reminisced.

"Are you sure it was talc?" Babs asked and laughed.

"Well, in my experience..." Marianne joined in, "... all men are pretty much idiots with nothing much on their minds apart from tits. My ex couldn't walk past the lad's mags without dribbling- life is better without them."

"Oh *my* ex-husband used to pick at his teeth after eating *anything*," Lou piped up joining in on the man-bashing spirit, "We had to buy packs of tooth picks and if we ever ran out he'd roll up bits of newspaper or magazines or envelopes… anything he could get his hands on and sit there poking away in his mouth…" she shuddered, "and his morning breath- ugh!"

Sophie momentarily wondered if she was at the right event.

A small group of men who had shuffled in by themselves were now standing around the bar awkwardly with their hands in their pockets looking over nervously to the group of women who seemed to be having a ball already. They politely made small talk as the laughter filled the room.

"I'm a bit reluctant to give up my freedom a second time around anyway," Babs continued, "I'm having too much fun *and* I'm not so sure anymore if there is one perfect man for me… I used to think there was but I'm 46 now and no sign of him yet!" she smiled sympathetically at Sophie who was still looking troubled, "There might be for you though. What kind of man are you looking for?"

Sophie considered this for a moment. "Well, I have a son so someone who doesn't mind children for a start as that has scared a guy off before. And then, you know, just someone *normal*."

Lou interrupted. "My friend has led a very quiet life!" she teased.

"I've met a few guys off the internet," Sophie continued, "and I just don't think that's a good place to start. I thought this would be better, because you can get an idea about someone instantly rather than building up an ideal picture of them before you meet and then finding out that they're actually nothing like it and the photo they have on their profile was taken when they were ten years younger!" she took a breath, "I'm not sure exactly what kind of man I'm looking or but I'll know him when I see him… and my sister met her fiancée speed dating…"

"She's a brave lady."

A bell rang from the bar and a young woman dressed in a black suit with a pink scarf round her neck and holding a clip board cleared her throat loudly.

"Excuse me! Attention please! Thank you!" she cast her eyes around the pub which had suddenly filled up with an assortment of singles, "Gather round!" she indicated for everyone to come in closer and so Sophie, Lou and their new friends picked up their drinks and belongings and went over to join the rest, Sophie subtlety checking out the men as she went. The woman waited while the small crowd of reluctant daters shuffled round to listen. She counted heads and then checked this against her list. "Just waiting for one… there's always one…" A flustered looking man came out of the toilets, letting the door bang behind him and drawing the group's attention over to him, "Ah here he is…"

Lou sniggered and dug Sophie in the ribs. "Flies," she hissed.

The man suddenly realised he'd forgotten to zip himself up and retreated back into the loos, re-emerging seconds later, ignoring the fact that everyone in the pub was now watching, the place seemingly only occupied with speed daters.

"He's here every month too!" Babs whispered to Sophie, "I'd give him a wide berth."

The woman briskly ticked a name off her list. "Come on Tony, we don't have all night! Right. Hi everyone, my name is Abby. Pleased to see so many new faces tonight! Some of you will be familiar with the drill…" she looked at the aforementioned Tony, "…but if you're new then listen in."

She explained the procedure. Sophie listened like her life depended on it. Around the edge of the room were single tall tables, each with two bar stools. There were enough tables so that each lady had one to herself. As she was talking the woman went round the group handing out pieces of paper which were printed with a numbered table. The men were given numbers to tell them at which table they should start and from there they would move round each lady, having a three-minute date with each.

Sophie and Lou made their way to two tables near the door.

"It's boiling in here," Sophie complained, fanning herself with her hand out. She noticed the worried look on Lou's face. "Oh I feel really guilty now I've dragged you out!" she said apologetically.

"You don't need to feel guilty!" Lou replied, "I didn't need to come. It's just making me realise how much I love Simon…" her voice trailed off and she looked off into the distance wistfully for a moment. Sophie decided not to remind her that only five minutes ago she was complaining in no uncertain terms about his oral hygiene. "Anyway!" Lou continued, "It'll be fun. It's only three minutes twenty times."

"Three minutes!" Sophie responded, "It's not long is it? You'll hardly get to say anything in three minutes; I can't imagine what it'll be like."

"Put your boobs away anyway," Lou looked at Sophie's cleavage. Sophie looked down and realised she was flashing half of her bra. She pulled up the front of her dress.

"Oh I *knew* this dress would be a problem..." she complained, "I've had it for years but never worn it... now I remember why..."

"It's quite a brazen technique," Lou joked, "They'll all choose you if you flash your boobs at them." Sophie continued to pull up her top self-consciously and then noticed that her first date had silently arrived at the table and was watching with great interest. She gave her top one last big pull up and folded her arms tightly across her chest.

"Hi!" she smiled broadly.

Abby checked that everyone had a partner and a pen and announced that the dating was to begin. Sophie and Lou exchanged one last worried look.

The man who had been transfixed by Sophie's wardrobe malfunction hesitantly hovered at her table, as if waiting to be invited to sit down. Sophie instantly thought that was odd due to the nature of the reason they were all there. She patted the chair next to her.

"Don't be shy," she joked, feeling empowered by the feeling of being in control, being the one with the table. The man sat down as directed. He was, Sophie thought, a fairly normal looking guy. A bit older than her maybe, slightly greying hair and nothing at first inspection that made him stand out from the crowd. His whole look was fairly grey she slowly observed, grey hair, grey suit, grey complexion... she decided she'd just write 'grey' alongside his number when he'd moved on.

"Hi!" she said again and smiled warmly, determined to make the best of the evening.

"Hi," he replied.

Silence.

"So!" Sophie continued, desperate to fill the silence with words, "Have you done this before?" she looked hopefully at her first date, feeling like her opening line was quite feeble and one that she had promised herself she wouldn't use due to its dullness but justified in the absence of any better conversation from him and finding the set up much more awkward than expected.

He shook his head.

Sophie sat waiting for some further details but none were forthcoming.

"I've not either," she replied, "I'm Sophie, by the way. Nice to meet you," she beamed.

"Graham," he extended his hand.

Sophie pulled her sagging dress up at the front again and realised that this three minutes could be the longest of her life so far. She wondered if anyone did just sit in silence if they didn't particularly like the look of their date. Her mind was suddenly blank of all stimulating conversation, sapped by Graham's lethargy, and Sophie wished that she had paid more attention to the radio that day for interesting topics. Graham sat with his eyes blatantly fixed on Sophie's chest.

"It's really hot in here…" Sophie observed and puffed, "they could do with some air conditioning …"

Graham nodded but offered no thoughts on this.

"Actually, if you don't mind, I'll just open this a bit more…" she leaned back twisting round and pushed the window behind her so that it was open further, partly to fill some time, and then realised that by this movement she'd exposed half of her bra and hurriedly hoisted her dress back round. She continued to chatter to try and divert his attention. "I've never even been to this pub before actually, and I've lived here for about six years! It's not as nice as the wine bars along by the water… It's near the town though isn't it, this pub… quite close anyway… but we didn't come that way… well, we kind of did…" her voice trailed off and she took a deep breath and composed her thoughts, her brain suddenly void of any interesting topics. "It's been really hot today especially… for October… I hate the summer, look forward to autumn so I feel a bit cheated when it gets hot at this time of year, when we get an Indian summer- it should be cold!" she laughed feebly. You're not funny, she thought. "So, anyway, Graham, what do you do for a living?" Sophie felt bored by her own conversation. Graham looked like he was too but was offering none of his own. He reluctantly moved his eyes to meet hers.

"Marine conservation."

"Wow!" Sophie said a little too enthusiastically, glad of some input from Graham, "That sounds great! So… what does that mean exactly?"

A bell sounded to move the dates along. Sophie breathed a sigh of relief, not feeling too bothered that she would never get the low down on what a marine conservationist actually did. This was harder work than she thought. She was slightly puzzled as to why Graham had bothered turning up, he didn't seem that into it and she made a face at Lou, who was entertaining him next, to try and convey the message that he was hard work. She wrote down 'Grey and socially inept' on her paper. Another man of similar appearance appeared at her table and Sophie smiled with new enthusiasm. He tried to look at what she'd written and she guiltily folded up her paper, not wanting to seem too harsh.

Out of the corner of her eye another man caught her attention, or at least his bright pink tie did. She glanced over and saw that he also had a yellow flower in his button hole. Very dapper, she thought. His well-spoken voice wafted across the room and she frowned as this sounded familiar. She stared idly at him trying to remember where she might have seen him before, his face now seeming familiar too.

"I wouldn't bother with him," the man hovering by the table sat down, "he's way too old for you! Unless you're after the older man! I'm Felix," Felix extended his hand and grinned making Sophie smile too.

"I'm Sophie," she tried not to smirk too much as he looked like he was quite a bit older anyway.

The conversation with Felix flowed much better although Sophie was slightly distracted by the peals of laughter that were coming from Lou's table where Graham sat animatedly talking. His flow of conversation paused briefly and Lou dissolved into uncontrollable giggles. Sophie stiffly sat trying to ignore them, wondering what it was that Lou had that she didn't.

Felix seemed quite happy with her company though and was extremely complimentary, a little too much perhaps and he had something of a Carry on Film actor about him but a one hundred per cent improvement on Graham. Sophie wrote down 'Good for self-esteem' next to his name when he left thinking that another date with someone who only said nice things about you couldn't be bad. She glanced over again at the man that she thought she recognised but still had no inspiration and turned her attention back to her next date. She was pleasantly surprised to see a younger looking guy waiting to be invited to sit down and Sophie smiled warmly at him and indicated to the chair next to her. He spoke with a slight accent and he looked nervous, Sophie thought, his hands thrust deep in his pockets of a jacket that was slightly too big. His name was Carlos and they chatted easily. Sophie felt herself start to relax into the evening. Carlos looked too handsome to be at the event, Sophie thought, sure that someone like him wouldn't have any trouble finding a date and he appeared to be much younger than everyone else too. Maybe he likes the older woman, she thought.

"Pick me," he said as he jumped off the bar stool at the end of the three minutes and made his way over to see Lou. He *must* like the older woman, Sophie decided and wrote 'Possible toy boy' on her paper.

She looked up to observe her next date heaving his weight onto the barstool next to her, a pungent smell accompanying him. Sophie sat back in her chair to try and avoid breathing it in. She recognised the man as the one who'd forgotten to zip up his trousers and started to breathe through her mouth. The man looked as greasy as he smelled. His hair looked like it had been washed in chip fat and his skin had an oily sheen. She balked at the sight of his nose, the sides of which was covered with very noticeable black heads. Three minutes, she thought.

"I'm Tony," he said and extended his hand towards Sophie who managed to avoid shaking it by feigning a coughing fit, not wanting to go near his unclipped dirty finger nails, "I work at the bakery counter down the road," he nodded his head towards the pub door. Sophie was unaware of any nearby bakeries but couldn't quite believe that any place serving food would have such a dirty looking employee, "I'm 48 and live with my mum." Three minutes stretched ahead of her like an abyss. A moment of utter silence passed while Sophie drenched her thought banks for some inspiration.

"Cool... I love cakes!" she said finding some and performed a monologue about carrot cake and the various different frostings to be found on different supermarket makes, deciding to fully embrace tedium and detailing her Top Five carrot cake brands. Tony seemed to enjoy the subject though and reluctantly moved on to Lou when his time was up who looked at Sophie in horror.

Kevin was next, a fairly young and cool looking mobile phone salesman. Sophie wasn't sure if there was chemistry between them but she managed to negotiate a new cheap contract for when hers ran out the following month.

"I tell you what I'll do for you Sophie," he told her, "If you come in this weekend- Saturday- and arrange that contract with the phone I've just suggested then I'll credit your account with £90. Actually, tell you what, make it 120. I need to get some more sales in by the end of the week."

"*Really?*" Sophie asked incredulously, thinking the offer sounded way too good to be true. "Great! I think I'll be able to…"

"Don't miss out on it, Sophie; deals like this don't come along every day."

"Uh, OK," she replied dubiously and then smiled, "Great! Well, at least if I don't get a date out of tonight I've got a cheap phone contract, thanks!"

Kevin saluted and moved on.

Ellis followed, a taller man Sophie had never seen. Six foot nine he told her which was apparently taller than most door frames. To satisfy her curiosity they stood up and she felt miniscule even in her five inch heels. It was a problem meeting women being so tall, he told her although Sophie couldn't think why, she thought that she would feel safe and protected by him and he was very sweet looking. At the end of his time Sophie watched him walk away, his head bent down slightly so that it didn't touch the low ceiling, and she idly wondered how having such a tall boyfriend would practically work. He'd have to pick her up to kiss her she mused. She wrote down 'Super tall'.

As the next date approached her table Sophie suddenly remembered who it was. Oh crap, she thought. The man sat down and beamed at her in a good humoured fashion and then the light dawned on him too.

"Well I never! Sophie! Miss Bridges! How delightful to see you, I *thought* I'd seen you somewhere before! I hope you didn't bring Enid with you?"

Donald, principle of Saint Andrews school, looked round worriedly in case Sophie was accompanied by her senior. He looked visibly relieved that she was not. Sophie squirmed with embarrassment.

"Why is such a pretty flower here?" he asked with horror, "such a waste of beauty! What's it like working with Enid, she's quite a formidable woman!" Sophie opened her mouth to speak but Donald held up his hand to stop her. "Oh but let's not speak of work, so dull, tell me all about you," he looked at her with eager eyes. Sophie wanted the floor to swallow her up. He noticed her hesitation. "Don't worry, I won't tell if you don't!" Sophie laughed despite herself, that Donald might be as scared of Enid as everyone else.

"I'd love to see her face…" she thought out loud, "… if she knew I was socialising with you! I think she had her hopes pinned on dating you herself...!" Sophie said looking at Donald mischievously.

Donald raised his eyebrows. "Ah so she is a single woman...?" he asked, "I had wondered! I think it would require quite a man to take that woman on… she looks like she eats men for breakfast!"

"She might do," Sophie replied, "she's in the office so early though nobody knows what she has for breakfast. I only start at half nine so I wouldn't have a clue!"

"I think that's a much more civilized time to start," Donald agreed, "work is work."

Sophie considered this. "Not for Enid. Work is life for her… She's in the office from dusk until dawn making heavy weather out of nothing and I doubt she ever gets thanked for it…maybe that's why she's such a miserable co…" she stopped herself abruptly realising she might now be crossing the line of professionalism. The bell rang and Donald held his hands up in despair.

"Three minutes wasted talking about work!" he wailed. Sophie smiled apologetically. "Maybe I could swap with the next man...?"

"Nope, my turn now," the next man swept past him looking sheepish, like he was embarrassed to be at such an event.

Sophie looked at him with a new feeling of optimism. He looked like he was of Philippine descent and Sophie wasn't sure if she had ever seen anyone so stunning. His skin looked perfect, without a wrinkle or blemish and his eyes were deep brown and looked at her softly. Donald pretended to wipe a tear from his eye and moved on reluctantly.

"I'm just here with my friend," the man told her as he sat down, as if to say don't think about being interested in me because I'm only doing my mate a favour. Sophie felt a little disappointed. "I'm Jude anyway, nice to meet you."

Sophie grinned. "I want to say 'Hey Jude' but I guess everyone says that, I don't want to be a cliché."

"No say it!" he smiled good-humouredly, "Nobody's ever said that before, certainly not tonight anyway… apart from the six women before you and every other person I've ever met in my life… but go ahead, it's only fair that you should get to say it too."

Sophie laughed, the first time a genuine laugh had left her mouth all evening. She met Jude's eyes and was lost in their beauty for a moment.

"So!" she brought herself back to reality, "There's not much use bothering to *try* and chat you up then, I guess, if you're only here for your friend…"

A smile started to play on Jude's lips. "Weeell…" he said reluctantly, "I wouldn't say that exactly… there's never any harm in trying…"

At the half way point in the evening there was a break and Sophie reconvened with Lou and the women she had met at the start. Excited chatter filled the ladies' loos and then the group made their way outside to sit and enjoy a moment of evening sunshine before the next round of dates started. Some of the men they had met in the first round came over and tried to impress them with humour and drinks but Sophie wasn't interested in what any of them had to say, nobody had particularly sparked any interest in her.

"You were getting on like a house on fire with Graham!" she said under her breath to Lou, "He could barely look me in the eye!"

"Which one was that?" Lou asked thoughtfully, "I can't remember one from the other now! I've not been writing down comments," she whispered to Sophie, "I'm not doing it. I'm sure nobody will pick me anyway."

"What did you think about the bakery counter guy?" Sophie said still in hushed tones, aware that most of the guys were sitting in close proximity.

"Oh he was *horrible!*" Lou replied, "He could have at least *washed*! I would have thought that would have been the minimum entry requirement for this evening. And who still lives with their mum at 46? And anyway, if they do who *tells* everyone about it?"

Sophie laughed at her friend's bluntness. "So you wouldn't go for him then."

Lou made a face of extreme distaste making Sophie giggle.

"Can I join you ladies?" Tony sat himself down at a spare seat at the table not waiting for his question to be answered. Lou's expression made Sophie choke on her drink and it required all of her self-control not to splutter the liquid in her mouth all over herself.

Carlos came over and sat on the other side of Sophie and seemed keen to have her attention. He showed great concern when she appeared to be choking and offered to get her another drink.

"No! No it's fine," Sophie croaked, waved off his concern, not particularly wanting a fuss made and wishing that the ground would swallow her up as her drink dribbled down out of her nose. She accepted the napkins that Lou thrust in her face gratefully and took a deep breath to try and stop the giggles that were still threatening.

Donald brought over a drink for Sophie and told her that the only reason he took the Elm Tree's contract was so that he could see more of her and he complimented her dress reminding Sophie to adjust it again. Ellis also approached the table and Sophie realised just how tall six foot nine really was. Nobody was going to get near her though with Carlos guarding her sides. His chair was squeezed tightly in between the tiny gap that had separated her chair from Lou's and he was now leaning towards her, blocking out her view of her friend.

"Are you leaving now you've met me?" he asked with a smug look on his face, "You're going to pick me, right? I mean, look at those guys! I could take you out for a quiet drink now, get away from here?"

"Certainly not!" Lou burst in much to Sophie's relief, "I need a lift home so Sophie's not going anywhere!"

Carlos considered this. "I could get you a taxi? Or you could come too… I guess?"

"No thanks!" Lou responded shuffling her chair in further to try and squeeze him out, "I'm too old to be playing gooseberry."

Sophie spluttered her drink again. She was not enjoying the spotlight of attention and started to feel claustrophobic, wishing that Carlos would bugger off and let her chat with her friends but being too polite to say.

She caught sight of Jude who was sitting with his friend at a table on the other side of the outside patio idly watching her. He shrugged and shook his head with regret when their eyes met, indicating to the men who were buzzing around her, as if he wasn't getting a look in.

***

Sophie considered her list of dates. Carlos had been changed from 'Mediterranean' to 'Needy'. The second part of the evening had been much the same as the first, although she had been given a random safety pin by Babs at least keeping her top in place, but nobody had sprung out as someone Sophie would have particularly wanted to see again. She decided she needed to pick one though as this was the only way she would get to see who had picked her and this would be a good self-esteem boosting exercise if nothing else. She looked down the names.

Graham- Grey. Socially inept

Felix- Good for self-esteem

Carlos- Possible toy boy. Needy

Tony- Bleurgh

Kevin- phone contract!!

Ellis- Super tall

Donald- OMG

Jude- Hey

Peter- Pointy shoes

Gary- Too many ex wives

Alan- Weird

Barry- Dodgy bloke

Glynn- Bit slimy

Nathan- Gay surely

Martin- Sweaty

Reese- ???

Chris- Wiry hair

Roger- Really??

Richard- Dick

George- Not Clooney

She studied the list now not being able to really remember any of the men and wishing that her descriptions had been more exact. One of the other women there had written a paragraph on each one and Sophie now regretted scoffing at her diligence behind her back. She wracked her brain to try and remember details about Reese but she could not picture him at all. How her sister could go speed dating *once* and meet the man she was to marry Sophie had no idea. Probably because she's pretty damn perfect, she huffed to herself. She looked up and down the names again willing one to jump out at her as worthy of a second date and her eyes stopped at Jude. Hey Jude, she thought, intriguing Jude. The more she considered him the more she thought it might be quite fun to see him again. He had slipped under the radar somewhat, not making a nuisance of himself as many of his counterparts and not hassling her for another date. The fact that he hadn't been a pest became the main reason he got chosen although she did remember that he had made her laugh. She put him as her top pick and randomly threw in Ellis as Number 2 as there had essentially been nothing wrong with him apart from his freakish height. She submitted her choices and waited to learn who had picked her. Pictures of all the men appeared in a column all with green ticks identifying they had chosen her in their Top 3- except for two.

"Bastards!" Sophie exclaimed, "Why not?" Suddenly the two who hadn't chosen her became more important than the 18 who had. "Bloody Graham, what was his problem anyway?"

Ellis had also not picked her and Sophie felt devastated. Why not, she thought, he was *lovely*. She sulked for a moment.

Once her indignation had subsided she realised that she had a match with Jude and felt a flutter of excitement, knowing that this meant their contact details would have been automatically swapped.

■■■

***

Sophie parked her car along the road from the pub that they were to meet at and sat tight for a while until Jude showed up. She hadn't spoken to him since the night before and the fact that he didn't have a mobile made her feel slightly nervous, like he might forget to meet her at all and have no way of letting her know. She was pretty sure that he was intending to meet her by the conversation they had had it was just that these days not having a mobile seemed most irregular. How hideous and embarrassing, she thought, if everyone saw I was all ready for a night out and then got stood up. She shuddered at the thought and decided to stay in the car until he had showed rather than get out and wait at the corner as arranged. Hey Jude, don't stand me up, she hummed in her head, although I a-a-am really e-e-a-rly.

With five minutes to go though he suddenly appeared around the corner, looking extremely dapper in a shiny grey suit and positioned himself at their agreed meeting point. He stood up tall and straight and looked around, checking his watch and adjusting his collar. Sophie watched him for a moment, not wanting to jump out of the car and appear too keen to see him although she really was. She had forgotten how perfect his features were and smiled as he smoothed down his hair and did what seemed to be a quick odour check. He then thrust his hands in his pockets and waited, looking around all the time, nervously Sophie thought.

Deciding that she'd made him wait for long enough she picked up her bag from the passenger seat and got out, ducking down behind the parked cars so that he couldn't see her approach until he turned away and she briskly walked across the road, holding her tummy in and standing up tall. She casually swished her hair and smiled as he turned and saw her.

"Hey!" she said as she approached then laughed, "Oh, I mean, 'Hi'! I should try not to say that; I've been singing that song since we arranged to meet up!"

Jude laughed. "You'll get bored of it soon," he leant towards her and kissed both cheeks, "Did I say, 'wow'? You look *amazing*!" He looked like he genuinely meant it.

Sophie smiled and for once accepted the compliment without her usual self-depreciating comment. "Thank you," she said simply.

Jude offered her his arm to hold. "So, do you want to go in here or to the White House? Have you been in there before? It's been newly done up," he offered helpfully.

"Oh I don't mind. Whatever you think!" Sophie replied, "I don't usually come to this part of town. In fact, I rarely come into town at all these days," she said honestly, tired of pretending she was something different to what she really was.

"Let's go to the White House then," Jude suggested, "We might get a seat in there and it's quiet, we might even get to talk to each other. And it's *much* more civilized than the pub we met in…"

Jude escorted Sophie along the road. She took his arm, glad to have something to hold onto in her heels but also touched by the civility of it, that Jude was such a gentleman.

"So, I thought you weren't looking for a date?" Sophie asked, teasing him slightly, "and yet here we are…"

"Is this a date then?" Jude asked teasing her back.

Sophie smiled bashfully. "Oh, um, well I thought…" she started to mumble, feeling ridiculously silly now for suggesting it was. Jude laughed.

"Well, you know, I have to protect my street cred… as I'm sure you do too. Speed dating…" he started to talk under his breath, "… isn't something I was shouting about. Male pride and all that… so, were *you* actually looking for a date?"

Sophie felt her cheeks redden and started to mumble again. Jude laughed.

"I bet everyone picked you anyway. I only said I wasn't bothered in case nobody picked me!" Jude smiled down at Sophie as they walked along arm in arm. Sophie felt like they had stepped back in time to the 1950s but felt comfortable in Jude's company. He was so easy going and unassuming and for the first time in a long time she felt like she was being herself. "Did everyone pick you?" Jude asked again.

Sophie smiled bashfully. "Well, a few did."

"A few? Or everybody?" Jude laughed, "You were showing quite a lot of skin. Just wondering who my competition is that's all."

Sophie looked up into his beautiful eyes and couldn't believe he was so lovely. Maybe she had prematurely judged speed dating and it was all going to turn out well in the end after all.

"Well, actually a few did choose me... but I only chose you," she smiled up at Jude hopefully.

"Well, I am honoured in that case," he told her, "although clearly you are mad and need your eyes tested!"

Sophie laughed. "Don't be silly..."

"Here we are!" Jude announced, interrupting her, "this is it... will this be suitable for madam? Shall we?" he opened the door for Sophie and stood to the side to let her walk in first. She looked at him with faint amusement not quite believing that there was any man left out there who was such a gentleman. He then proceeded by buying her a drink and pulling out a chair for her to sit in. He waited for her to take her seat before sitting down himself and they chatted amicably and Sophie enjoyed Jude's random conversation.

"Do you give much thought to the meaning of life?" Jude asked and looked at her with interested eyes.

Sophie considered this for a moment. "Not *really*... well, not at the moment. I'm too busy to be thinking about *that*! I have more pressing questions like 'What's for tea' or 'How come we've run out of socks, *again*'!"

Jude nodded seriously. "Yes, I see, those are important questions…" he thought again, looking up to the ceiling as he did. Sophie watched him thinking how cute he was. He turned his attention back to her. "What about existence… I often wonder if anyone else exists apart from me… you might just be a figment of my imagination…"

"Well, that would be a shame!" Sophie replied, warming to him with every second as he nervously rambled, "I did philosophy at university so I *have* given these things *some* thought- although that was a while ago!"

"I don't believe it," Jude replied, "that must have only been last year."

Sophie laughed. "Don't try that old trick- flattery won't get you anywhere! That was too many years ago to mention."

"Well, I don't believe that," Jude responded, "but that's very interesting, that you studied philosophy… I'm very interested in it; I've not been to Uni though, just done my own research," he nodded thoughtfully, "maybe I could interest you in a trip to the Dog and Duck one day… they have excellent leather sofas in there which are *perfect* for settling down into for the evening with a beer and some good company to put the world to rights and have great philosophical debate… It's just a thought!" he laughed at himself, "You will learn to ignore me!"

Sophie smiled at the suggestion of a second date.

"So, I never got out of you what you do… for a living?" Sophie asked, bringing the conversation back to boring mundane work. She didn't want to sound dull, although as soon as she asked the question she thought that was exactly what she was, but she liked to know what people did for a job.

"Ah, well, I was wondering when you'd ask about that…" Jude suddenly became a little cagey. "Well, I *did* work for an oil company…" he started, "…but then… I decided that life was too short to be stuck behind a desk in an airless office every day with people that I despised doing a job that bored me senseless and that I *knew* I wouldn't get thanked for in thirty-five years' time- or however long it would be- when I retired and realised that I'd wasted my whole life staring at walls when I could have been out there in the world living… so I gave it up and started a band."

Sophie was momentarily speechless. Jude didn't look like the sort to be in a band.

"Wow," she said, "What kind of band?"

"Ah well that is the question," Jude looked thoughtful, "We're a kind of fusion between good old fashioned rock and roll and modern day jazz… with a twist of the new romantics in there and a little bit of electronica."

Sophie was rendered speechless again.

"Oh. Wow," she struggled for words for a second, "Wow, well that's pretty cool. I'd love to hear what you do. Do you play guitar?" Jude seemed so laid back that she could imagine him maybe with a bass guitar, standing at the back of the stage quietly doing his thing.

"Yeah I play… I'm also the singer."

Sophie felt like the conversation was becoming slightly disjointed as Jude kept baffling her. She couldn't imagine him being a front man.

"Wow! That's cool. So… I'd love to hear what you do? I can't imagine what rock and roll new romantic modern day electronic jazz sounds like… actually!"

Jude looked impressed. "Well done for remembering all that! Yeah well you can look us up online… we're no secret! We quite often play in here… but not tonight… usually mid-week is our slot. You'll have to come along next time; we have some gigs coming up. Look us up," he reached inside his jacket, taking out his wallet and felt inside it, pulling out a receipt and flattening it out with his hands on the table. He then took a pen out of another pocket and wrote something down on the paper. Sophie thought that he was the most organised man she had ever met. "Here, this is our website," he passed the small piece of paper to Sophie, "You can watch our videos… not that they're up to much but at least you can see what we're about… and I would be *very* interested in your feedback!" Sophie inspected the web address feeling slightly impressed that Jude was in a band but trying not to show it.

They stayed in the pub until about ten and then Jude escorted Sophie back to her car. She had told him that she needed to be up in the morning as Ollie was getting back then and he had seemed fine with that. As he was walking back to his flat she offered him a lift, feeling safe in his company and he gladly accepted telling her that any exercise was too much for him. His flat was about a mile out of the centre of town in a new-looing block along a leafy road where expensive cars were parked. Being in a band must pay well, Sophie thought, or he had a lot saved up from his time in the oil industry. She pulled in where he directed and stopped the car, leaving the engine running. She had had such a lovely time with Jude that she could have sat with him all night. She looked at him and smiled.

"So… I've had a lovely time. Thanks," she smiled again not sure what else to say, not wanting to seem overly keen but not wanting him to think she wasn't interested at all. Dating is so complicated, she thought.

"Me too… I'll give you a call yeah?" Jude asked.

"OK!" Sophie nodded and carried on smiling.

The two sat momentarily in silence, looking into each other's eyes. Sophie felt like time stopped for a second as she waited to see what he was going to do next. She felt a longing to be kissed.

Jude lurched forward and pecked her on the cheek and pushed his door open.

"I'll call you then, bye!" he said hurriedly. He paused for a second then held up his hand in a wave and got out of the car, leaving Sophie still longing for a proper kiss. She sat as the door was slammed shut and Jude strode up his path, turning round as he entered his front door giving her a last wave. She waved back and pulled out of the parking space now confused as to the extent that he liked her. Enough to suggest further meetings but not enough to give her a proper kiss… She analysed the evening all the way home, as she got ready for bed and as she drifted off to sleep. A peck on the cheek, she thought, what does that mean? She analysed the depth of the kiss, the look in his eyes as he kissed her. Did he look like he wanted more of a snog? Should *she* have initiated a more passionate kiss? Questions tumbled round in her head.

The next morning Sophie was straight on the computer looking up Jude's band. She couldn't imagine what kind of band it would be; he didn't *seem* to have the charisma of a lead singer. She found the website and followed one of the two links to watch their videos. There didn't seem to be much to the website or much in the way of a back catalogue but she was hopeful that they were going to be the next big thing. She waited for the video to start with excitement, warming to the idea of being the girlfriend of the lead singer in a band.

The video was fairly grainy and it was difficult to tell that it was Jude. He stood at the front of a small stage that appeared to have been set up in a school gym hall, holding a guitar with another guitarist beside him and a drummer behind. As she waited Ollie padded into her room pulling Mr Ted along on his duvet behind him.

"Hi darling!" Sophie said warmly, "Jump in with Mummy. You're up early!"

"What are you watching?" the boy asked.

"Oh just one of mummy's friends plays music so I was going to see what it's like. Let's see…" she turned her attention back to the computer as a din of sound started and she could hear what sounded like a hippo having all the air violently squeezed out of it but not so tuneful. For a moment Sophie and Ollie watched in stunned silence as horrible noises came out of the computer. The person making the noises, apparently Jude although the quality of the video was so bad it was difficult to tell, droned loudly with no particular awareness it seemed to the rhythm of the music accompanying him and with no real attempt at singing actual words. She made a face of disapproval.

"I don't like that sound Mummy," Ollie stated, "It sounds scary."

Sophie stopped the video. "Yes it's not a very nice sound is it? Oh dear, but Mummy might have to pretend that it is…"

***

She later told the girls what a pleasant evening she had had in Jude's company but what a quandary she was now in as he was the worst singer in the world.

"I don't know what to say to him now! He emailed me and asked if I was free tomorrow night, which I am, and I really *do* want to see him again but his *band* are *hideous* and I can't quite believe that he's left a good job in the *oil industry* to be in some crap sounding student band- his two band mates are quite a bit younger than him and at college… He said that he advertised for people to join his band… he should really have advertised for a singer as well…"

"Is it really that bad?" Lou asked.

"Yes. Absolutely. Listen…" Sophie got up and went to fetch her computer to let the girls have a listen.

"Bloody hell…" Lou said as the tuneless moaning was played.

"Mummy!" Ollie's voice was heard shouting from his room, "Mummy I don't like that sound, it's *scary*!"

"OK darling!" Sophie called up and snapped her computer shut, "See! It's beyond hideous. And he gave me the website to listen to it so he'll be asking if I did."

"Just pretend that you've not had a chance," Joules offered helpfully.

"I know, I could but I can't do that indefinitely. I'll just have to pretend that I thought it was good…"

"Other people might like it…" Tina said.

"He sent me an email this afternoon at 4 o'clock saying that he'd just woken up because when he'd got in last night he's gone back out to have a 'jam'… He's 34!"

The girls laughed at Sophie's horror.

"There must be something about him though, if you're going to see him again?"

A smile started to play on Sophie's lips. "Well, yeah…" her smile broke into a grin, "he is lovely… even though he sounds like a beached whale calling his pack, or whatever lots of whales are called. I could have spoken to him all night; he's so interesting and *really* funny. He's *such* a gentleman too- he opened the doors for me and pulled out my chair… and really cute too," she grinned contentedly at her friends who smiled indulgently back, happy that their friend was beginning to make progress.

"Well, he is an honoured man…" Lou told Sophie, "Not many men get a second date these days!"

Chapter Sixteen

With the prospect of a new man on the horizon Sophie decided that it was time she tried to get Ollie out of his habit of coming in to bed with her at night. This practice would make it very awkward of I ever met someone new, she thought. It was a weekend that he was with her and she broached the subject with him on the Saturday morning as he lay spread out like a star fish, taking up most of the bed.

"Darling…" she had said, clinging onto the sheets for fear of falling out, "Darling you know that you have your own bed…?"

"I like your bed," he told her matter of factly.

"Yes, well I can see that!" she said lightly, "but bigger boys normally do sleep in their own bed… because you're getting so big that there's not really enough room for both of us…!"

"Yes there is… look!" he pulled his arms and legs in and made a space again for Sophie.

"Well, yes there is now… but it is something that you can't do forever…" she decided to resort to her trump card, "Mummy will buy you anything you like, today, if tonight you will try and stay in your own bed…?"

The boy considered this and seemed to view the suggestion favourably.

"What, *anything*…?"

"Well, yes, if I can afford it! I mean a toy or something…?" she looked at him hopefully ashamed of her bribing technique.

"Can we see what they have...?" he asked hesitantly, hedging his bets.

"Yes of course, let's see."

They found themselves at the shop in the country park. A small place that sold everything you might need to play in the park- bats and balls, kites, footballs, Frisbees, yo-yo's, water pistols big and small, sets of bowls, skittles and then some other random stuff, some large inflatable objects being amongst them- hammers, water beds and a four-foot dinosaur. Sophie could see that Ollie's eye had spotted the dinosaur as soon as they went into the shop and she tried to divert his attention, knowing that it would just burst one day and cause tears and probably be used to hit her.

"Ooh what about this darling, a bouncy ball!"

"Nah..." he said, transfixed by the large inflatable dinosaur.

"Ooh what about *this*...!" Sophie held up a long corrugated green tube, "It makes a funny noise when you swing it round and round...?" she did so in the shop much to the displeasure of the sales assistant. Sophie stopped and put it back in the display.

Ollie scrunched up his nose. "Nah..." he said, still inspecting the inflatable section, deep in thought.

"Wow look at *these*! Bugs!" Sophie showed him a transparent tube filled with plastic mini-beasts.

The boy remained unimpressed.

"Nah... I'm too old for those now."

"Ooh darling, look!" Sophie tried again, "Kites!"

"Can I have *that*?" Ollie pointed to the four-foot inflatable dinosaur ignoring his mother. Sophie sighed. "You said I could have *anything*!"

Sophie 'shushed' him aware that the sales assistant was listening and now probably judging her on her lack of parenting skills.

"That is true…" she whispered, "Well… OK but you must promise that you will try your absolute best to stay in your own bed…?" she raised her eyes challengingly to him, wanting his promise to try hard. He considered this before giving his response.

"I promise," he said solemnly, "I promise to try."

"OK then darling, pinkie promise…?"

The boy held up his pinkie and linked it to hers.

"Pinkie promise."

"Great!" Sophie said. That was easy, she thought. "Which dinosaur would you like then…? That one…? OK let's ask the lady to get it down for us…"

They left the shop hand in hand, dinosaur in tow.

Ollie was tucked into bed that night with the dinosaur being used as a constant reminder of his solemn promise.

"Now remember darling, you did promise! Mummy bought you the dinosaur so now you must try and stay in your own bed, OK? OK darling goodnight."

She pulled the door to and went to get herself ready for bed, deciding to read for once and have an early night. It wasn't long before she was sound asleep.

The next morning Sophie woke up in bed with her son and the four-foot inflatable dinosaur. Bribery, she thought, is never the answer.

***

Jude came round to Sophie's house on the Sunday night. She decided that rather than leaving it for another whole two weeks before she saw him again when she didn't have Ollie that he was trustworthy enough to be allowed to come round to her house. Her text system with Pat and Peter next door seemed to be rigorous enough to protect her from any dangerous situations that may arise having a 100% success rate, although it had only been tested once before.

He arrived on time in a smart suit and wiped his feet on the door mat. He had a cup of herbal tea and talked about what he had read in the Sunday Times. OK so not until he had got up at tea time but at least it wasn't the Sunday Sport. He seemed to be an odd combination of impeccably mannered, well-read gentleman and lazy lay-about. The evening passed quickly though and they spoke about all manner of subjects.

"I looked you up on the internet… you're band I mean!" Sophie told him. She found him easy to talk to, "It was, um, really good. So, how long have you been a, erm, singer?"

Jude looked slightly smug. "Well, not for long actually! But thanks! I was originally going to just write the songs and be more of a manager really. I couldn't find anyone with lead singer attributes though and so in the end I thought I'll just do that myself because actually, I was pretty good. There would be nothing worse than having to manage a bad singer with a huge ego!"

Sophie looked at him with wide eyes and nodded silently.

They spoke about children…

"I'd love to meet Ollie, I think children are amazing. How cool is it to have a little version of yourself!" Jude gushed, "He sounds great, from what you've said, I bet he's a right little character and…" he paused and gazed at Sophie, "… he must be really cute…"

Sophie felt her tummy do cartwheels.

He spoke about philosophy and fate.

"I really believe that there is one person for me… that in the world there is only one person that I am supposed to be with. That's why I've been waiting… for the right woman. I've never wanted to be with just anyone, you know, I only want to be with the right one. I think that it's already determined who I'll be with and I think that fate will bring us together… I just don't know yet…" he looked at Sophie again with his beautiful big brown eyes as if it was she he was waiting for.

He spoke about the library.

"Sometimes I just need peace, you know, to gather my thoughts. I write in the library a lot, I read there, obviously… I think there," he laughed, "It's a great place as it's generally deserted!"

"I like taking Ollie to the library…" Sophie responded, "He likes the story time there." She stopped herself for a moment and thought about what her friends would say if they knew she was talking to her date about the library.

Jude then talked about work.

"I just thought one day that there was more to life than sitting in that office… I wasn't going anywhere. Well, you know, I was heading for *promotion* but that wasn't

everything to me. I could have been quite successful…
well, *really* successful! I was about to be offered a
company Audi and there had been talk of moving me to
Houston for a while then maybe Norway… both places I
would have liked to have gone and the pay to do that would
have been about four times what I was earning… but
money isn't everything."

Sophie nodded trying to look enthusiastic at his thinking.

As the evening went on though she liked him more and
more. He was definitely a 'grower' she thought. As time
got later her eyes started to focus increasingly on his
mouth, wondering if he would kiss her at all tonight. This
chatting is all very well, she thought with increasing
frustration, but what about a little snogging action now?
She glanced at her watch and saw with surprise that it was
heading towards twelve. The evening had passed without
her realising Jude being so easy to talk to. As her body
realised how late it was she started to yawn and made
attempts to hide this. The sensible side of her head worried
about getting up in the morning.

Jude continued to talk and Sophie watched his mouth as he
did, it's shape and movement making her wish that he
would kiss her this time. He was warming to his subject
though and she sat listening as he went into great detail
about a philosophy theory that he had recently read about in
the paper. His words started to pass through her as she
increasingly longed for his kiss. Deciding to take matters
into her own hands, as it was getting late now, she subtly
started to move closer to him. Her rational brain counted
how many hours she had until it was time to get up for
work.

Gradually she slid her arm along the back of the sofa where
Jude's arm was casually draped. He was sitting in the

corner with his body turned slightly towards her and Sophie now edged her way towards him, millimetre by millimetre to the point that Jude then started to back away, an increasingly petrified look on his face. She made a point of not encouraging his conversation anymore as she slowly shuffled her way closer to him until she eventually brushed his hand with hers. The touch sent electricity through her body and she longed for him to join in, for him to come towards her and kiss her passionately. Instead his petrified and now shaking body pressed harder and harder into the corner of her sofa and Sophie was sure that he had started to perspire slightly. Bloody hell, she thought, I'm not that scary! Eventually she was so close to him that any closer would require her to sit on his knee but her approach seemed to have upset him and he looked on the verge of tears to the point that she now felt guilty and leant forward to give him a cuddle.

"Oh I'm sorry!" she wailed, "Have I upset you? I *really* didn't mean to…" she sat up and looked at his face, the look of sheer horror softening slightly.

"No, it's OK," he said, "You've not upset me… I'm just, you know… just not used to this kind of thing…"

"Oh!" Sophie said, rather taken aback, "Ahhh…" she was relieved at least that it wasn't *her* that was scary but the situation. "Well, I'm not going to hurt you…" she looked at him hopefully and smiled and then waited to see if he could muster up the courage to make a move on her, she was practically on top of him now and she had given him a fairly good indication that she liked him so she decided to see if he could manage the last bit.

They gazed into each other's eyes for what seemed like several minutes; Sophie determined now to let him take the lead. He was a stunningly good looking man and close up he looked flawless, the whites of his eyes were so bright and pure next to his brown skin. Sophie parted her lips in an indication that she would like him to kiss them and tried to pout seductively, she wasn't sure if this was helping but Jude was now staring at her mouth with what looked like intent. Slowly but surely he lifted his body out of the corner of the sofa and started to lean towards her, all the time staring at her mouth, as if with his eyes on the target and not wanting to look elsewhere and miss it. As he moved towards her though he also started to open his mouth but he opened it and opened it and opened it until it was wide and now approached her like a deep chasm, clamping his open mouth over hers as if trying to perform C.P.R. and giving her little opportunity to do anything that resembled a kiss, her whole mouth now covered by his. She pulled away slightly to survey the situation and see if she could initiate a better kissing position but Jude's mouth was open so much that there was nowhere that she could kiss, there was just a gaping black hole that looked as if it was trying to engulf her. She tried to kiss his lips but his mouth was open so wide there wasn't much to kiss, unless she nibbled her way all the way round she thought. Deciding to go with it for a moment she allowed his mouth to cover hers and felt his tongue going round and round and round like a mini washing machine, a mouth valeting system. She tried to join in some way but there was nothing there for her to kiss but space so she gave up and sat, letting him get on with whatever it was he was doing.

I'm too old to be teaching my boyfriend how to kiss, she thought, I'm not at school. Any passion and longing that she had felt disappeared in a flash and she decided to make her excused as soon as she had been released.

***

"It's not *that* serious a problem… is it?" Lou asked her the next day at school, "I mean, so far you've met some right numpty's and this one sounds like he's OK?"

"Yeah he *is* OK…" Sophie agreed.

"And what if he had kissed you and it had been *amazing,* what would you have felt like *then?"*

Sophie considered this. "It would have been… better," she thought some more, "Yeah, I mean, I could have spoken to him all night and he really made me laugh… he sounded keen to meet Ollie and that wasn't an issue… he's *really* attractive, I think… yeah I really liked him. The kiss though…" she shook her head and shuddered, "Honestly, that was something else!

***

Sophie found that having someone else now demanding her time was quite a struggle as most of her time was accounted for already. She communicated with Jude by phone, she loved talking to him, and email but the next time she actually saw him was two weeks later when Ollie was away by which time she had partially forgotten about the sloppy nightmare that was his kiss. They met outside the pub that they had gone to when they first met and Sophie was quite relieved that he went back to pecking her on the cheek for now. She expected him to say something about how awful the kiss was or how embarrassed he was about it but no apology was forthcoming.

"So, how was work?" he asked her with a smile, "What time did you have to get up this morning?"

"Oh, about seven o'clock!" she replied, slightly crossly as he had increasingly started to wind her up about this subject, taking great delight in the fact that he didn't need to get out of bed early, if at all if he didn't feel like it as he didn't have to go to work, "We had band practice at five yesterday so I had to get up about four… quite early for me but we needed a session."

Too bloody right, Sophie thought remembering the last offering she had watched.

"Did you get stuck in traffic?"

"No," Sophie said flatly, tired of the subject and beginning to find out that there were some things about Jude that were really irritating, "So how long is it that you gave up work? Do you think you'll go back at all?"

Jude considered this. "Well, there is a chance I could go back…" he mused. Sophie's ears pricked up at this news, beginning to wish that he just had a normal job.

"Oh, really?" Sophie asked with renewed interest, "When could that be?"

"Oh… I'm just waiting to hear… I don't know if I want to… that's what I'm waiting for… to decide if I do. Anyway…" he added hurriedly, "… do you want another drink?" Do you fancy going somewhere else?"

Sophie still sometimes had to get used to the fact that on some nights she could do whatever she felt like; she didn't need to go home for Ollie tonight. A feeling of liberation passed through her.

"Yeah, OK!" she said with enthusiasm, "Where shall we go?"

Jude looked wickedly at her. "How about clubbing…? If you don't think we're too old!"

Sophie was offended by the use of the 'O' word.

"Hey!" she said comically pushing him away, "Are you saying I'm old? Let's go clubbing then, I'll show you who's old!"

Jude laughed. "Look forward to that then!"

They gathered their belongings and made their way out of the pub and towards the nightclub which was about a mile away. Sophie was glad of the fresh air and felt like a walk would do her some good, dismissing Jude's suggestion of hailing a taxi and grumblings about having to do some exercise. Jude took Sophie's hand and they walked like this in silence Sophie feeling funny to be part of a couple when she had been single for so long but happy that she could stop looking for a man for a while. She enjoyed the peace of walking with someone who didn't feel they had to fill each moment with chatter. Eventually Jude spoke. He cleared his throat as if it was something important that he had to say.

"So, I've been meaning to tell you something..." he started.

Oh here we go, Sophie thought. She looked up at him with interest. Jude cleared his throat again, summoning up the courage to speak.

"I've just been meaning to tell you something about my job..." he started. Sophie was suddenly all ears. "I've not been *exactly* truthful with you... about my job. About why I left..."

Sophie felt the doom imposing. She didn't speak, waiting for Jude to let it all out as he appeared to need to do.

"Yeah... so... I didn't *exactly* leave my job... well I did, but I didn't want to. It was all a bit of a misunderstanding," Sophie continued to look up at him without talking, wanting him to get to the point. Jude looked at her and sensed her keenness to know.

"There was this woman who worked in the same office as me… she was a really annoying cow actually."

Sophie was shocked, the word 'cow' not sitting well with Jude's vocabulary or suiting his polite and gentlemanly image.

"Yeah she was a right annoying cow. I'd only worked there for about a year but felt like I was on my way up and I really enjoyed it, the only thing was that she kept making little digs at me, kind of racist she was actually but I think she thought she was being funny. So, anyway… I just decided one day that I'd do the same back to her and as she was a woman I thought it would be funny to, like, you know, kind of harass her… but just as a joke!"

Sophie couldn't quite believe what she was hearing. Jude seemed to be on a roll now and carried on without many pauses for breath.

"Yeah so I know it sounds stupid now but I just wanted to shake her up a bit, so that she knew what it was like to have someone draw attention to something that was a bit different and as it was a mainly male office I thought that her womanly attributes would be a good place to start…" he looked at her with pleading eyes, wanting her to believe that his intentions were honourable. Sophie had nothing to say at this point though anyway and so he carried on.

"So, anyway… I pinched her bum and said a few things… and then squeezed past her sometimes and touched her a bit… I guess the last straw for her was when I squeezed her boobs one day at the photocopier… Yeah…" he nodded sheepishly, "I know, really stupid… She complained about me and, well, it's actually going to trail but I *know* that they'll decide against me because I had only been there for a year… last in first out and all that…"

"No!" Sophie suddenly said, "Not last in first out at all- you were sexually harassing her? There must have been a better way of dealing with the situation, a more grown up one? So you got suspended for sexual harassment pending a hearing…! That's just great."

Jude listened to her outburst with wide eyes as if not expecting that reaction at all.

"You've been sacked for sexual harassment and lied to me about it from the start!" Sophie continued, "Is that it?"

Jude looked at her dumbly for a moment then shook his head. "Um… yeah. That kind of sums it up."

***

Jude's revelation was one too many for Sophie and she had made her excuses and gone home early, not in the mood for clubbing anymore. Is there nobody just *normal* out there anymore, she thought at work the next week as she listed her dates so far, there being a lack of anything else to do. She took out her Elm Tree note pad from her desk drawer and wrote 'Dodgy Dates' at the top of the first page and then two more headings- 'Pros' and 'Cons'.

Paul was friendly and quite funny but had terrible wind. Dan was gorgeous but knew it and shagged anything that moved. Phil was *also* gorgeous and made Sophie laugh but he had a weird obsession with shoes. Christian had been perfect until it came to light that he was engaged and now indeed married. Charles had *looked* lovely but was incredibly rude. Jon was cute but was now being done for attempted murder. Will was great with Ollie but Sophie just didn't *feel* anything for him. Mick was sweet but manically possessive. She could have talked to Jude for hours but he had lied, kissed like a tumble dryer and was really an office sex pest… Sophie sighed. Does everyone out there have a fatal flaw, she wondered, have all those who have 'settled' done so because they have found the best of a bad bunch? She looked at the list in front of her and wondered if she could settle for any of these flaws or was she, in fact, better off by herself.

***

December came with the prospect of a break from work and new opportunities to meet members of the opposite sex with several Christmas meals and outings planned. Mick however had different plans for Sophie and also came, with a Gucci diamond collection two and a half thousand-pound watch. He had gradually nudged his way back into her consciousness with a few short and sweet messages online and then some text messages and soon they were amiably chatting again on the phone. He sounded more grown up, as if he had been doing some thinking on the naughty chair about his behaviour and seen the error of his ways. He told Sophie that he liked her so much that he really wanted to make a go of things. He had never met anyone like her before and that she was just right for him. Sophie believed him when he said that he understood what she was saying, that she could manage to go into pubs without wanting to have sex with every other man in there and that when she said she was having a night with her 'friends' she actually meant 'friends' and not 'random men who I've picked up just to have a quick orgy with'. She was happy to let things ride and see what happened, tired now of her quest for a man and flattered that someone had thought she was worthy enough to come back and say sorry.

Approaching Christmas though 'The Watch' was becoming quite a topic with Mick dropping it into their conversations at every opportunity.

"I'm not telling you what I've got you for Christmas..." he told her as soon as he had a whiff of an apology acceptance, "... but you'll love it... oh OK, it's something that you can tell the time on- but that's all I'm saying!"

"I'd never get you some cheap rubbish, you're worth much more than that... oh OK I'll just tell you that I have a favourite designer for women... but that's all I'm saying!"

"I know you don't like wearing gold... but what about white gold, eh? That looks like silver but is *much* more expensive."

"I noticed you never wear diamonds... is that because you don't have any?" Mick asked and smiled, "Well, watch this space..."

Sophie began very quickly to worry about not what he had bought, as this was plainly clear, but about how much he had spent. She browsed designer diamond watches and saw that they cost from hundreds to thousands of pounds and with Christmas being just weeks away she now had a serious dilemma- what do you buy for a guy you're at the beginning of a relationship with, you're not really sure how that's going to go but you do know that he's spend a serious amount of money on a very special gift for you. A pack of comedy boxers just wouldn't do the trick. Sophie's budget was always tight and she struggled to buy very much for Ollie so the prospect of having to match a seriously expensive gift from Mick was troubling and she cursed him for coming back before Christmas and not after.

Mick though did seem to be making a massive effort and they managed a few nights out without him having a meltdown about other men. Sophie didn't even notice other men looking at her, if they indeed were but made sure that she kept her eyes fixed on him at all times. She did find it very difficult not to inadvertently offend him, though, and this did cause her minor exasperation.

"Even if Gary Barlow walked into the room…" she told him one day to try and quash his fears, "… I wouldn't even notice."

The bristling appearance of jealously started to twitch on his features.

"What, so you have a thing about Gary Barlow then?" he said with much offense.

"No! Don't be silly!" Sophie exclaimed slightly impatiently, "As if he's going to walk in anyway… I *meant* that I only have eyes for you, it doesn't *matter* who else were to walk in the room. Gary Barlow was just a random name that I pulled out of nowhere… I think he was on the radio this morning so that must have put him subconsciously into my head…"

Mick considered this and nodded. "Ah right, OK. So you don't fancy him then? Most women do."

"No! I'm not most women," Sophie replied, looking for a quiet life, "that was just a random reference."

Mick also made such an effort with Ollie that it was hard for Sophie's heart not to start melting. Sometimes it did seem like she was looking after two children but the lengths that Mick went to make friends with and include Ollie was something that she hadn't witnessed until then and she saw what an important part of a new relationship that this would be. Up until then she had tried to keep the two apart and she didn't want Ollie thinking that she had a different boyfriend every week but she realised that anyone that she wanted to be with would have to accept that she came with a little boy.

A few weeks before Christmas though Sophie, already stressed out about what present to get Mick, did nearly throw in the towel on the fledgling relationship when the three of them went out together to a Santa's grotto- a normally happy event with her son. Amongst children and children's things Mick suddenly began to act very much like a child and showed all the worst attributes of childhood- tantrums, impatience, attention-seeking and egocentrism.

With life as it was she hadn't managed to book tickets for anywhere or check times or prices but Lou had mentioned that there was a grotto in town and so on Saturday afternoon two weeks before Christmas the three of them had set off for some festive fun. There was a chill in the air and Sophie felt a sense of total completeness, getting into the spirit of the season with her son and a man who was working very hard to make the two of them feel special.

They arrived at the grotto at two and were met by a queue to end all queues. The little wooden hut, covered with fake snow and fairy lights, was on the ground floor of a huge open plan shopping centre bustling with Christmas shoppers and Sophie cast her eyes to the queue that they were about to join. She could see where it ended at the grotto and tried to follow it back as it wound round and round the little hut and then around the shopping centre floor, a seemingly endless snake of grumpy and restless-looking people laden down with bags bursting with seasonal contents. A rather fed up looking elf stood at the door of the grotto checking his watch at regular intervals and trying at all costs to ignore the children biting at his heels.

"Did you book a ticket then?" Mick asked, "So we can jump the queue?"

"Um, no…" Sophie said realising the first error of her way, "I didn't think it would be so busy…"

"What?" Mick huffed. "So, what, we have to queue up?" he looked at the line of people that stretched ahead.

"I'm sure the queue will go down quickly," Sophie tried to reassure him. "You can go and have a look round the shops for a while if you like, while we're waiting?"

"What leave you?" Mick said and pointedly looked at the man standing in front who held the hand of a little girl, possibly about three Sophie thought, "Nah you're alright, anyway, I might want to see the big red man too you know. He might have a present for us."

Sophie considered this. "I don't think so…" she said doubtfully, "I think it's just for children…"

"What at ten pounds a shot?" Mick asked, indicating the sign that had just been revealed having been previously obscured by the queue.

"Ten *pounds*?" Sophie asked incredulously under her breath, not wanting to spoil Ollie's surprise as he was still very much a believer, "That's a bit much isn't it, especially as they know everyone's children will want to come? Oh well, it's only once a year!"

The queue moved slowly. Ollie sat down on the ground and happily drove the little car that Sophie had brought for him along the lines of the tiles on the floor. Mick was not so easy to amuse. He huffed and puffed and shuffled his feet impatiently.

"God I wish they'd bloody hurry up!" he eventually complained.

Sophie was quick to jump on his use of language. "Watch your tongue mister," she said half-jokingly but meaning it, using the same affectionate term as the one she used for Ollie, as if Mick was her little boy and not her lover, "Go and have a walk round if you're bored."

"Nah, you're alright…" he told her and continued to shuffle his feet around, "Did you bring a drink with you? I'm thirsty!"

Sophie took a breath. "No, no I didn't… do you want one? Here, take this and go and buy…"

Before she had a chance to finish he had pushed her money back towards her and shook his head. "Nah its fine thanks. I'll get one later."

"Well we'll be here for a while… you might as well get a drink if you want one, you're not going to miss anything!"

Mick continued to shake his head, a look of firm resolve now on his face that he was going to stick this out and not move away least Sophie should get chatted up.

"Your army training should maybe help you stick it out…" Sophie started hopefully.

"Hey!" Mick suddenly shouted at a woman who appeared out of nowhere in front of him, "Hey what do you think *you're* doing?" he asked her accusingly. "We've been waiting here for about half an hour, you can't just *push in*!" he spat. The woman looked visibly shaken by the manner in which Mick had spoken to her. The man with the little girl got involved.

"Excuse me young man. My wife is joining us, if you don't mind, to see Father Christmas with her daughter. It's not exactly going to hold *you* up?" he looked at Sophie, possibly wondering what she was doing with such an idiot, and a young one at that. Sophie moved away slightly, absolving herself of any responsibility.

"Oh right, sorry," Mick mumbled and continued to stand in silence.

Sophie rolled her eyes to the roof of the glass building. She wished that she had just come with Ollie as it was rapidly becoming clear that going out with Mick was like going out with another child.

As the minutes ticked past Mick began to look restless again. He eventually broke his silence with a bang.

"God that bloody *music*!" he said, sounding like that was it, he'd had enough.

"Mick!" Sophie whispered sharply, "*Please*! It's Christmas time, they're playing Christmas carols," she looked towards the brass band that was playing close by.

"Well maybe next year they can practice," he said petulantly.

Sophie looked apologetically at the man in front who looked round when he heard Mick's outburst.

"I'm really thirsty…"

Ollie's ears pricked up. "I'm thirsty too!"

Great, Sophie thought, look what you've started now!

"We didn't bring a drink darling," she said calmly to Ollie, "We can get a drink after seeing Father Christmas?"

Ollie seemed happy with this and continued to drive his little car along the floor.

"I can go and get you a drink if you like?" she told Mick, "You stand here?"

"Nah its fine," he replied.

"Right, then…" Sophie told him not taking any more nonsense, "… if you won't let me get you a drink and if you won't go and get one then please stop complaining about it!" she said with finality in her voice. She looked at the man in front with a look of resignation on her face. "Teenagers," she said to him then cut off Mick's response by asking Ollie if he was alright, in the most patient voice she could manage. She hadn't imagined that she would have had to bring amusements for the twenty-six-year-old as well as the six-year-old.

The queue shuffled forward by about ten inches and Mick let out a huge sigh. He sat down on the ground next to Ollie.

"God this is boring," he complained.

"You should have brought a car," Ollie stated simply.

Mick laughed. "Yeah. Yeah I should have," he nodded his head, "I actually need the toilet…" he looked over to the grotto where the elf was manhandling a young child away from the door.

Mick stood up restlessly. "It's a bit crap, isn't it? You can see inside," he said to Sophie, indicating to the grotto, "I mean anyone can see that it's not *real.*"

"Shhh!" Sophie practically clamped her hand over his mouth, "Will you *shut up*?" she hissed. "If you don't want to wait then go away, really, go shopping for a while. If you spoil this for Ollie I will *never* forgive you! There's a long queue so if you're staying you'll just have to put up with it."

The man in front gave Sophie a sympathetic and understanding look.

About forty-five minutes later Sophie, Mick and Ollie were at the front of the queue. Mick looked like he was on the edge of a breakdown and Ollie was engaging the elf in conversation.

"How long have you been Santa's helper?" he asked suspiciously, "Last year it was a lady elf…"

The elf looked bored beyond boredom. Sophie reckoned that he only replied as she was giving him evil eyes from behind her son. He sighed deeply.

"I was probably… erm…" he looked helplessly at Sophie.

"Lapland?" she suggested.

The elf's eyes lit up. "Yeah! That's it! I was in Lapland last year!" his face displayed relief.

Ollie considered this and nodded his head in acceptance.

"Were you looking after Santa's reindeer?" he asked, looking like he was trying to think of the most difficult question ever to ask this sullen elf, "How many reindeers are there…?" he looked at the elf challengingly. The elf looked at Sophie in bewilderment. I bet he thinks there's just one, Sophie thought.

"Oh that's a good question!" Sophie praised Ollie, "That's so good, can *I* answer that one?"

"There's just one, isn't there?" Mick asked, "Rudolf, isn't it?"

Ollie looked at Mick with disappointment, as if he'd gone down a few notches in his estimation. Sophie judged him, maybe unfairly, on his lack of festive knowledge.

"No! Of course there's not just *one* reindeer!" she told a bemused Mick who expected kinder treatment after standing in the queue for so long, "There are *nine!*" Sophie said triumphantly and was about to name them all when there was movement by the grotto door and the elf, relieved to have been let off the hook, told them that Father Christmas could see them now.

"At last!" Mick said and pushed his way past.

Sophie followed him in with Ollie bursting with excitement, the boy almost shaking with anticipation. They entered the small grotto door which Sophie had to stoop for and into a brightly lit interior with a Christmas tree, a white wigged woman who Sophie imagined was Mother Christmas and Father Christmas himself sitting on a small plastic chair that was far too small for his plentiful behind and a sack of presents between his legs. Mick was already deep in conversation by the time Sophie got in with Ollie and they had to wait for several minutes before Father Christmas could get a word in and asked Ollie if he had come to see him or did he mean to go to the bear factory.

"We came to see you," Ollie told him, "I know you're not the *real* Father Christmas- he's in Lapland. Where are your reindeers?" he asked seemingly stuck on that subject. "How many reindeers do you have?"

The group looked at the fake Father Christmas and waited for his response.

"Oh Santa's a bit forgetful these days," Mother Christmas joined in, "He'd forget to change his pants if I didn't remind him!" she chuckled hoarsely and Sophie thought they needed to work on their act a bit more.

***

The one thing about going out with Mick was that if it could be bought then it wasn't too much to ask for. Sophie *could* start to feel slightly claustrophobic at times as he was so super possessive but if they stayed at home, which they increasingly did, then that wasn't so much of a problem, as long as she watched what she said. For example, watching telly was fine but saying that the presenter was cute was not. This was a small price to pay though, Sophie rationalised, for being treated at times like an absolute princess.

Mick desperately wanted her to open her present before she went away for Christmas but she insisted that she didn't believe in opening presents before the actual day and said that it would spoil the surprise. The night before she left for Scotland to spend a festive week with her parents he turned up with bags full of gifts all wrapped up with tags and bows. Sophie was touched at the effort he had gone to for her and Ollie. She was glad that in the end she had put an MP3 player onto her credit card and filled it with the songs that he had put onto disks for her hoping that this would seem like a thoughtful present and as expensive as she could manage. She did feel very awkward though that Mick appeared to have bought so much.

"You shouldn't have bought us so many presents…" she had started to say but he waved this off.

"I wanted to, that's how special you are to me," he told her.

"You've bought so much for Ollie too…" she looked around at all the parcels with snowman paper covering them, in contrast to the silver wrapped presents for herself, "What have you got for him?" she whispered keen to know too what the boy was getting.

"Aha!" Mick said and tapped his nose, "I thought you didn't believe in opening presents before Christmas! You'll see!"

Sophie couldn't wait to see after the huge build up and so when Mick had gone she peeked at her present. As she went about her chores she felt the small package calling to her, 'open me, open me!' it cried in her head. She ignored it for so long and then caved into temptation deciding that actually, although rather childish, nobody would know. She carefully unpeeled a piece of tape, slid the velvet box out of its wrapping and slowly opened the lid which felt heavy and stiff. She gasped as she saw the diamond encrusted Gucci watch. It had a white mother of pearl face with diamonds all around and a white crocodile strap. She pulled a disapproving face and felt a slight disappointment as she didn't really like it then felt guilty, ungrateful and then, worst of all, trapped.

Immediately she rushed up to her room to see if the watch was still on the Gucci website and was horrified to see that it cost two and a half thousand pounds. Her mouth dropped open in shock.

"Oh my God!" she said out loud, "What...? Two and a half *thousand...*?" Suddenly the little MP3 player she had bought for Mick seemed grotesquely insignificant but even that had broken her bank. If he was going to spend *that* much, she thought slightly selfishly, I wish he'd asked me to *choose.* She snapped the box shut and carefully wrapped it up again.

When she arrived at her parents and started to put the presents under the tree her mother had commented on the quantity.

"What are all *those* for?" she asked with interest and Sophie told her, "He must really like you. Is he coming to your sister's wedding?"

"Oh the wedding!" Jo came into the room holding a plate with a piece of Christmas cake on it, "There's only five months to go Sophie, we have so much to do!"

"Well…" Sophie said, "… tell me what to do and I'll do it. I thought I'd nearly done all my duties…"

"Well, no, we still need to decide what we're doing for the hen weekend, thanks for booking the cottage though. Have you decided about your hair yet?"

Sophie realised she had been neglecting her bridesmaid duties somewhat.

"I promise that I'll get onto it all this week, I've been so busy! I might at least have my plus one though…"

"Oh that's great!" her sister clapped her hands, "Is he definitely coming? If so I'll have to alter the seating plan because at the moment you're by yourself."

Sophie considered this for a moment.

"I'm not sure… I suppose he will be if he's still around…" she wondered what her family would think of Mick, "He is a little bit younger than me… I'm not sure what you'd think of him…"

"Do you like him?" her mother asked.

"Well, yeah… he's a bit possessive but apart from that…"

"Well at least he cares enough to be possessive! Better that than someone who doesn't care at all...?"

Sophie nodded slowly. "Yes... yes I guess so."

"Does he treat you well? Do you think he might love you?"

Sophie nodded her head definitely. "Oh yes," she replied, "Just wait until you see what he's got me for Christmas..."

***

Sophie always went back to her parents for Christmas, loving that they did everything exactly the same as they always had.

On Christmas morning Ollie dived under the tree and grabbed all the presents that he could see with his name on as soon as he was allowed downstairs, having been awake since 5am. Sophie felt that she had done well to contain his bursting excitement until just after seven by which time she was well awake having been persistently asked every ten minutes if it was time to get up yet.

"Calm down darling, you have all morning to open them!"

"I want to see what Mick's got me!" Ollie replied as he started to rip wrapping paper. Sophie wondered why he was so particularly excited and then realised when she saw what his first gift was.

"Look Mummy!" Ollie said with glee as he held up a massive box containing a much smaller toy, "He's got me a Transformer!"

Sophie sighed. This particular present was on Ollie's extensive Christmas list but was the one thing she had decided not to buy as when she looked at it in the shop the toy didn't look like it would live up to its £50 price tag. She fixed a smile on her face totalling up the money that Mick had spent so far.

"Ooh lucky you," she told Ollie, "What else did you get?"

More paper was ripped open. "Wow Mummy *look*!" And Ollie held up a football kit with his name and age on the back.

"Wow… that must have cost a fair bit… can I see it for a minute?" Sophie inspected the top and saw that it was official merchandise. She looked at her sister worriedly, "He must have spent a *fortune*…"

"What's this Mummy…?" Ollie held up what looked to Sophie like a computer console.

"Let me see…" she replied taking the object from him, "Bloody hell it's a DS!" she exclaimed then remembering her language, "I mean, gosh it's a DS. I can't *believe* he's bought Ollie one of those…"

"What did he get you then Sophie?" Jo asked and Sophie dutifully opened her gift and passed it to her. Jo's jaw dropped open as had Sophie's in surprise and she stayed like that for a moment as she inspected the watch. "Oh my *God*!"

"Language!" Sophie's father interjected.

"Oh my *goodness!*" Jo had corrected herself, "I wonder how much *that* cost?"

"Two and a half thousand pounds…" Sophie told her in deadpan tones.

***

Going back to work after the Christmas break was always a massive come-down, drudgery personified. Cold, grey weeks stretched ahead without the prospect of anymore time off for the foreseeable future and what had become a horrible memory over the festive break was brought back into sharp focus when Enid snapped her first set of orders at Sophie within seconds of her walking through the office door. Not so much as a, 'How was your holiday?' passed her lips before launching into a tirade of 'things-to-do'.

"We've been awarded a new contract..." Enid barked, seemingly in a bad mood already, "... council money..." she almost spat, "...to do some training in the areas of *regeneration...*" she said haughtily in a way that made Sophie think that Enid wasn't too hot on the idea, "... so I thought that *you...*" she thrust a huge pile of paperwork into Sophie's hands, "...*you* can sort it out, you need *something* to do..."

Sophie gladly took the bundle of papers and hugged them to her chest while listening to Enid's directions. She wondered if Enid had had a nice Christmas or if she had been in the office for the whole time.

"So, we have three areas of so-called regeneration. The sorts of places you have to hide your valuables when you leave your car for any amount of time... or indeed wave goodbye to your tyres... The kinds of places that nobody gets up to go to work..."

Sophie listened making no comment, always amazed at how unprofessional Enid was.

"We're going to be going into the *schools* in these areas and getting involved with some of their in-house training..." she looked repulsed by the idea. "We will, in fact, be teaching the teachers. Telling them things that they should know already about why 'play' is important in a child's schedule. Children in these areas are apparently not playing enough and we now have money to encourage them to do so. It all seems a waste of time to me as in the end they'll all be on benefits anyway but as the city's *leading* provider of first class education we have been deemed to be the most suitable people to tell these other hapless schools what to do. We will be running play sessions too which you can do, Sophie, I know you enjoy working with children, not being ambitious..."

Sophie ignored most of what Enid was now saying, suddenly feeling hopeful that she was actually getting some proper work to do and might be allowed out of the prison for once. She wanted to show her excitement but held back, thinking that Enid might withdraw the offer if she appeared to like the idea too much.

That evening she worked on the training that she was to deliver, taking her paperwork home to continue with what she had started the day finding the whole project inspiring and at last something to show off her talents and actually make a difference to some people's lives. As she worked away her phone rang and she saw that it was Mick. Her initial thought was to ignore it but then she remembered about the watch and felt obliged to answer. She sighed.

"Hi!" she said brightly, "Are you OK?"

"Oh you do remember me then?" Mick sounded more than a little fed up, "Like your present then?"

"Yeah, I said 'Thank you'?" Sophie replied, "Didn't I?"

Back at home with her family Sophie's life of dating had seemed like a distant memory and she had tried to get into the wedding spirit with her sister, feeling guilty that she might have been neglecting her duties as a bridesmaid slightly. They had organised the hen weekend, decided on a hairdresser for the day and accessories to match the colour scheme and Jo had gone through Sophie's duties with her and Sophie had nodded her head and tried to take it all in. She had left her phone off for most of the time but text Mick every now and again to satisfy his need for contact and had sent a text on Christmas day saying what an amazing present and thank you wasn't enough. The present had been so over the top that a mere 'Thank you' seemed a bit feeble.

"Yeah I know but I've not seen you since you got back. Are you around now?"

"Well I am at home but I'm working tonight, I've been given this new project which is really great! I'm getting to go into the worst areas of the city, areas of regeneration, and…"

"I need to see you!" Mick burst in, interrupting, "I need to speak to you about something."

"Can you talk to me now then, quickly?" Sophie said, hoping that it would be quick so that she could get back to her project.

"I'd rather see you," Mick told her, "You were away all Christmas, I could pop up now."

Sophie looked at her watch. It was already almost nine; if Mick came up he wouldn't get there until after ten and then they'd be up until all hours.

"Tell me now and then you can come round another night… maybe Thursday…?" she said hopefully.

Mick relented.

"OK, I guess it is quite late to be driving up… I could come back early in the morning…" Mick tried his luck but got no response. He cleared his throat. "Well, I wanted to talk to you about my job…"

"Oh, yeah?" Sophie replied casually, flicking through her papers, "What about it?"

"Well, my posting's coming up soon… I need to choose where to go next…? I could stay where I am cos I'm doing well here but it's so far from you so I thought maybe I could get posted nearer to you… or Scotland…? I know you'd like to move there…?"

Sophie was dumbstruck for a moment, not quite sure what she had heard as she hadn't had her full attention on the conversation.

"Sorry, say that again?" she asked suddenly all ears.

Mick patiently went through it all again. He told her that he had the choice of where to be posted next, that because he was in the corps that he was he could choose his next posting, something to do with the number of years he had served in the army but Sophie didn't quite understand, she thought that soldiers got told where they were going to be sent. She listened as he explained his three options, to stay where he was which was better for his career, to be moved to a base that was a twenty-minute drive from Sophie's or to be posted to Scotland so that Sophie could move there, to be close to her family.

"What d'you think?" he asked eagerly.

Sophie was lost for words. "Oh! Umm… I'm not *really* sure… that's not really my decision is it? I mean, it's *your* career so you should do what's best for you...?"

"Yeah I know that, but what do you think I should do? I mean, what would you want me to do?"

"I'm not telling you!" Sophie replied immediately, "It's not my career, it doesn't matter what I think and I'm not going to say anything to alter your judgement."

"Or I could just say, send me to Afgan…"

"Oh don't be so silly!" Sophie said crossly, "Are you seriously saying that if I don't give you my opinion you'll go for that?"

"Well, I'd ask for Afgan if we didn't work out…"

"Oh don't be ridiculous!" Sophie exclaimed, "Really, it's your career; it's for you to decide. You only met me a few months ago… you really shouldn't be asking me what I think you should do with your career. I know what I think but that's for you to decide! I mean, clearly you should do what you want to do! If we were married, then maybe my opinion would count more but at the end of the day you still have to fulfil your own ambitions...?"

Mick's interest was sparked by the mention of marriage.

"We could get married…" Mick said and left the sentence hanging.

"What? No! I mean… not yet… I mean, you only just met me!"

"We could get a nice house, married quarters and all that...?"

"I have a house already!"

"I know you do but… well… do you think one day...?"

Sophie stopped for a moment and wondered how a simple conversation about jobs had turned into what sounded like a marriage proposal. She brought herself back to reality with a start.

"Right listen, Mick. We met a few months ago, I really like you and you bought me an amazing gift- thank you again- but your career is just that, *your* career! I don't think that after such a short time that you should be asking me what I think that you should do with it! I think that you need to decide what *you* want to do and we can sort it out from there. Now, I really need to go and finish this work before it's too late. How about we go out this Friday? Ollie's away this weekend so we could go to the cinema or something? There was that romantic comedy that you thought we should see...? Why don't we do that?"

***

Enid looked down her nose at Sophie's training ideas and scoffed at her plans for play sessions but dates were put in the diary for her to be allowed out to implement them and she was left for the rest of the week to finalise her first presentation. This had been scheduled for the next week. She reached Friday for the first time feeling like she was working on something meaningful and was actually getting paid for doing something other than photocopying and left the building for once feeling like it might not be so bad after all. She checked her phone to see if anyone had got in touch while it had been in the box under Enid's desk and saw a message from Ben that had been sent just after she had started. It just said, 'Call me please'.

Here we go, Sophie thought. She called him back.

"Hi! Are you alright?" she said chirpily, "Sorry I've been in work all day. Did you call?"

Ben was silent for a moment and then started speaking, quietly and hesitantly. Sophie thought that he sounded like he had been crying.

"Hey, Soph," he said. "Yeah… not so good. Listen…" his voice broke as he spoke and he took a second to compose himself, "It's my Mum… Remember she'd had high blood pressure before…?" Ben's words were difficult to make out.

"Yeah…" Sophie replied, "Oh Ben, is she OK?"

Ben started to sob loudly.

"No. No she's not…" he managed, "She had a heart attack early this morning… she's… passed away!" Ben cried uncontrollably and Sophie felt his sadness. She had still been in touch with Ben's Mum as despite their problems she was still Ollie's Grandma. The last time she had seen her was at his birthday and she thought back to that afternoon when his Grandma had been so proud and so happy that Sophie involved her in these events. Sophie quickly remembered that Ben was to have Ollie at the weekend.

"Oh Ben I'm so sorry… really sorry. Listen, don't worry about Ollie. I'll have him this weekend, of course. No problem. Let me know when everything is, you know, sorted out. Don't worry about Ollie anyway, he'll be fine. I'll tell him if you like… I mean, he'll be devastated but, yeah, don't worry about the weekend."

"Thanks Soph," Ben replied sounding like he truly meant it, "Tell him I'll see him soon yeah?"

Sophie rushed down to her car now running slightly late for the school run and text Mick as she went.

'Can't do tonight, really sorry! Ollie's Grandma's died. Talk later.'

She reached her car and hastily threw her bags in the back, getting in and closing the door, driving off as she was still stretching the seatbelt across her.

It wasn't until she got home with Ollie that she saw she had recent phone activity, texts and missed calls. She'd expected maybe a text from Mick about their planned night out but her phone was showing eight texts and six missed calls.

Oops, she thought, and had a look to see who they were all from. Mick's name was listed several times along with her voicemail. She started to listen to his messages but he sounded so angry that she stopped and looked at the texts. They got longer and increasingly angry sounding as she went through each one, the crux of the matter being that he was fuming that she had cancelled their date and that he never got to see her, her ex always seemingly came first.

Sophie couldn't believe that his reaction was so extreme and read the text that she had sent to see if it was a bit abrupt and didn't explain the situation that well. She sent another just in case although she thought that her original one was fairly clear and she wanted to tell Ollie about his Grandma.

'Really sorry- Ollie's Grandma died unexpectedly and I have to tell him. I told his Dad that I would have him this weekend as he's obviously upset and probably has lots to sort out. We can go out any other night?'

She left her phone in the kitchen and went upstairs to find Ollie. He was sitting under his cabin bed looking through his box of treasure; various jewels and trinkets that had been collected over the years from various places- old jewellery, Playmobile gold coins, foreign money, charity shop tat and Sophie's once loved polished stone collection. She crawled under his bed and watched him sorting for a while. She couldn't bear to tell him about the realities of life, that his beloved Grandma was dead. Tears started to fill her own eyes and she looked up to the base of his bed and took some time to compose her thoughts and work out what she was going to say. She had no idea how he would take it, if he would even understand.

"Darling…" she said hesitantly, "Darling Mummy has something to tell you."

The boy looked up from his treasures and held up some fool's gold that they had bought one day at the seaside for her to see, his eyes sparkling with wonder.

"I've been choosing my favourite treasure!" he told her with delight, "It's this one, its *real gold*!" he started rummaging again, "and this is my second favourite, it's a crystal. Grandma got me this one for my birthday."

Perfect timing, Sophie thought.

"Darling… Mummy needs to tell you something about Grandma."

"Is she coming to see us?" his eyes lit up at the prospect of another crystal.

Sophie shook her head sadly. "No darling…"

"Is she dead?" he said immediately, "Joshua told me that his Granny died because she was old. My Grandma's not as old as his Grandma though, his Grandma was nearly *one hundred!*" he looked into Sophie's eyes and then saw that they were wet with tears and his own eyes filled with tears too.

Sophie looked sadly at her son and nodded her head now. "Yes darling… Oh darling I'm so sorry, Grandma has died…"

There was a few moments pause while Ollie digested this information before the flood gates well and truly burst open.

"Grandma!" he cried, "Grandma! Grandma! Grandma!" his little face soon was red and soaked with tears and Sophie held his sobbing body tight.

"I'm sorry darling," she told him softly and kissed his soft hair, "I'm sorry. Grandma had something wrong with her heart and it made it stop. Oh my darling boy Mummy is so sorry…" her own tears came again, sad for her nearly Mother-in-law and her son whose heart was breaking in her arms.

"Does that mean Grandma has gone to heaven, Mummy?" Ollie croaked, "Does that mean I won't see Grandma again? Daddy said that Grandma was coming to see us soon."

"We won't see Grandma again darling…" Sophie breathed deeply to control her tears. "Grandma is in heaven now…"

Ollie looked up to the sky and blew a kiss and then another.

"That's one kiss for Grandma and one for Joshua's Granny because I don't know if he blows her kisses…" his little face smiled and then crumpled with grief once more, "Grandma!" he sobbed and climbed onto Sophie's knee, burying his head into her neck.

They sat for some time, Sophie hugging Ollie's shaking body tight and rocking him gently, whispering, "I'm sorry, I'm so sorry…"

***

Later on in the evening when Ollie was tucked up in bed and finally asleep, Sophie having sat stroking his head until he dropped off, she turned her thoughts back reluctantly to Mick's strop and went to locate her phone which she had eventually switched off and left in the kitchen. She flicked through the many texts that he had sent during the duration of the evening, not reading any in great detail but getting the general gist that he was mightily upset that their date had been cancelled and why did her ex's Mum dying mean that Ollie couldn't go to his Dad's this weekend? The last words that she read were, 'What about me?'

Sophie switched her phone off and threw in down on the kitchen side where it bounced off and smashed on the floor sending the back and battery skidding under the fridge. I'm not even going to bother replying to that, she thought shaking her head, you can have your stupid watch back I just can't be bothered with your whining anymore. Leaving her broken phone she took herself upstairs, checked that Ollie was still soundly sleeping and went into her room craving some peace. Flicking through her pile of CD's she found a classical collection and put it in the player, switching it on and adjusting the volume so that her room filled with the slow and steady sound of the tune that she knew from a cigar advert when she was little. The music began to bring stillness to her troubled mind. She jumped onto her bed and propped herself up with pillows and closed her eyes, allowing her head and thoughts to be drowned in the music so that nothing else was there. The music washed through her body and she felt relaxation and calm at last, her body still and nothing else in her head but sound. As she listened she began to feel a sense of aloneness creeping in to her consciousness and she willed it to leave her, I don't need to be scared of being alone now, she thought, I am better off being alone. Over and over in her head she repeated the mantra, I am stronger alone, until she started to believe it again. The music came to an end and another classic started and Sophie continued to sit, her mind flicking through her various recent experiences and she felt a pattern forming, that it was other people who were bringing stress and bad feelings into her life, that when she was alone she was fine. She suddenly opened her eyes as if she had had an amazing revelation but really, she thought, it was quite simple, I am the only person who can make me happy… I don't need anyone in my life that makes me sad. I was perfectly happy being alone.

Chapter Seventeen

Ben appeared on Sunday afternoon, his face all puffy and his eyes red, a very sorry sight and one that made Sophie's heart hurt a little. She tried to ignore the involuntary feelings.

"Hey," she said and smiled sympathetically, "Are you alright...? Silly question... of course you're not. Have you come to see Ollie?" she looked at Ben's sorrowful face.

"No, Sophie... I've come to see you..." he said, "Well of course, if Ollie's here then of course I'll see him too... I just wanted to talk to you quickly maybe, if he's busy...?"

"We've just put together his train set in the living room. Look!" she stepped back and let Ben look into the front room where the track wove around the whole floor space, under the table and around the stools, disappearing into the kitchen...

"Ollie wanted to play with his train so we've used the entire track!" she checked that the boy was busy playing and lowered her voice, "He was so upset... about your Mum, of course... I've just been trying to keep him busy and distract him with lots of fun things! I spent a fortune on him at the beach fun fair yesterday when it was raining; we were the only people there!" she smiled at Ben who laughed at the thought.

"You're such a great Mum Sophie..." Ben told her, "You always do the best thing for him don't you? He's absolutely your number one priority..."

Sophie was taken aback by his niceness. "Well, yeah of course... He's my number one... I'd do anything for him..." she smiled again at Ben and now felt sorry for him; he looked like a broken man. He pressed his finger and thumb on top of his eye lids to stop anymore tears and breathed deeply, composing himself.

"Listen, Soph. Sophie. I've been doing a lot of thinking lately and thinking about us and Ollie. I don't know, I'm confused... you always look great when I see you and I always think, what did I do walking away from her and my boy...? Ollie means the world to me too and I miss him every day we're apart, I want to be a part of his life, I want to wake up in the morning with you and have him jump into bed with us and wake us up," he smiled and laughed at his own soppiness. "I want to take him down the park on a Saturday morning to let you have a long lie cos I know you work so hard in the week... I want to pick flowers with him to give to you because you're the best Mum... I want to see him growing up and be there for all the special days he's going to have... his birthday's and Christmas... family times... normal Sunday afternoon's when we have to go shopping and he moans about it... I just want to be a family with you two, that's all I want in my life... I didn't realise what I had until it was gone..."

Sophie listened to this speech feeling numb; scared to allow herself any feelings in case they were to completely engulf her, this being what she wanted when Ben had left but now having come to terms with being alone. She looked at him and frowned, rubbing her forehead in frustration. Ben stood there on her doorstep looking at her with hopeful eyes, pleading with her to let him back into her heart.

They stood for several minutes in silence, Sophie rubbing her forehead to the point that it started to feel like she was actually rubbing the skin away. The moment was eventually broken by Ollie who, on noticing his Dad was at the door came running out and clamped himself around his legs.

"Daddy!" he cried happily and then remembered about his Grandma and looked up solemnly, "I said a prayer for Grandma last night... and for Joshua's Granny... I don't know if Joshua says prayers."

"I didn't know you said prayers!" Ben said and looked at Sophie, "See, I want to know these things..."

Sophie stopped rubbing her forehead and checked in the mirror next to the front door that she still had skin left. She suddenly felt irritated by Ben's presence, remembering when he had come back after abandoning her and Ollie and their wedding plans and stood in the very same place, telling her that he'd met someone else.

"Listen, Ben. I need to think, OK? I'm not saying 'no' or 'yes'... I just need to think about things for a while... it's been a rough few days for everyone."

Ben nodded his head with understanding. "Yeah, well... of course I didn't expect you to decide right now! I just wanted to tell you... and maybe one day you'll decide that I can come back and share Ollie with you, like it's meant to be."

Sophie closed the front door and stood leaning against it for a while, now deep in thought, her mind that had been so certain about being alone now racing with thoughts of a proper family with Ben. She eventually shook the thoughts from her head muttering, 'men!' under her breath. I need a girl's night urgently, she thought and picked up her phone to arrange one for the following week.

***

By the time Friday came, after the week she ended up having, Sophie was ready to hit the bottle. She had been made to look like a fool during her first presentation on play as Enid, who had come to monitor events for her first one, kept interrupting her with, what Sophie thought, were stupid questions and ended up asking Sophie one that she didn't know the answer to. As Sophie 'um-ed' and 'ah-ed' and went increasingly red, Enid had stood up, smoothing down her suit as she did and walked to the front of the room declaring that she would carry on the presentation from there and continuing with what Sophie thought was utter nonsense but because she was a total bitch she seemed to get away with it, leaving Sophie now demoted and sitting down at the back of the room feeling hot with anger and frustration and knowing that she would have been fine had it not been for Enid who had it in for her for some reason. Then there was the proposition from Ben that she was still confused about, Ollie's grief and texts from Mick who went from pleading to be taken back to demanding that she return his watch.

"So my peace was short lived," she explained to her friends as they listened to her account of the last week, "I was absolutely sure that I actually was better off alone and then Ben comes round with that!"

"I'm not sure anyone is necessarily better off by themselves…" Lou thought aloud, "… but probably better off by themselves rather than be with the *wrong person*."

"I'm not sure if there is a '*right person*' anymore though," Sophie replied, "I mean, how, out of the billions of people who live in the world can you find your perfect match?" she took a mouthful of the proper beer in her hand, Ollie having been picked up by Ben and she having decided that for once she needed something stronger than a Coke. "I'm *happy* by myself, when I'm by myself nobody makes me unhappy, well, apart from Enid but the money at the end of every month dulls that one a bit… I should send the watch back too as at the moment it's making me feel obliged to go out with Mick but that's just such hard work!"

"But what about Ben?" Joules asked, "He must really mean it Sophie, this time...?"

"Why exactly?" Lou challenged her, "He's a bit late! He shouldn't have left them in the first place! He can't just come back now and expect her to welcome him back with open arms!" she put on a high pitched squeaky voice. "Oh Ben, Ben I've missed you *so* much I'm *so* glad you've come back!"

"I don't really sound like that, do I?" Sophie asked, horrified.

"No, not really!" Lou laughed, "Allow me some artistic license!"

"What gets me, though, is that he's never actually said 'sorry'! If he would just say that then I might forgive him but he never has, like he doesn't actually think that he's done anything wrong!"

"Maybe his Mum dying has had an effect on him...?" Joules wondered, always seeing the good in people, "Maybe he just is telling the truth and just hasn't really thought about your side of it but really does mean what he says...?" she looked at Sophie with wide questioning eyes. "Maybe...?"

"Maybe…" Sophie said.

"What about the funeral? Are you going to that? Ollie's not, is he?" Tina asked, "I can have him if you need to go."

"No it's fine, Joules has offered already!" Sophie smiled, "Thanks though. It's luckily on Monday at three in the crematorium just outside town… well, I mean luckily because otherwise I probably wouldn't have been *allowed* to go! It will literally take me ten minutes from work and I'll already be in the dark suit! I don't need to go of course but I do want to, she was a big part of my life and Ollie's so I want to say my last goodbye."

***

Sophie made it to the crematorium with five minutes to spare after being delayed in the office by Enid for ten minutes for no apparent reason. What is her *problem,* Sophie wondered as she parked her car and jumped out, eager to find Ben and say how sorry she was again before the service? She strode up to the crematorium doors thinking about Enid's delaying tactics, sending her around the school on a wild goose chase to find a document that was actually in the top drawer of her desk. Entering the building she saw that as she was so late the seats were almost all taken and she was forced to sit right at the back of a small balcony overlooking the room with no time to see if she could catch Ben. She craned her neck from her high up seat and was dismayed to see him and his family now walking in, taking their sets solemnly at the front, Ben twisting his head round looking at all the faces there for his Mother but not seeing Sophie sitting above his eye level and behind a tall gentleman who had rather large hair. Sophie leant over to see and stood up slightly so that she had a view of Ben. She froze and felt her stomach lurch when she saw him kissing the woman next to him who then tenderly pecked him on the nose and cupped his chin with her hand, someone she had assumed was his family but now she realised that it must be Sarah, a woman she had heard so much about from Ollie but never seen- someone who looked not dissimilar to Sophie but fatter, much to Sophie's great pleasure. The sight of them kissing made Sophie feel panicked, like she suddenly knew that it was Ben that she wanted to be with. Oi, she thought, keep your flipping hands off him I'm the mother of his child! She slumped down in her chair, at least behind the hair do she couldn't see the canoodling and looked around where she was. She could see to the front of the lower level where a large screen had been placed and was now doing a slide show of random photos from what appeared to be the family album. Sophie was touched that there were several of her and Ben before Ollie had come along and some of

Sophie and Ollie together after Ben had left, Ollie having been the apple of his Grandma's eye.

It was with mixed emotions that Sophie sat and gazed at the images flashing past- the happy pictures contrasting with the reality of what their lives had turned out like, the memory of Ben leaving rising to the forefront of her thoughts. Sophie sighed and dismissed the memory, nothing can be done about the past, she thought philosophically, only the present we can live and the future we can change.

There is nothing like a funeral to make you realise what is important in life. As Sophie sat watching the images of family life flash past on the projector she yearned to have her own family back together. A random photo taken at Ollie's first birthday when the hurt had been forgotten for a while took her breath away, Ben holding the birthday boy while Sophie stood next to them smiling broadly holding onto the first birthday cake, both wearing party hats and their full attention on their little boy. The image took Sophie back to that day and she closed her eyes and remembered how, for moments, they had been like the perfect family unit, despite the fact that Ben's new girlfriend had had to be asked permission for him to attend. Sophie felt the hurt and anger rising up in her heart again. The love of her life had been stolen away from her, maybe it was time for her to fight back. What Ben had said the other day started to echo round in her head; I just want to be a family, I didn't realise what I had until it was gone, we all make mistakes. Sophie sat up straight so that she could watch Ben sitting down below. He stood up and adjusted his suit and made his way to the front, stepping up beside the projector clutching a piece of paper from which he started to read. He cleared his throat several times and looked out into the congregation of gathered friends and family with sorrowful eyes. He cleared his throat again and fixed his sad eyes on his paper. Sophie's heart skipped a beat, he looked so young again, like when they first met, but now vulnerable and it took her all her strength not to jump up from her seat and rush to be by his side to offer him the support that he needed at this hideous time. She felt a jealousy that she had never felt before that there was someone else there now giving him that. He mustn't have told her that he's thinking of coming back to me, she thought, I guess he's waiting for my reply.

Ben's reading was short and heartfelt, a piece that he had composed himself. Sophie couldn't remember hearing anything more poignant and she breathed deeply and willed away the tears, a passage for the woman who gave him life. A section caught Sophie's attention, 'As Mum's family meant the world to her my family means the world to me. I may have made mistakes in the past but if I can do anything for her now it will be to always strive to be the perfect son and now, the perfect father'.

He bowed his head and hurried back to his place, sitting down and receiving a squeeze of the shoulder and a few words from Sarah. Sophie felt like an outsider when really she wanted to be down there, giving the man she loved the support he needed.

At the end of the service she held back to allow the throng of people leave before her, wanting to say some words in private to Ben before she left. She hung around just inside the doorway and watched the line of mourners shuffling past the family, shaking their hands, embracing, some saying a few brief words to which Ben would nod solemnly or others talking for longer, even making Ben laugh through his tears. She absentmindedly remembered how much Ben could always make her laugh, even when she had had the worst day or felt ill or felt sad he had always had the ability to put the smile back on her face. She stood sadly thinking that she couldn't actually remember the last time that she had laughed properly, the sort of laugh that makes you double over and hold your sides and make tears appear in your eyes. Nobody had ever made her laugh like he did.

As the line started to get shorter Sophie joined the end of it and made her way towards the family to give them her sympathy and hopefully say a few words to Ben. She felt strange lining up to speak to his family as she had once been engaged to be married to him and been so close to them. Sarah was standing next to him clutching his arm, what was she doing there anyway, Sophie thought, when all he wants to be is a family with me? Sarah looked so close to him, was looking at him so fondly. They didn't look right together though, Sophie thought, she's taller than him for a start, he must be waiting for me to get back to him with my response. She kept catching his eye as she approached and tried to convey her thoughts to him; that she would like to try again if that's what he wanted. She felt an impatience now to get to him and tell him that she had thought about it and that was all she wanted too, wanting to push past the few people now in front of her and run into his arms and say, yes I do want you to come back and to have her family complete.

At last she reached Ben's Dad and clutched his arm and said how sorry she was. He gratefully nodded and asked her how she was getting on and how was Ollie? She moved onto his brother and sister who received her condolences and asked after Ollie, Sophie replying briefly, now just wanting to get to Ben. As she approached him Sarah whispered something in his ear and walked away, pulling her long black cardigan tightly around her waist and heading off down the path towards the garden of remembrance where she sat on a bench and watched from afar.

Sophie reached Ben and instantly cried, feeling like she had been bottling up years of emotions. She hugged him tightly and told him how sorry she was about his Mum and that she had been thinking since he had come round. The rest of his family looked at them awkwardly and subtly moved away as Sophie, it would seem, had a bit of a breakdown.

"I've also been thinking about what you said, Ben, the other day and I just want the same! I don't want to have Ollie one weekend and not the next! I want what you said, for him to jump into bed with both of us on a Saturday morning! To raise him together, that's all I ever wanted from the moment I met you, to get married and have your child. Please, *please* let's try again?"

Ben stood stiffly while Sophie sobbed into his black collar and hesitantly brought his hand up to rest on her waist, hardly touching her with his feeble attempt at a cuddle. She suddenly realised that she wasn't getting anything back from him, that this was a one sided display of need. She lifted her wet face to look up at him and the look on his face told her everything she needed to know. She pulled away from him, wiping the tears from her eyes.

"Sorry," she said, "Not the time or the place is it?" she cast her eyes around and instantly felt stupid. "Apologies. I've just been thinking about what you said and I was so excited to tell you that I wanted what you wanted too… but now clearly isn't the best time…"

Having had enough of Sophie hanging off her boyfriend, Sarah appeared at his side and asked him if everything was OK.

"Yes we're just talking," Sophie said bravely thinking, who do you think you are asking that? She looked frantically at Ben as if to say, what are you going to do about *her*? Both women now looked at him demanding some kind of input.

"Tell her!" Sarah demanded.

Ben cleared his throat as he had a tendency to do and looked awkwardly at both before speaking, addressing Sophie.

"Listen, Sophie, we've had some news," he looked at her hoping that she would tell him what he was about to say so that he wouldn't have to say it. Sophie stood in frozen silence as if the world had stopped spinning, waiting but also knowing exactly what he was going to say. She watched Ben's mouth moving as she had watched them years before when he told her that he'd met someone else, now telling her that Sarah was pregnant and that they were going to move away, about an hour away; still close enough for him to drive down and collect Ollie every other weekend but time for them to get on with their lives and not live in each other's pockets anymore. Sarah stood clutching her tummy smugly, watching Sophie with steady eyes.

Sophie's heart exploded in her body, a pain that she had never felt before, a second blow like no other. Her chest feeling like it might burst as her breathing took over her whole being, the tears welling up and the sadness and hopelessness of the situation making her want to scream and thump Ben's chest and cry, 'Why? *Why? Why are you doing this to me again?'*

She looked at Ben through the tears that were threatening to tumble down her cheeks, gazing into his for an answer as he looked back, maybe a trapped man now but not one who deserved her love or who deserved her tears.

"Right," she said and turned on her heel, briskly walking back to her car which was parked at the bottom of a gravel drive. She crunched away, her eyes now so full of tears that she could barely see where she was going. She tried some deep breaths to delay the torrent that was threatening; at least until she was back in the confines of her car, away from the eyes of Sarah and Ben, not wanting to let them know that she actually cared.

Getting into the car she hurriedly tried to put her keys in the ignition so that she could drive away and wail elsewhere but she fumbled and the tears that were threatening tipped over the edge of her eyes and started to stream down her face. She threw the keys angrily into her lap and dropped her forehead onto the steering wheel and allowed her body for once to cry, to let the toll of the past be released from her soul.

"Men!" she cried, "Bloody stupid men! What am I *doing*? Why did I *listen* to him again? What was I *thinking*, taking him back again? Let her have him, let *her* worry now if he's going to stick around! I don't care anymore; I just don't *care*!"

She cried until she could cry no more, until her whole body felt exhausted and there were no more tears to fall. A calm resignation now washed over her. That chapter has ended, she thought, it's time now to move onto the next.

Chapter Eighteen

Jo's hen-do weekend was held in March, a year after her invites had gone out and with enough time, she said, between then and the wedding for her to get back from wherever the girls were going to send her.

"Don't be silly!" Sophie had told her, "We're not going to do anything *horrible*! That's for the men to do to the *groom*!"

Twelve had been invited, from Jo's school friends who she was still in touch with to University friends and work colleagues. The cottage that they had hired was in the Borders, more like a country house and had six double rooms and plenty of seating areas plus an extensive garden with a hot tub, perfect for the time of year Jo had said. Sophie had planned a quiz about her sister and was busy in the kitchen preparing a meal for the group as they all gradually arrived, chattering excitedly with Jo. Sophie didn't really know any of them that well, remembering some vaguely from school but was pleased that Jo seemed so happy that all her special friends were together and got on with being the mother of the house taking it upon herself, as chief and only bridesmaid, to organise events and run a smooth hen-weekend.

Sophie had arrived at Edinburgh airport with Ollie where she had been collected by her parents. Ollie was to stay at a nearby B&B with her parents while she was to stay in the hen house, as it was named for the weekend. Her Mum was going to come over on the Saturday night, leaving Ollie and Granddad to fend for themselves.

As the ladies started arriving Jo popped some pink champagne and filled up glassed for everyone but herself.

"Have a drink, ladies, while you unpack!"

Her friends had gladly taken a glass each and gone off with their cases to sort their sleeping accommodation out. As Sophie stirred a huge pan of pasta she could hear the animated voices discussing who was going to sleep where.

"Are you not having a glass, Jo?" she asked, thinking that it was unlike her sister not to indulge in a tipple.

Jo checked that there was nobody around and moved to Sophie's side and whispered in her ear.

"I think I'm *pregnant!*" she hissed and then stood back looking at Sophie with wide eyes.

Sophie dropped the spoon into the pasta.

"Jo!" she exclaimed, "What? Does Andy know? What about your d*ress?*"

Jo poured a glass of champagne and pretended to sip it.

"Just like the time we went to Italy with Mum and Dad and I pretended to smoke," she smirked at the memory and Sophie laughed.

"Oh yeah, I'd forgotten all about that!"

"Well, I'll just have to pretend again and not *eat* anything! So that I don't get too fat…"

"You can't stop *eating*! If you're pregnant…!"

"Ssh!" Jo looked around furtively and whispered again, "I don't want *anyone* to know! I'm not sure exactly, I'm just a bit late… but it might be all the stress of the wedding… but we have been *trying!*"

Sophie held up one hand so that she was spared the details and fished the pasta spoon out of the pan with the other. She always though it odd that people should announce that they were trying for a baby, they may as well announce that they were at it like rabbits at every possible chance.

"You timing is impeccable," she told her sister.

Proceedings had taken on a rather civilized air and the ladies enjoyed a supper on Friday night with Sophie's quiz and then general chat followed by some hill walking on Saturday afternoon. A table had been booked at a nearby country pub for a meal on Saturday evening where Sophie's Mum was going to join them. She had had constant text updates about how Ollie was which Sophie loved, allowing her to enjoy the time away. They had bought a new Thomas the Tank Engine DVD that afternoon, Sophie's Mum had said, so that Ollie and Granddad had something to do.

"I'm going to pop over to the cottage to see Ollie before the meal, if that's OK?" Sophie had told her sister, "I could get a taxi back over with Mum?"

"I think Mum was going to meet us at the pub...?" Jo thought out loud, "I *think!* She was rather vague actually. But it doesn't matter, it's all booked. Why don't you give him a call?"

"I just want to see him, it's not far away. I'll get ready to go out and then pop over- I'll be back within the hour?"

Sophie's taxi dropped her off at a tiny B&B on the edge of a hill and she strode up the driveway. Her Dad looking slightly flustered and Ollie were waiting at the door for her, having received the text that she was on her way.

"Hi!" she said happily and scooped up Ollie, his little legs dangling down as she cuddled him tight, "Hi, Dad! Where's Mum? Is she upstairs getting ready?"

"No you're Mum left a little while ago, said she had something to sort out, probably a cake or something?"

Sophie looked at her father with a perplexed look on her face. "Yes…" she said slowly, "… *probably* a cake! Are you OK? You look like you're a bit stressed out. Ollie I hope you're being good for your Granddad!"

"I am!" Ollie replied indignantly.

"Oh he is being a very good boy," her Dad reassured, "Granddad's just getting a bit old for climbing trees…"

"Oh Ollie! Not climbing trees without Mummy! Poor Granddad!" she felt relieved that it was now nearly bedtime and that they would be safe indoors watching Thomas.

Once she had set the two up with their portable DVD and a huge bag of popcorn Sophie had called another taxi to take her straight to the pub where the rest of the group were now waiting.

"What's the occasion?" the taxi driver asked with keen interest, "We don't usually see such classy ladies around these parts. Here," he passed his business card over his shoulder, "call me later if you need picked up."

"OK thanks, we will do!" Sophie said, "My sister's Hen do." She rummaged around in her bag to find her phone for the name of the pub and called her sister.

"Mum's here!" Jo said, "Where are you? Why didn't you come over together?"

"Mum had gone already when I got here!" Sophie had told her, "It's just a mix up I won't be long! Where are you again...?"

Sophie's taxi arrived at the small lonely pub, right out in the middle of nowhere quite some miles away from the nearest town. She got out and breathed in the fresh country air and looked around at the stunning scenery in awe. It seemed like so long since she had seen proper countryside and mountains. Where she now lived she saw buildings and cars unless she took Ollie to one of the organised green spaces, how lucky to live somewhere like this she thought. She paid the driver and stood while he drove away from the pub, the sound of the taxi slowly getting quieter leaving her in the wonderful silence.

"Come on!" Jo's voice rudely broke her peace as she yelled out of the front door of the pub, "We're all waiting for you before we crack open the champers!"

Sophie laughed and waved and made her way over to where her sister stood.

"I think we're about to spend more in this dive that they normally take in the *year!*" her sister whispered loudly. She dismissed the look of concern on Sophie's face, "Not your fault, we had no way of knowing, their website was crap. At least we're all here! Come on!"

They tottered past a bar where two old men sat and a bar man stood behind. Everyone stopped talking and watched as the sister's walked past them and through into a back room.

"They've hidden us in here; I have no idea why because they clearly have no customers out the front! Never mind, at least we can make a noise!"

The seated group cheered loudly when Jo appeared again with Sophie, most wearing some kind of hen-do attire; glittery cowboy hats, pink feather boas and badges that flashed, 'Jo's hen Do'.

"I got the badges!" Sophie claimed, "But have *nothing* to do with the rest!"

"It's fine, Claire got married the other month; these are left over from *her* hen do," Jo looked pleased as punch that everyone was now together, "Let the party begin!" she shouted and raised her glass of champagne, Sophie watching as she tipped it towards her lips and let the liquid touch them but didn't drink a drop.

As the meal went on the ladies swapped seats several times to allow everyone a chance to talk to each other. The pub owner couldn't believe his luck as they ordered drink after drink after drink, bottles of wine and champagne being poured dry again and again but none entering the body of the hen herself. By the time they reached desert he had fully entered the spirit of the evening and brought Jo a huge bowl of different coloured ice cream festooned with sparklers and cocktail umbrellas.

"You don't get that in the city," he had told them, indicating to his creation.

Jo tapped her full wine glass to bring the table to attention.

"Ladies! Ladies!"

The now drunken company jeered her, enjoying their conversations now too much to listen to a speech from the bride to be.

"I just want to say 'Thanks'!" she told them with mock crossness. The door to their room opened and a policeman popped his head round, looking serious.

"I've had a complaint…" he started.

The table of women looked aghast.

The policeman came in and closed the door.

"This is the right place, isn't it? I'm looking for a Jo Bridges?"

Jo looked at the policeman worriedly. "That's me, officer. What's up? I don't *think* we've been *that* loud…"

The policeman moved around to Jo's side of the table and started to loosen his collar.

"What about if the complaint was that you weren't being loud enough?" and with that he whipped his helmet off and started to rotate his hips in, what Sophie thought, was a rather disturbing way.

The collection of women screeched and screamed and hollered, wolf whistles started as he thrust his groin in the direction of a horrified Jo.

"Sophie I will *kill you!*" she yelled and pushed her way past the stripper and out of the room, followed by Sophie whose chair fell to the ground in her haste to catch up with her sister and tell her that it was nothing to do with her.

Sophie found her sister locked in a cubicle in the ladies' toilet.

"Jo? Jo it's me!"

"Go away!" Jo shouted petulantly, "I *told* you I didn't *want* a stripper*!* How could you? You *knew* that I would hate it*!*"

"I didn't book the stripper!" Sophie told her sister patiently through the cubicle door, "He's nothing to do with me! I *promise!* It must have been one of your friends…"

"My friends wouldn't do that to me!" she said stubbornly.

"Well I wouldn't either! What kind of person do you think I am?" Sophie stopped and thought, suddenly realising who it could have been, "Oh God… Mum…!"

Jo's door swung open to reveal her sitting on the closed toilet, now shaking her head.

"Mum…"

"Maybe *that's* why she wanted to come early…" the awful realisation dawned on Sophie, "She kept going *on* about getting a stripper! The only difference with her idea thought was that it had been for the fire service…"

The ladies looked at each other seriously and then both started to laugh.

"Oh God…" Sophie managed before collapsing into giggles, crouching down on the floor and holding her sides, as if to prevent herself from splitting in two. Jo held her head in her hands and shook it from side to side.

"Mother, mother, mother…" she said and then laughed some more.

"Come on, we'll miss it!" Sophie said.

"No! I'm not going back in there until I know he's gone! There's no *way* I'm eating jelly beans out of his cod piece…!"

Sophie wondered how Jo had this information if she was so against strippers but let it pass.

"I'll go and pop my head round the door then, see if he's decent," she smirked, "Maybe I can pull him and bring him to the wedding… It's OK! I'm *joking*!" she reassured her sister who looked horrified as she made her way back out to the party.

Sophie slowly pushed the door and peered through the gap to see the policeman still tugging at his collar but now with little else on apart from a little piggy cod piece to hide his modesty and to Sophie's utter horror, her mother on all fours at his feet wearing a leash.

"Oh my God…" she said under her breath and let her head fall against the door frame which caused the door to creak open and reveal her hiding place. The stripper who was twisting his nether regions around in a rather disturbing manner looked at her with worried eyes, concerned that he had spoiled the event in some way and Sophie looked back, using all of her willpower to maintain eye contact and not look down, at all. She smiled at him.

"It's OK, it's not you. My sister just didn't want a stripper…"

Sophie went to the toilet again to retrieve her frightened sister and sent her back in to be with her friends.

"I'll go and deal with PC Plod," she told her, "I'm guessing Mum's paid for him already. Whatever you do, do not let him know that was our mother!" she shuddered at the thought of what she had seen and went off to see if the stripper was still around. She found him dressed again and nursing a pint of lager at the front bar, alongside the two elderly gentlemen who Sophie supposed propped up the bar every evening.

"Hi, there," she said and smiled as he looked up at her. "I'm sorry again about my sister. She really didn't want a stripper. I don't know who booked you but I hope that they paid…?"

"Yeah they did. They just all chipped in now. I think the older lady booked and paid the deposit but they all thought they should help out... I'm Neil," he extended his hand to Sophie who shook it, thinking that it was funny that he was quite so formal now. "How do you do.? It's good really... that you ran out... it's never happened before actually, you know, even if they say they don't want it they normally do once I start. I mean, most women can't resist such a fit body..."

Modest, Sophie thought. The man clearly wanted to talk.

"... but it's just a job... I do it to make some extra money while I'm at University... I'm doing a degree in Ancient Philosophy and, well, gave up a pretty good job to do it but it's what I'm interested in and I thought, if I don't bite the bullet now and do it I'll probably never get round to it... I've always wanted to go to University but never had the chance after school as we really couldn't afford it... but anyway, this came up and it's quite easy money really, you just rock up, take your kit off and leave. Two hundred pounds, thank you very much... at least!"

"Two hundred!" Sophie exclaimed, "Wow..."

"Well, I'm one of the higher class performers... I've done other things and got more though, escort and that sort of stuff..."

Sophie must have looked fairly horrified as he quickly explained.

"Oh, I don't *do* anything you know... not *that* kind of escort. Just having dinner with a lady and having a chat...

listening to her… that's what's wrong with most relationships it seems to me, people don't listen to each other anymore. The ladies who come to me anyway say that and that's what most of them want, just a listening ear," he looked at Sophie who was fairly sceptical about what he had just said but decided to let it go, "Some might try it on a bit but then they find out that I'm actually a *thinker…*"

That must be disappointing for them, Sophie mused.

"I've gone back to University so that I can maybe one day be taken seriously, like the intellectual person that I am… not just someone who has this great body!" he said matter-of-factly. "You have been the *only* woman, though…" he continued, "… who hasn't even *looked* at my body… when you came back in and I was practically naked you looked into my *eyes*…into my *soul*… Nobody has ever done that before… I wish they would, you know, just look into my eyes…"

Well don't take your clothes off then you twit, Sophie thought and tried to expel the image of his gyrating groin out of her head.

***

The one good thing about being single, Sophie thought as she tumbled out of the house shoes in hand and still tucking herself in the morning after getting home from the hen do, is that it doesn't matter one jot what I look like. She saw Ollie into school, realising that he hadn't cleaned his teeth and telling him that they would do it twice later. She smoothed his hair down in an attempt to make him look smart. As she dashed back to the car she read a message from her sister saying, 'Not pregnant, bugger'. Sophie laughed despite herself and felt a little sorry for her sister who had had a dry hen do now for nothing.

"Heavy weekend?" Enid had asked when she saw the state Sophie was in as she burst into the office. Sophie muttered under her breath that she had been to her sister's hen do as she sat down at her desk and shoved her coat and bag underneath.

"Oh *dear*!" Enid had said sneeringly, "So there will be a wedding coming up then?"

Here we go, Sophie thought; don't *bother* to cancel my leave!

"Yeah, it's in May? It's on a Friday, I've got the day booked off. I had it confirmed ages ago."

"Did you now... well, I hope it lasts!"

Sophie looked at Enid with steady eyes, why say that she thought? You really are a total bitch aren't you?

"Hang up your coat please Sophie, if it was supposed to go under your desk we would have put hooks under there. You may have slovenly habits at home but here we have high standards. Then you'd better get started on your next presentation. Mrs Wright seems keen for you to do another..." Enid looked at her with a puzzled look on her face, "I'm not sure why... Anyway, I have a meeting downstairs so will leave you ladies to it! I'd like to see a draft of your training plan on my desk by lunchtime, Sophie. All the details you need are on your desk."

With that Enid breezed leaving Sophie bewildered.

"I must have done something alright, if Mrs Wright wants me to carry on with the training?" she asked nobody in particular.

Ruth rummaged under a huge pile of paper and pulled out several sheets, passing them over her monitor to Sophie.

"Here, take a look!" she told her.

"I don't think that we should be passing pieces of paper to each other..." Laura started.

Sophie took the sheets ignoring Laura completely, getting fed up now of pointless procedures and secrecy.

"In my last office we *shared* so much information!" Sophie said to Ruth, "It was so great because that's how we learnt and all did our jobs properly! Anyway, thank you. Let me have a look..."

She saw that they were evaluations.

"These came back by post, after your last training session? It then turned out that Enid had been hiding the rest in her desk drawer- they're all good! Everyone loved your training and the ones that Enid had hidden said that the only way you could have improved was if you had shoved a sock in the annoying woman's mouth that kept interrupting!" Ruth beamed at Sophie.

Sophie happily leafed through the training evaluations and read all the positive comments for herself, feeling a great sense of achievement and pride for the first time ever in the job.

"Wow! Very clear… good information… a good balance of listening and doing… really interesting… wow everyone thought that it was good…"

"Great," Ruth corrected her, "Everyone thought that you were great."

"So why has Enid been hiding all of these…?" Sophie wondered out loud, "… if we were so great then why didn't she want to tell Mrs Wright…?"

Ruth shook her head at Sophie's naivety.

"It's nothing to do with 'we' being great, Sophie, it was *'you'* who was great- you're competition to Enid and she doesn't like it one bit!"

"I hardly think so…" Laura muttered from her desk.

"Oh stop it Laura, you know that Enid likes everything her way and likes the power that she has. The fact of the matter is, though, that any one of us could run this office and Sophie, here, happens to be fabulous at delivering the training- that's Enid's job and she won't give it up without a fight!"

"But I'm not trying to take over Enid's job…" Sophie said worriedly, "They asked me to do the training and so I did it… it was nice to be asked to do something for a change rather than the photocopying!"

"Mrs Wright wants the best… Enid *really* didn't want her to see how great your training was. She hid the evaluations that she collected but didn't bank on the rest being posted back! I made sure that Mrs Wright saw them all as soon as I opened them, they were addressed to the training team and not Enid thank goodness!"

Sophie thought back to the presentation.

"She did seem hell bent on sabotaging it… Enid, I mean. She interrupted *continuously* with *impossible* questions! By the end of it I felt absolutely frazzled and was sure that everyone had thought I must be so stupid…"

"Put your C.V. next to hers and you'll see why you're competition to her… she actually has no teaching or training qualifications at all, your C.V. wipes the floor with hers but so far she's managed to stay where she is by bullying and harassing everyone until they leave. How Mrs Wright doesn't notice her high staff turnover is anyone's guess… If you can stick it out long enough then maybe you'll get a promotion," Ruth smiled wickedly at Sophie who grinned back and embarked on her new training plan with a newfound enthusiasm.

***

For the weeks before her sister's wedding Sophie became immersed in her work, finally having a project to focus on and determined to show her employer what she could do. Pay rises were random at the Elm Tree but were awarded for performance and could be well over any other a similar employer would award. If you could stick the job for long enough, Ruth told Sophie, then you could reap the benefits. She was given a block of twelve training sessions to plan, prepare and present in different schools in the city plus a tool kit for others to use to implement similar training. Mrs Wright, who never seemed to have any real idea about how long anything should take, gave her until the summer to arrange her training for the new school term in September and awarded Sophie a new contact with pay rise attached. That was to be her sole project for the forthcoming months and Enid was fuming.

The brown envelope was waiting on her desk when she arrived one morning to an empty office. She was inspecting the writing on the outside as Enid breezed in and stopped in her tracks when she saw what Sophie had in her hand.

"Not *everyone* gets a brown envelope…" she had said and hovered as Sophie began to open it.

"Maybe it's my notice…"

"Maybe…" Enid said with what sounded like hope in her voice.

As Sophie pulled the paper out of the envelope that hid its contents she audibly gasped as she saw the figure that was printed at the top and she continued to read the rest of the contents with her mouth hanging open.

"Anything interesting…?" Enid said casually from her side of the desk, pretending to look busy but clearly *bursting* to know what the letter said.

"Oh not really… just contractual stuff…" Sophie replied and slid the letter back into its envelope and hid it away in her bag. Enid looked irritated that she wasn't going to get a satisfactory response and briskly got up and put her jacket on. "I'll be back in a while." She said and flounced out of the office.

Sophie slumped back in her chair and allowed herself a smug smile.

Eat that Enid, she thought triumphantly. Sophie now had a new title, 'Off-site training co-ordinator'. 'Off-site' was *so much* more important than 'on' she thought happily and switched on her computer to begin a productive day of planning.

With her new responsibility came a new-found enthusiasm for work and the feeling of needing to meet someone gradually disappeared, Sophie managing her life as she had once before, this time in a rather more comfortable manner. She arrived at her sister's wedding venue a month later a new person. Professional, sorted, happy.

The wedding was taking place at a small converted castle just north of the border, a beautiful ancient building which was now a hotel in the most breath-taking surroundings. Months before Sophie would have arrived feeling melancholy that it was not her own wedding or that she was there by herself but now she walked in with her head held high, proud to be there with Ollie and proud to be supporting him herself with her new important job.

She arrived on the Thursday evening, having gone straight to the airport after collecting Ollie from school. They were greeted by a rather frazzled looking Jo in the foyer of the hotel.

"Sophie! At last! We're waiting to have dinner!"

Sophie looked at her with glazed eyes. "Uh, OK… we've just got here! I didn't know you were waiting for me…" Why am I always late for *everything*, she thought?

"Well of course, everyone's here! The family! You're in the room next to me, look, here are your keys. Dump your bags and come down. We'll hang on for a bit longer."

"Oh don't wait for us!" Sophie said, "We probably could do with chilling out for a moment...? And Ollie really needs a bath...!"

Jo looked like this wasn't an option. "We've been waiting until everyone is together, we've not all been together like this since… well, since Mum can't remember! Come on, just hurry up!"

***

Fifteen minutes later and Sophie had managed to quickest turn-a-round she could remember with the boy freshly bathed and she freshened up. They made their way down to the plush carpeted lobby and headed off down a corridor signed to the dining room to find the family gathering. The soft carpet under Sophie's feet felt luxurious and gave her confidence while wearing her super heels, making it very easy for her to walk; much better than the polished floors in cocktail bars, she thought, this is much more like my idea of a good weekend.

She stopped under the doorway of the bar clutching a tired Ollie's hand, a stone walled and floored ancient room with low ceilings and tapestries hung on each wall. The bar was dark wood and stretched down the inside wall towards another archway where Sophie could see a log fire roaring on the far wall beyond and heard the sound of voices drifting through.

We must have booked the whole place, she thought as no other people seemed to be around.

"Come on then darling, I think everyone must be in there," they continued through to where Sophie's whole family sat in a cosy back room.

"Sophie!" her Dad was the first to notice them and jumped up out of his seat to embrace his youngest daughter and gave Ollie's hair a ruffle which he instantly sorted out back to its original style, "You made it! How was the flight? Sophie's here everyone!" he said to the assembled group, "What shall we get you to drink?"

"Hi, Dad," Sophie said and looked around at the faces now having broken off from their conversations and looking at her fondly, "Yes please we'll just have some water, the flight dries me out and I'll have to look perfect tomorrow!" she smiled at the company. "Hi!" she said to everyone and waved around the group, "Nice seeing everyone again! I hardly see you all now I live so far south! Where shall we sit...?"

Sophie's Dad hurried off to find a waiter for another drinks order and the group all shuffled round and found extra chairs. Soon Sophie was in amongst a table with her sister, mother, two cousins, an aunt and uncle, catching up, it having been years since she had seen the members of her extended family.

"We're planning *our* wedding for next year!" her cousin announced over the table, "Who shall I address your invite to...?" she asked mischievously.

Sophie took it in good humour. "Oh, just write it to me for the moment and Ollie if children can come. *Don't* put 'Plus One' on it please as it puts too much pressure on me to find a partner and a year just *isn't* long enough to find one, trust me I know!"

Sophie's Dad appeared with a waiter who went round the assembled group taking another extensive drinks order.

"I'll just have some sparkling mineral water please... I'm quite boring..." Sophie joked as the rest ordered wine and brandy, "and a small apple juice for my son? Thank you," she smiled warmly at the waiter.

"Sophie, do you remember everyone?" her father went round the group, "You know your sister Jo and your Mother, of course..."

"Yes..." Sophie laughed at her Dad patiently.

"And you know your Aunt Bea and Uncle Tony... and Uncle Gerald and his partner *Patricia*... and Cousin Bob and..."

"Yes dad, I do remember my family!" Sophie joked, sparing her father from introducing the *whole* group needlessly.

"Have you said hello to Aunt Hilda and Elizabeth...?" her dad asked.

Sophie moved across to a table by the fire where two ancient ladies sat. She crouched down on the arm of their sofa and took a withered hand, kissing Aunt Hilda's powdered cheek which had the unmistakable scent of crème powder puff careful not to leave a sticky mark of lip balm behind. She hadn't seen these Aunts since childhood. "Hi!" she said enthusiastically and extended her hand to the other too, "It's *so* nice to see you again!"

"Who have you brought with you dear?" Aunt Hilda asked.

"Oh it's just me and my son... this weekend... Ollie, come and meet Aunt Hilda and Elizabeth!"

"Is your husband working this weekend, dear...? Some do, now-a-days; some of the young people do work *awfully* hard!"

Sophie wasn't sure if she should make something up but decided against it, tired of the assumption that everyone was happily married.

"No my husband-to-be left us when Ollie was a baby and so it's just us. I work myself to support him," she said defiantly and then realised now that not only was she in disgrace for being a single mother she had also let it slip that she had actually had her baby out of wedlock anyway.

"Nice seeing you anyway!" she chirped and made her way back to a more forward thinking table.

"What is the young man wearing tomorrow then? Has he gone for the whole Scottish ensemble or the more modern tartan trousers...?" Sophie's uncle asked, addressing Ollie who looked suddenly cheated because nobody had mentioned that he could wear trousers.

"He's being *forced* to wear the whole ensemble, I'm afraid," Sophie said looking at her son apologetically, "Kilt, shirt, jacket, tie, sporran and proper little shoes... everything down to the itchy socks! Although..." she corrected herself, "... we did have to draw the line at the skean dhu!"

Ollie sulked at the memory of being in the kilt shop and his little eyes falling on the glass cabinet which contained various slim pewter knives intended to be worn inside the sock when wearing full Scottish dress. His obstinacy at being made to wear such an outfit could have been placated if he had been allowed one of *those* but Sophie had had to point out the sign that she was thankful was there to back her up, that the contents of the cabinet should not be handled unsupervised by anyone under the age of 18. From that moment the socks had become increasingly itchy.

"We're going to put a pair of specially purchased long cotton socks under the itchy ones though..." Sophie explained, "... and after the wedding service I suppose you can take them off and put your trainers on if you like!" she smiled at her son amused that he was also extremely embarrassed that under his *itchy* socks he would be wearing some *girls'* ones.

"What have you been doing with yourself then, Sophie, since we saw you last?" her lovely Aunt asked, always sympathetic to her situation as had been a single mother herself many years before.

"Oh just working hard. I've started a new job, well, been doing it for about eighteen months now but at first it was pretty awful but I've got a new project on the go now and had a pretty good pay rise so that's all good. My hours are perfect too- half nine to half two so I can drop Ollie off and pick him up... I have to work Wednesday night's too but I have a really amazing babysitter..."

"I'm not a *baby*...!" Ollie interrupted, having been sat silently leaning sleepily against her side for the duration of the conversation.

"*Child minder*," Sophie corrected herself, "That's all I do really, now, take Ollie to school, work and pick him up. I've ventured out there again, into the world of dating, but really..." she shuddered, "... it's not all it's cracked up to be."

"You seem to be doing fine by yourself," her aunt said supportively, "Men are over-rated anyway" she dug her husband in his ribs, disturbing him from his drunken dozy snooze. "The right one will come to you, take my word for it, when you least expect it," she tapped the side of her nose, "You don't need one and that is the best position to be in."

Sophie took Ollie back to their room about ten leaving some of the group still assembled and started on the whisky. The wedding wasn't until 3pm the next day but she knew that Ollie would be a grump if he didn't have his proper sleep and it would be hard enough getting him into his outfit without him being tired too. She was also hoping to get up first thing and go for a run while he was having breakfast with his Grandparents. She set everything out for the next day; hung her dress up and laid out her shoes, set her make-up out on the dressing table and located her brand new underwear and stockings and hung them in a bag on the dress hanger. She had a tiny clutch bag that she was going to use in the evening and put a lip balm compact in there as well as a tissue in case of wedding tears. Already, she thought, how quickly a year passes.

***

There had been no rehearsals for the wedding or any directions as such as to what Sophie was actually to do; she was just to be ready by one.

"Just follow me," Jo had said, less than helpfully Sophie thought, during the family dinner the night before, "Or Hamish… He's the best man and he has been *told* to look after you… although, I wouldn't let him look after my *dog…*"

"You don't have a dog…" Sophie had pointed out.

"Well, if I *did*… I wouldn't ask him."

And that was that, Sophie's instructions. She had read a book on etiquette which had a chapter on 'Weddings' but there weren't any details about what a bridesmaid should *do,* just what she should *wear* and who should pay for it. She thought to the only other wedding she had ever witnessed, that of Lady Diana Spenser and Prince Charles, when she did remember that the bridesmaids did have to sort out Lady Diana's dress and train and so she geared herself up for that. Her Uncle had also told her just to stand around 'looking pretty' which he thought had been quite hilarious but mainly, she thought, as he had consumed quite a considerable amount of whisky.

At eight o'clock she got up with Ollie, got them both dressed, her in her running kit and delivered the boy to her parents for breakfast needing some fresh air before the day's events. Getting back to the hotel an hour later she quickly retrieved her swimming costume from her bedroom for a quick cooling dip in the luxury pool before her preparations began. She never stayed in such plush surroundings and so was determined to make the most of it. She collected a fluffy white towel from the reception as it said to do if using the pool and made her way off to find it. As she reached the changing rooms the sound of her sons excited cries and shouts of 'Granddad!' made her smile.

"Hello you two!" she waved as she reached poolside and lowered herself into the warm water.

"Look Mummy! Look what I can do!" and with that Ollie climbed out of the pool and dive bombed back in.

"Wow, look at you!" Sophie said, "Are you *allowed* to do that...?" she dubiously asked her dad.

"I'm not really sure… but he's enjoying himself," her dad replied.

"Yes," Sophie said dubiously, "But make sure he's careful. I guess he'll have to behave later though so better that he's noisy now!"

"Shouldn't you be doing 'girl's stuff'?" her dad asked slightly concerned, "Your sister was at breakfast this morning flapping about her veil. I think she needs your help with it…"

Sophie looked up at the clock on the wall above the pool.

"It's only just ten we have loads of time yet… I guess I'll go up soon… I don't want to get ready *too* early though otherwise my make-up will look all crap by three…"

"Language…" her father reminded her.

"Sophie!" another voice screeched her name from the changing room doorway. Her sister in white towelling dressing gown with a towel wrapped around her head, "What are you *doing*! We have a *wedding* at three!"

Sophie inhaled deeply and guessed her bridesmaid duties had begun. She swam over to the other side of the pool to talk to her sister.

"It's alright, Jo, look it's only ten! I'll be ready in an hour… OK, I'll get out now," she turned towards Ollie and his Granddad, "I'll see you guys later! Mummy has to go and be a bridesmaid! Be good for Granddad!"

"I will!" the boy called happily and dive bombed into the pool again. She exchanged a worried look with her Dad.

"Maybe get out before he gets too crazy, remember we need to dress him too… which actually I hadn't factored into my plans… right I'd better go!"

Sophie sped back to her room to get ready. She popped her head round her sister's door to reassure her that everything was in hand and then to her own to shower and change. It felt like a long time since she had made such an effort and it not being for the benefits for some random date.

"For me now, nobody else…" she though as she applied her make-up, sitting at her dressing table wrapped in her own white towelling dressing gown, feeling a little bit Marilyn Monroe.

She looked steadily at her reflection in the mirror, into her own deep brown eyes.

"This is not your day… but your day *will* come…" she felt the emotion of the occasion start to rise in her chest and closed her eyes and breathed. She exhaled willing the emotion to leave her body, "No tears… enough tears…" There was a knock at the door and she got up to answer it, pulling the dressing gown cord tight. She opened the door to her Dad and Ollie, the boy shivering now, wrapped in his towel with wet spikey hair.

"And here is my plus one!" she said happily, "Come on darling, we need to get ready we have a wedding to attend!"

By half past two the company were ready. The make-up lady had been for the bride and the girls had all had their hair done. Jo was in the bathroom applying finishing touches having been tied firmly into her dress by Sophie.

Sophie stood admiring her son who looked so gorgeous in his little Scottish outfit, cotton socks under the itchy ones and a sporran full of jelly beans.

"Try not to get it all sticky though…" she had said worriedly, "… because it is only *hired*…"

Ollie appeared to feel very grown up in his attire and looked at his mother proudly. Sophie wondered how she could have ever wanted a different plus one. She looked stunning in her deep pink full length silk dress and soft curls in her hair. The hairdresser had pinned a section up and put a flower in her hair and Sophie admired the results in the mirror. Her Dad, also in full Scottish dress, stood proudly next to his Grandson while their photograph was taken and Sophie's Mother bustled in with last minute orders.

"And where's your sister?" she asked Sophie, "It's probably time for photos!"

"She's in the bathroom," Sophie told her, "She's having trouble with her veil but won't let me help… I *did* suggest that I do it but she said that she knew how to do it best… though how she's the best person to put something in the *back* of her hair when she can't see it I don't know…" Suddenly she felt like she was eight years old and telling tales on her big sister.

Her Mother went and knocked on the bathroom door. "Jo! Jo! Darling! Can we help! Your presence will be needed soon!"

Jo's voice was heard from within swearing, something about the veil was what Sophie heard. She tried not to smirk.

"I think she's having trouble with the effing veil…"

The bathroom door swung open and her sister's freshly coiffed hair was now slightly askew as she tried to ram a comb in to keep the veil in securely.

"It won't stay in..!" she wailed as the comb slipped out pulling another section of her hair out of the neat roll it was in.

"Do you want me to try?" Sophie asked gently.

Jo looked at her petulantly. "Oh *OK*. But the hairdresser showed *me* how to do it…"

Well you obviously weren't looking properly, Sophie thought and took the comb and forcibly shoved it into the back of her hair, very slightly making her hair look a bit taller but with the effect that the comb was going nowhere.

"There," Sophie said firmly, as if she were talking to her son.

"Ouch…!" Jo said and worriedly inspected the results in the mirror.

"It looks fine," Sophie said, "Right, it's now twenty to three. The master of ceremonies will be here soon, time for some photos," she organised the group for the photographer who had been hovering, deciding that her bridesmaid duties might also have to include jollying the bride along.

***

The hotel wedding planner, a rather flamboyant gentleman, came to give the group the news that all the guests were in place and wished Jo the best of luck.

"The groom looks *gorgeous*, good choice!" he said, "*And like he's bricking it*"

The registrar came to give the occasion a blessing.

Sophie and Jo then darted to different mirrors and did a final hair and make-up check.

"What beautiful daughters I have!" their mother told them, "And a handsome Grandson, must be the good genes…"

"What beautiful daughters *we* have!" Sophie's Dad corrected her.

Final photographs were taken and Sophie Mother darted away to join the gathered guests in the wedding room.

"Good luck," Sophie said to Jo, "You look lovely, by the way, completely stunning. Andrew is a lucky man."

Jo squeezed Sophie's hand. "You do too. Thank you for being my bridesmaid. Right…" she looked at the clock and the celebrant nodded, "Come on then, it's time for me to get married!"

Chapter Nineteen

With Jo and their Dad leading and Sophie and Ollie behind, the group made their way downstairs, through the lobby, past reception and down a corridor to the wedding room. As the sound of the wedding march could be heard- played off Jo's MP3 player as the hotel had had a late technical hitch early in the afternoon and it had been the simplest solution- they steadily entered the room where the gathered guests turned to see. The bride groom turned to see his bride and smiled proudly, turning back to whisper something to the best man who also turned around now to watch. He wasn't watching the bride though, Sophie realised, as their eyes met and he fixed her stunned stare as she followed her sister down the aisle, now conscious of her every movement and starting to tremble somewhat. Jo had not told her how handsome Hamish was and standing there at the top of the aisle in his full Scottish dress he fairly took Sophie's breath away. Her heart started to thump in her chest, she couldn't believe what was happening, the daydream that she had had all that time ago… it couldn't possibly… could it…?

By the time they reached the groom Sophie didn't know where to look, completely transfixed by Hamish and stunned by his gaze. She smiled feebly at him as she took her seat and he winked, smiling, which made his eyes wrinkle up in a most attractive fashion.

Oh my God, Sophie thought as she sat down, what is happening? Her chest heaved as her breathing had quickened, she puffed her cheeks out and blew air out cooling her face then stopped herself as was very aware it was not a good look. Is it possible to fall in love at first sight?

As the celebrant spoke she casually looked at the back of the best man's head and was horrified as he glanced around, again catching her stare and making her blush again furiously.

How is it, she thought, that after so many dates I still do not know how to deal with this kind of situation?

Hamish grinned at her and turned back round to pay attention to proceedings.

Vows were said and time for Ollie to produce the rings. Sophie gently pushed him towards the celebrant, not realising his sporran was still open after searching for the rings amongst the jelly beans and several of the sweets fell out on his way casing him to stop and bend down to collect them thus making even more fall out.

"Get them later!" Sophie hissed and he scampered up to hand over what had been his precious treasure.

Hamish watched him and laughed in good humour at his antics. Sophie's heart skipped a beat.

Maybe this is why I've had such a time of it dating, she thought, because God intended me to meet Hamish.

When the ceremony was done and the register signed the bride and groom walked down the aisle, husband and wife followed by Sophie and Hamish, new acquaintances.

Hamish extended his arm to Sophie and she took it, wondering if this was what he was *supposed* to do as the best man or if he was just being nice.

"How do you do?" he whispered, "You look amazing, by the way, upstaging the bride a little bit but of course I mustn't say that."

"Thank you," Sophie smiled shyly. You don't look bad yourself, she managed not to say. "Do you know what you're doing...?" she asked and then hastily added, "... I mean, about being best man! I mean, I have no idea what I'm supposed to be doing..."

Hamish smiled down at her. "Just stick with me young lady; I have been to all the rehearsals."

"Rehearsals?" Sophie said in dismay, "I didn't know there were any rehearsals!"

"Oh no, not really, but I think it's fairly simple. Whatever *they* do..." he said indicating to the bride and groom, "... *we* do... just a few minutes later," he winked at her again.

Sophie fixed her stare ahead and concentrated on walking in a straight line, her faculties suddenly leaving her.

***

The photographs were something that Sophie hadn't realised would have taken quite so long but she enjoyed every second as it meant she could have Hamish mostly to herself. Jo and Andrew were soppy newlyweds and Ollie was happy in between photos running up and down the garden paths. The family shots were taken first in the grounds at close proximity to the castle and then the five man wedding group were taken by the photographer deeper into the gardens where the flowers were starting to bloom. It was more secluded there.

Sophie chatted easily to Hamish in between shots, feeling comfortable in his amiable company and like she'd known him for some time.

"I think after this…" he told her helpfully, "… then we can all get a drink in the foyer… see, I know when all the drink breaks are anyway. *Then* we go in for the meal and then it's the speeches. That's why I'm keen for the drinks beforehand!" he laughed.

"Are you very nervous?" Sophie asked, "Us women have it easy, not having to make any speeches. I'd *hate* that…"

"Would you? I heard that you're an *excellent* public speaker!" Hamish said.

Sophie was taken aback.

"Your sister tells me you do the best childcare training in the country!"

"Oh ha ha! Well, you know…" she smiled at Hamish, "Yes, yes I do," she laughed, "Probably in Europe actually, but I don't like to talk about it."

"Of course…" Hamish said nodding his head seriously, "us experts don't like to brag. I'm probably the very best solicitor in the country but, you know, I'm quite modest...

but, back to your original question, I am *very* nervous! Hence the hip flask…" he took the aforementioned container from his belt and took a swig, offering it to Sophie who refused.

"No thanks! I'll save myself for the toast. What's in there anyway…?" she asked curiously.

"Whisky," Hamish said and took another swig, "Good strong stuff."

Blimey, Sophie thought, he's going to be *wasted.*

When Hamish and Sophie's attendance was no longer required for the photographs Hamish suggested they go and find a drink.

"You look parched," he said and grinned, "I think you need to know where the bar is… We'll go and get a drink then!" he called to Andrew who was being manhandled by the photographer into position. He smiled with resignation and tapped at his own hip flask.

"Do you know what else we have to do…?" Sophie asked as they made their way back along the enclosed paths, hedges lining them on either side.

Hamish considered this. "Well… I think that *your* duties are pretty much over… apart from looking pretty and accompanying me for the first dance… you may have to receive compliments during the speeches too… and I guess circulate and pretend you find your drunk old uncle *extremely* amusing…!"

They crossed the grass that surrounded the castle and past the aforementioned relative who held his glass aloft to them.

"You've met him then...?" Sophie asked.

"Oh yes..." Hamish took Sophie's arm and led her inside where people were gathered in the hotel lobby sipping drinks as a waiter circulated with a tray of champagne glasses. Hamish grabbed a couple and gave one to Sophie as he indicated for her to follow him. "Now, *my du*ties on the other hand are not *nearly* over as I have to, of course, make a hugely witty speech..." he looked slightly worried about the prospect, "... and that is why..." he said flamboyantly indicating to the room he had led her to with his glass in hand, "... I have taken you to the bar!"

Sophie laughed at his boyish enthusiasm.

"Can I get you a drink...?" Hamish asked, "... although you do have one already!" He looked at her with a sudden look of concern on his face, "Sorry, you must think I'm a right alcoholic! I'm really not, just getting a top up..." he patted his hip flask.

Sophie sipped her champagne. A combination of giggling and champagne was making her feel decidedly lightheaded.

"Maybe not just now thank you," she said hesitantly, "I don't think my sister will want me getting hammered so early on..." she laughed at her own sensibleness. "I'm quite boring really..." she said by way of explanation.

Hamish shook his head. "Of course you're not. There's nothing wrong with not wanting to get hammered… something to say for it really. You don't have a speech to make though so if you don't mind…" he indicated towards the bar and took his own supply over for a top up, the bar tender seemingly on first name terms with Hamish and retrieving the correct Whisky without being asked. Sophie idly gazed at him as he leant against the bar chatting, inspecting his dark slightly messy short hair and broad shoulders. Her eyes drifted down to his bare legs, shown off as he wore a kilt. She began to wonder about the rest of him…

"Mummy!" Sophie's thoughts were interrupted by Ollie who hurtled round the corner into the bar holding what looked like a catapult and with a huge smile on his face, "Look what Granddad made me!"

"Excellent!" Hamish joined them, "What a great toy for a wedding!" Sophie wasn't so sure.

"Oh why did Granddad give you *that*?"

"He didn't *give* me it Mummy he *made* it!" Ollie told her, "With a stick and an elastic band."

"A classic design," Hamish agreed, "Your Granddad must be really cool to make you that! You need to get some cans now and line them up then shoot 'em all down!"

"Yeah!" Ollie said with excitement, "Where can I get some cans?"

"Oh if you ask my friend behind the bar…" he said indicating behind him, "…he might be able to help… he sells a lot of things in cans so maybe he has some empty ones."

"We might need to go through soon though darling, for our dinner. Where are you playing?"

"Outside with Granddad."

"Sophie! *There* you are!" her Mother bustled in, "You're *needed*!"

"Oh… am I…? Sorry I didn't know…!"

Hamish looked apologetically at Sophie's Mum. "I am *so sorry* Mrs Bridges; this is entirely my fault. I was showing your daughter around but had no idea her presence was needed elsewhere. That must mean mine is too…" he glanced worriedly at Sophie.

"Well, yes I think you are… the photographer isn't entirely finished."

"What! Still not finished- he's been here for over an hour already…!" Sophie wailed, having had quite enough of posing for one day, even if it was with Hamish.

"Well that's what you do at weddings," her Mother told her curtly, "Now off you go, both of you. Ollie, you can come with me…" she held up her hand to his protestations. "No thank you young man, Granddad has now been deployed elsewhere. And thank you, I will look after *that*," and with that she confiscated the catapult, took the boy by the hand

and marched him out of the bar leaving Sophie and Hamish alone.

"We'd better go then," Sophie said, "Sorry about Mum."

Hamish laughed good- humouredly. "No need, she'll just want the day to go smoothly, and who wouldn't. I'm sorry I've been leading you astray," he extended his arm again for Sophie to hold and they went off together to find where the photographs were still being taken.

By the time they sat down for the meal Sophie didn't feel like she was there alone, Hamish was stuck to her side and didn't seem in any hurry to go elsewhere. Sophie was happy for such good humoured and easy company. They chatted as guests found their seats, both knowing that they would be at the top table and taking their seats straight away. Ollie was deposited next to Sophie by her Mother who told them that on no condition should he be given the catapult back. Both Sophie and Hamish sympathised with him when she had gone.

"That's bad luck," Hamish told him and Ollie listened to him in awe, "But I guess it's not the *best* toy for a wedding... well, that's what some grown-ups think... not me but I do get their point. Maybe after dinner we can find you something else to play with...?" Ollie nodded obediently and was placated with a bread roll that the waited sneaked him. Being the only child at the reception he was getting preferential treatment.

The meal went like a breeze, conversation flowing along with the wine. Sophie sipped her champagne. As the time passed Hamish appeared more and more nervous about his forthcoming speech and gradually became quieter. Sophie turned her attention more to Ollie as didn't want to be a pest and hog all his time, although she didn't think that he was minding as he kept initiating new conversations with her.

Coffee was served and with that came the speeches. Sophie's Dad had been a regular public speaker in his younger days and delivered a funny but efficient speech, thanking all those who had to be thanked. The groom then delivered a belter; having the audience in stitches and saying a lovely piece about his new wife which made Sophie get a lump in her throat and wish she had someone to felt the same about her. She felt the pressure now on Hamish as he stood up, now a little the worse for wear but still, at least, coherent.

He made a shaky start, Andrew's speech being so good that following it was always going to be a tall order, but his audience warmed to him and gradually he found his flow. Sophie gazed at him as he spoke, lost for a moment as she enjoyed the sound of his faint Scottish burr. She didn't hear what he was saying particularly until her attention was grabbed by the sound of her own name.

"And, while the groom has commented on the beauty of the bridesmaid I would just like to part from tradition and add my own compliments and say that she is tremendous company as well and…" he turned towards Sophie and raised his glass, "… it is a pleasure working with you," he winked at her and the room toasted her good company. Sophie wanted to slip quietly under the table, hating being the centre of attention, and felt her cheeks burn. She smiled and shook her head modestly. The happy couple were then toasted and the reception got into full swing.

Sophie excused herself and took Ollie back up to their room for a moment of reflection and to powder her nose. She took some cars out for Ollie to play with who proceeded to 'brum' them round the carpet. After all the excitement so far Sophie thought they needed ten minutes at least to gather their thoughts. They had some time, anyway, while the band were setting up, so Sophie sat down at the dresser and inspected her reflection. She was pleasantly surprised that she looked tastefully made up still and was not the red shiny mess she had expected, the attention from Hamish making her feel a little flustered to say the least. She tried not to get too excited though, her year of disastrous dates making her tread carefully. Deciding to play it cool and let him come to her she sat for a while longer, powdering her nose and applying a little additional make-up for the evening. Ollie was happy playing with his cars and he had been so well behaved up until then she decided not to try her luck by rushing him away from his game.

"It's half past six now darling. We should go back down at seven because that's when the party starts. In fact…" she suddenly remembered something that Hamish had said, "… we can't miss the first dance!"

"Ooh party," Ollie said without enthusiasm and carried on 'brumming' his cars.

***

Just before seven o'clock Sophie told Ollie that they really should make their way back down; wanting to make sure that she was in place in case Hamish really did want the first dance. She allowed a car to come down with them and they made their way back to the reception hall. The lights had been lowered and tables moved to the side, new guests had arrived wearing more glamorous eveningwear and Sophie didn't know a soul. She stood in the doorway looking lost, trying to locate her own family. Just as she spotted a table where her parents and cousins were sitting she also saw Hamish, waving at her from the other side of the room holding up a bottle and pointing to it. She looked at him with a puzzled expression and he put his hand up to his mouth and said, with exaggerated movement, 'Do you want a drink' and lifted the bottle up again.

Sophie sighed happily and nodded, happy to see a friendly face at the least and feeling fairly overwhelmed that Hamish still wanted to speak to her after she felt she had monopolised his attention for the last few hours already. She looked around the room and saw what she thought were a couple of single groups of females, some of whom she recognised from the hen do. Amazing, she thought, that he still wants to talk to me when a new load of women has turned up. She smiled at her own negativity, a year of dating has made me into a cynical old sod, she thought.

She took Ollie over to the table where her family sat and made him comfortable for a while with a pad and pen, aware that everyone would be up for the first dance soon. She stood next to the table and watched as the band settled down in to their places and saw Jo and Andrew entering the room, chatting happily and greeting random people as they passed. Their attention was taken by one of the band members who called something to Andrew who indicated that he'd heard and led Jo onto the dance floor.

The gathered guests stood and watched as Andrew and Jo danced to a waltz played by the Scottish country dance band, Sophie watching impressed with their moves, Jo had told her they were going to have some lessons. She was suddenly aware of a presence next to her and she turned round to see Hamish, brandishing a bottle for her.

"I'll put this down here...?" he said pointing to their family table, "… while you come with me…" The band indicated that others could join the happy couple and he took Sophie's hand and led her onto the dance floor, leading her with his arm around her waist.

Sophie had never danced properly like this with anyone before, the only times she had danced in the past was when her bag had been down at her feet and she'd bounced around a nightclub with Ben. She rested her hand on Hamish's shoulder and tried not to swoon at his close proximity, pretending that this was a common thing, being swept professionally off her feet.

"Did you take lessons too...?" she asked him as they danced.

He smiled down at her. "Maybe one or two… Andy asked if I wanted to go too…!"

"You're such a cheat!" Sophie said, "But I'm glad you did." She melted into his touch and allowed her body to be moved and twirled with his.

The scent of his aftershave was strong, as if he'd almost just sprayed it. His body felt warm under her touch, she supposed he must be boiling and uncomfortable now in his kilt and jacket. His arms felt strong around her delicate body and she looked up at his mouth and imagined if he just looked down at her now, the slight growth of stubble would feel rough against her skin if he kissed her. She hastily looked away, over his shoulder and watched the others pass them by. She noticed a woman watching them from the side, one of the few not dancing. I wonder if anyone thinks I'm with him, she thought absently.

The dance came to an end and everyone stopped and applauded. Sophie did so too and thanked Hamish for the dance.

"No worries, the first of many I hope! You're not off now are you, like Cinderella...?" he actually sounded disappointed.

"No, it's not midnight yet," she replied and smiled.

"Good, then maybe you would like to dance...?" he led her back onto the floor for the next dance… and the next… and the next.

A good hour later and Sophie was actually feeling dizzy, not entirely with the feeling of desire for Hamish but because Scottish county dancing was so frantic and exhausting. She excused herself for a while to get a drink and have a sit down.

"You carry on though...?" she said, wondering if he would like to dance with anyone else.

"Nah... I might have a rest too! You've tired me out!"

"*I've* tired *you* out?" she joked, "I think it's the other way round. It's so hot in here; I might get some air for a moment," she fanned herself with a stray menu that had been left on the table. "These shoes were not *t*he best choice for dancing either..." she said rueing the day she had chosen heels over flats for the occasion. "I might take a seat outside."

"Would you mind if I joined you...?" Hamish asked, suddenly seeming unsure of himself, "If you don't mind, I could do with some air too."

"Of course," Sophie said, feeling smug now that the best man clearly did want her company. She noticed a few women on the other side of the room watching them and wondered if they were like her, singles, just waiting for the wonderful moment when you meet someone and feel the chemistry is just there.

The band announced a break. "Perfect timing," Hamish noted, "I might take some water out with me, do you want a glass?"

"Oh yes please, that would be lovely," Sophie said and glanced around to see if she could see her son anywhere. As everyone sat down for coffee and cake Sophie saw him, throwing some shapes on the dance floor, his jacket now discarded on the floor, bow tie untied and hanging down with the top of his collar unbuttoned, his shirt untucked, his socks rolled down to his ankles and a rather red sweaty look about him, now playing air guitar to nothing, the band having dispersed for a while.

"Fits in perfectly," Sophie said to Hamish as he handed her a glass of water, "I think he'll be fine for a minute!"

The two made their way down the carpeted corridors and through the lobby to the front door. It was a crisp clear evening and the sky was full of stars. A few random smokers stood just outside the door and Sophie and Hamish passed them and made their way to a bench that was across the grass they were photographed on earlier, on a small patio area surrounded by hedges that formed part of a maze.

"Let's not try that now..." Sophie thought out loud, "... I've never been that patient with mazes and we'd be gone for the rest of the evening...!" she laughed and glanced at Hamish, wishing that they could do exactly that.

Sophie sat on the edge of the bench, not wanting to make any marks on the bottom of her beautiful dress and the bench looked decidedly grubby, while Hamish paced around the paving slabs, like a man with something on his mind. He took several deep breaths of the fresh spring air.

"Ah the peace..." he said, "... weddings can be quite full on. I have another one in a few weeks... not the best man though. So, you don't sound very Scottish?"

"Yeah, I'm not sure what's happened to my accent really, too much time spent living in the South of England I expect! I am though, one hundred per cent. I'd love to move back up here though one day; I've just found myself settled down there..."

"Your son's pretty cool... Kids are funny. I love how they don't care about stuff like we do, like your son back in there- totally rocking out, not giving a monkeys. Sometimes we worry too much... about stuff, stuff that's not really important," he stood with his hands in his pockets and back now to Sophie, staring out into the black of the night.

Sophie sat perched, happy to listen to Hamish's thoughts. For a while he stopped speaking and the two enjoyed the time of companionable silence, feeling comfortable enough now with each other that they didn't feel the need to fill each second with talk. He eventually turned around and looked at Sophie whose ivory skin radiated in the moonlight.

He opened his mouth about to speak but was interrupted by Jo, calling for them from just outside the foyer. He swung around at the sound of his name and Sophie who had become mesmerised by his presence was brought back to reality with a bump.

"*There* you are!" Jo shouted over at them and, holding up her dress slightly so that it didn't trail on the ground she marched over to where the two sat, "What are you two *doing?*" she asked crossly, "We've been trying to find you for *ages*!" she looked at Hamish accusingly, "People will start to speak."

What's wrong with that, Sophie thought. "We're just getting some air," she told her sister, now feeling bad for clearly demanding too much attention from the best man. He probably has further duties she thought and stood up, gathering her own skirt up. "I guess we'd better go back in then; sorry Jo I didn't know we were needed. I'd better make sure Ollie is OK anyway."

Hamish followed her in and, despite the telling off from the bride, still wanted to be at her side. As the band started up for their second half he asked her for a dance and she accepted, thinking that dancing must be allowed.

"I don't know what's up with my sister…" Sophie said to him as they danced, "… I guess it must be stressful, being a bride…"

"It shouldn't be…" he said, "… it should just be the best day of your life…"

Later the couple circulated together, Sophie holding onto Hamish's arm as he introduced her to some of his male friends at the bar.

"He's got you man marked!" one of Hamish's friends whispered to Sophie as she went past.

Man marked, she thought, what's *that*? She did think that Hamish was being very attentive but had taken it to mean that he wanted to spend time with her. He definitely didn't seem to want anyone *else* spending time with her as he followed her round casually when she chatted with her family and circulated the room, chatting to those old friends she knew. By the end of the evening she felt like *they* were the married couple, looking for each other when they got separated, introducing each other to those they knew and choosing each other's company over anyone else. Sophie couldn't think of a time when anyone had ever been quite so attentive. As the clock got closer to midnight she wondered what was going to happen, wondering if it was possible for dreams to actually come true. If so then in a minute he would steal a kiss, just after making the coin appear from behind Ollie's ear.

The reception room gradually emptied of guests and Sophie was aware that Ollie was now beyond tired and needed to be put into bed. She hung around for a moment longer so that she could say 'goodbye' to Hamish who had disappeared suddenly.

"Are you taking the wee man off to bed now?" her Dad asked as she frantically looked around the room for sight of Hamish.

"Oh, yes… just in a minute… I was just going to say 'bye' to someone…"

"He's *very* tired!" her Dad told her, "But he's been a *super* boy," he smiled proudly.

"Yes, yes he has… I'll just take him up in a minute…" Sophie looked beyond a group of guests who were on their way out, exchanging last farewells and hugs. She impatiently stood on her tip toes to see past them to where she thought she had caught a glimpse of Hamish. She saw him now, deep in conversation with Andrew who was holding him by the shoulders and giving him a stern talking to by the look of things. Hamish was looking towards the floor, pinching the top of his nose between his fingers.

Sophie was concerned that things were alright but happy that now she had located him again and hurried over so that she didn't miss him to say goodbye. She arrived at their side and suddenly felt awkward, not sure what to say. Both men looked at her seriously. She was lost for words for a moment and then remembered what he had said earlier, about not worrying about silly things.

"Hey found you! I was just going to say 'bye'… Ollie needs to go to his bed…" she looked at Andrew as if to say, bugger off and leave us alone, but he didn't take the hint.

For the second time that evening Hamish opened his mouth to speak and was interrupted before he got his words out.

"*There* you are!" this time not Jo but a woman that Sophie didn't recognise approached looking more than a little irritated. She gave Sophie a withering look of extreme pity. She held up some keys and dangled them right in front of Hamish's face.

"Come on, you've done your best man duty now. It doesn't extend to taking her to bed," she cast Sophie another look then turned her attention back to Hamish, who now suddenly looked like a broken man, "Home!"

He was led away before Sophie was able to say her 'goodbye'. Jo, who had been watching proceedings nearby, came over to Sophie's side.

"I *told* you that I wouldn't trust him!" she said.

Sophie stood, her heart feeling like it had been crushed again, her feelings trampled on, not worthy of care it would seem. She suddenly felt nothing, nothing at all for the man who had just wasted her whole day.

"You told me you wouldn't trust him with your dog..." she mumbled, "How was I supposed to know that meant he was a total and utter shit...?" Her brow furrowed. "Right, where's Ollie? He needs to go to bed, as do I... Congratulations, you two..." she remembered to say, "I hope you'll be very happy together. What a lovely time I've had..." her eyes started to moisten.

"Oh *Sophie!*" Jo said, "He's not even *worth* it. Bloody Hamish does it again!" she said crossly to Andrew who was looking at Sophie now with concern. "Why did *he* have to be your best man? Why couldn't you have asked *Martin?*"

Sophie didn't want their first marital rift to be about her and so made her excuses and left, saying that it was really her own fault.

"I think..." Andrew said, as if by way of explanation, "... that he really *was* trying to be the very *best* best man... maybe doing too good a job..."

Jo shook her head at her husband. "Bloody idiot." she said and flounced off, nobody sure exactly who the comment was directed towards.

Sophie managed to make it to her room before the tears started but only just, not managing to wait until Ollie was asleep as she normally did when life got too much. She flopped, face down on her bed and started to sob, a year's worth of encounters with the opposite sex finally taking their toll, her self-esteem at an all-time low. The men she didn't like liked her, the ones she did didn't and the ones she *really* liked treated her like whatever she felt wasn't in the slightest bit important.

"Are you OK Mummy?" a still wide awake Ollie asked with concern.

Sophie sat up and indicated for him to come and give her a cuddle. She wiped at the tears that were pouring down her face and sniffed loudly, her tumbling curls now getting stuck to her soaked face and her perfectly applied make up smeared below her eyes.

"Mummy's just a bit sad," she said in explanation of her sudden state, "Mummy is just a little bit fed up because lots of people have made me feel sad… like I'm not important…" she broke down again and Ollie stroked her hair, not sure what to say to his mother but doing what she would do to him.

"You're important to me…" he said and went to collect the box of tissues that were sitting on the dressing table. He pulled one out of the top and handed it to her. She took it gratefully and blew her nose loudly then with another wiped away the tears from under her eyes, causing her mascara to smudge yet further.

"Do you remember what it was like when it was just you and me...?" she asked, "I loved it then, I was so happy then! When Mummy didn't spend her *whole time* trying to find her handsome prince...? When I didn't spend my whole time *worrying* about the way I *look*!"

"I think you look pretty," Ollie stated, "I think you look pretty *now* and you have snot coming out of your nose…"

Sophie quickly wiped at her nose again.

"I love you my darling," she told him fondly and kissed him firmly on his nose, "Love you love you love you. You are my handsome prince, I am so lucky that I have you!" she cuddled him again tightly, Ollie relenting and allowing it just for once, wanting his Mother to be happy again but carefully watching her nose unless the contents should go anywhere near him.

"I've wasted a *whole year* of my life!" she exclaimed, "What have I been doing? No more!"

"Does that mean you'll have more time to play…?" Ollie asked hopefully. Sophie felt terrible that she might have had less time.

"Yes, I have all the time in the world for you."

"Can we play a game tomorrow…?" he asked.

"Of course!" Sophie said, wiping her eyes again and taking a deep breath, "What game shall we play…?"

"We could play 'hotels'… when we get home…?" Ollie asked making Sophie laugh.

"Oh yeah…? How do you play hotels then mister…?"

"Well…" Ollie started, "We each have different jobs…"

"Yes…" Sophie said, "What sort of jobs…?"

"Well!" Ollie said, warming to his topic, "You could be the cleaner and the cook and the waitress… and the receptionist and the lady who makes the beds… and the person who carries the bags and the bar maid…" he clearly had been paying attention to what everyone's job was.

"And what about you darling…?" Sophie asked, deciding that her son had had a very comfortable upbringing despite the separation of his parents, "What will you do?"

"I'll be the guest!" he said, as if this was obvious making Sophie laugh.

"Yes, let's play that tomorrow, what a good game," Sophie said and gave her nose one final blow, feeling her composure return.

Chapter Twenty

A feeling of optimism entered Sophie's life when she returned home after the wedding and she felt a renewed energy to make something of her life, for her and for Ollie, and not let anyone waste her time again. Her job was going great now that Mrs Wright had given her some responsibility and she didn't need to sit in the office for so long anymore being bullied by Enid. The feedback from Sophie's training sessions was so good that her employer was keen for her to continue, having an eye for talent that she could use to make her school more profitable if not great management skills. The pay rise that had accompanied her new responsibilities meant that budgeting was a little easier and she actually had money spare at the end of the month now and started to save for a holiday for her and Ollie in the summer. Where her life may have lacked in some areas it was rich in others and she began to relish the time she had alone. She didn't even mind the arrival of another wedding invitation, this time to her cousins wedding and addressed to just her. The absence of 'Plus One' made it a lot easier to digest. Ben came down every other Friday afternoon to collect Ollie and had him until Sunday night and during this time Sophie started to do more of the things she loved and generally enjoyed being alone instead of wasting it on useless dates. I can do anything I like, she thought happily, and I don't need to check it with *anyone.* She had her friends and a new man in her life, Mike the washing machine man, who had subtly got back in touch with Sophie having seemingly kept her number. He was proving to be a genuine nice guy though and was always there for her at the end of the phone when she felt like a chat even though he now seemed to have a special lady in his life. He even managed to find her a new washing machine that another customer, who clearly had too much money Sophie thought, had bought and then replaced almost immediately and he installed it for free.

In the office Sophie seemed like a breeze of fresh air and everyone noticed her new positive attitude to work.

"You're in a very good mood these days..." Laura had said almost accusingly one day, "Can we take that to mean you have met a man...?"

Sophie scoffed at this as she was gathering up her hand outs for a late morning training session at Saint Andrew's school.

"No you certainly cannot take it to mean that!" she said crossly, "Why would meeting a man make me *this* happy? I'm happy because I *don't* have a man!"

"I'd watch out talking like that..." Laura said, "... you're becoming quite like Enid, you know, working all hours, bringing up your boy alone, hating men..."

"I don't *hate* men..." Sophie said, "... but what about Enid...? I certainly don't want to be like her!" she looked worriedly at Laura who made a face that indicated she had said too much already. Sophie looked to Pam for further details.

Pam looked at Laura for confirmation. She lowered her voice so that Sophie could barely hear her words.

"Enid's husband had an affair... a long time ago..."

Sophie was shocked that she'd ever *had* a husband but let it pass.

"He worked away a lot... and he had an affair and left her when her two boys were tiny, they're twins. They must have been about six months when he dropped the bombshell..."

The room fell silent as they heard footsteps and breathed a sigh of relief as the cleaner came in to empty the bin. They all watched her and she eyed them suspiciously and hurried out of the office once she was done.

"So, anyway, Enid then had to work full time to support herself and her sons... and her boys are all grown up now and she's *still* bitter... and twisted... and so cynical! When I met my Keith she told me it wouldn't last... she tells Ruth all the time that her husband is away a lot... and all *she* does is work... I don't think anyone's going to thank her, either, when she gets to retirement... Mrs Wright will just get the next one in; she doesn't care about people, just profit..."

Sophie felt sorry for Enid but not enough for it to justify the way she treated everyone.

She made a face at Pam. "I don't want to end up like *Enid*!" she said and smirked, "I'm not *entirely* anti men... I'm just not going to go out looking for them anymore..."

She put all her paperwork in her Elm Tree briefcase and snapped it shut.

"I'm training at the posh school now, and they're a billion times nicer than anyone here... present company accepted. See you after lunch!"

Sophie drove to Saint Andrews in the little red clapped out Micra, much preferring this to the massive black tanks that everyone else swanned around in. It was the first time she had made the journey since visiting the school with Enid. She arrived with time to set up the room before the training started at eleven and hoped that she would also manage to catch a word with Donald, after she had turned him down speed dating- an event that had been put to the back of her mind, filed under 'to forget'.

She had seen Saint Andrews on her list of venues when she received her new contract and felt hugely embarrassed that she might have to deal with Donald again after encountering him that night. Now standing at the front door to the school she couldn't think of a more awkward situation, her year of dating having left a few casualties in her path. She stood cuddling her briefcase waiting for the door to be opened.

It was opened now by someone unfamiliar who welcomed her warmly and took her into the school and through to where her training would be, offering tea and coffee. Sophie asked for a glass of water and started to lay out her resources wondering if she had offended Donald so much he was now having to avoid her completely. She wondered idly as she readied herself if this school had a visitor policy and smirked, hoping that her trainees would not all arrive in a skirt as she doubted that she would be able to keep a straight face if they did.

At the end of the morning when she was packing up she suddenly noticed that Donald was hovering at the doorway, watching her. She smiled sheepishly and struggled to know what to say. He continued into the room and praised her event enthusiastically.

"I don't know if you saw me… squeezed in at the back...!" he said with a twinkle, "I didn't want to put you off… I mean, I know it may have been an embarrassing situation for you… but we're all adults and so I hope we can forget about our… brief encounter...?" he smiled amiably.

Sophie back, a politer man she didn't think she had ever met.

"Of course!" she said.

"I was, of course, disappointed but… I'm just an old fool!" he laughed at himself and shook his head, "I must ask though, did you have any luck…?"

Sophie shook her head, keen to forget the whole episode. "No! No luck at all. Well, really I'm afraid I found the whole thing a bit odd and then I just decided that I actually didn't need a man in my life after all. I shouldn't have gone in the first place…" she smiled at Donald and continued to pack up her stuff.

"Ah well, we must try these things… Nothing ventured, nothing gained! But, onto more pressing matters- your presentation was really very good, Ms Bridges," Donald told her changing the subject swiftly, "You know, and I shouldn't say this really, but if you ever wanted to come over to the dark side and do training for us…" he raised his eyebrows, "… you'd be *most* welcome!"

"Well, um, I…" Sophie fumbled her words.

"It's fine; I don't want an answer now. It's something I'd like to develop here and you're clearly very knowledgeable and confident. The class really responded well. Why don't you just take my number… just in case? I think you would find that our pay is very competitive and we have a good team here, very supportive place to work."

Sophie agreed and took out of her bag the first piece of paper that came to hand, the invite to her cousin's wedding.

"This'll do…" she said and scribbled Donald's number on the back.

He smiled and extended his hand. "I do mean it. We are developing our own training ideas and could do with someone on board who knows what they're talking about… we could all learn a lot from you!" he held his hand up in a wave and made his way out of the room. "I've got to dash now, meetings… but bear it in mind. You have my number."

***

"Come on darling!" Sophie called up the stairs to the boy who had been told ten minutes ago that they were just going, "What are you getting now? We're just going down to the park, come on!" she took her keys out of her bag and jingled them for him to hear, "I'm going then, see you later!"

"No wait!" he cried and she could hear his footsteps clattering to the top of the stairs where he appeared holding his four foot inflatable dinosaur, smiling broadly, "Can Deeno come too…?"

Sophie was about to object when Ollie added 'please' to the end of his sentence.

"Oh OK then, seeing as you asked so nicely. He's quite big for Mummy's car though…"

"Nah it's OK, look, he's squashy."

Sophie smiled indulgently. "Come on then Deeno, if you're coming with us."

"Yeah!" Ollie said and gave the toy a high five on his puny dinosaur legs, "You can go on a swing!"

Sophie sighed happily as if she didn't have a care in the world, just happy that Ollie was happy. They had just had a trip to the supermarket, Ollie dressed fully in his Buzz

Lightyear gear, running up and down the aisles and zapping anything he came across at the end of each one with his super laser shooter, whether this was a trolley, display of breakfast cereal or old lady. She loved his imagination and zest for fun and felt that she had rediscovered the joy of motherhood after a year of maybe losing sight of what was important in life.

The wind had picked up and Sophie hoped that they would avoid the summer storms that had been forecast for later that evening.

"I hope the storm doesn't come early!" she said to Ollie, "It feels quite windy already down here by the sea…"

Ollie showed no concern that the wind had picked up and ran with Deeno across the grass towards his favourite play area, heading for swings. As he went Sophie felt a strong gust of wind and watched as it swept Deeno out of Ollie's arms and up into the sky for a moment before depositing him down again several meters away.

"Deeno!" Ollie screamed and hurtled after his toy.

Sophie broke into a run to retrieve it before it was lost forever or burst on some nearby prickly hedges, not wanting her boy to have any more heartache. The wind carried Deeno away, faster and faster as Sophie too picked up her speed now and chased the run-a-way toy. As the wind took it away from them Sophie saw that it was now blowing toward the perimeter road around the park and frantically looked to check that there were no cars coming.

"Bloody thing!" she swore as she sprinted faster still. She called after Ollie to let her get the toy but he didn't hear and carried on running towards the flyaway Dinosaur and the road.

Someone else in the park had also witnessed this and out of nowhere a man appeared, his legs rapidly making their way towards the escapee and before Ollie or Sophie reached it he caught the dinosaur squarely and stood waiting for the two to arrive and claim it.

Sophie and Ollie reached him and stopped, both panting happily now, overjoyed on Ollie's part and relieved on Sophie's that Deeno was back in captive hands.

"Oh, wow, thank you so much!" she gushed to the man who she thought she did recognise vaguely, "Wow Ollie, say 'Thank you' to this man! Deeno say 'Thank you'!"

"Thank you," Ollie said grinning from ear to ear.

Sophie took Deeno's tiny arm and waved it at the amused looking stranger.

"Thank you!" Sophie said in her best squeaky dinosaur voice. The man laughed.

"Well, after all that thanks I'm happy to help!" he said and handed Ollie his dinosaur back, "Hold on to him, it's really windy now!"

"Yes…" Sophie said apologetically, "I had no idea it would be quite so windy down here when we left the house… Thank you so much, he'd have been devastated if we'd lost him, or… perish the thought… if he'd got *burst!*"

The man laughed. Sophie realised that he was in his training gear and that he must have broken off from a run. She suddenly realised that she had seen him in the park before, leading the running club.

"Oh I'm sorry," she said, "we've disturbed your run…"

"It's fine, really, I was finishing up anyway!" he wiped the sweat from his forehead and smiled amiably.

"Are you the guy who does the running club...?" Sophie asked, "I'm sure I've seen you before...?"

He nodded. "Yeah, just doing my own run now but yeah that's probably where you've seen me."

"Ah!" Sophie exclaimed, "I keep meaning to come along actually... you run on Saturday's don't you...?"

"Yeah, Saturday and also Tuesday and Thursday evenings. Come along! Have you run before?"

"Oh yeah, I run all the time... between six and ten miles normally, depending on how I feel. But running can be quite dull sometimes, on your own when you do the same route again and again and again! I'd been thinking it might be fun to run with other people."

"You probably don't need my little club..." he said, "You sound like a pro already. I do run an advanced class though too. Are you training for something?"

"Oh no, not really..." Sophie replied, "I just run! The reason I do those two distances is purely because I have two routes that I like... not very professional at all!"

"Well, if you were interested we're all going to do a run next weekend...? It's up north a bit so there are a few cars going... It's an eight-mile cross country run... it can be quite muddy but that's half the fun! The distance won't be a problem for you though."

Sophie felt excited at the prospect of doing something a little different.

"Yeah, that sounds great! I think I can come..."

"Do you have some paper...? I'll write down the details for you if you like...?"

"Oh yeah, I do somewhere..." she fumbled in her bag and felt a card at the bottom. With a puzzled look on her face she pulled it out and saw that it was her cousin's invite with Donald's number scrawled on the back. "Oh, I've been *looking* for that! The invite, I mean... Anyway..." she folded it over so that the blank inside page was face up and passed it to the man, "You can write it on that... it's an invite to my cousin's wedding but I seem to be using it as a notepad...!"

The man wrote down some details on the card and passed it back to her.

"There you go. I'm Anthony, by the way. If you don't make it to the club this week then you can either meet us down here on Saturday morning or meet us at the race...? I've put brief directions but you can just look up the race online...? I've written the name."

"Great thanks! I'm Sophie. How do you do?" she extended her hand and he took it looking slightly amused by the formalities. She looked at his instructions and put the invite back in her bag. She suddenly felt like she was holding him up. "Well, I might see you then! And thank you from both of us for saving Deeno! If anything had happened to him, I don't know what we would have done...! I owe you one!"

"No worries! See you!" he held up his hand in a wave and broke into a jog. Sophie watched as he disappeared off.

"Well thank goodness that we met *Anthony*!" she said to Ollie, "What a nice man for saving your dinosaur."

"I can't be late tonight girlies!" Sophie declared to her friends as they sat in her garden making the most of the warm summer evening, "I've to be up early tomorrow for a run!"

"You always go for a run," Lou pointed out, "Why does that mean we have to go early?"

"Because it's not just a run but a *race*! I bumped into a guy who takes a running club and he told me about it. Its eight miles' cross country and I need to leave at eight o'clock in the morning!"

"You're mad…" Joules said, "That sounds like hell to me."

"I can't wait! And I might meet some of the people in the club, unless they're all finished before me, which is quite possible…! I think they do this sort of thing quite regularly. I was feeling a bit bored with my regular running route anyway so I just thought I'd give it a try," she beamed at her friends.

"I don't think I've seen you look so happy Sophie!" Tina observed, "It's great and you look great. I was getting worried about you as you seemed quite stressed a while ago."

"I think I was just trying too hard… to meet a man or to keep them happy. Meeting a man had taken over my life and honestly, after that guy at Jo's wedding…! I consider that I have wasted a whole year of my life going on dates. If I ever meet anyone in the future, then at least I can be glad that up until that time I have been leading my own life and am clear about who I am and what I want out of life."

"That's very sorted of you…" Lou told her, "I hope I can be like that. I feel lousy at the moment."

"You will," Sophie said adamantly, "I'm sure of it, give it time." She noticed that Joules was absently twisting a ring on her finger. "Hey, is that your *normal* ring...?" she asked as she went over to inspect it. "Blimey, that's a *huge* rock! I've not noticed that before...?"

Joules looked at the sparkler on her finger fondly. "It's from Steve..." she said, "He gave it to me for our anniversary... which was yesterday. He's taking me out for a meal tomorrow..." she held her ring up for the girls to see.

"Wow..." they all looked at each other.

"Do you think he's trying to make up for something...?" Tina teased.

Joules looked crossly at her friend. "No, I don't *think* so! I think he's just remembered how much he loves me...!"

"Aw well that's lovely," Lou said slightly cynically, "*Some* men are thoughtful..."

"I do think..." Sophie said, addressing the group philosophically, "... that there must be *some* men out there who are worthy of our love... and that some of us have found one but at the time of going to press they are very few and far between and so we..." she looked at Lou, "...shall not waste our time on them anymore," she raised her glass in a toast, "Here's to us and our spare time and doing what we want to do in life!"

***

Sophie managed to prise herself out of bed in time to leave for the race in the morning. As she had been advised that she would get covered in mud anyway she dispensed with the morning shower and got straight into her running kit, pulling her hair up into a pony tail. She considered briefly forgetting about it and going back to bed but managed to stay true to her resolve and buzzed around the house collecting what she needed.

She took the map that she had printed from the internet, a bottle of water and her bag and set off on what felt like a little adventure. The journey took her north and into the countryside. She realised that she rarely left the town normally and loved seeing the countryside change and the houses and buildings get less. The villages became quainter with each one that passed until she got to one that she thought must be near her destination. She pulled over at a red telephone box briefly to inspect her map, half expecting an old classic car to chug past. Nearly there, she thought and stuffed the map back in her bag clear now about where she was going.

Past the village she spotted a bright yellow sign directing travellers to the race, an arrow pointing upwards saying 'Race 100m ahead'.

Great, Sophie thought and felt a tingle of excitement, why have I never done this before? She slowed down as she approached another yellow sign this time pointing to the right that said 'Race Parking' and Sophie indicated, pulling into a field and drove slowly along a bumpy track. Marshals in neon yellow raincoats directed Sophie to where she was to park and she pulled to a halt at the end of a line of parked cars.

What looked like hundreds of people milled around in the muddy field and she looked around to see if she recognised anyone or could see Anthony. She felt slightly conspicuous as everyone else seemed to be in a group but then decided that nobody else was bothered and so she shouldn't be either. She decided to make her way to the start line and worry about finding the running club later, if she found them at all as the race time was drawing near.

**

Running the race was the best thing that Sophie could ever remember doing. Her body felt ready to run the distance and she pushed herself round the route, having no idea about pace or time just running as fast as she could until she saw something that resembled a finish line. The terrain was off road and muddy and some sections took the runners through bogs and streams, up slippery hills and along grassy verges and she loved every second, not minding the mud that caked her trainers, splattered her face and got into her hair.

At some points along the way groups of supporters stood. As Sophie approached a couple who were waving a charity flag she heard the voice of the man.

"There's the first lady!"

Sophie continued past her mind racing now as well as her body.

First lady, she thought, first *lady*! She looked behind her and couldn't see anyone close but sped up just in case, the thought that they were talking about her put an extra spring in her now tiring steps.

She saw ahead a large crowd of people and focussed on them, being sure that she must be getting close to the finish line by now. As they came into view she recognised Anthony, clearly finished the race as he was covered head to toe in mud and called, 'How many more miles?' desperately to him, her body feeling now as if she had pushed it for as long and hard as it was going to take for today. Anthony pointed his arm and shouted, "Down there, another hundred meters or so!"

Sophie looked ahead and in the far distance saw the inflatable finish archway bobbing around in the gentle breeze and found a last reserve of energy to see her through to the end. As she ran over the finish line she felt a surge of emotion as she heard people around her cheer, congratulating the first female finisher. She stopped and stood, relieved now to be finished, looking stunned as random people congratulated her and someone put a medal round her neck.

Later on, wearing her medal proudly, she idly wandered back down the finish straight to see if Anthony was still there, runners still passing. She was unaware of the fact that her face was obscured by sweaty smears of mud and her hair was falling out of its pony tail, straggles now hanging down and getting stuck to the side of her face.

Anthony spotted her first and waved amiably.

"Hi! I *told* you that you were a pro!" he teased, "Fastest lady, good job!"

She smiled modestly. "I must have been the only lady running then...? Were you first man?" she joked.

Anthony looked bashful. "Ah yes well..." his smile gave his position away.

"What, you *won*?" Sophie said in complete admiration, "*Wow*! What was your time?"

Anthony waved his hand dismissing her question. "Oh I don't know... I don't do times really...! You are one impressive lady though, turn up at your first race and win it! That's awesome!" He looked at his watch, "Listen, I don't mean to sound cheeky… but could I catch a lift back with you…? Whenever you're going back…? I got a lift up here with a mate but he was going on somewhere else and the guys were going to give me a lift back but when I saw them at the start one of them had dropped out so they'd only brought one car… long story really but you'd save me getting the train like this…" he indicated to his mud covered body.

"Yeah, of course…" Sophie said dubiously, thinking about her beautiful car and wishing she'd brought a change of clothes and wondering if Anthony had, "I wish I'd brought something clean and dry to wear on the way back…" she mused, "but of course, I owe you one anyway for saving Deeno."

Anthony looked confused for a brief second and then remembered the dinosaur episode. "I tell you what…!" he said, "If you give me a lift I will supply two protective seat covers…?" he smiled and took a roll of black bin bags out of the front zip pocket of his ruck sack.

"Great! You're on!" Sophie said and took one, "Well, whenever you're ready really. I'm in no rush. I might grab a drink on my way to the car though if you want to go now?"

Anthony looked to see if there was anyone approaching the finish line.

"I think I'd be OK to head off now; the other guys will be together but they said not to wait as I was going to be getting the train. Thanks so much for that, I didn't really fancy sitting on a train in this!"

The two made their way back to Sophie's car.

"Did you run with your bag…?" Sophie asked.

"Not this time, I do sometimes, if it's a longer run," Anthony told her, "But they had a bag drop at this one so I just left it there."

"Ah OK…" Sophie said. "This is so cool, I love it! I've never done anything like this before!"

"You must be a natural then," Anthony said and smiled. He offered her a packet of jelly beans that he had taken out of his bag and took his phone too having heard a text alert.

"Thanks!" Sophie said, "I'll be more prepared next time!"

As they arrived at the car Anthony's jaw stiffened as he finished reading a text and he shoved his phone back into a pocket of his bag. He carefully smoothed his bin bag over the passenger seat and lowered himself in, careful not to get any mud on the car interior. Sophie did the same. She looked in her rear view mirror and was horrified by the way she looked. Her sweaty hair stuck to her head and with mud smeared over her face. She smoothed her eyebrows in an attempt to make herself look better but immediately realised that this was going to be useless. She applied some lip balm and laughed at herself.

"Oh my God what a mess!"

"I don't think so," Anthony said simply.

The two sat in companionable silence as Sophie slowly drove out of the bumpy field and back onto the open road. Anthony's phone beeped again and he sighed and rolled his eyes at Sophie, retrieving it from his bag. He read the message and sighed again.

"I will *never* let a woman control me again," he said defiantly without warning.

Sophie raised her eyebrows not sure quite what to say.

"Sorry!" he said, "just been a bad day."

Sophie glanced at Anthony and wondered if she should ask him what the problem was or just leave it, having only known him for about ten minutes.

"Well you're safe with me," Sophie said light-heartedly, "I've given up on men so have no desire to control one!" she laughed, "Although, why anyone would want to control another person is beyond me...? You're right not to want that. That's like when someone tries to *change* you..." she looked thoughtful and slightly confused then shook the thought from her head. She looked sideways at Anthony and laughed again, self-consciously this time as he was looking at her. "I think we're both looking rather splendid, don't you?" she said changing the subject, "I'm *loving* this look!"

His serious features broke into a smile momentarily. "Well, one of us looks splendid," he looked serious again.

"Do you want to talk about it?" Sophie asked as she slowly started to drive, "*Believe* me, if you have a story to tell I will *bet* that I have one to match because, never mind being controlled by a woman, I have recently had the *worst* year with men. *Most* men, present company accepted for now, are a waste of space so tell me *all* about it!"

Anthony started to chuckle. "I'm fine actually, are you sure it's not *you* who needs to talk...?"

Sophie looked apologetic. "Oh yeah... I probably do."

"Well my problems are all forgotten now. I want to know about your year!" Anthony said, "Sounds intriguing!"

"Well, I wouldn't say that..." Sophie replied.

"So tell me," Anthony said a smile now playing on his lips, "Why are we such a waste of space?"

"Well," Sophie started, now sure how much detail she should include, "Well… what would you think of a man who made you think he *liked* you but neglected to also tell you he was *engaged* and the first you knew about it was when you saw him tagged in his own *wedding photos* after turning up at your house in the early hours of that very morning making it quite clear he did like you and then came *back* to you after his *honeymoon* telling you that he thought he was *in love* with you? Is that *normal*?"

"I'd think he needs to sort his sexuality out…" Anthony laughed.

"Oh yeah… I don't mean with you...!"

"He sounds like quite a shit," Anthony agreed, "unbelievable really."

"Yes thank you, that's what I thought. Here's another one. What would you think of someone who chatted you up *all night* at a wedding, literally, wouldn't let a *soul* near you but then at the end of the evening find out that their *partner* is there waiting to take them home...?" Sophie opened her eyes wide in utter amazement that someone had done that to her. "Or, this one cracks me up, a guy who even gets *jealous* when the *bar man a*sks me what I want to drink!" Sophie laughed mockingly, "I mean… come on…"

"Are these real people?" Anthony asked, enjoying the diversion from his own problems.

"Oh yes…" Sophie shuddered, "Very real. I've met the stripper who takes it personally that everyone looks at his *body* and not at his *intellect*!" she guffawed, "The guy who spends more than *£2500* on a woman he's known for five minutes. The guy who tells you after a few dates, quite casually, that he was sacked for sexual harassment! The one who wants to lick your shoes and gets arrested for pleasuring himself outside a cheap shoe shop during the early hours of the morning. The guy who shows you a photo of all the women he's slept with in a year. The one who thinks it's OK to eye up other women while on a date. The one who asks you out and then looks *bored* the whole night and I can tell you it wasn't *my* company that was boring. The one who spends the whole evening telling you what you should *change* if you *ever* want to meet a man. The one who stalks your house when you're on holiday and when you get home you find they're in prison for attempted murder...!" she stopped talking abruptly aware that she had gone off on one and that Anthony was watching her with a look of worry on his face.

"I think you need to be much choosier when it comes to dating..." he told her, looking concerned at the last contender.

She nodded in agreement. "Yes well I doubt that I will ever go dating again! But you seem to have caught me at a bad moment..." she said and smiled across at him, hoping that he didn't think she was a complete nut case, "When you see me coming to your running group next week you'll probably make everyone hide until I've gone, there's that mad woman again..."

"Not at all..." Anthony said kindly, "Promise me you'll not go on any more dates, it sounds dangerous out there!"

"Yes, yes it is," Sophie confirmed, "Anyway, *you* were saying..."

"Oh well nothing as interesting as you..." he started, "No dodgy dates, I was just trapped in a marriage when I was 19 and am only, at the age of 36, managing to extricate myself from it. I have nothing to show for it, seventeen wasted years... but I should get some money soon, out of my house... I was thinking of blowing it all on cosmetic dentistry...? What do you think...?"

Sophie furrowed her brow worriedly. "Why would you want to do that? There's nothing wrong with your teeth?"

"Well apart from being all crooked!"

"They're not crooked!" Sophie told him, noting that he must mean the tiny overlap of his front two teeth which Sophie thought was rather cute, "anyhow, if you did change them then you wouldn't look like you anymore. So I don't think you should."

Anthony nodded, listening to her advice. "Cool, that's good to know, you've just saved me about twenty grand!"

"What! Well I should get fifty percent of that now!" she joked.

"I've actually got my eye on this holiday when my divorce comes through. Well, not a holiday exactly, I'd be leading groups up mountains basically... in Scotland, Wales, Europe, Asia... wherever the company sends me! I've never been *allowed* to do anything so as soon as I can I'll let them know. It would be for a winter season but there is a chance that it could be permanent. I kind of like the idea of being an old man of the hills..."

"Wow..." Sophie said thinking it all sounded quite drastic, never been one to venture too far from home, "What do you do at the moment then?"

"I work for the police," Anthony said, "And at the weekend if I'm free I do stuff for the T.A- the Territorial Army. It's through that that I found out about the mountain leader opportunity."

Sophie jaw nearly dropped right open at his revelation that he possessed the top two uniforms from the top five. Wait until I tell Tina, she thought.

"But, yeah, anyway all my life I've been looking for the big adventure and now's my time to have it," he continued, unaware that his occupations were detailed in Top Five uniform a list.

"Wow, well that's great…" Sophie said, slightly dubiously.

"Yeah, really can't wait…" Anthony said.

"Well…" Sophie said, "…all the best!"

"Thanks…" Anthony replied.

"Got to take these chances when you get them…"

"Yeah…" they exchanged glances.

***

During idle moments Sophie found herself thinking about Anthony more and more. There were things about him that as time went by fascinated her and his eyes and the way he smiled just made her melt. He also had a strong idea of what he wanted to do in life and this was very attractive to her. She joined the running group and through that became his friend online and she started to fall in love. She fought it at first and she definitely tried to contain it but over time the feelings in her grew.

Anthony was the face of professionalism at the running club and Sophie almost felt like he almost tried to avoid her sometimes but she wasn't surprised after her outburst about men in the car. She felt annoyed with herself for being so thoughtless, why would you tell someone you like about all the dates you've been on, she thought, although I didn't know I liked him at the time? When she arrived at the club he usually said a curt 'Hi Sophie' and ticked her off his list, continuing to chat to the other members. Sophie was fine with it though; the others had been going for so much longer they all knew each other quite well and she reminded herself that she was there to run. At the end of the class they did some stretches to finish off and Anthony asked for volunteers to come up and demonstrate each one, except he never asked Sophie to do it which confirmed to her that he must truly think her to be a little bit weird. The other members seemed to get a lot of encouragement and praise but Sophie was lucky to get a brief, 'good job'. She loved running with the others though started to make some friends, watching Anthony from afar and just feeling a little bit sad that he would be going away soon, on his big adventure.

The night she had been dreading came a week later when he announced to the group at the end that he had been given his date for his new job and so he's be leaving the club.

"I'm asking around to see if anyone can take over... in the meantime you guys can keep up your running yourself! You've all made so much progress and achieved so much, hopefully you'll all keep going."

Sophie listened sadly and wished that she had joined the group the year before, when she had seen them in the park that day instead of wasting her time like she did being preoccupied by useless dates. The thought that every week for the last year and longer Anthony had been right there, so close to her and now she'd met him he was going. I wouldn't control you, she thought, I'd let you have your adventures.

She hung around at the end and waited for all the other runners to leave with the pretence of taking over the club when he was gone.

"It might sound silly…" she said, "… but I love coming here and now that I've found it I don't want to stop…" her eyes looked into his and she wanted to tell him that now she had found him she didn't want him to leave, but that might sound controlling she thought. For a moment they stood like that, each deep in their own thoughts, as if searching for answers in the other's eyes.

Anthony snapped himself out of the moment and switched his professional façade back on.

"Well, that would be great, for now… I mean, you might need to do some kind of course… but for the moment just to keep everyone together then that would be amazing and I think they'd respect you seeing as you were fastest lady!" he smiled and looked happy with the outcome, "I could come back on leave and see you again… you all again. Maybe before I go we could catch up and I could let you know a few things, show you the paperwork and stuff? Do you have a first aid certificate…?"

Sophie nodded, waning to see him again for whatever reason. "Yeah I have one through my work."

"Great! That's perfect. Well, you have my number don't you…? Text me yours… I have some stuff to sort out but then I'll get back to you and we can meet up before I go…?"

"OK cool," Sophie said casually, "Speak soon then."

"Yeah, speak soon," they stood and smiled at each other for a moment before Anthony said, 'bye' again and they went their separate ways.

It was later that evening when Sophie was idly scrolling through Anthony's photos on the running club website that she realised she really did have it bad. She had switched on her computer to make up a power point presentation for work but got distracted and for about half an hour without realising she gazed at her favourite photo of him. There were various photos on the website showing the club taking part in different activities, general photos of them running in the park and then others of organised events like the one Sophie had gone to. The one that caught Sophie's attention was one in the mountains and Anthony was pictured inspecting a map in a way that his chin doubled slightly in the most gorgeous way. Sophie suddenly realised what was happening.

Oh my god, she thought, and looked at his chin rationally. It doesn't look *that* attractive… *does it*? She sat back in her chair and felt a horror enter into her, I was meant to be forgetting all about men, she thought, and now I've gone and fallen in love. She felt a sadness sweep over her. He doesn't want a woman in his life though, she thought, he doesn't want to be controlled.

***

The thought of Anthony going away now just as she had met him made Sophie feel so miserable that she decided that she would rather have him in her life as a friend than not at all. They had started to text each other to arrange a time to meet up and just the sight of his name on her phone filled her heart with joy. Enid also had been so world-weary at work that Sophie realised she didn't want to be like her at all, she needed the happiness that another person brought into her life even if it was just platonic. She wanted to stay in touch with Anthony even just as a friend.

***

Anthony had his leaving date and they arranged to meet on the Friday before so that he could pass over all the necessary paperwork to Sophie. He told her that he would collect her on the way as he had to drive past her house anyway and asked her when a good time would be. She gave him a large time band to choose from, not having any preference herself.

"Anytime between, oh I don't know, from seven or eight or nine... I'm around all evening so whenever you like!" she didn't want to appear to be too keen.

"I'll be around at seven then," Anthony said, "Then we'll have more time together."

This sentence played round and round in Sophie's head all week. 'Then we'll have more time together', what did that *mean*, she wondered. Did he mean that they would have more time together to plan stuff or did he mean they'd have more time together...?

Just after Ollie was collected by Ben on the Friday night Sophie got a text from Anthony saying that he was on his way. He realised that he was rather early but he was looking forward to seeing her. The text confused her even more. She rushed to finish getting ready and considered her reply. She really wanted to text him and say that she couldn't wait to see him and that she had been thinking about him since the last time they met but quickly dismissed that idea. In her haste and excitement, she sent a text back, in jest, saying 'What am I doing- you told me not to go on anymore dodgy dates'.

As the minutes after she sent it passed she regretted sending it.

What a stupid text, she thought, why did you even send that...?

She was expecting him to arrive early but the clock reached seven and he was not there. She got on with a few jobs, busying herself as this was just a business meeting and nothing else but now full of a horrible dread that the mention of the 'D' word had made him change his mind. She tidied away the tea dishes and cleaned the kitchen sides, making sure they were spotless. The weekend washing was put on and she straightened out Ollie's room, it being the only time she could ever give it a proper tidy-when he wasn't there. She then looked around for other things to do and eventually started on the bathroom, doing all her normal weekend jobs but trying not to get herself messed up in the process. She tried to put her stupid text to the back of her mind; he's not going to stand me up because of that is he, she thought? He was very clear that he didn't want to be controlled though, maybe he had got cold feet at the thought that Sophie might be thinking it was a date.

By eight she was in tears, cursing her stupidity. She felt so upset that she might have spoiled everything that she eventually picked up her mobile and tried to call him but his phone was switched off. Great, she thought, I've pissed him off so much he's switched his phone off. He's not coming because you just can't shut up about stupid dates, she thought crossly, the one last time you might have got to see him and you've blown it. She tried to use her computer to send him a message seeing as he wasn't using his phone but for some reason her internet connection was down and she realised her landline was dead. With no means of communicating with the one man who had been making her feel happy without him knowing she threw herself down on her bed and cried.

The weekend passed in a blur. She felt as low as she ever had, even Ben noticed something was up when he dropped Ollie off and showed concern.

"Hey Sophie, you look *awful*. Do you want us to have Ollie for a few more days...?"

Sophie shook her head and tried not to cry again. "No. No I'm fine thanks; Ollie is the only thing that can make me feel better."

Ben looked at her with concern. "Listen, Sophie, I've never said sorry..."

Sophie shook her head and held her hand up for him to stop. "Its fine, please don't. That's not what's wrong with me anyway..." the tears started to well up in her eyes and she took a moment to compose herself, "Everyone's getting on with their life, that's all, everyone except me..." she didn't want Ben's pity though and told him to go. "I'm fine, really. We all have our bad days; just you don't normally see mine," she smiled through her tears and gave Ollie a hug, "Mummy is just being silly. What shall we do tonight darling? Shall we watch a movie?"

"Yeah!" Ollie said and scampered up to choose one to watch.

Ben called 'Bye' after him and told Sophie to give him a call if she needed.

"We're fine," she said, "Kerry's got him tomorrow; it's the first week of his holidays isn't it? We're away next week, but we spoke about all that."

Ben tapped his head. "It's all up here," he said.

"I hope it's written down too!" Sophie scolded him, "We're away over your weekend but you're having him the next...?"

"Don't worry Soph, I have it all written down at home. Well... bye then... have a good time!"

Pat next door pulled into her driveway and Sophie waved at her. She called up to Ollie that she would just be outside and hurried over to see her before she disappeared into the house.

"Hi! Hi Pat!" she called, "Is your phone working OK? Mine's not been working all weekend! I can't get on the internet either!"

"No, not since Friday…" she said, "But Peter said that the men were working on the overhead cables yesterday… they never tell you anything though, do they, about what they're doing… no word either when it might be fixed."

***

Sophie felt like she was just going through the motions again, the glimmer of love in her life which had been instantly extinguished took her enthusiasm away once more and she felt numb and tired. Her eyes felt raw after a weekend of crying and her face still puffy and red. She tried to be rational and remind herself that Anthony was just going to be a friend but it felt like little consolation, she just wanted to see him again.

Kerry came round to the house the next day at nine to have Ollie for the day while Sophie worked it being the first day of the holidays. How amazing, Sophie thought, to be a child and have the long summer ahead. She told Sophie that they would probably just play in the garden but if it was alright they might walk up to the park. Sophie agreed and gave Ollie his instructions for the day to stay with Kerry and hold her hand at all times.

"I will!" he said automatically being used to his mother's concerns.

She found Enid in a foul mood at the office to add to her own sense of misery.

"Someone's had a bad weekend," Enid said as if twisting the knife on purpose. Sophie didn't reply for fear of crying again, "Well you'll be pleased to know that we've put an extra session in for you today, at eleven. It's here, for our staff."

Sophie looked squarely at Enid. She couldn't believe that she had arranged something like that without giving Sophie any notice.

"Great, so now I've got an hour to sort it out…"

"You should just be able to use what you've got already…" Enid said sneeringly, "Mrs Wright wanted to see for herself how *great* your presentations were."

On autopilot Sophie moved around the office collecting the resources she needed for her presentation and went through to photocopy what she needed. Ruth appeared and closed the cupboard door.

"Are you alright…?" she said with concern, "You know Enid's a bitch but you'll be fine won't you?"

Sophie looked like she might crumple into sadness. "I just don't feel like it today, any of it. It sounds silly, I know, but I thought I'd met someone really nice and I think I blew it and I just want to sit in a dark cupboard for a while now and cry… and maybe in a few days I'll feel better but Enid has really picked the wrong day to be a bitch…"

The cupboard door opened and Enid appeared. "Come on ladies, work time now. I'm a phone short in the box, Sophie; I don't think I have yours...?"

Sophie dropped the photocopier lid and marched through to the office to relinquish her phone. She threw in into the box under Enid's desk.

"There you go. It causes nothing but problems anyway," and she went back to doing her photocopying.

A while later when she was finished she went through to the office to get the rest of her resources and take them down to set up her room. Enid was on the phone and Sophie thought she heard her name.

"Yes, yes we're very busy today! That's right. No well she shouldn't be taking personal calls at work anyway. Let them know she finishes at half two," she said and put the phone down, looking at Sophie challengingly.

Sophie wasn't in the mood anymore for Enid's bullying. "Who was that?" she asked.

"I don't know," Enid said flatly, "Personal calls should not be taken at work."

Sophie stared at her momentarily and decided she couldn't be bothered wasting her time anymore. She turned on her heel and ran down the stairs to the main office. She burst in interrupting a heated conversation between Mrs Wright and Tim about pencils.

"There's just been a call for me. Who was is?" she demanded.

Enid followed close behind Sophie.

"Miss Bridges, you are training in less than half an hour. When you are within these walls then work is the main focus."

"Can you control your staff please, Enid, this is becoming quite tiresome!" Mrs Wright spoke impatiently.

Tim bravely spoke up. "I think we need to pass on the message," he said simply, "Sophie, it was your child minder."

***

Sophie hurtled back up the stairs to retrieve her phone out of the box and saw that it was flashing with messages. She sensed an urgency to get back to her boy.

She listened to the frantic messages that had been left by Kerry and her body froze as she listened, the world around her stopped, she was conscious of her own breathing getting heavier and heavier and a panic she had never felt before bursting out of her heart.

"Ollie!" she cried and frantically tried to call Kerry but her phone rang off, "Oh my God, Ollie!" Sophie cried as tears started to stream down her face, "No!"

She grabbed her bag and sprinted downstairs again completely forgetting her jacket, frustrated that her legs could not take her faster. She cursed her work for not passing on the message, she cursed Enid for being such a bitch and she cursed herself for leaving Ollie with a babysitter while she went to work. She pushed past Enid who stood in the entrance and left the school without as much as a word to anyone. She blindly ran, reaching her car and realised that she didn't know where she was going and listened to the messages again.

'Hi!' the first one said, Kerry's voice sounding upset. 'Hi Sophie I've tried to call you at work but they've said that you're busy. We went to the park and Ollie was climbing a tree and he fell out. Oh Sophie I'm so sorry, I was right there underneath but he just slipped and I tried to catch him…' there was a pause, 'I'll try and call you at work again.'

'Hi!' the second message said Kerry's voice now hysterical, 'Hi Sophie I can't get you at work. I'm taking Ollie to the hospital, right now! I'll stay with his until you get here. Please Sophie, please hurry!"

Sophie's brain stopped working and her movements became uncoordinated. She hit her head getting into the car and dropped her keys in the foot well, suddenly unable to perform the simplest of task.

"Stop it!" she said and took a deep breath, "Keep it together," she indicated and pulled out and made her way to the hospital, the thirty speed limit being painfully slow. She tried not to think of what had happened to Ollie, tried not to think the worst.

"Oh my boy…" she said under her breath, "…my precious boy…"

By the time she reached the hospital her concern for petty driving laws was forgotten and she abandoned her car outside accident and emergency and ran inside to where she saw with dismay a queue of people standing in an orderly fashion waiting to talk to the nurse. She ran up to the desk completely oblivious to the needs of the others.

"My son is here!" she blurted out, "He's fallen out of a tree… I don't even know what condition he's in… I don't even know if he's here…!" she broke down and sobbed- her distress not abating the members of the queue who looked at her disapprovingly for pushing in.

"I'm sorry, madam…" the nurse behind the glass started to speak but another appeared behind Sophie and assured the other that she would take care of it.

"Miss Bridges…?" the nurse asked, "I was about to try and call you again… your babysitter has been trying all day…"

Sophie sobbed. "I know. I've got the message. That's my stupid work; we have to put our phones in a box under the desk… But they didn't even pass the message on…" she felt a blind fury bubble up inside her, "They didn't even let me know… we have to put our phones in a *box!* Where's my son…" she sobbed again and the nurse led her away from the crowded reception area and through some double doors.

"Your son is down here…" she said guiding Sophie's sobbing body away from others coming towards them. "…he's conscious now…"

At this Sophie broke down completely and wailed. "Oh!" she cried, "Oh! I thought… I thought…"

The nurse led her further into the depths of A&E and eventually they got to a room. The nurse paused outside and squeezed Sophie's arm.

"I think you've had a bad day…" she said softly, "…but he's fine now, he asked for you when he woke up and was upset that you weren't here but your babysitter has been wonderful. He's just a big bandage on his head… but he's absolutely fine."

She opened the door for Sophie to go in and she ran over, her sobbing only made worse by the sight of her little boy bandaged up in a hospital bed, the skin that she could see looked rather bruised and sore. Next to his bed was a can of coke and a chocolate bar.

Ollie spotted that he had been found out and blamed the babysitter.

"Kerry got them for me," he said, "She said they'd make me feel better."

Sophie laughed through her tears and covered his face with kisses, careful not to hurt him further and then thanked Kerry profusely, explaining about her work not passing on the messages.

"Well, I got it that they were a bit funny..." she said, "... so that's why I left messages on your mobile... I'd have stayed here until you came!"

"Oh you're amazing, I own you at least quadruple time...! No, more than that... I don't know what to say... thank you."

"S'alright," Kerry said and collected her stuff. She refused the money that Sophie tried to put in her hand, "Pay me later. You'll need that for in here, it costs about a fiver for a cuppa!"

Kerry told Ollie to look after himself and left them to it. The boy was examined by a doctor and moved out of the accident and emergency wing and through to a room in the children's ward where Sophie could stay with him.

"He'll be fine with us for a while, though, if you want to get anything from home...?" Sophie was told by the nurse, "Is there anyone else you'd like to call...?"

"No," Sophie replied, "Nobody else just now... well, I should call his Dad but he lives an hour away... I'll nip away and come back and call him later." The nurse smiled understandingly.

Sophie was reluctant to leave Ollie after what had happened the last time she left him but the nurse insisted that he would be fine. She promised Ollie that she would be back within the hour and asked him if there was anything he would like her to bring back. The boy seemed happy enough sipping his coke and playing snakes and ladders with the nurse.

"Can you bring Deeno?" he asked before she left, "*Please...?*"

Sophie laughed. "If it's OK with the nurse, you can have whatever you like."

***

Sophie went home and collected her stuff for the night and Deeno. She parked her car legally this time and walked back through A&E with the four-foot inflatable dinosaur eager to see her son. Just as she reached Ollie's room she heard footsteps behind her and a voice calling, 'Excuse me! Excuse me!' Sophie turned and saw another nurse running towards her.

"Excuse me!" she panted, "So sorry!" she stopped and took a moment to catch her breath, Sophie amazed that someone who worked in the health profession could get so exhausted by running a few feet.

"I'm sorry," she said again, looking rather flushed, "Do you mind...? I'm with a gentleman who has been here since Friday. He was in a rather nasty crash... well, self-inflicted if you ask me, brought down a telegraph pole apparently... but, that is by the by! He had what the doctor thinks is temporary amnesia and can't remember a thing about what happened... They found his wallet, but he still can't remember... but he's just seen you... well, rather, your dinosaur... and become rather agitated about it. He says that he remembers it but I can't see how... but I can't get him to calm down until he sees it... could I borrow it please...?"

Sophie felt her heart beating faster at what the nurse was saying. She looked beyond her to the room that she was indicating to and started to move towards it, as if there were a magnet inside pulling her in. The nurse scuttled after her.

"We don't want him to get too excited..." she said, "... he is in quite a delicate state... I think it might be better if I take the dinosaur...?"

Sophie looked at the nurse with irritation and gripped Deeno tight.

"No, no it's fine... I might know your mystery man."

Sophie stopped in the doorway of Anthony's room and saw him lying in bed in a similar state as Ollie but with additional bandages around his right arm and his legs.

The moment their eyes met the realisation spread over his face and Sophie dropped Deeno, who bounced on the floor and landed on his nose, tail aloft, and ran over to where he lay. She took his good hand and, forgetting herself, kissed his nose.

"It's you!" she cried happily, "It's *you*!"

"Who am I?" Anthony asked, grimacing at the pain he clearly felt, "Ouch..."

"I thought you'd gone...!" Sophie said, "I thought you'd just... stood me up... although... it wasn't ever a date..."

She looked at him wanting all the answers. She felt an impatience now to know what had happened. A look of realisation started to spread over his face and he started to smile.

"I wouldn't have minded if it was a date…" Anthony said. "I was hoping that it might be…? I'd have been an improvement on your other ones! It's all coming back to me now!"

Sophie laughed and wiped her now running nose and eyes with her sleeve. "But you didn't turn up…" Sophie said and then smiled with realisation, "Oh yeah, maybe because you had a crash…?"

"I stupidly tried to read your text; I shouldn't have when I was driving. I'll get into trouble for that…" Anthony replied and reached over painfully to his bedside table to pass a box of tissues to Sophie.

"Did you read it…?" Sophie asked, gratefully pulling one out of the box.

"No, no… I picked up my phone from the seat but the second that my attention was diverted was the one that my car decided to skid on the wet road… I was driving over to you the back way, it had been raining so much though the road was so slippery with wet leaves- this is what the ambulance man said anyway- I skidded and went straight into a telegraph pole."

"So *that's* why we've not been able to use our phones for the weekend…!"

Anthony looked impressed with the devastation he had caused. "Wow, I had no idea about that! Well, I guess that was me… But I woke up in here yesterday and I couldn't remember a thing… but then…" he smiled and indicated to

Deeno who had been picked up and diligently placed next to the other side of the bed by the nurse in a hope that it would trigger Anthony's memory further, "… then I saw this thing walking past my door and it rang some bells…" he smiled fondly at Sophie whose heart nearly burst with happiness.

"Ollie's in the room down the corridor… in a similar condition…" she told him, "… it's a long story!"

Anthony looked concerned.

"He's doing fine," the nurse interjected, "Brave wee lad."

Anthony took Sophie's hand and looked into her eyes.

"I was driving too fast, I wanted to reach you and tell you something… All my life I've been looking for the big adventure, the next challenge, the perfect job… but then I met you… and I started to realise… all I want is for someone to love me, the adventures I planned were to fill a big void in my life. I used to think that true love was just something that happened in the movies but then I set eyes on you… all sweaty and covered in mud, the smile on your face when you realised that you'd won that race was something I'd never seen before, such pure joy… if it's possible to fall in love at first sight then I did, right then… I was rushing to tell you that because I've wasted so much of my life being unhappy, I was impatient and didn't want to waste another second…" he looked at her suddenly worried that he'd said too much but Sophie laughed through her tears.

"But I thought you didn't like me!" she said, "You were always so…"

"Professional," he stated, "and scared… scared that you wouldn't be interested in me. It sounded like you'd had quite enough of men anyway!"

Ollie's nurse popped her head into the room having heard that she was back in the building.

"I'm just off now but my colleague is with your son until you get back...?" she looked at the two quizzically, wanting to know more.

"Oh thank you so much!" Sophie said happily, "I will be there in a minute, sorry, I seem to know a lot of people in here today!" She reached down and rummaged in her bag, eventually finding the wedding invite that was now in a tattered condition at the bottom of it.

"I hope you've written that date down…" Anthony said, "… that invite has seen better days!"

"Oh yes… I hate weddings anyway!" Sophie said happily and pointed to the number she had written down.

"Is that your little black book?" Anthony joked.

"No!" Sophie said indignantly, "Certainly not. I just have two very important numbers written down. One is yours and one is business and I just need to make a quick phone call…"

The End

Printed in Great Britain
by Amazon